Zoë Rice grew up in Brooklyn and now lives in Manhattan. She graduated cum laude from Yale, where her friends thought she should have majored in art history. She then spent four years editing while her friends told her she should write. She hopes they're happy now.

Pick Me Up

Zoë Rice

little
black
dress

First published in the USA in 2006
by NEW AMERICAN LIBRARY
A division of PENGUIN GROUP (USA) INC

This edition published in Great Britain in paperback in 2007
by LITTLE BLACK DRESS
An imprint of HEADLINE PUBLISHING GROUP

A LITTLE BLACK DRESS paperback

1

978 0 7553 3952 5

Typeset in Transit511BT by Avon DataSet Ltd,
Bidford-on-Avon, Warwickshire

www.hodderheadline.com

For my parents,
Rena and Shel

There's art in beauty.
Hi, Beauty. I'm Art.

Rushing up Seventy-third Street toward the gallery, I can think of only one thing. I've let Deidre Gayle down. Deidre Gayle, the nicest, most genuinely enthusiastic art lover I've ever known. The collector who regularly buys fifty-thousand-dollar paintings without batting an eyelash. The woman to whom I owe my upcoming promotion.

When I woke up this morning, the large, red digital alarm clock that usually sits by my head was on the floor, its cracked display flashing twelve o'clock over and over again. Robbie must be branching out to plastics. I'm not sure he loves me as unconditionally as I love him, because when I screamed, 'Robbie!' he just slunk out from under my bed, blinking with indifference. I was a whole hour late, and he might as well have been shrugging his guilty little kitty shoulders.

Now it's ten forty-five a.m. Deidre has been waiting for me at the gallery for forty-five minutes. She may be a ballet legend, but Deidre Gayle still prizes every second she can use to improve her technique, and look how many precious seconds I've wasted! I feel so guilty I may as well have thrown a bucket of water at her prized Picasso drawing. And the worst thing is, she'll forgive me instantly.

I bound up the stairs to the Emerson Bond Gallery,

which occupies the bottom floor of a stately limestone town house near Madison Avenue. The Old Man used to live here, as I understand it, back in the forties. I always have this romantic picture of Emerson Bond in some dashing tuxedo mixing highballs where my desk is now, while he waits for his wife to descend the marble staircase in her white chinchilla coat. Although my boss, Freddie, thinks it would be a more accurate picture if the maid were mixing the drinks, young Emerson Bond were working at his desk, and the wife were out on the town with another man. And he's pretty sure that our office was used as a larder. But probably a fancy larder.

'I'm here! I'm here!' I cry breathlessly as I throw open the door and nearly trip over the threshold. 'I'm *sooooo* sorry!'

The Bond's assistant, Kimmy, peers at me curiously from behind the reception desk, her spiky dark purple hair contrasting nicely with the red Warhol silk screen hanging behind her. It's from the Old Man's private collection, and the only piece we've ever shown that predates the eighties. 'It's okay, Izzy,' she says cheerfully. 'Deidre left half an hour ago. I told her you had a family emergency. A nice bouquet is already on its way with a note of apology in your name.'

'Kimmy!' I can feel the adrenaline leaving my body in a whoosh. 'You're a star.'

'No problem, doll,' she says nonchalantly, marking something in her ever-present notebook. 'Although Deidre did say she hoped I was covering and that you were actually – how did she say it? – recuperating from a night of passion in the bed of a new lover.'

I let out a strangled laugh. My recent luck with men has been like my past luck with men: absolute crap. 'We both know I'd be more likely to spend the night farming beetles in the deserts of Egypt.'

'That's not true!' Kimmy protests eagerly. 'You're afraid of bugs.'

Kimmy has the coolest clothes I've ever seen. Today she's wearing a sleeveless black dress, with a trompe l'oeil of a strand of pearls painted on the front. What she doesn't make herself she buys only from obscure downtown designers. Every day's like an alternative fashion show.

'My cat destroyed my alarm clock,' I say bleakly, resting my elbows on the ledge in front of Kimmy's desk.

'That's because your cat's crazy,' she answers.

'He's not!' I object, though Kimmy squints doubtfully. I peer down at her notebook, where she's been drawing an elaborate, fantastic dragon with a tail spiraling down the page. Kimmy just graduated from NYU, where she majored in fine art. She's working now on a fantasy graphic novel, and her greatest dream is to get it published. Considering her talent, I'm sure it will happen. I asked if I could be a character, and Kimmy said she'd give me a long billowy empire-waist dress and a big cone hat with a veil. How cool is that?

Kimmy reaches over the reception ledge to hand me a bagel wrapped in foil. 'I figured since you were late, you wouldn't stop for breakfast. It's your favorite – sesame with chive cream cheese. Hopefully the tinfoil kept it warm.'

'Oh, Kimmy.' Honestly. Anyone who says the New York art world is nothing but a stomping ground for spoiled socialites should spend an hour with Kimmy. I know few people who are as devoted to their work, their art, or their friends. 'I got you something too.' I reach into my tote bag, grinning mischievously, and pull out a jar of golden honey.

'You didn't.' Her eyes shine with delight.

'They weren't going to miss just *one* . . .'

Kimmy throws her head back in laughter. The jar of honey I'm holding was part of an invite-only event hosted by the Eaton Bosc Gallery in Chelsea on Saturday night. The Eaton Bosc is known for stealing other galleries' artists. They've been after ours – unsuccessfully – for years. On Saturday, performance artist Elspeth Worth, one of their stolen stars, put on a show where she was covered from head to toe in honey and then lowered onto a bare mattress. When she arose, the form of her body was left in a gooey imprint. Audience members were asked to toss a personal memento onto the honey as a symbol of the outside influences an artist must internalize – a mighty unsubtle symbol, if you ask me – after which, the whole mattress was covered in shellac, soon to be hung on a wall and sold for hundreds of thousands of dollars.

Cassie Arnell, the Eaton Bosc's director, added a handwritten poem to the honey, spread open for us all to see. *My soul is stuck*, she wrote, *like this body, on which it lies prone. We merge. We are as one.* Poor Cassie. She's always trying so hard to appear deep and intellectual, but in the end all she appears to be is trying too hard. The crowd of artists and gallerists made fun of her the entire night. I felt so bad, I went right up to Cassie and told her I thought her poem was a really brave and moving gesture. Unfortunately, she took my interest as a sign that I wanted to hear the rest of her poetry, recited without pause, for over an hour. Lordy, her soul has been through a lot.

For my own contribution to the mattress, I chose something that would add a sense of humor to the piece, like in the Pop Art of Claes Oldenburg or the Dada of Marcel Duchamp. Thankfully, Elspeth Worth loved it. When my turn came, I took a little yellow-and-red plastic figurine out of my pocket and nestled it down happily for eternity. Because, really. Who else would love a bed full of honey more than Winnie the Pooh?

'Thank you for my souvenir.' Kimmy hugs the jar to her chest. 'I shall treasure it always.'

'And thank *you*, my dear, for breakfast.' I shrug off the jacket of my new cream linen suit, which has already wilted in the intense June heat. 'Any messages?'

'The shippers are running two hours late.' Kimmy points to the four paintings stacked against the wall behind her desk, all wrapped in acid-free glassine paper to protect them from scratches. These are the final paintings from our last show to be picked up and sent to their new owners. Their combined worth tops a million dollars.

'If it becomes more than two hours, let me know.' I scan through my other messages. A curator at the Hirshhorn in

Washington, D.C., wants to exhibit one of our artists. The *Village Voice* needs a press packet for our new show. D. W. Faulkner wants to arrange payment for the sculpture he just bought. Business as usual.

'Miss Izzy, look at you,' Kimmy exclaims, holding up the title list of our current show, which just opened last week. She's talking about all the red dots that litter the page, indicating a piece has sold. The artist, John Teller, transforms the shapes of body parts into freestanding artworks, using wax, foam, latex, and rubber. Truthfully, I'm not a huge fan, but Freddie thought we needed some sculpture. And the weird thing is, people seem to like it. I sold the six-thousand-dollar foot first. Although, in that case, I have a feeling the buyer was less interested in art than he was in . . . well . . . feet.

'I mean,' Kimmy says, her voice rising in disbelief, 'you even sold *Nose*! How'd you do it?'

I grin. 'The buyer's a plastic surgeon.'

Kimmy shakes her purple-spiked head. 'Man, you're good.'

'Ooh, girls!' I hear behind me. Freddie swoops in, holding out his Prada briefcase in front of him like it's a religious offering. Frederick Barnes is our boss, the gallery's dealer. He's thirty-eight and adorable – pudgy and bald, with cheeks you just want to grab hold of and wiggle. I've never seen Freddie wear anything but black – it's slimming, he says.

'Freddie, what happened?'

'Izzy, I've found our next big thing.' He takes out a large bound folder from his briefcase and starts to untie it. 'And let me tell you, he's good.' This is what Freddie lives for – the thrill of discovering new talent and introducing it to the public. For him, the art world isn't about the parties or the status. Few people know this, but Freddie's real name is *Frederick Barnakofski*, and he comes straight out of the Bronx. He spent his twenties working his way through Yale art school not to become a star himself, but to champion the work of others. Really, I think he deserves a medal.

(Something in platinum. Freddie's always saying gold's not his color.)

Freddie and I head through the two main exhibition rooms toward the office, which lies behind an elegant set of glass-paned French doors. It's an airy space, decorated with works from our more successful shows. Freddie has a gorgeous antique desk that lines the back wall. Above it hangs a piece from last year's industrial-collage exhibition – a large work, crafted with steel and other metal alloys, bent and twisted into something both foreboding and beautiful. Although I really hope the canvas never falls, or Freddie's in for major head trauma.

My desk sits across the room from Freddie's. It's small and gray, but I've got nice office supplies and custom stationery, and my computer's a pretty blue color. Since Freddie's the dealer, the grandeur is rightfully his. I'm the gallery director – which means I do a little of everything. Mostly, I'm the go-to person for our collectors and the press, but I work with the artists too, especially when a new show goes up. Freddie discovers the talent; I make sure their paintings get on the wall. I consider the job very good practice for when I have my own gallery someday, which I've been dreaming about since I was an assistant, more than four years ago. I hope to do what most galleries won't risk doing: represent young, unknown artists who don't necessarily come with the right connections or a built-in list of buyers. About half our shows at the Bond are unknowns, like the one Freddie's so excited about now, and they're always my favorites. An artist's first show inspires a unique sense of hope that makes the collaboration seem more worthwhile.

'I saw his studio last night.' Freddie does his happy dance, shaking his black-clad hips around. I haven't seen him this overjoyed since Taye Diggs came into the gallery. I love that Freddie isn't all stuck-up like every other major dealer in the city. For most of them, arching an eyebrow is a wanton display of pleasure. 'I've already got the show laid out in my mind. They're great, monumental paintings.' He drops dramatically into his chair, throws his head back, and winks at me. 'He's a honey too. Twenty-nine, brooding, the works.'

'Freddie!' I wander over to the coffeemaker and pour him a cup, heavy on the milk. 'I don't know how you can date artists. They're so angsty.' Artists make the worst boyfriends ever. All they ever talk about is how their work is going, and how their competitors' work is going, and 'Why is his work selling better than mine, that talentless little bug who wouldn't know innovation if it came and bit him on the nose?' Okay, so I had one bad experience: my college boyfriend Seth, who enjoyed sleeping with his models a hell of a lot more than he did painting them.

'Moot point,' he says as I perch on the edge of his desk. 'He's on your team.' Freddie holds up the coffee. 'Skim, right, darling?'

I nod, as I do every day. He likes the reassurance.

'His colors, Izzy. They vibrate like a Rothko. Such subtle gradations, you could stare at them for hours.' Freddie's eyes sparkle. 'You wouldn't know it, but each image is a detail from a product label, blown up hundreds of times. Only when they're unrecognizable can they be beautiful.' He rifles in his briefcase and brings out a small box of slides. 'Lookie. That second one is Skippy peanut butter, and there's a Ben-Gay in there too somewhere.'

I hold them up to his desk lamp one by one. Freddie's right. The colors are haunting and luminous, interrupted by varying lines, some sharp and jagged, some round and cartoonish. Nice, indeed. And thank God they are. Freddie's timing couldn't be more ideal. The next artist we're showing, French collagist Adelaide Fortù, just phoned last week to say her show 'ees not weady yet' and that she had to 'staht ova again, dahling.' Freddie nearly had a heart attack. We've been planning that show for three months. I spent forever getting the press release worded just right – a fitting tribute to her whimsical, crafty paper collages. Now Freddie'll have to take advantage of every press connection he's got to start the buzz on this new painter, whose show we'll have only two weeks to plan. He can do it, though. He's that good.

'Of course the slides don't do them justice.' Freddie pulls a piece of paper out of the now unbound folder. 'Can you believe the Old Man himself asked me to take a look at this guy's work? Got the memo right here.'

'Get out!' Aside from his yearly visit – which I love because we get all this really amazing wine and cheese imported from France – we don't hear much from the benevolent Emerson Bond. From what I understand, no one does. Not the press, or his foundation, probably not even his family. Sequestered away at his Connecticut estate, the Old Man's the poster child of reclusiveness. Well, the poster senior citizen anyway.

For decades, Emerson Bond has been one of the country's most generous patrons of contemporary art. He personally supplied the grants that allowed Chuck Close and Cindy Sherman to pursue their work toward fame and fortune, and he still offers dozens of grants and scholarships a year. As far as the gallery goes, he pays for most of our expenses so we can afford to offer our artists eighty percent of the sales price rather than the usual fifty percent. Plus, we get our space for free. Most of New York's other contemporary galleries are in Chelsea. They're really cool-looking, with glass fronts, bright white walls, and stark lettering. I don't think I could ever work in those galleries, though. I smile too often, and I don't wear any vintage accessories. And when people accidentally wander toward the office, I don't say snotty things like 'Excuse me, you can see the office when you fill out a *job application*.' No, I like our spot on the Upper East Side. Less glamorous, perhaps, but definitely more homey. Truly, I've got one of the best jobs in the business, working for a billionaire who cares more about artists than about profit, and a dealer who cares as much about his employees as he does his artists.

'This is your chance, Izzy.' Freddie leans forward, his elbows on the desk blotter. 'In the past six months, you've already increased our sales by thirty percent. Now just sell the heck out of this show, and the Old Man will be sure to approve the budget increase for a new gallery director. You'll be promoted to associate dealer. I'm sure of it.'

Associate dealer. God, I never thought it could happen so fast. When I sold my first hundred-thousand-dollar painting to Deidre Gayle six months ago, Freddie promised if I continued to make blue-chip sales, he'd ask the Old Man to create a curatorial position for me. And he's right – I've done well. But to be an associate dealer! I'll get to travel to all the art fairs in the U.S. and around the world. I'll have the authority to recruit talent and mount my own exhibitions. And if I'm successful, I'll be light-years closer to having the clout to woo investors and open my own gallery. In fact, I'll be so disappointed if the promotion doesn't go through, I don't know if I should even allow myself to hope.

'What's he like, the new guy?' I ask. We've been lucky in the two years I've worked here. Artists can have the most inflated egos ever, but ours have been pretty low-key. The closest we've come to a diva was Janson Lloyd, this photographer who worked only with Polaroids. He got all snippy when we wanted to mat and frame them – said it would interfere with the purity of the object. He sure changed his mind, though, when he saw how few of those pure objects were selling.

Freddie shrugs. 'Like all artists, he's Narcissus incarnate. But trust me, it'll be worth it.'

'Well, then' – I hop off Freddie's desk – 'I think you should buy me lunch to celebrate.'

'Oh, yes. And then I'm off to Barneys to buy myself a little treat.' He claps his hands with the childlike glee adults reserve for upscale retail.

We return from our extended lunch with two Barneys signature black shopping bags. I couldn't help but get myself a little something too – a great pair of red corduroys by Earl. To be honest, I thought the beige ones would go better with my auburn hair, but my best friend, Dix, is always saying I should buy the opposite of what I want. According to her, my wardrobe is like a chip without salsa – definitely in need of some spice.

Freddie and I stop by the front desk to show our wares to Kimmy, who's sitting beside a pile of art publications, clipping reviews of the Teller show. Unfortunately, we didn't receive the one review we'd been hoping for. Only a rave from the *New York Times* can make a show legendary. But I guess with all the high-profile, end-of-season shows still up, the competition for review space was just too fierce.

'Do you guys ever lunch together without shopping afterwards?' Kimmy chides us, collecting stray cuttings.

'The dessert with no calories, darling, it's perfect.' Freddie holds up his new black fedora and the matching cashmere gloves.

Kimmy laughs. 'It's, like, eighty million degrees outside.'

'They were on sale!' Freddie does his happy dance for probably the tenth time today.

I pull out my new cords, and Kimmy whistles. 'Those'll make a few hearts race,' she says.

'Oh, stop.' I shove them back in the bag.

'Those pants make her legs look two miles long.' Freddie looks me up and down. 'Bitch.'

The fax machine starts to buzz, and Kimmy trots over to it in her little black dress. 'Incoming.'

'Are your congratulations on the way already?' I pat Freddie on the shoulder. 'We haven't even announced your newest find and you're already getting buzz!'

Freddie waves it away. 'Way too soon, love. No jinxing, now.'

'Guys,' Kimmy says, standing over the fax machine.

'Don't tell me,' Freddie says. 'Press release announcing that the Eaton Bosc Gallery has recently been awarded the Wee Kissass Award.'

But Kimmy's not smiling. 'It's the Old Man,' she says.

'Ooh, early visit?' I perk up. 'Do we get Brie?'

'He's coming?' Freddie raises his eyebrows. 'Then it *has* to be for the new painter.'

'No,' Kimmy says, still holding the inky paper. She looks up at us. 'He's dead.'

Is it hot in here or is it just you?

As I stand on the boiling subway platform waiting for the 6 train, I feel a prickle of guilt. A great man died. That's what's important. But here, squeezed in among the masses of rush-hour commuters, I find myself preoccupied not with grief, but with worry. Selfish worry. Could the Bond family shut down the gallery? We've never been the Old Man's most profitable endeavor, but we do turn a profit in the end. Usually. Oh, stop imagining the worst, Izzy. Surely the family wouldn't want to close down their beloved patriarch's pet gallery. The Old Man always said it gave him so much joy – or at least, I'm sure that's what he *would* have said had he been the talkative type.

After the fax today, the phones didn't stop ringing for one minute. Freddie thought it best to keep our mouths shut until we heard from the family, and so Kimmy said nothing but 'no comment' all day. And anyway, what could we say? I'd seen Emerson Bond twice, and he didn't speak much either time. All I know about him is what everyone knew: He loved art, he kept to himself, and even at his age, he had a great head of hair.

'Oh, no!' I hear a female voice call out, and my attention snaps back to the grimy platform. I see the contents of a purse rolling past me toward the train tracks, and I lunge to catch a Chanel lipstick before it gets past.

'Thank you!' I hear behind me. I turn around to see a youngish Latina woman reaching madly for her belongings, now littered in between people's shoes. 'That jerk ran me over.' She gestures toward a man in a burgundy T-shirt and baggy jeans whose back I can just make out as he surges down the platform, still shoving people right and left with no regard. 'Slams into me, then doesn't even turn around to apologize. I'll be bruised tomorrow.'

'Jeez, are you okay?!' I grab a roll of Tums and hand it over to her with a look of sympathy. I can only imagine how embarrassed I'd be if my bag spilled open, revealing its hundreds of gum wrappers, receipts, and movie stubs. My friend Jamie calls my purse 'The Black Hole of Crap,' because somehow, what goes in there never seems to come out again.

'I wish I could give that guy a piece of my mind,' she says, patting my hand in thanks. 'What people get away with!'

'Att-n-lad-n-g-mn,' a woman's garbled voice announces over the ancient speakers as my new acquaintance vanishes into the crowd. Translation: *Attention, ladies and gentlemen*. Like most New Yorkers, I'm fluent in subwayese. 'We are ex-ing-ext-m-d'l's due-t-s-nal-ml-f-tions.' *We are experiencing extreme delays due to signal malfunctions*.

The sweaty horde of people presses inexplicably forward. *But there's no train*, I feel like crying out. And now I'm smashed up against the hairy man in the too small 'I ♥ NY' T-shirt! The one who doesn't love New York enough to spare us his hairy midriff! Suppressing a gag, I give up my prime real estate by the tracks. I'll miss the next train, but that's okay. I'll just find someone cuter to wait next to.

Hmm, like that guy. He's tall, if a bit slouchy, in a burgundy T-shirt and baggy jeans . . . *Hey!* My pulse starts quickening. That's *him!* That's the rude jerk who knocked over that poor woman! I'm sure that's him, straining forward to glimpse down the tunnel. Pushed any babies yet, dickwad?

I feel a sudden rush of indignation, tempered only by the tiny voice of reason trying to sneak into the conversation. It's not your battle, Izzy. You should mind your own business. But the voice of injustice pipes up again, louder and more insistent. He should know what he's done. He should be made to regret it. He should *apologize*.

Before I can reconsider, I'm two inches away from the offending back, jabbing at it with my finger. 'Do you always shove people to the ground?' I hear coming out of my mouth.

'What the –' He turns around, recoiling from my finger. His face is only a few inches above mine: a prominent chin under a frowning mouth and blue eyes blazing with annoyance. 'What's your problem?'

'It's not *my* problem!' I cry, ready for a fight. That's right! I'm standing up for the downtrodden, for the put-upon, for every victim of subway rudeness everywhere! 'You wouldn't shove into someone waiting for a table at Jean Georges, would you? Of course not! They'd throw you out! That's not the way people *behave*.'

His head is tilted now, his forehead all wrinkly. 'Are you *crazy?*'

I take a mental step back and realize how I must sound. 'Back there' – I point toward the scene of the crime – 'you pushed into a woman, and her purse fell down. Her Chanel lipstick nearly rolled onto the tracks!'

'*Chanel?*' He places a hand to his heart. 'The horror!'

'That's not the point,' I say brusquely. 'You might have hurt her. You didn't even look to see if she was okay.'

He narrows his pale blue eyes at me. 'Look, Princess,' he says with scorn, 'I have no idea what you're talking about.'

Really! I'm not usually one for confrontation, but it's like he's willing me to retort with those self-satisfied eyes. 'Are you always this rude?'

The stranger draws his thumb lazily across his jaw, his voice gravelly. 'Are you always such a spoiled brat?'

I'm so angry I can't even talk. *I'm* spoiled? I try to think of some clever response, but before I can even react, I hear the sound – the first *kachink* of the track, the first *whoosh* of compressed air. The silver train is swooshing into the station, already too packed to accommodate the massive crowd waiting for it.

I watch as a handful of people struggle to exit the front car, and the conductor's voice shouts, 'Let the passengers off first!' But one person refuses to listen. He's throwing his arms at anyone who gets near him, pulling hair, kicking. Really, did he sleep through evolution? I crane my neck toward the hubbub, trying to get a better look. Instantly my breath catches. It's him! Shoving Guy! But . . . how'd he get over there so fast? My eye passes over the telltale baggy jeans, the burgundy T-shirt, the messy hair. Except, wasn't his hair darker a minute ago? A sinking feeling gnaws at my stomach. Then the guy reaches back to elbow a child, and I catch sight of his face. A face I'm seeing for the first time. Oh, God. It's not him. I mean, it *is* him. *That's* the jerk who knocked over Nice Purse Lady. I've been running my big fat mouth off at the wrong guy.

My cheeks burn with shame. I was so rude! I was even a little mean! I turn around, expecting to find my Shoving Guy – who really didn't shove anyone at all – so I can apologize profusely. But he's vanished. No doubt he couldn't wait to escape that crazy, shrill woman who jabbed at his back with her finger only to yell at him about Chanel lipstick and Jean Georges restaurant. That crazy, shrill woman who should be banned from ever talking to strangers again.

The train pulls slowly out of the station, carrying more passengers than I would have thought possible. I can see them, smashed up like bugs against the windows, adding so much extra weight that the cars can barely move. I empathize with this train, chugging fitfully by. Like me, the great silver beast should've just kept its mouth shut.

If I follow you home, will you keep me?

'Meeeww!'

I don't know how, but as soon as I start walking up the three flights to my apartment, Robbie always knows it's me. Even when I vary the sound of my footsteps, he still cries out in excitement. Food Lady's home!

'I'm coming, buddy,' I call out, unlocking the bolted door.

I walk into my teeny entranceway and instantly, he's pacing against my ankles, purring like a luxury car engine. Tossing my keys on the white end table near the door, I bend down to scratch the tufty black fur behind his ears. Robbie looks up at me with his big green eyes, and I want nothing more than to pick him up and squeeze him tight – which would no doubt lead to frantic clawing and kitty hysteria. So instead I drop a kiss on his pink nose and rub my face in his bunny-soft coat. 'Hello, baby.'

For the past three years, I've lived in this studio apartment on the Lower East Side. What was once the poorest, most crowded neighborhood in New York now boasts more trendy bars and shops than almost anywhere else in the city. My particular building is situated between a tattoo parlor and an avant-garde clothing boutique. The tattoo parlor's owned by a guy named Puffer, a wiry, olive-skinned artist who has a gold tooth and always wears a tight wool cap, even in summer. He may look tough, but Puffer's a sweetheart, and usually waves to me on my way home – even when he's sticking needles in people. The boutique is run by this very skinny Swedish girl. I don't think she's so nice, but maybe she's just hungry. One time last winter, when her heat was busted and it was frigid outside, I brought her a cup of hot cocoa on my way home. She sort of gave me this look and said flatly, 'How sweet.' I guess what she really needed was a steak dinner.

My building used to be a tenement, overstuffed with immigrants struggling to scrape by. But, like most of the neighborhood, it's been renovated for the young and artsy urban hopefuls who now occupy its tiny studios. I adore my apartment. All 350 square feet of it. Every little niche and corner makes me happy: the white tiled kitchen nook and breakfast bar. The baby-pale yellow walls, lined with glass vases from Pottery Barn. My wrought-iron bed, with its extra-fluffy white comforter and throw pillows. And my white bookcase, which holds all my treasures, including my scrap-book collection and my Victorian dollhouse. It's not that I don't like my best friend Dix's interior-decorated SoHo digs or Freddie's minimalist two-bedroom in Chelsea, or even Kimmy's illegal, almost uninhabitable loft space in Brooklyn. But somehow, amid the twee yellow and white, with my one big window and my beloved tabby feline companion, I feel all warm and pretty. My apartment is kind of my guilty secret. Like Jamie's passion for the musical *Rent* (he knows all the words), or the Monet key chain in Freddie's desk (given to him by his first boyfriend), or Dix's beloved high school yearbook (filled with our own commentary). Sometimes what's not so cool is what you love most.

I kick off the heels that have been torturing my feet all day and shrug off my suit jacket, which has become almost unrecognizable after my time on the sweltering Seventy-seventh Street 6 train platform. Ever-smiling Mr Chung at the local dry cleaner is going to have a field day when he finds out that black streak on my skirt came from lunging in subway dirt. He likes a good challenge. 'Cleaning clothes is like raising children,' he says. 'Must be at same time gentle and tough.'

The late spring evening sun streams through my window, making the yellow roses in the wall vases glisten. I breathe in the scent of lavender, which I keep in sachets on the nightstand, and try to relax. After all, it was an honest, understandable error. Mistaken identity. Happens all the time. Just watch any episode of *Days of Our Lives*. And I would've apologized if given half a chance! I can still hear his words rattling around in my head. *Look, Princess . . . at least I'm not a spoiled brat.* Ooh, I hated hearing that. He could've called me impulsive, irrational, misguided, or – let's face it – a lunatic, and I would've had to agree. But . . . *spoiled?* Stop, Iz. Don't let some stranger get to you. Besides, I think with a stab of sadness, my mind should be focused elsewhere. I may not have known the Old Man well, but I know how much he did for contemporary art. He was a good man. And now he's gone.

Reaching into my nightstand drawer, I select a shiny black CD, place it gingerly in my stereo, and press PLAY. Robbie Williams fills the air, warbling with emotion. *'We've got stars directing our fate,'* he sings. *'And we're praying it's not too late.'* My eyes close involuntarily, and I begin to sway to the music. That's right, Robbie. You've got to live every day because you never know when the game's all up. My own Robbie jumps onto the bed and meows at me, clearly jealous of his namesake. He turns over on his back, and draws his front paws up to his chest, as if to say, *Hey, I'm cute too.* But Robbie Williams is more than cute. With his heartfelt pop music, impish sense of humor, and perpetually lonely eyes, he's nothing short of a dream. Okay, so I have more than one guilty secret.

Most Americans haven't even *heard* of British pop sensation Robbie Williams. I hadn't either until Dix's music industry connections got us free tickets to his U.S. tour a few years ago. As soon as he hit the stage, I felt drawn back into the past, as if I were staring at a memory. Dix saw it too. The short black hair, the piercing green eyes, the playful smile . . . we could swear we were looking directly at Jared Anders, my first love – and my first heartbreak. 'Damn,' Dix said. 'If that's how Jared's grown since high school, then you really did miss out.' For two hours, I couldn't take my eyes off Robbie. When he danced, I danced. When he laughed, I laughed. When he jumped off the stage and threw himself lustily into my arms . . . oh, wait, that part was in my head. And, well, I got kind of hooked.

I've been thinking a lot about Jared the past couple days, ever since I heard my cousin Mimi's voice on my answering machine. Mimi, with her perfect, Jared-stealing chestnut hair and rosy cheeks. She and I grew up together, only four months apart, in Park Slope, Brooklyn. We were inseparable when we were little, sharing everything – even my Strawberry Shortcake dolls and her Brooke Shields makeup head. But then Mimi's father, Uncle Pete, became a senior vice president at some big foreign bank, and his family moved into a fancier brownstone near the mansions on Prospect Park West. After that, Mimi would only play *Little House on the Prairie*, so she could be Nellie Oleson and brag for hours about how much richer her family was than mine.

The last time we spoke, months ago, Mimi called to tell me (and probably nine hundred other people) about her new job working for one of Manhattan's most desirable interior decorators. Dix says I shouldn't call her back this time. 'Why give Mimi the satisfaction,' she said, 'of bragging about the tiles she put in some famous person's bathroom? Everyone knows it's only what's in the medicine cabinet that counts anyway.'

As I lean against the downy pillows on my bed, my mind reaches back thirteen years ago, to my freshman year of high school. The mental picture's less than cute. At fourteen, I was shy and quiet, with unfortunate bangs, oversized clothes, and a chest flatter than cardboard. By then, Mimi and I weren't exactly bosom buddies (although she, at least, *had a bosom*), but still, when I received an academic scholarship to attend the same ritzy school as Mimi, I was relieved. At least there'd be a familiar face in my new class.

I didn't yet know that my cousin would wind up dating my first real crush. The boy I gushed about to her every day. The boy Mimi promised she'd help get to notice me.

Just thinking about it now brings back a rush of feeling – the kind I usually get only from watching *Oprah*. Come on, Izzy, don't be silly. Jared Anders is ancient history. I mean, I don't get all choked up thinking about when Danny Carlucci stole my mittens in kindergarten, do I? The knit ones, shaped like little puppies, with pink tongues on the palms? Gosh, I loved those mittens.

The phone rings on the night table, startling me into the present. I turn down the stereo, bidding adieu to Mr Williams. It's probably my mother, calling to tell me to have more sex. Somehow, that's her solution to everything. *You just picked a fight in the subway, darling? Clearly you haven't been getting yours lately. Try some nooky!*

'Hello?' I say into the receiver, sitting back down on the bed.

'*Iz-zy.*' My heart drops about a foot in my chest as Cousin Mimi's nasal voice surges over the phone line. 'How long has it been? Aren't I just the worst at keeping in touch? It's okay – you can *totally* tell me I am.'

The girl has an eerie sense of timing, like she knows to call at the exact point when I'm feeling most vulnerable. Dix doesn't understand why I talk to her at all. But whether I like it or not, Mimi's family. And besides, high school was a long time ago. Mimi barely affects me anymore. Well, almost barely. 'Mimi, what a surprise.'

'Silly girl. Didn't you get my message?' I'm not sure whether she's chiding me or asking for real.

'Oh, you know how busy it gets,' I say, trying to sound casual. 'For us all. Here in the city. Living our lives and . . . stuff.'

'Of course I do!' she says enthusiastically. 'So tell me everything, and don't leave out one tiny detail.'

'Um . . .' I push at a slipper with my toe. We're not supposed to mention anything about the Old Man's death until the newspapers break the story tomorrow. And to Mimi, secrets are like hot coals: something to get off your hands as soon as possible. 'Work is going really well,' I say. 'I'm, um . . . developing new artists and working with some really cool collectors, like this one ballet dancer—'

'Aren't clients so fun?' Mimi squeals, satisfied with my one tiny detail. 'Like, the other day, David Bowie and Iman called us to decorate their New York flat, and I've already started arranging showings.' Mimi drones on for another five minutes or so, during which I zone out, until she says, 'And how's the love life? Anyone special? You can tell me!'

There it is, the dreaded question – the one where simply answering 'no' makes you feel about two inches tall, especially considering who's doing the asking. Okay, I confess. No matter how much I love my apartment, one crucial element is noticeably missing: the man I love helping me hang picture frames, or chopping vegetables, or throwing up his hands and crying, 'You're dragging me to Pottery Barn *again*?' I know Mimi can't wait to hear that I haven't found him yet. She can't wait to click her tongue and exclaim, 'Poor Izzy!' I even hear her breath quickening with anticipation. But you know what? I don't want to play along this time. Robbie struts over, yawning, and plops himself down at my feet. I bend down and scratch him under the chin. 'Well, I am seeing this one guy,' I say vaguely.

'Oooh, what does he do?' she coos. Mimi translation: *How much does he make?*

I say the first thing that comes to mind. 'He's a columnist. For the *New York News*.'

I hear Mimi take in a breath. 'Coup for you, Izzy! What's his name?'

'James D. Hunter,' I say, wincing. I shouldn't use Jamie this way, trying to impress my least favorite relative.

'Never heard of him,' Mimi says. 'Should I have?'

Well, actually, no. My friend Jamie is the least-known regular columnist at the *News*. Most of the people he *works* with haven't even heard of him. He got the job – his fifth in two years – only because Dix convinced Silas Burman, the *News's* publisher, that he could learn a thing or two from her reporter friend James D. Hunter, New York's equivalent to Don Juan. Silas Burman wanted Dix so badly, he would have gone to a swamp planet looking for Yoda if he thought it would help. So he hired Jamie. (And still didn't get a date with Dix.) For the past couple months, Jamie's been writing a biweekly column at the *News* that's supposed to explain women to men, decoding the eternal puzzle and revealing the key to a woman's heart. Or at least her panties. The column's called 'Getting It.' Problem being, Jamie isn't. He's about as far from Don Juan as Kermit the Frog is from singing. 'It's not easy being orange.'

'Well . . . maybe not,' I admit. 'But he's really up-and-coming! You should definitely keep an eye out for him! And . . . anyway, enough about me.'

Mimi giggles. 'I am *so* transparent, aren't I? I'm sure you could hear it in my voice the absolute minute I called. Can you *believe* it?'

'I guess not . . .,' I say hesitantly. What has she done now? Could she have stolen my job? Did she buy out my building, and she's going to raise my rent?

'Isn't it the greatest, most wonderfulest thing in the world?' Mimi continues to gush.

'Mimi,' I say carefully. 'I think I've missed a step.'

'Of course you have. Silly me!' She mock laughs at herself. 'Remember Trevor? The hottie-shottie banker I was dating last time we talked?'

I sure do remember – Mimi met him when he came to pick up her roommate for a blind date. Guess who he wound up taking out instead? Last time she called, Mimi spent five minutes telling me about his Lexus, another five minutes about his parent's home in Greenwich, and a good ten on how high his GMAT scores were and which business schools were at the top of his list. Her voice got so squeaky at the mention of Stanford and Harvard that I had to hold the phone away from my ear.

'Izzy, it's marvelous,' Mimi squeals. 'Trev's *sooo* good to me. He wakes me up every morning with a kiss, and he's always buying me some sweet little trinket. Nothing outrageous, just a bottle of perfume or a book of poetry.'

'Mmm-hmmm, that's super.' I force a smile, even though she can't see me.

'He can't leave for work in the morning without telling me how much he loves me, and how beautiful I am,' she continues.

'How great for you,' I say, feeling loneliness settle in, like a distant relative who needs a place to stay.

'*And*' – Mimi pauses dramatically – 'you absolutely *have* to see the size of the rock on my finger! Izzy Bizzy, I'm engaged!'

Hold on. *That's* not how it's supposed to happen.

Would you like to eat my pretzel?

During our first few months of high school, whenever I moaned that Jared Anders was out of my league, Mimi would say all I had to do was have the right attitude. I thought she was a saint, the way she let me go on about him. Even Dr. Phil would have yelled, '*Shut up already.*' So when my cousin passed me a note in algebra class that read 'I have news and it's *soooooo* fabulous!' I couldn't possibly have guessed her news would be that she'd been dating my crush for over two weeks. Or that she could look so gleeful while absolutely breaking my heart.

But without the whole Mimi-Jared fiasco, I might never have become friends with Dix. I knew her then only as Dorothea Dixon, the name our homeroom teacher used during roll call. The first time we met, I was crying on the school's bathroom floor. Dix wasn't the first to see me there, but she was the first to ask what was wrong. She was wearing a hooded black sweatshirt and tight black jeans, her hair cut short and choppy, black eyeliner around her eyes, and black Doc Martens on her feet. She was the coolest thing I'd ever seen.

Sitting with my back slumped against the cold tile, I told Dix how my cousin was dating Jared Anders – the boy I loved so much, I'd joined the cast of *The Crucible* just to be near him. Jared was the star; I was Crazy Screaming Witch Girl #3. But at least I got to talk to him. We had even become friends! Until my cousin swooped in.

'It's that Mimi chick, isn't it?' Dix had scoffed, rolling her eyes. And then she said something that I've always remembered. Something that comforts me even to this day. 'You'll find someone better than Jared Anders,' she assured me. 'A man who's intelligent, dashing, and classy in a way Mimi will never be. Trust me. I'm never wrong.'

My friendship with Dix began that day – a real, lasting friendship that I still marvel at. When I (finally!) bought my first bra, Dix was the one to pick it out – a lacy, lilac number that she said made me look like a 'hottie.' And when her parents divorced a few months after we met, I was the one to wipe away all that smeared black eye makeup, the only one who saw her cry. But my sharpest memory of our early friendship will always be on that bathroom floor. Standing there with her punk haircut and her big black boots, Dix was impossible to doubt. I did trust her, one hundred percent. I still do.

But there are times when I begin to doubt Dix's optimism. Like right now. Does Mimi have the right idea? If you're all schemey and self-absorbed, then you get everything? I'm twenty-seven now, and no closer to finding my perfect love than I was with Dix in the school bathroom. Not that I place the same importance on cars, houses, and business school that Mimi does, but kisses in the morning, books, perfume, and being adored so entirely sound kind of blissful.

Suddenly, my apartment doesn't feel so right. The place is too quiet. The dinner crowd hasn't yet hit the street outside, and my usually noisy neighbors all seem to be out. Even the yippy little dog upstairs must be sleeping. It's actually kind of lonely. And when I stop to think about it, lately I've been feeling that way more and more.

Come on, I think, pushing away images of Mimi. I've got one of the best jobs in my field, right? How many people can say that? Except . . . that could all change now.

There's no more Emerson Bond to come and eat cheese with us. No more Old Man watching our backs. Oh, God, when I go into work tomorrow, will I even still have a job?

The phone rings again, and I jump. What now? Did Mimi forget to tell me that *David and Iman* are importing all their furniture from Morocco? Did Trevor just surprise her with a *second* Lexus? But when the voice comes on the answering machine, it's not Mimi at all. It's Dix, and she sounds concerned.

'Iz, we've got a situation,' she's saying.

I look around desperately for the cordless, which I seem to have thrown down in frustration. There it is, under my comforter. I grab the phone and press TALK. 'Here I am!'

'Iz,' Dix says, 'meet us at HOME as soon as you can. It's happening again.'

'What?' I ask. 'What's wrong?'

She doesn't need to explain, though. I know what it is the minute she says the words.

'It's Jamie.'

We're sitting on a gargantuan plush red velvet sofa unlike any I've seen in someone's actual home, drinking our third round of multicolored cocktails. Dix has her heels on the upholstery and one hand propping up her head. Her high school punk days far gone, Dix is now a bombshell with the curves of a forties pinup icon. Next to her, Jamie looks as dejected as I've ever seen him, all hunched over, with his curly dark hair falling into his face. My heart goes out to him.

As far as guy friends go, Jamie's the best. He'll help paint your apartment by day and wash dishes after dinner by night. He'll go with you to a Merchant Ivory film when no one else will. He doesn't mind being the default date for weddings or cocktail parties. And, best of all, he can always sense when you need a hug. Jamie would make the best, most supportive boyfriend ever. If Dix or I could ever commit friendcest with someone who's nearly a brother, one of us would have snatched him up long ago. But whenever Jamie's around a girl he likes, he just loses it. He goes mute. He sweats. The stress makes him break out in hives. Poor, sweet Jamie hasn't been on a date in over six months. He *had* been dreaming about this one girl for weeks – a waitress at his favorite brunch spot – but she recently got deported to Poland. And just when Jamie'd finally mustered up the courage to say hi.

Needless to say, his column about women hasn't exactly caught on like wildfire. Or even like a damp match. And now it's about to end.

'Are you sure the *News* is going to ax you? Maybe you're just being paranoid.' I rub Jamie's khaki-covered knee. 'What'd your editor say?'

Jamie groans. 'He asked if I was gay.'

'Ouch,' Dix says, raising her head.

'Your time is coming,' I say brightly. Although to be honest, I'm not exactly sure it is. Jamie gets fired so often, the unemployment office sends him Christmas cards.

Dix points to all the beautiful, tipsy women around us. 'Dearest,' she says to him, 'it's time *you* started coming.'

And, well, she's usually right.

'How about that one?' Dix nods at a girl in a crop top and low-slung jeans.

Jamie lowers his head into his hands. 'This is making me feel worse,' he says. 'I can actually feel the waves of pity washing over me.'

'No, no,' I say quickly, continuing the knee rubbing. 'We're just trying to help.'

'Izzy,' Jamie says through his hands, 'it's a pity *tsunami*.'

'What about Internet dating?' I toss out, brainstorming. 'You haven't written about that yet.'

'Actually, I have.' Jamie slouches down even farther. By now, his chin's almost resting on the cushions. 'When I turned the column in to my editor, he held up a copy of *Time Out* with the exact same story on the cover. I am a fountain of craphole ideas. It's over. I'm toast.'

'Well, if it makes you feel better . . .,' I say in a small

voice, squirming uncomfortably on the red velvet sofa, 'this time, I might be joining you.'

'What?' Dix bolts upright, her shiny black ponytail swinging behind her. 'What are you talking about?'

I've kept the secret for a whopping five hours, but my friends are nothing if not discreet. So I tell them. And finally saying it out loud, how the Old Man's gone forever, and the gallery's in jeopardy, makes me really sad. The end-of-an-era kind of sad. The kind where you know that your life is going to change, and probably not for the better.

'We don't know much right now,' I say, trying to sound positive. 'We're waiting to hear from the Bond family lawyers.'

'God, I feel like an idiot.' Jamie shakes his head ruefully. 'Here I am moaning away, and *you're* the one who actually needs comforting.'

'No!' I say. 'Jamie, don't feel bad! I mean, *do* feel bad.'

He gives me an odd look.

'I mean, we can feel bad *together*.'

'No way.' Dix shakes her head. 'Not while I'm around.' She swings her feet off the couch and smooths down her clingy dress. 'I'm getting us more drinks.' And with that, she heads to the bar, which in accordance with HOME's theme is disguised as a kitchen counter.

'Look, Jamie, don't worry about me. I'm sure everything will be fine.' And as I say it, I almost believe it, like the words themselves are infusing me with optimism. 'And you'll be fine too! You've got one more shot, right? I mean, your boss told you to go ahead with the next edition of your column. So maybe this one will be a huge hit!'

Jamie shifts his weight, stretching his lanky legs in front of him. 'How on earth am I supposed to do that? How can I write about women when I can't even *talk* to them?' He leans his head back, his glasses reflecting the dim light above. 'Hell, I just *look* at a girl and I get all self-conscious, which makes *her* self-conscious. And you try having a conversation when both parties feel like they're giving testimony before a Senate committee.'

I nod understandingly. The thing is, I know what Jamie's feeling. I know what it's like to be so nervous when talking to a guy, you can't even hear what he's saying, so you just laugh and hope he was telling a joke. And then, when you realize he's expecting a response, all you can say is, 'Yeah,' because your words, like Elvis, have left the building. There's nothing harder than connecting with someone. No matter how big the city is, no matter how many different kinds of people live in it, and no matter how many friends you have here, it's still possible to go home at the end of the day and feel alone. I just think that Jamie – with his big heart and floppy hair – feels it a little more keenly than the rest of us. I smile and reach my arm around his waist. 'For what it's worth, *I* think you can do it.'

Jamie tilts his head until it rests on top of mine. 'Thanks, Iz. It's worth a lot.'

Dix returns then, plopping herself down on the sofa next to Jamie. 'That was *pathetic*,' she says, crossing her long legs. 'Not to interrupt your tender moment or anything.'

Jamie straightens up, blushing. 'We were just talking about current events.'

Dix nods. 'Uh-huh. So. I'm paying for the round, and this guy' – she points to a skinny straw-haired man sitting at the bar – 'pokes me on the arm and says, "Can I get you a pretzel?" I mean, "Can I buy you a drink?" is boring enough, but they give out the pretzels for free. I can get my own damn pretzel.'

I take a sip of my overflowing lychee Martini, thankfully made with Skyy, the only vodka I can drink without grimacing. 'He seems to really like those pretzels, though,' I say. And it's true. The guy has, like, four bowls lined up in front of him.

Jamie sighs. 'And of all the women here, Dix, he wants *you* to eat his pretzel.'

Dix runs a hand through her long ponytail and grins. 'Now, if he had said, "Would you like to eat my pretzel?" that would have been a different story.'

I look over at her snack-food-loving suitor. 'As long as he's being funny, and not icky.'

A waitress in a tight black dress appears before us just then with a giant plate of shrimp cocktail, Jamie's favorite, and a glass cup of chocolate mousse, my favorite.

'You guys need to fucking cheer up,' Dix says with a hopeful smile.

God, Dix is the best. She never underestimates the healing powers of chocolate. My mouth waters at the sight of the fluffy mousse. But shockingly, Jamie isn't paying any attention to the food *or* to the attractive waitress.

'You mean,' he says, leaning forward eagerly, 'if awkward pretzel guy had said something cheesy like "Hey, you want to see something swell?" he would have had a chance?'

Dix pops a shrimp in her mouth and tilts her head to one side. 'Make me laugh and let me know you want my body. That's why they invented the pickup line. It's that simple.'

Jamie turns to me, his glasses nearly slipping off his nose. 'It is?'

I shrug, not knowing the effect my words will later have. 'Well, if you put it like that, sure. I guess it is.'

Jamie blinks twice. Within seconds, he's saying good-bye. In another minute, he's out the door. The shrimp cocktail never stood a chance.

Dix throws up her hands. 'It's like he *tries* to go home alone.'

*Do you believe in love at first sight,
or should I walk by again?*

I never realized New York had so many newspapers.
We've got them all spread out in an inky mess over the
reception desk. I'm reading the Old Man's obit in the *New
York News* while Kimmy peers over my shoulder,
munching carrots. Today, she's surrounded her eyes with
shocking purple shadow and is wearing a black empire-
waist gown, no doubt a sign of mourning.

> Industrial magnate Emerson Bond, 87, died
> Tuesday of a heart attack. The publicity-shy
> billionaire – who first made his fortune refining
> steel for airplane wings in the Second World War –
> was a lifelong philanthropist and patron of the arts.
> Upon founding the Emerson Bond Gallery in 1989,
> Mr Bond offered this now famous tidbit when asked
> how he managed a lifetime of success: 'I don't listen
> to fools. And I don't talk to them either.' It would be
> his last interview. Mr Bond is survived by a son and
> two grandchildren.

Poor Emerson Bond. To go to sleep one night, just like any
other, with your warm milk on the night table, your
slippers at the bedside, your butler downstairs in a pink

ruffled apron, washing the silver (the things you read in the gossip columns!), only to never wake again. And on top of that, Freddie says the Old Man hadn't spoken to his only son in almost ten years. I wonder what the son is thinking now – if he regrets never having healed old wounds. I know I would.

'Dahlias for my dahlings,' Freddie exclaims, heading toward us from the exhibition rooms. His face is hidden behind a massive arrangement of the showy pink flowers. The office is full of memorial baskets and bouquets. I've been avoiding them as much as possible, though I appreciate the thought. Don't get me wrong – I love flowers, but somehow, they make the office feel like a hospital room.

Freddie places the dahlias on the ledge in front of the reception desk, and they actually do look kind of cheery, like dozens of carnival pin-wheels. 'Look,' he says frankly, 'I know you're feeling gloomy right now. I am too. I wish I could make things better.'

'Aw, Freddie,' I say, giving him a little hug. 'We'll buck up.'

'Totally!' Kimmy pipes in, nodding her head. 'I've even got good news! Grady Cole called. He's stopping by today.'

'Ooh!' Freddie's eyes dart open, and he claps his hands together. 'Goody!'

'Who's Grady Cole?' I wonder if he's next in the long line of Freddie's boyfriends. The last one was named Joseph, but it was pronounced 'Zho-*zef*,' like the French. When they broke up, Freddie spewed out an hourlong diatribe on the abnormal shape of his moles. 'There's one on his hip,' Freddie said, 'that's shaped like a donkey. As if that wasn't enough to warn me he's a jackass.'

'Grady Cole is my *star*, darling, the new artist.' Freddie splays his hands out on either side of his head, like Judy Garland in *A Star Is Born*.

'The cute one, right?' Kimmy gives a purple-lidded wink. She's got a boyfriend – this very nice punk rocker named Flick – so the wink must be meant for me. But after

my college boyfriend, Seth, the model-boinking painter,
I've sworn off artists forever.

'Mm-hmm,' Freddie purrs, wiggling his eyebrows like
Groucho Marx.

The phone rings, and Kimmy deftly lifts it to her ear.
'Bond Gallery,' she says, sitting down behind the dahlias.

Everything feels so normal. The three of us, joking
around instead of working. Freddie and Kimmy in their
dramatic black outfits, me in my yellow sundress, talking
about boys . . . and art, of course.

'Freddie,' and suddenly, Kimmy's voice sounds
anything but normal. 'It's Andrew Gold, the lawyer for the
Bond family.' She raises her head. 'He says it's urgent.'

I take in a sharp breath, and I see Freddie's mouth
tighten. For a second, he doesn't say anything. He just
looks at me. I give his hand a supportive squeeze. 'Go on,'
I say, hoping I sound positive. 'It's all right.'

'Sure it is.' But he sounds hopeless. 'I'll be in the office.'

I watch Freddie maneuver through John Teller's waxen
body parts and then disappear. For a moment, the only
sounds are the cars whooshing past outside, the faraway
tinkle of an ice cream truck, Kimmy's computer eagerly
announcing 'You've got mail.' She and I seem to have a
tacit agreement not to talk about the phone call. In fact, we
seem unable to talk at all.

Then, just as Kimmy's mouth opens and I lean in
expectantly, I hear a floorboard creak behind me. *Someone
else is here*. Oh, *no*, I think. They've come to shut us
down. I'll turn around, and there'll be a lawyer there
with a shutdown notice, or whatever it is lawyers use, and
he'll change the locks and repossess the art, and it'll all be
over.

There's nothing I can do. I've got to face him.
Clenching my fists to steel myself, I spin around on my
heel. For a moment, I'm stunned. It's not a lawyer. It's
nowhere near a lawyer. My eye is first caught by his old-
school Puma sneakers, then by the worn jeans hanging on
his hips. Continuing upward, I see his faded T-shirt,

prominent chin, blue eyes, and messy brown hair. Wait. There's something familiar about that hair, the way it sticks out at random ... *No*, it couldn't be ... Oh, fuck, oh, *fuck* ... it's the guy from the subway! Mistaken-Identity Guy, who I yelled at for no reason! Oh, my God, did he have me followed! Is he here for *retribution*?

But aside from a slight flinch that I could've imagined, there's no sign that Mistaken-Identity Guy even recognizes me. So ... could he be a collector? Granted, our collectors tend to buy new clothes once in a while, but what if he's here to buy art? What should I do! I should apologize. Right away. Before anything bad happens. Either that or act like I've never seen him before. Biting my lip, I sneak a glance at the guy's face. Nothing. No sneer of hatred, no widened eyes of shock. Could it be possible that he doesn't remember?

'Is Freddie around?' he asks Kimmy, ignoring me entirely.

Kimmy hesitates. 'He's unavailable at the moment.'

'I'm the director,' I say carefully. 'Can I help you?'

Mistaken-Identity Guy turns reluctantly to me, his eyes taking on a familiar glint of confrontation. 'So do you have the contract I'm supposed to sign?'

You're kidding. You've got to be kidding me. Somewhere, the Fates are looking down at me and laughing. 'Grady Cole?' I say, really more of a statement than a question.

'Yeah,' he says, his eyes narrowing like a hawk's.

My heart pounds in my chest, but I muster up a smile and hold out my hand, hoping beyond hope that I can sound sincere. 'Hi, I'm Isabel Duncan, and I've been so looking forward to meeting you.'

Grady Cole looks at my hand like it might explode at any moment. Then he stuffs his own hands in his pockets. Either he's giving me the silent treatment (what are we, *three*?) or he's just plain impolite.

'Listen,' I say, using my professional tone. 'I don't know if you've heard, but Emerson Bond passed away yesterday.

I want to assure you, though, that your show is still a priority for us.'

'Yeah, I heard.' He turns his back to me, thereby displaying the gaping tear in the back of his jeans, and starts to walk toward the office. 'Is this where the contract is?'

'Wait!' I feel a moment of panic. All we need right now is for our next big thing to walk in on Freddie crying over the loss of the gallery. 'I'll get it for you. If you wouldn't mind waiting in the private salesroom.'

Kimmy places a supportive hand on my shoulder before I head after this man, my nemesis, our new champion painter. I've dealt with egos before, even a tantrum or two. But this guy . . . well . . . he's just *rude*.

I usher Grady Cole into the small room just off our main exhibit space, where we show work not currently up for view. He sits on the ivory sofa, spreading his arms out on either side of him and resting one leg on his knee. Honestly, the man looks like he's sitting on a park bench. After a long night of drinking. And not washing his hair.

For a moment, we don't speak. Can I actually pull this off? I mean, when you think about it, I must have looked different on that boiling subway platform, with my hair plastered to my head, my clothes a sodden mess, and my face all red. Now my hair's up in a ponytail, and my dress is bright and crisp. I'm a different person! And anyway, what kind of perspective can you get when it's so crowded that you're pressed up against someone like a LEGO? So really, why *would* he recognize me?

Boy, that's a relief. So he's just a difficult artist. *That* I can handle. I'll focus on selling his work based on the images themselves rather than the artist's winning charisma, and I won't expect any cooperation when it comes to getting his paintings out of his studio and into the gallery. He'll be a nuisance, yes, but at least he won't realize that the director of his gallery is actually the infamous 6 Train Assaulter.

Grady finally raises his eyebrows and gives me a slow, mischievous grin. 'Well, Princess?'

Crap. *Crap*. He knows.

'I'm sorry!' I cry out. 'I would've apologized then, but you left so soon. You were the wrong person! I mean, I thought you were someone else. From the back. Which wasn't your back. Well, yes, it was, but it wasn't the back I thought it was. See?'

Grady Cole neither cracks a smile nor says a word.

My mouth feels dry, and all of a sudden, I don't know what to do with my hands. This is my big show! The show that's supposed to get me promoted to associate dealer, if that's even a possibility now that the Old Man's gone. I've got to fix this, but if Grady won't accept my apology, what else can I do? Drop to my knees and beg forgiveness? There's got to be another way. My mind fixes briefly on all the fruit baskets in the office – because that etiquette handbook I got in my Christmas stocking *did* say that regifting was totally fine in some situations. I try to remember – was death one of them? Hmm, probably not. Besides, I've got a feeling it would take more than apples and walnuts to win over Shady Grady Cole.

'So, Isabel,' Grady says, somehow turning my name into a rebuke, 'is that Chanel lipstick you're wearing?'

'What?' I say, taken aback. 'No, actually, I think it's –' Oh. Right. Not funny.

'And I was thinking' – Grady tilts his head pensively – 'you, me and Freddie should go out somewhere for dinner. You know, to celebrate our new union.'

'We should?' I don't like where this is going.

'How about Jean Georges?' Grady's eyes bore into mine. 'Although if we have to wait for a table, I might just shove everyone in the place.'

Oh, God. He's enjoying this. That's why he won't accept my apology. He knows how awkward I feel. And he's going to rub my face in it, night and day, until the end of his show.

Grady Cole's eyebrows rise sardonically. 'What do you say, Princess?'

'I'll just go get that contract,' I mutter. The click of my

slingbacks sounds unusually loud as I make my way toward the office. As agitated as I am by Grady Cole, I'm even more vexed by what Freddie might be going through right now. Do I knock? Or just walk in? What if he's in the middle of some dramatic confrontation? I wish I didn't have to interrupt, but the thought of entertaining Grady in our tiny private salesroom for even ten minutes makes me feel prickly with dread, and who knows how long this phone call will last?

I rap lightly on the glass French doors and then crack them open. Freddie's sitting at his desk, writing down notes, holding the phone in the crook of his neck. He looks up when he hears me, but his expression is unreadable. That's *very* un-Freddie-like. Not a good sign.

'Can you hold one minute?' Freddie says into the receiver, pressing HOLD before turning to me.

'Contract?' I ask, trying to sound bright. 'Grady Cole is here.'

'Oh, good,' Freddie says wearily. 'I want you two to get to know each other.' He reaches into his desk for the legal papers, giving me a quick smile that I hope isn't a cover-up. 'You'll love each other. I'm sure of it.'

'I'm sure we will!' I say enthusiastically. The last thing Freddie needs is something else to worry about.

He nods, pointing to the phone, and I kiss the top of his head before closing the doors firmly behind me. I take a few deep breaths and try to think positively. But inside, I feel all fluttery. I know Freddie. Things are not going well.

I collect myself, pressing my fingers against my temples. I am going to raise my head and march right in there. I'm going to hand Grady Cole these legal papers with a cheery smile. And as I do so, I must say I feel quite proud of myself. I guess what they say in entertainment works for galleries too: The show must go on.

Silently, Shady Grady takes a pen, signs his name several times, and hands the contract back to me. This is when the artist usually shows his excitement – like, with a happy handshake, or even a hug. But this guy just puts the pen down and asks, 'That it?'

'Yes,' I say, unable to hide my frustration. 'That's it.'

'Okay, Princess.' He stands, finally smiling a fraction of an inch. 'See ya.'

'We have champagne,' I say hesitantly. 'I mean, with most of our new artists, we toast to a new partnership, great show, all that. . . .'

Grady peers at me, his ice-blue eyes sharp and focused, as if trying to whittle out my every motivation. It's not hard to see he disapproves of whatever he thinks he sees.

'I don't think so,' he finally says, edging toward the doorway. 'I've got to go.'

'I'm sorry to hear that.' My voice has a sarcastic lilt that I'm not used to. 'Would you like me to walk you out?' I say, sitting firmly on the couch and crossing my legs.

'Sure,' Grady Cole says. But he's already walking away.

Once he's out of sight, I let my head fall into my hands. Well, one thing's certain. Next time there's a subway delay, I'm taking a cab.

6

*Do you mind if I end this
sentence in a proposition?*

I can't believe it. I just cannot imagine it. I feel like I'm
on *The Facts of Life*, and Mrs Garrett is about to leave,
and even though Cloris Leachman is coming to take her
place, everyone knows Peekskill will never be the same.

After he got the news yesterday, Freddie didn't come
out of the office for over an hour. Dear, wonderful Freddie.
The Bond will go on, but without him. I never would have
thought, not with all the years Freddie's given the gallery,
or the rave reviews his shows have gotten, and that's not
even considering how much fun we all have together. But
the family has a new dealer in mind, one schooled in
Europe and long admired by Raymond Bond, the Old
Man's son. I guess Frederick Barnes from the Bronx – one
of the most devoted, sharp-eyed dealers in the art world –
just isn't good enough for him.

Freddie and I spent today calling all our artists and
collectors to tell them that next week will be his last. I had
hoped that repeating the words over and over would
somehow deaden their meaning. It didn't. Each time I told
a client that Freddie was leaving, I felt the same
constriction in my chest, like I'd just been pinned under a
cartoon anvil. He was so noble about it too. After the
lawyers fired him, Freddie didn't say one bad word about

the Bond family. His priority, he said, was letting them know how necessary it was to keep Kimmy and me. That's just so Freddie. Here he is, cut afloat in the middle of the ocean, and his first instinct is to make sure we get life jackets.

'We were a good team,' I say sadly. And it's true – we were great together. Now who's going to advise our artists on the best way to realize their creative vision? Who's going to know by sheer instinct if there's a market for an artist's work? And after the close of a tough sale, who will be there shaking his hips in the happy dance? Gosh, I'll miss that dance. The new guy probably won't even have a happy foot tap.

The new guy. Oh, jeez. Just thinking about him fills me with anxiety. The lawyers told us that his name is Avery Devon, and we're to expect him next Friday, a week from tomorrow. He's currently in Berlin, where he's the dealer at a respected avant-garde gallery. Beyond that, we don't know much. Although according to Kimmy, anyone named Avery Devon must have a foot-long stick up his you-know-what.

'I'm sorry,' Dix says compassionately. We're at an outdoor café table, gazing over Union Square Park, where people are walking their dogs or lying out on the grass enjoying the early June evening. Dix still has on her work clothes, a white Armani pants suit, as do I, a pleated gray skirt and fitted T-shirt. 'But you know the arts are a field of upheaval. If you'd wanted a stagnant career, you would've chosen accounting.'

'What if he fires me?' I stir my mocha, melting the whipped cream into swirls. For all we know, Avery Devon could be bringing a whole new staff with him. 'What if he wants a director who's more official? Someone with slicked-back hair, ramrod posture, and boxy little glasses.' My spoon drops to the saucer with a clatter. 'What if he wants someone more *German*?'

'Calm down, Iz.' Dix reaches out her hand to touch my arm. 'You've got a week to prepare. Just make the best of it.

Study your past sales. Take a few extra clients out to lunch. Solidify plans for the next show. Make yourself even more indispensable than you already are.'

'Right.' I nod my head firmly. 'Indispensable.'

'And then, when this Avery walks his ass into the gallery next Friday, you'll greet him in some sophisticated outfit, with your hand outstretched for a confident handshake.' Dix leans in, her brown eyes warm and focused. 'Just worry about the first impression. The rest will fall into place.'

I want to believe her. I want to believe I have nothing to worry about. That the new guy will be generous and understanding, with a vision for the gallery that matches my own. But I can't ignore the nervous, high-pitched voice in my head – the one that's screaming, 'Danger! Abort!' over and over, as if I'm about to launch myself into space, but I've forgotten my gravity suit, and the life support doesn't work, and we're out of Tang. 'Dix,' I say, twisting my napkin around my fingers, 'what if the new guy doesn't like me?'

She smiles sweetly. 'Then I'll have to hurt him.'

God, I love her. With a grateful smile, I take a nice big gulp of my mocha and savor the tastes of coffee and dark chocolate mingling on my tongue. Mmm. Nothing tastes better than drinkable chocolate. Except maybe for assorted chocolates. Or truffles. Or chocolate mousse – 'Hey, wait,' I say, my head snapping up.

Dix nods. 'I knew you'd remember.' She reaches into her leather Dior bag and pulls out a copy of today's *New York News*. Jeez, how could I have forgotten?

Dix spreads open the paper to a page toward the back, where I see the name *James D. Hunter* under the unlikely title 'Getting It.' Here it is. Jamie's last hope. I cross my fingers while I read.

Twenty thousand years ago, prehistoric man grabbed a fistful of prehistoric woman's hair and dragged her behind him into the cave. After hours of pleasure, he impregnated her and started new generations of men with fists and women with readily grabbable hair. And so it went. Man wanted Woman, Man let Woman know, Man got what he wanted. Until Woman decided to make it difficult.

One day, some poor Neanderthal schlub grabbed the nearest nubile cave wench, and she turned around and decked him. Never again would Man be assured of getting Woman into his cave. Humanity's eternal dilemma was born: If hair grabbing is out, how does Man let Woman know what Man wants?

Enter the first Neanderthal genius, lounging in a Stone Age bar, chatting up newly independent Woman. 'That's a nice pelt,' he says. 'It would go great with my dirt floor.' She blushes. She giggles. Then, something miraculous happens. Back into the cave she goes. Sometimes we forget it, men, but the pickup line is our friend. .

' "Nubile cave wench"? Is he for real?' I scan the column again. The voice is confident and funny; authoritative, even. Sounds nothing like Jamie. This guy I'm reading here – who goes on to talk so glibly about making retro-style romance hip again, with all its bouquets and heart-shaped chocolate boxes – this guy could be a stranger. 'Listen to this,' I say, reading toward the end. ' "Give it a try. If you wind up with a drink down your shirt, send me the cleaning bill. And if you wind up beneath her five-hundred-thread-count bedsheets, well . . . remember who got you there." ' Hey. How does Jamie know about girl sheets?

Dix shrugs her shoulders, brushing a teeny piece of lint off her suit. 'If you ask me, he'll be regretting his words when he gets those cleaning bills. Pickup lines are a cute idea, but the cheesy guys already use the worst ones, and the decent guys haven't got the balls.'

Poor Jamie. I'm already mentally planning ways to

cheer him up – (No strippers this time. I'll never forget the look of embarrassment on Jamie's face that time Dix and I bought him a lap dance at Scores. But how else do you cheer up a guy?) – when my eye is caught by a man at the table next to ours. He seems to be in his twenties, with dark hair and a preppy Izod shirt. At another moment, I might think he was cute, but right now all I notice is that he's got his nose buried in the *News*. And I may be mistaken, but it looks like the same page as Jamie's column.

'Look!' I whisper.

Dix follows my eyes and leans over surreptitiously to see what page he's reading. She raises her eyebrows at me in disbelief.

'Get out!' Immediately I swivel my head around, checking out the other tables. It's a gorgeous evening, and still before sundown, so the café's outdoor seating is filled to capacity.

'Izzy!' Dix gasps. I see it too. At least four guys and one woman around us have Jamie's column splayed out on the tables in front of them. 'My God,' I whisper, looking up to see if pigs are flying. 'It's a miracle.'

For once, Dix and I are at a loss for words. We've known Jamie for five years – Dix met him when she was still a PR assistant and he was a fledgling (and soon-to-be failed) entertainment reporter. Since I've known Jamie, he's covered everything from the Tribeca Film Festival (where they threw him out after he accidentally stepped on Kate Hudson's foot) to the Democratic convention (where he couldn't get in because someone stole his press pass) to the opening of Brooklyn's first Barnes & Noble (which he finally found after getting lost for two hours). But I've never seen anyone actually reading one of Jamie's articles. *Ever*. Until now.

'We have to tell Jamie!' Dix reaches for her cell phone, but before she even dials, it lights up and starts shaking maniacally. Dix always keeps her phone on vibrate – she's convinced the ring melodies will give her seizures.

'Yu'huh?' she says into the tiny silver phone. 'Oh, fuck. What? No. Tell him to clam up, keep his head down, and push his way out of there. Does he have a hat? Shit. I'll be there in a minute.' She slams her phone shut, rolling her eyes.

'What happened?' I wonder which of Dix's celebrity clients might have done what. Though the bulk of her clientele is still B-list, Dix is quickly becoming known as New York's top publicist for the young and brooding. Perhaps Stephen Dorff was spotted ordering a Happy Meal?

'It's Tanner.' Tanner Field is the client that made Dix's career and still her one full-fledged star. He was the 'rebel' member of the boy band Second to Nine until Dix pushed him to solo success. He's also denser than lead, which keeps her on her toes. 'There's a group of paparazzi hounding him at Bliss SoHo.' She's grabbing her corporate platinum AmEx out of her bag and struggling into her blazer at the same time.

'Bliss Spa?' I flag down our waiter for the bill. One of the perks of hanging out with Dix is that no matter how many times I try to pick up the bill, she absolutely refuses. For her, socializing is a tax write-off.

'Yeah. Fucker was getting a facial. *People's* going to go nuts – "Toughie Tanner seeks softer skin" or better yet, "Tanner Field fights fine lines." ' She pens her bold, swirly signature on the bill, pockets the receipt, and strides onto the sidewalk.

'You'll fix it,' I say.

Dix winks, but I can see her mind working. 'We'll give him a love interest. He was visiting a mystery lady at Bliss, well-bred socialite, identity unconfirmed. Resident bad boy meets uptown girl of his dreams, who of course will not last long enough to alienate his ten million adoring female fans.' As Dix and I walk to the corner, she's already got her phone open again and her hand out for a cab. 'Bye, dearest, I've got a romance to create.'

'Can you throw in an extra one for me someday soon?'

I kiss her cheek and in two seconds, Dix is speeding west on Fourteenth Street.

I head the other way, thinking I'll walk home since it's so nice outside. Ordinarily, I'd be ecstatic right now. Only New Yorkers know the joy of a late spring day in the city. The population thins as the upper crust flocks to the Hamptons, and the rest of us walk along treelined streets in a happy glow, passing up the cabs and subway stations to spend a few extra minutes in the sun and the breeze. I live for this time. Whenever I hear that song, 'I love New York in June; how 'bout you?' I can't help but say – out loud – I do! I do! So as I head east around Union Square Park, I notice the soft rustle of the trees and the warm sun on my face. But I can't revel in it. My mind is too occupied with worry, and with grief. My head drops as I walk, touching on all the what-ifs. What if Avery Devon is a goblin? What if he axes me? What if I never find a gallery job again? What if I wind up on one of those commercials for art school, asking, 'Can you too draw this cartoon turtle?'

Suddenly, my pessimistic thoughts scatter as I hear the sound of wheels on pavement just inches away. One of the teenagers skateboarding around Union Square is flying by right in front of me. 'Whoa!' I say, taking a step back. He rises in the air, spins around, and falls to the ground with a loud clatter.

'Are you okay?' I call to him, even though I know he'll ignore me. The skater boys never speak to anybody – it's against their code of cool.

But the kid pops up his skateboard with his foot and, to my surprise, seems to be heading exactly my way.

'Hey,' he says to me. He's got on a black Metallica T-shirt and camo pants, and his head is shaved. Close-up, I can see he's carrying under his arm, of all things, a copy of the *New York News*.

'Um . . . hi,' I say.

'I just wanted to know,' he says, scanning me up and down. 'Did you wash your skirt with Windex? Because I can really see myself in it.'

I don't mean to laugh, but I do, loudly. I laugh until tears spill from my eyes, until my shoulders finally relax and my jaw unclenches. I laugh like I've needed to laugh since Emerson Bond died two days ago.

'Sorry,' I say to Skater Boy, wiping my eyes with the back of my hand. 'But I think what you really need is some fabric softener.' And with that, I'm off.

7

*You must be Jamaican,
because Jamaican me crazy.*

'Conway Archer,' Kimmy calls out, nibbling on the top of her pencil.

I scrunch up my nose. Conway Archer, the dealer for the Berger Archer Gallery, has the habit of sucking all the air out of a room just so he can blow it back out talking about himself. At one of our openings (for this dazzling photographer who takes portraits of Southern drag queens) he spent half an hour telling Freddie how his gallery's show was more mature and thematically deeper than ours. Freddie – bless him – just looked Conway Archer blankly in the face and said, 'At what point did you think I'd care?'

Seeing me shake my head, Kimmy crosses out yet another name. We've been fine-tuning the guest list for Freddie's going-away party next week: the artists, minus the ones he's dated; our major collectors, minus the obnoxious ones; and the dealers, minus the ones he can't bear to be around. 'Well,' Kimmy says, looking up at me with her smoky-kohled eyes, 'that leaves us with about forty.' Truthfully, I'm surprised there are that many. But at least Freddie will be sent off by the best of the best. He's owed that.

I swing my legs up on my desk, which is finally free of fruit after I sent the baskets to a local soup kitchen, and for some reason start rolling and unrolling the bottoms of my Capri pants. Nerves, I guess. Freddie's not in yet. We don't even know if he's coming in at all today.

Kimmy's sitting on a corner of his antique desk, writing in her notebook. She's wearing an adorable slip dress (well, probably just a slip from the looks of it) a few shades lighter than her spiky purple hair. Next to her lies the huge bouquet of white roses we got for Freddie, his very favorite flowers. Okay, so actually we just plucked them out of all the memorial bouquets we've got lying around. But Freddie'll love it, and that's what's important.

'Well,' says Kimmy, sticking out her tongue as she crosses out one final name, 'I think that about does it.'

'Lemme see?' I reach out my hand.

Kimmy clatters over in her stacked heels and hands me the notebook. My eye passes over the list of familiar names. Deidre Gayle, my favorite collector. Andre Roth, a curator whose pecs, Kimmy says, should be bronzed and put in the Museum of Mm-Mm-Yummy. Gosh, these names are making me feel all nostalgic – how could I forget that time Freddie's grad school buddy Xavier Firth came out of the closet and admitted he was straight? – until, with a start, I reach one glaring, irritating exception. Oh, God, I should have known. We can't exactly throw a party for Freddie without inviting his final *star*, can we? Even if I do secretly hope that star goes supernova and blows up.

Ugh. A whole night with Grady Cole. This is going to be worse than the time my parents invited my eighth-grade math teacher, Mrs Hoffheimer, home to dinner. At least then, all I had to do was talk about fractions. Now I'm going to have to be all smiley and sweet-talky. I might even have to *sit* next to him.

The sound of the front door closing interrupts my thoughts, and Kimmy cranes her neck to look out the glass doors. 'I'd better go back out there,' she says, and then gives me a knowing, sidelong glance. 'You can't escape him, Izzy. He's your artist now.'

'Of course he is!,' I say too quickly. 'I don't want to

escape anyone. He'll get my full, undivided attention. Like any of our artists.' I hand Kimmy back her notebook with a sharp nod, for emphasis.

'Uh-huh,' she says, heading out the French doors.

'And besides . . .,' I call after her. 'I don't even know who you're talking about!'

So I don't like the guy, and I still have to work with him. Worse things have happened. In the end, we want the same thing: to sell his paintings. I'm sure we'll just shake hands, have a drink, and one day even laugh at our former animosity. Of course we will.

With a deep cleansing breath, I push back my chair, resolving to smooth out my differences with Shady Grady, if only for the gallery's sake. And for Freddie's. I let my finger run over the silky petals of his roses, hoping they'll make him smile. Such a small gesture, I think, and yet what else could we do?

Walking through the gallery toward reception, I pass a woman taking in the John Teller exhibition. She's quite elderly, with blue-gray hair, bent posture, and a sweet expression that makes me think she's got lots of grand-children. I look over to smile at her, but she's busy staring intently at a wax and foam sculpture of a young woman's hand. She looks down at her own wrinkled, age-spotted hand, and her face just falls. That is so sad. God, how did this place become a vortex of melancholy? Tuesday, only three days ago, we were celebrating the anticipation of our next big show, shopping at Barneys, happy dancing all over the place. Now some inappropriately placed stick-bearing Avery Devon is on his way to become the gallery's wicked stepdealer, and Freddie's left floating in the abyss. I mean, where's the fairness in that? And please, don't just say, 'Life isn't fair'. Because it should be. Everyone should get what they deserve. Life *should* be fair.

'Kimmy,' I moan as I pass the final waxen body part. 'Do you sometimes get that . . . not so cheery feeling? And can you cure it with vinegar and—'

I choke on the last word, sending me into a coughing

fit. There, leaning against the ledge at reception, with his arms crossed in front of him, is Grady Cole. Smug-looking, T-shirt-and-cargo-pants-wearing, nary-a-comb-using Grady Cole. He's looking at me with one corner of his mouth raised, seeming very pleased with himself, while I'm hacking up a lung.

'Jeez!' Kimmy rushes forward, rubbing my back. 'You okay?'

I clear my throat a few times, endure one more round of hacking, and then nod sheepishly, wiping at the corners of my eyes. 'I guess I just . . . swallowed wrong.'

'Yeah, swallowing can be tough,' Grady says wryly, lowering his face out of view. I swear, if he's laughing at me, I'll . . . I will *so* . . . oh, who am I kidding? I won't do anything. He's our artist. My job's to keep him happy.

'Grady,' I say, hoping my voice doesn't sound as resentful as I think it does. 'To what do we owe this . . .' Pleasure. Say *pleasure*. '. . . visit?'

'Well,' he says, stuffing his hands in his pockets and pushing at the floor with his toe. 'I wanted to see Freddie. Pay my respects and all.'

And to his credit, he seems genuinely upset. Like he'll miss our Freddie. At least we have that in common. 'He's not here, but I'll tell him you stopped by,' I say softly. 'I know he'll appreciate it.'

Shady Grady narrows those eyes of his – honestly, with all this eye narrowing, he's due for some crow's-feet – and squints at me. 'If it's all right with you, I'd like to wait for him.'

'It could be a while.' I bite my lip, trying to sound politely firm. 'In fact, he might not come in at all today.'

Grady plants his feet on the floor, as immobile as an oak tree. 'How 'bout I give it a try.'

For one long, drawn-out second, no one speaks. Grady's sending me all these defiant eye signals, I'm too afraid of what'll come out of my mouth, and Kimmy's staring at us like she's watching her favorite soap opera. I swallow – the right way, this time. 'Of course. Can we get you anything? Coffee?'

Kimmy's shaking her head at me, her purple spiky hair cutting through the air. What's she worried about? Does she think I'm going to poison his coffee? I give her an 'It's okay' look, and she gives me one back that says 'Oh, no, it isn't.'

'Actually' – the tension in Grady's shoulders seems to ease – 'I'd really love a cup of coffee, thank you.'

Kimmy just stands there with a pained expression on her face. 'We're kind of . . . out of coffee,' she begins, as if what she's about to say will hurt me more than her. 'But I'm happy to run out and get you some.'

That's it. From now on, we're growing our own coffee beans. Right here in the office. I'll water the plants myself.

'I'll take anything but Starbucks,' Grady says, turning to me and – for the first time – giving me a full smile. 'I'm sure Isabel can entertain me while you're gone.'

I give a tight-lipped smile. 'Of course I can.' By stapling your hand to your head. 'No problem.'

'Okay, so I'll be right back! I promise!' Kimmy vanishes out the door, and then there we are, just the two of us.

See, if life were fair, Freddie would be swooshing through the door right now to take Shady Grady off my hands. I close my eyes for a hopeful second. Come on, you Fates up there . . . work with me . . . But when I open my eyes again, there's no Freddie. Just Grady. And me. And strained, awkward silence.

'Would you like to sit?' I offer.

He flashes that smug smile of his. 'I'm good.'

I've got a sinking feeling he's trying to make this hard for me. 'So . . . um . . . it's sure hot outside, isn't it? Only June, but it feels like August.'

Grady Cole's face remains expressionless, but he exhales in a huff. 'The weather? You've got to be kidding me.'

'Well, what am I supposed to say?' I ask before I can stop myself. My hands are all fidgety, and I keep looking down at the floor to avoid his narrow, icy-blue stare. 'What do we have to talk about that won't end in you calling me "Princess" or me saying something I'll regret?' I shift my weight, wishing I had worn heels today instead of ballet flats. Grady must think I look like a child, in my little Capri pants and Peter Pan collar shirt, with my auburn hair back in a ponytail. But that doesn't mean he can bully me.

Grady mutely walks around me in a semicircle, until I'm forced to turn, or else leave him staring at my back. So now when I look at Grady, I see Teller's body parts behind him – a forearm sticking out behind his left ear, an upper thigh next to his right hand. I almost burst out laughing at the absurdity of it. In just a couple weeks, these rooms will be filled with Grady Cole's paintings. We'll have his biography at the front desk, along with a list of prices and slides of his past work. Since Grady's never shown before, I'll have to work extra hard to make his name known by collectors and press alike. He'll be an unavoidable presence, just like he is now, every day for as long as his show remains up. I've got to learn to cope with him. I've just got to.

'Okay, Grady . . .' I say, clasping my hands together. 'I've been writing your press release, which we'll be sending out next week, but I could use a few more personal details. Why don't you tell me something about yourself?'

After a moment's contemplation, he shrugs. 'My work speaks for itself. Freddie's got my bio. Beyond that, there's not much to tell. Nothing that would interest you, that is.'

What's that supposed to mean? That his life is too complex for me to grasp? That he's got the tortured soul of an artist, like poor, earless Vincent Van Gogh, and only another artist could possibly understand? 'You'd be surprised,' I say with conviction, 'at what things *do* interest me.' Crap, that came out wrong. Thankfully, though, Grady has no chance to respond. Because the nice elderly lady shuffles out of the Teller exhibition just then, and she looks so bent over and fragile that I can't help but rush over to her.

'Thank you, dear,' she says in a raspy voice as I guide her past Grady toward the exit. 'Tell me. Will your next show be so . . . grim?'

I place my hand lightly on her back, opening the front door. 'No, ma'am,' I say soothingly. 'I assure you, the next show will be truly exquisite.'

She gives me a grateful smile and squeezes my hand gently. 'You're a lovely girl, dear.'

I keep watch as the woman makes her way down the stoop stairs. 'Thank you, ma'am,' I call after her. 'We'll look forward to seeing you again.' And I mean it too. Not because she's a potential buyer – the elderly locals never are – but because she's come especially to see our show, and I think that's worth something. Higher-end galleries tend to forget that the art is there for people to enjoy, whether they take it home or not.

'That was nice of you,' I hear behind me, closer than I would've imagined. And when I turn around, there's Grady Cole, not two steps away.

'Which part?' I retort, not sure if he's being genuine. 'Helping out the lady or praising your show?'

He gives a short laugh, his eyes crinkling again, only this time without malice. 'I guess both.'

So, Grady Cole, I call your work exquisite and now we're buddy-buddy? That is *so* typical. Show me an artist without a massive ego, and I'll show you a basketball star who could extra as a Munchkin. Pushing past Grady, I leave the intimate entranceway and return to reception. I don't like being that close to him. 'Yeah, well, just doing my job.'

He stands there in the entranceway, still holding the door open. 'Hey, Isabel, I uh . . . I think . . .'

I've got every finger and toe crossed that he's gotten tired of waiting for Freddie. Come on, Grady. You're almost out the door. Just a few more steps . . .

'Hellooo!' a shrill voice calls out behind him. 'Izzy! Izzy *Bizzy!*'

My blood freezes. It couldn't be. There's no way. Please, tell me there is *no way*. But in an instant, framed by the open doorway, stands a nightmare I am entirely unprepared to handle.

'Ex*cuse* me! I'd like to get through the door, *please*. You shouldn't just *stand* there.' And then there she is, materialized next to what I'd thought was the horror show, but was really only the coming attractions.

Grady Cole and my cousin Mimi.

Side by friggin' side.

*I'm a thief, and I'm here
to steal your heart.*

'And so *then* I told her, "What do you want? To have a floating bookshelf without bookends?" ' Mimi rolls her eyes and huffs. 'Hello? *Madness!*'

I nod, trying to seem rapt. We're clustered around the ledge in front of Kimmy's desk, and all I can think is, *How long can it take to get a cup of coffee?* 'She's lucky to have you as her designer, Mimi.'

'Um, *yeah*, she is!' Mimi laughs her tinkly laugh, throwing her head back with a wave of her hand. The hand not holding the giant Louis Vuitton bag, that is.

Meanwhile, Grady Cole's stroking his chin and giving us a haughty expression, like a French king surveying his subjects and thinking, *The masses can be so amusing!*

'So! Are you a friend of Izzy's?' Mimi turns her attention to Grady, and I feel a knot of panic. 'Not only are we cousins, but we also went to school together – since *kindergarten*, if you can believe it! But I bet you can't! Can you?'

This is super. All I need is for Mimi to start telling Grady about that time I got detention for triumphantly shouting out 'Cock!' in chemistry class after writing out the Lewis dot diagram for potassium oxide, or 'K-O-K,' on the blackboard. Or the time I dressed up as Raggedy Ann for

Halloween and wound up with indelible-marker freckles all over my face for a week. I feel like I'm in *Buffy the Vampire Slayer*, and the gates between demon dimensions have just been pried open. I mean, that's the whole *point* of different dimensions – they're not supposed to commingle! Ever!

'Grady's our next artist,' I say before he can respond. 'His show goes up in less than two weeks. We're very excited.'

Mimi's eyes go wide, and she swats at Grady's forearm. 'Ooh! I should *know* you!'

Grady recoils. 'You should?'

'Well, *of course*.' She makes a show of shuffling through the artist biography and price list on the reception ledge, as if assessing our current exhibition by its titles alone. 'I've got clients looking for contemporary art. Clients with a *lot* of money! That's why I'm *here*.' Mimi turns to me, rolling her eyes again. 'Why *else* would I be here?'

Could it be? Could Mimi finally be paying me a compliment? 'Mimi,' I say, feeling tenderness well up inside me. 'I'm touched.' She didn't have to come to the Bond for her clients. But Mimi had faith in me. She wanted to support me. I'm not sure she's ever done that before. Well, unless you count the time she bought tickets to all my performances of *The Crucible* in high school. But when it came time for the curtain call, she was throwing her roses at Jared Anders, not at me. If I remember correctly, that's also when she threw him her phone number. And her panties.

'I'll be touched too when I see the discount you'll give me!' Mimi gives a little squeal. 'My boss will be kissing me *all over*.'

Oh. Of course. Silly Izzy. She's not here because she trusts your taste or your business acumen. She's here because she expects you to cut her a deal.

'And here I thought it was a social call.' Grady leans casually against the ledge, his arms crossed and his messy hair falling in his face. He nods, as if tipping an imaginary hat in my direction. 'Dropping by for a little conversation with me and Izzy here.'

Wait a second. I never said he could call me Izzy. Only my family and friends call me Izzy.

'Actually!' Mimi leans in and winks. 'There *was* one more reason for my visit . . .' She scrunches up her face with glee and shoves her arm out. I notice her white silk blouse hasn't got a single sweat mark, despite the one-hundred-degree weather outside. Is that what she wants me to see? That she's too refined to even sweat?

'Remember Heather Taylor? The richest girl in high school? Guess what! *My* ring is bigger than hers! Well, her center stone, at least.' The ring. She came all this way to show off her engagement ring. 'Is it *too* big?' she asks joyously. 'You can *totally* tell me if it is. I mean, it's *only* three carats.' And now she's fishing for compliments!

'That all depends on too big compared to what?' Grady says lazily, his eyes glancing up under their heavy lids. 'Guys buy flashy cars to make up for their deficiencies in other, shall we say, "delicate" areas, so why not rings too?'

'Oh, no!' Mimi shakes her head vigorously, reaching into her LV-logoed bag and pulling out a wallet full of pictures. 'Look, see? That's Trevor's car. No deficiency there! It's a *Lexus*.'

I snort with laughter before I can stop myself. 'Sorry, Mimi. I, uh, swallowed wrong.'

'She's not a very good swallower,' Grady adds, and I'm about to shoot him a dirty look when I see he's also choking back laughter. I just wish I knew whether it was directed at Mimi or at me.

'See? That's *Trevor*.' Mimi shoves the photo in my face with a satisfied grin. 'Isn't he the handsomest thing you've ever seen?'

And I have to admit, Trevor's a dish. Tall and well built, with bright green eyes and lush dark hair. 'He seems . . . lovely,' I offer. 'Very hunky.'

Mimi sighs, clutching the wallet photos to her chest.

'My handsome husband. Well, *almost* husband. He loves me soooo much.'

I stare down at my fingernails, wishing they were a bit better manicured, like Mimi's. The magazines are always saying the key to looking put together is doing away with ratty cuticles. Maybe that's the key to *being* put together too? Like, you get a shiny coat of nail polish, and suddenly nobody laughs at you, and the awkward silences melt away, and when you walk down the street, there's music playing in the background, and people turn to gape at you like in one of those shampoo commercials?

'Mimi,' I say sincerely, 'I'm really happy for you.'

She beams back at me, and for a moment, it feels like we're kids again, dreaming about the future. Except in those dreams, I had someone too. Someone who loved me absolutely and entirely. Like Trevor and Mimi. Okay, so technically, I *also* had a four-bedroom penthouse apartment with a balcony overlooking Central Park. But no good New York fantasy excludes real estate.

'And guess *where* we're getting married!' Mimi squeals, bouncing up and down.

Grady presses a finger to his ear. 'Somewhere with dull acoustics, I hope?'

But she doesn't seem to hear him. 'At the *Puck Building!*'

'What?!' I exhale, dumbfounded.

'With white lilies everywhere, and green vines twisted around the columns, and a champagne ice sculpture fountain, and both a string quartet *and* a swing band! Just like we always dreamed, Izzy Bizzy!'

We? Not we! *Me.* Just like *I* always dreamed. What Mimi's just described is the fantasy wedding I've had ever since I went to Kathy Rosenbaum's bat mitzvah at the Puck Building, my absolute *favorite* historic landmark in New York. It's a huge building, but it has all these private rooms, and there's one on the top floor that's painted entirely in white, even the floor-boards, with white columns that are just aching to be twisted with ivy. And the ceiling follows the slanting lines of the roof, and there's no fussy marble or gold gilt, and it's the most upscale place in the whole city that could also be called rustic and intimate. Mimi *knows* I've always wanted to be married there. I've told her a hundred times. She *knows*.

'Mimi,' I say, distressed. But she won't let me continue. She's busy rattling off her plans for the wedding – where she's trying on dresses, what color the invitations will be, how many bridesmaids she'll need.

Inside, my heart is just sinking. Every girl dreams about her wedding. It's a rite of passage, like wanting to be a ballerina at age four, or picking out your prom date from the freshman face book. It's not the same as my dream of having my own gallery, or even my dream of one day owning a Kandinsky. The perfect wedding is supposed to be something you hope for your entire life. Without the wedding fantasy, there's no big finale in my imaginary, autobiographical romantic comedy. There's no unlikely ending to the madcap adventures and misunderstandings that lead to the man I've always wanted. The whole elaborate picture is vanishing into smoke before my eyes. Champagne ice fountain. *Poof*. White lilies. *Poof*. String quartet and swing band. *Poof*. Oh, God, she's not going to have my father give her away at the altar, is she?

Mimi has paused, no doubt waiting for my wondrous reaction. 'Mimi,' I start again, trying to grasp what's happening. 'It wasn't your . . . I mean, I wasn't aware that you . . . wanted to have your wedding at the Puck Building too.'

'Well, *duh*,' Mimi says, rolling her eyes at Grady as if to say, *Isn't she a moron*? 'Don't be upset, Izzy.' She purses her lips in faux sympathy. 'I guess, in the end, I just got there first.'

I hate her. For the first time ever, whether she's a blood relative or not, I actually hate her. And I don't hate *anybody*, not even telemarketers. There's something in Mimi's detached, gray eyes – or maybe it's the twist to her lips, or the tone in her voice – that tells me she's aware.

She's aware that she's taking away a fantasy I've had since I was thirteen. And she's reveling in it.

Grady seems to sense the tension crackling in the air, because he shifts his weight uncomfortably, stuffing his hands deeper in his cargo pants pockets. 'Well, if you ask me,' he says flippantly, 'I wouldn't want to get married in *any* building that rhymes with—'

'I'm back!' Kimmy cries out, holding a Grecian-diner paper cup in front of her. 'I'm here! It's okay!' She hurries in, patting at her forehead with a napkin. 'Do you know how *hard* it is to find non-Starbucks coffee? It's like trying to find the eighth wonder of the world or something.'

Grady winces, meeting her at the door to take the cup off her hands. 'Hey, I'm sorry. I didn't realize . . .'

Kimmy shakes her head. 'No! I mean, it's fine, really!' She pauses to catch her breath, fanning herself with her hand. 'Although I could have done without the guy at the counter asking me if I liked my coffee as sweet as his love.'

'Thanks, I do prefer my coffee sans man love,' Grady says, peeling back the plastic cover.

I can't move. I'm just standing there, seething. I can actually feel my body temperature rising. And the thing is, if Mimi's actually serious about buying art, then she'll be my client. I'll have to take her to lunches, and show her pieces in the private salesroom, and cozy up to her like an Eskimo to a bear rug. I'll *have* to be nice to her.

'So,' Kimmy says cheerily, sitting in her chair and opening her notebook. 'What'd I miss!'

If I told you that you had a great body,
would you hold it against me?

Robbie Williams is pulsing doggedly through his third hour on my sound system. *'You think that I'm strong,'* he sings, infusing the lyrics with meaning. *'You're wrong. You're wrong.'* Wearing my favorite fuzzy blue bathrobe, I waltz around the apartment with kitty Robbie in my arms, spinning round and round ... until he lets out a feral *'Mrrrawww'* and madly claws his way back down. *Ow.*

The thing is, I'm starting to think that I'm not so strong either. I *know* I shouldn't let petty things bother me, like subway delays, and rudeness, and someone stealing a boyfriend I never had in the first place. Someone stealing a *wedding* I never had in the first place. But the point is, I *do* let them bother me. I just feel miserable. The thing about someone stealing your dreams is that you can't get them back. There's no arrest report to file, no APB to call over the police radio. And the worst part is, I'm actually starting to wonder if I've overreacted. It's not like I'm actually *planning* a wedding. In fact, I think with a pang of heartache, I can't say for sure that I ever will.

I say all this to Dix on the phone while I sink as deeply as I can into my down comforter, rolling one corner of it around in my fingers.

'If it were someone else getting married at the Puck

Building,' I reason, 'I don't think I'd be so upset. But it's Mimi.'

'The hag,' Dix interjects.

'It's like she lives her life just to spite me.' I pause a moment at the thought. 'But who *does* that?'

'Mimi's children will be the spawn of Satan,' Dix states decisively. 'Now, throw on that fabulous dress I picked out for you the last time we went shopping, and meet me outside your apartment in half an hour.'

Her tone says not to argue.

Shimmy doesn't look like it should have a velvet rope, but it does. And here Dix and I are behind it, trying to catch the eye of Brenda, the most notorious ice queen door girl in New York. On a normal Friday night, throngs of people circle Shimmy's nondescript doorway, praying to gain entry. But tonight, with a music producer hosting a strictly list-only party, the crowd is more like a cavalcade, spilling past the curb and into the street.

It's been a while since Dix and I had a big night out together. May is one of the busiest months for art events, so I've been preoccupied with work for the past few weeks. Besides the parties for the major contemporary-art auctions always held in May, there are also the more formal benefits – like the superfancy MoMA garden party or the Artists Space and Skowhegan benefits. These are fun and all, but mostly revolve around special exhibitions or – in the case of MoMA's party – identifying not only your salad fork, but also your fish fork, dessert fork, white-wine goblet, red-wine goblet, and sterling water goblet. Really, it's exhausting.

By now, though, the heaviest hitters in the art world have gone to Switzerland for the Basel art fair. Basel's one of the most influential fairs, even more so than New York's famous Armory Show. The Bond used to have a booth at Basel, until Freddie decided he'd rather focus on putting up a stupendous June exhibition in New York than on toting our best wares overseas. The hope is that since there are so few strong summer shows, we'll get a larger share of publicity and sales. If Shady Grady can behave himself, that is.

So after all this time, I'm glad to be out with Dix. But Mimi's put me in such a dismal mood, I'm not sure I can face a crowd tonight. I've still got her cold stare imprinted on my mind, and her triumphant voice rattling around in my head: *I got there first. I got there first.* I didn't even know we were racing to begin with.

Dix pulls me by the hand, nudging her way through the crowd toward Shimmy's entrance – a wooden door underneath a neon sign that cryptically says O'FLAHERTY'S.'

'Dix, I don't know . . .,' I whisper, tugging at her arm.

'Come on.' She gives my hand a squeeze. 'A night out'll cheer you up. Paris Hilton's supposed to be here. Maybe she'll flash a boob.'

'For the one person who hasn't seen it yet?' I manage a grin.

She laughs. 'That's my girl.'

We continue forward, maneuvering around girls with teeny tops, stiletto heels, Gucci or Fendi bags, and always long, blown-straight hair. As my hand reaches involuntarily to smooth my own wavy, reddish tresses, Dix halts suddenly. Two gangly guys in Ashton Kutcher-type Von Dutch caps are blocking our path. Stopped short, I accidentally step on someone's foot with my heel. *Ooops.* I look up to say a quick 'I'm sorry,' but instead, I'm speechless. He's enormous. Conan the Barbarian meets Incredible Hulk meets Jesse 'the Body' Ventura enormous. He's got cropped red hair, a red goatee, a black puffy jacket, and about twenty gold chains. I'm thinking now's not the time to clue him in to the eternal turnoff of male neck jewelry.

'So sorry.' I scrunch up my face as if to say, 'Oh, what a silly thing I just did! Please don't bludgeon me with your burly-man fist.'

Gold Chain stands back a bit and blatantly looks me up

and down. 'I'd give you a piece of my mind,' he says, leering. 'But I've got more of something else.'

'Heh, heh.' I shudder as – thank God – Dix pulls me forward. She looks amazing, I must say. She's got on a long black skirt that clings to her curves for dear life, and a seventies-style halter top. Her long, shiny black hair is pulled back into her signature high ponytail. The dress she picked out for me is an incredibly slimming off-the-shoulder number, with a print of geisha girls fanning themselves by a river. Not a bad life, it would seem – I'm sure there's no geisha door girl to get past at the river.

After another few minutes of squeezing around people, we finally get to the actual rope, the bouncer, and Brenda. She's wearing a retro cap over her curly blond hair. Two guys are shouting at her from one side of the crowd.

'Yo, our friend's in there. Go in and get Justin. He knows us.' The guy's wearing a button-down shirt and brown jeans. I didn't even know they made brown jeans.

'Yeah, our names are supposed to be at the door.' Another twenty-something, this one in a blazer and khakis.

From behind the rope, Brenda turns to them languidly. 'Loooook,' she says. Brenda speaks more slowly and with less expression than anyone I've ever met. 'You're not on the list. It's a private party tonight.' The boys protest for another few minutes, but Brenda's already given them her back. She glances at the layers of people straining forward, all trying to catch her eye.

'There he is!' Dix throws up her arm and waves.

I crane my neck in the direction of Dix's beckoning hand, and there's Jamie, in a blue button-down shirt and jeans, squashed between two fratty-looking guys in varsity jackets. He's got his arms wrapped around himself, and despite his obvious attempts to strain forward, he's only getting pushed farther and farther back.

From her post at the velvet rope, Brenda spots Dix, and I see the briefest hint of a smile. 'Hiiiiii, how are you.'

'Great hat,' Dix says, giving Brenda an air kiss. She points to Jamie, now barely visible. 'He's with us.'

Brenda lifts her hands, like Moses parting the Red Sea, and the masses reluctantly ebb. Jamie squeezes his way through, straightening his glasses.

'What took you two so long?' He's stretching his long arms in front of him, like a cat just out of a cage.

'I need time to look fabulous,' I say, giving him a quick hug. 'We can't all be as naturally beautiful as you.'

Jamie laughs. 'If that had been just slightly less obsequious, I might have actually believed you.' The two fratty boys scowl at him above their meaty football shoulders, and Jamie shudders. 'Um. Let's go.'

Dix gives a nod to Brenda, and she unhooks the rope for us. 'These three,' Brenda says to the gigantic, silent, sumo wrestler bouncer. He gives us a nod, and we're one step closer to the madness.

'Keep your head up,' Dix says into my ear. 'You look gorgeous, and I want everyone to see it.'

What would I do without her? Dix winks, gesturing with her hand as if to show me the way forward.

What appears to be a pub on the outside looks like an Indian paradise within. To the left of the door, in the narrow front room, people recline on benches adorned with colorful silk pillows. Rugs and tapestries cover the walls, accented by dozens of small mirrored disks. A dimly lit, gilded chandelier casts a golden glow over everything and everyone. Dix lets go of my hand and she and Jamie make their way to the bar opposite the tapestried walls. She turns to me, and her face radiates with warmth. I have a feeling that every man in the place is about to fall in love with her.

Dix returns first, bringing us two red wines. We squeeze ourselves onto a bright orange cushioned bench in the corner, and Dix stares down the clearly inebriated woman next to us until she gives us more room. Then she smooths down my dress over my knee and pats my cheek like my mom used to when I was a girl. 'I wonder,' Dix says wistfully, giving me a strange look, 'if I don't hold you back.'

I scrunch up my forehead in surprise. 'What on earth do you mean?'

Dix just laughs and sips her wine, avoiding the question. 'So, Jamie!' she exclaims as he appears in front of us, sniffing at his drink.

'Damn it, they gave me the crappy vodka,' he moans, taking a tentative sip and making a face. He downs half of it anyway.

'Instant fucking sensation.' Dix turns to me, pursing her lips. 'He's booked for the *Today* show next Friday.'

'Get out!' I exhale. 'So your editor's off your back?'

'Are you kidding?' Dix tosses her ponytail behind her shoulder. 'His editor is all *up* on his back. Only this time, he's kissing it like crazy. The *News* hasn't gotten this much publicity since they published that photo of Julia Roberts sucking on a water bottle two years ago. Every media gossip columnist in the city has pounced on the story of our Jamie's overnight success.'

Jamie swats the air with his hand and gulps down the rest of his drink. 'Stop! You're making me feel self-conscious. It's really nothing –'

'He'll be on "Page Six" soon for sure,' Dix continues animatedly.

'Please, Dix.' Jamie rubs his eye with his knuckles. 'I don't think I can handle this. . . .'

'Izzy' – Dix rises like Venus from the sea and puts her arm around Jamie's waist – 'in less than a week, our boy has become a phenomenon.'

Huh. Jamie, a phenomenon. Who'd have thought? Some light has been shed, however, on the mystery of his sudden good luck. Seems infamous radio shock jock Howard Stern (*Howard Stern!*) caught sight of Jamie's column yesterday morning and made it a part of his show. He ventured out on the street looking for average guys who'd be willing to try their best pickup lines on a couple of Penthouse Pets in his studio. One of the guys, Michael Brewer, a computer analyst visiting from Illinois, said to Pixie Stix (whose breasts, according to Stern, resembled succulent manna sent from boob heaven), 'Want to see my hard drive? I promise it isn't three-point-five inches and it sure ain't floppy.' Apparently – though I can't imagine it's *too* difficult to pick up Stix – it worked. Mr Brewer's detailed description of his sexual escapades with Ms. Stix, which he enthusiastically credited to Jamie's column, started forwarding yesterday from inbox to inbox at the speed of 'send.' I've already gotten the e-mail twice. And let me tell you, that Pixie sure is limber. The *News* hasn't sold this many copies in years.

'Jamie,' I say, standing up. 'How is it that you're not freaking out?'

Jamie slaps at his forehead, sending his black curls swinging. 'Who says I'm not? The television appearance alone has me out of my wits. I don't have anything to wear!' His voice reaches a frantic pitch. '*Nothing!* I'll be on national television in my boxer shorts! Man, I need another drink.'

Jamie's lean frame awkwardly wades through the throngs of scantily clad women and lusty-eyed men. 'Meet us in back!' Dix calls after him.

He turns to us and nods meekly, giving a thumbs-up sign before bumping smack-dab into a tall brunette wearing a lacy wraparound top and tight jeans. At the sight of her, Jamie takes a step back, lowering his head and apologizing profusely. I watch him, keeping my fingers crossed. Come on, Jamie. Talk to her. He glances sheepishly at me and Dix, and we both nearly explode in hand gestures. We're pointing at her and making chatting signs, like two deranged puppeteers. Jamie shakes his head vigorously no; we nod ours enthusiastically yes. I feel like I'm in a silent film, and there's a black screen with sepia lettering saying 'I can't! I can't!' followed by 'You must! You must!'

Finally, with a sharp sigh, Jamie turns back to the brunette, and we see him mouth, 'Hi, I'm James. James Hunter.' To which *she* mouths, '*The* James Hunter? Of the *News*?' And, honestly, I'm not sure which of the two of them looks more shocked. After a bug-eyed pause, Jamie nods his head, the brunette coyly offers him her hand, and I nearly burst out into applause.

I feel Dix next to me, leaning in to whisper in my ear, 'Your turn now.'

'I don't think so,' I tell her. I mean, I don't even write a column!

'Just follow me,' she purrs.

We head to the back room, where there are tables and a DJ. The place is filled beyond capacity. Some people are trying to dance, even though there's barely room to wiggle. A waitress squeezes past us, carrying three bottles of Grey Goose toward a huge gathering at a table in the very back. Probably a celebrity entourage. Dix and I find a pocket of space against a wall by the DJ, where Aerosmith and Run DMC's 'Walk This Way' blares out of the speakers. Dix surveys the crowd behind me and then screams something into my ear.

'What?!' I lean in toward her.

'THAT GUY WAS CONCRETELY BOOKING YOUR ROVER,' Dix yells.

'WHAT?' I say, just as the song ends and the moment of silence amplifies my scream ten thousand times.

Dix takes me by the arms and swings me around so our positions are reversed. Directly in front of me is a man in a James Dean-style leather jacket and dark jeans, his hair creatively mussed, like he's just gotten out of bed. He looks fit and muscular, and he's got this great jaw – as if it's been chiseled by a descendant of Michelangelo. Dix says again, 'That guy was completely looking you over.'

Can she be serious? I'm sure my eyes have gone wide and my mouth has dropped open, probably around floor level. Trying to regain my decorum, I laugh hysterically, as if Dix has just told me something very witty. She looks at me strangely. 'I'm going to see who's there,' she says, pointing toward the gathering in back. 'Might be someone I should know.'

She's leaving?! 'No!' I yell, a bit too loudly. Dix gives

me that wistful look again – like she's watching a fawn take its first steps – before she sashays away. Hey, I'm no fawn. And even if I were, it's not like Thumper left Bambi alone to fend for himself in the scary forest. So here I am, stuck like the proverbial deer in headlights, looking directly into a pair of gorgeous, intense eyes. Mr Sexy leans toward me, and it feels like my heart's doing a polka in my stomach. There's a slight stubble on that jaw, and I have an unexplainable urge to reach out and rub it.

'I hope you know CPR,' he says, ''cause you've just taken my breath away.' Only it sounds like 'C-P-AH' because this man with his muscles and his stubble and his rumbly, deep voice *also* has an accent just like Robbie Williams!

I desperately search for a brilliantly clever response. 'Hi.'

Mr Sexy nods toward the front room, where the music isn't as loud. As I follow him, I can hear Dix's voice in my head – *Keep your head up!* But reverting to old habits, my eyes begin their droop downward, where they happen to settle on Mr Sexy's bottom. His firm-enough-to-dent-metal bottom. An embarrassed flush spreads across my face. Head *up*, Izzy!

We stand against the wall, and I surreptitiously check my hair and lipstick in one of the tiny mirrored disks hanging beside me. I try to catch Jamie's eye from across the room, but he seems spellbound, as if he and the brunette are the only two people in the place. He looks so . . . radiant. His face has just lit up, and though she seems to be doing most of the talking, Jamie's nodding and laughing like a pro. He even looks taller. Gosh, does flirting make you grow?

I'm certainly not interrupting him any time soon. Even if I do feel like I'm about to hyperventilate. 'Where are you from?' I manage to ask.

Mr Sexy runs a hand through his hair. 'I'm Australian, but I grew up mostly in England.' Keep talking, please. 'I'm Cameron. What's your name?'

'Isabel.' I stare down at my empty wineglass, as if something witty might be written in the dregs.

'Isabel,' he repeats thoughtfully. 'So what do you do, Isabel?'

'I, uh . . .' Oh, come on, Izzy, this is an easy one. 'I work at a gallery.'

'You do? Which one?' He looks surprised.

'The Bond,' I say, with newfound poise. That's right, Mr Sexy. I've got a brain, and a good eye, and I know about art.

'Huh.' He leans his head back to finish his drink, a tawny liquor that looks like Scotch. 'I saw the industrial-collage exhibit you did last year. It was good.'

'Thanks,' I say, throwing my shoulders back and hoping it looks more confident than twitchy. 'It was one of our few group shows. Took months to curate, but we were pleased with the result.'

'Well, as someone in the industry, you might be interested to know' – he pauses for effect – 'I was one of the first to acquire a DeLaunay photograph. In fact, I own two.'

'Shut *up*!' I exclaim, totally unintentionally. So much for poise. But I've never met someone who owned a DeLaunay before! Matthew DeLaunay is the biggest star to come out of the art world in years. His bizarre, incomprehensible videos – and their accompanying eerily beautiful photographs – have won over celebrities, socialities, and art insiders around the world. Last season, he became the youngest artist ever to be featured in a solo show by the Guggenheim. 'From which series?'

'The "Hitchhiker,"' he says simply, waiting for my reaction.

'But it can't be.' My breath leaves my body. The three films in the 'Hitchhiker' series are mythical in themselves. In fact, I've never been convinced they even exist. Matthew DeLaunay has vowed never to show them, saying they're unfinished. But the rumors are that the fanciful characters DeLaunay portrays in these films are some of his most spectacular. The Guggenheim begged him for them. Still, he refused.

'I've had them for years.' Mr Sexy's deep voice intensifies. 'Right in my apartment.'

'I can't even imagine,' I say, reverential. 'I mean, no one's seen that series. Not even the *Guggenheim*.'

He leans in toward my ear. I can feel the stubble on my cheek, and I can smell his neck – a little sweet, and a little sweaty. 'I'm not in the habit of turning my apartment into a museum, but for you . . .'

Dix arrives back then, her ponytail swinging as she rushes to my side. 'Everyone's leaving,' she says breathlessly. And now that she says it, I can see Moby and Sean Lennon – always the last B-listers to leave a party – headed out the door.

'Dix!' I cry, struggling to calm myself. 'Cameron here was just inviting us to his apartment to see his DeLaunay photographs.' I turn shyly to Mr Sexy, my voice tentative. 'Is it okay if my friend comes too?'

'Of course.' He bows his head to her.

I'm hoping Dix'll get the secret eye signals that I'm shooting at her – *I want to go! I want to go!*

But she has this impish twinkle in her eyes and a sly twist to her lips. 'Can't, darling.' She air-kisses my cheek. 'After-party. But *you* go, certainly. And kiss Jamie good-bye for me.'

'What?' I grip Dix's arm. She can't go. This guy is so cute. He's got great taste in art. He sounds like Robbie Williams! He's a dream. How do you *talk* to a dream?

One by one, Dix pries my fingers off her arm. 'Bye, dearest,' she says, winking as she takes off.

Oh, God. This is just like the time Dix taught me how to cornrow my hair. After braiding half my head, she insisted I do the other half for practice. I would up looking like a cross between Bo Derek and Animal the Muppet. I just *know* I'm in for another Izzy-created monstrosity.

'So?' Mr Sexy looks me in the eye.

It feels like a rocket's been shot through my head and down into my shoes. What else can I do? I nod.

*

This apartment could not be any more intimidating. I walk through the doorway into a narrow hallway with a massively high ceiling. The slate gray walls tower above, like something out of a sci-fi prison movie. Mr Sexy takes my hand and leads me down the hallway. Any minute now, I fully expect some alien convict will jump out and attack us. But when we reach the main loft, I have to gasp. It's beautiful. The central room has lighter gray walls, and a lower ceiling. I notice a wrought-iron spiral staircase near a brick fireplace, and I assume it leads to another level. Perhaps the . . . bedroom? Quickly, I scan the walls, which are lined with enlarged, framed magazine covers. Carmen Kass on Australian *Vogue*. Gisele Bundchen on *W*. Some waify-looking girl on British *Elle*. Oh, dear. Does Mr Sexy have a model fetish? I stand on my tiptoes and strain my neck up, trying to look taller.

'You all right?' he asks.

I return my heels to the floor. 'Oh, yes, just, um, doing my stretches. For when I feel a bit stiff. You know, in the neck.' Argh.

He puts his hand on the small of my back, turning me toward the wall separating the main room from the hallway. 'Here,' he says softly. 'What do you think?'

'Wow,' is all I can come up with. 'Wow.'

The long wall is bare save for the two stunning photographs. In one, a wild satyr with silver horns – DeLaunay in costume – stands at a roadside in the middle of nowhere. The night sky pulses behind him with the moonlit sparkle of a thousand stars. In the other, it's daytime, and DeLaunay's again unrecognizable as some kind of futuristic wood nymph. His skin is brushed pink, and his long hair exudes a fiber-optic glow. These rare images would probably take in a few hundred thousand dollars each at auction. But what rivets me to the spot for at least a good fifteen minutes is their ethereal, otherworldly beauty. What a privilege, I think, to be given this opportunity.

'Thank you,' I say, my voice distant with wonder.

'Can I get you a glass of wine?' Mr Sexy's deep voice gently breaks the spell.

I follow him to his kitchen. Everything is shiny chrome and black, like a motorcycle. Jeez, even his kitchen is hot. He opens a sexy stainless steel cabinet and takes out a dark bottle, which he opens with a sexy bartender's corkscrew. Then he gives me a delicate black glass that he fills with red wine before grabbing himself a beer. As we head back to the main room, I cannot think of a single thing to say. I curse the fact that it's too late to pretend I don't know English.

'So, are they friends of yours?' I ask, pointing to the models on the wall.

'Nah, not really,' he says as we sit down on the big white sofa. 'I just took them.'

He just *what* them? Is that, like, Australian slang or something? I'm not panicking. I'm sitting next to a guy who takes models – and I sure hope gently – and his arm is around me, and he's coming closer now . . .?

'Only these three?' I ask, standing up so quickly that I almost spill red wine on his white couch.

He looks at me quizzically, and then breaks into a wide smile. 'I'm a fashion photographer.'

'Oh! Right. I figured. Nice work.' I walk over to the pictures, as if that's what I'd intended to do all along. They aren't bad. His approach has a directness that makes the models seem a teeny bit more human, like they're thinking.

'I've always wanted to exhibit.' He gets up from the couch and moves toward a bookcase. 'In fact, I met with the dealer at the Bond once, a few years ago. What's his name? Frederick something?'

'Barnes,' I say quietly. 'Frederick Barnes.' And there it is. The sadness. The fear. What will the Bond be without Freddie? Exactly one week from today, I'll have a new boss. If I'm even still employed, that is. I should be working now, preparing for his arrival. Or I should be finishing Grady Cole's press release. I've no right to be here, in some strange apartment, struggling to make small talk with a man I don't even know, no matter how many DeLaunays he owns. Honestly, what am I doing?

Mr Sexy returns to the couch with a big black binder. He gazes up at me with unexpected kindness, obviously sensing that something's wrong. 'You okay?' he says, all English and soothing. 'You needn't be such a stranger.'

So instead of making my excuses and heading out the door, instead of refusing Cameron's company at a time when I really need it, I simply drain the rest of my wine and head back to the couch, tripping on the white rug along the way. 'I guess I can stay just a little longer.'

Mr Sexy refills my glass and opens his portfolio. 'This is my own work.' He turns the book's pages. 'This is in Italy, and this Morocco.' The photos are black and white, and instead of models, the subjects are locals, in cafés or on dusty roads.

'They're nice,' I say, looking up at him. 'I particularly like this one.' I point to a shot of an old man sitting at a table, his worn face looking straight at the camera, his eyes precise and wise.

Mr Sexy smiles lazily and closes the book. 'Thank you,' he says sincerely. Then he leans down and kisses me.

And what a kiss. Warm, soft, not too much pressure, but enough to know he's into it. The exact way first kisses are supposed to be.

'Mmmm,' he hums as our lips part. 'I don't know what it is about you.'

I nibble at my thumbnail, getting shiny lip gloss all over it. My heart pounds loudly in my chest. 'What do you mean?'

'You're smart,' he says frankly, as if listing off the features of a new car. 'I could see that right away.'

He *could*? What gave it away? My inability to put two words together?

'And you're sweet, that's obvious. And captivating. And lovely. And I guess I just . . .' He gazes off dreamily at some point behind me for a moment before focusing again, entirely, on me. 'I guess I just want to get to know you better.'

'You do?' My voice sounds too high, like a little girl's. I feel completely light-headed, and realize I've been holding my breath.

He kisses me again, gently, and then says in that outstanding accent, 'I really, really do.'

Standing up from the couch, Mr Sexy offers me his hand, which I take. It feels like slow motion: I rise, move in toward him. I wrap my arms around his neck . . .

Then, in a heartbeat, I'm off the floor. Ah! Not so fast! *Hold on.* Is he thinking what I think he's thinking? No . . . I can't . . . *Why* did Dix have to leave? Who am I going to drag into the bathroom for an emergency debate? While Mr Sexy's busy nuzzling my ear, I imagine what she would say:

'*Look at him, Izzy. Why are we even having this discussion?*'

'*But I've barely said a hundred words to the guy.*'

'*Which, as we've seen, was already too much.*'

'*But Dix! I wouldn't even know what to do.*'

'*Iz, if it's been so long that you don't remember what to do, then you clearly need the practice.*'

'*I can't do this. I can't do this. I can't do this.*'

'*What can't you do – be with the most amazing man you've seen in aeons? Have him cater to your every need? Let him worship you like a goddess?*'

'*I can do this. I can do this. I can do this.*'

Cameron's swept me up and is walking toward the staircase. Okay, please don't tell me you're about to carry me up a spiral staircase. It can't be more than two feet wide. Rhett and Scarlett had, like, three yards. He takes the first step, turns himself – and me – the littlest bit left, then takes another step. My feet are bumping against the wrought iron railing. Step up, angle left, step up, angle left. Sheesh.

At the top, he puts me down and caresses my cheek with his hand. He makes a growly, rumbly sound – which has to be one of the sexiest sounds ever – and lifts my dress over my head. Bye-bye, geisha girls.

'You have a great body,' he says, and I sigh. Imaginary Dix was right – I could certainly get used to this.

10

*If you're going to regret me in the morning,
I'll let you sleep in until the afternoon.*

I'm awoken by a band of bright sunlight blanketing my face with a warm, yellow glow. The sheets are cool and fresh, and I reach my arms up behind me for a delicious morning stretch. God, this feels good. I can feel my smile before my eyes even open.

When I do open them, though, I find myself alone. There's no Cameron beside me, gazing fondly on my sleeping face, as I had imagined. Hmm, that's disappointing. But no matter, his side of the bed's still warm. He's probably just showering, or reading the newspaper, or calling all his friends to tell them he's just met the girl of his dreams. You know, usual guy stuff.

I allow my thoughts to slip back to last night, to falling asleep with my head on Cameron's shoulder and his arm around me. He had such a gentle touch, and a manner that put me – after my initial spazziness – at ease. I can't remember ever feeling so desired, not only for what I look like, but also for who I am. Really, I felt like someone in a romance novel. I can even picture Mr Sexy – no, Cameron – wearing a white billowy shirt blown open to display his chiseled form, and me in his arms, my auburn hair flowing behind me and my bosom heaving (which, I'm sorry, *always* means there's a push-up bra involved – it's not like a bosom decides to heave on its own). I feel flushed just thinking of his voice, alternately deep and soft, like James Bond meets Russell Crowe. Then, suddenly, there it is.

'Morning,' I hear coming up the spiral staircase. Cameron soon follows, carrying a sleek black tray holding two cappuccinos and croissants. He's dressed already, in a clingy gray T-shirt and waffle-fabric long shorts.

'Wow,' I exhale, as he sets the tray down on the bed. 'This is perfect.' I'm still wearing the soft, careworn T-shirt of his that I slept in, no doubt an old favorite. I bite into one of the croissants, and it's flaky, doughy, and warm.

I look up at his rugged face, probably with croissant crumbs all over my mouth, and he leans over and kisses me – somehow, even more tenderly than before. I don't understand how being with him can feel so right. I don't even know the guy. Yet, he made me cappuccino. He warmed my breakfast pastry. 'I've never done this before,' I tell Cameron, looking down at the foam in my coffee cup. 'I mean, I've never . . . you know . . . with a stranger.'

He brushes the hair off my forehead, gazing at me with warm eyes. Then he says, in that amazing Robbie Williams-y accent, 'I guess you must have trusted me.' And he's right. I do. For the first time in ages, I feel the way I've been so longing to feel: cared for. He's considerate. He's understanding. And, hello, have you *seen* him in boxer briefs? What was it Mimi said about Trevor? Kisses in the morning. Perfume and poetry. Is this my chance?

I shake my head a little, willing myself to stop imagining the what-ifs. I promised myself last night that I would be calm and cool today – 'the morning after' – and not the least bit obsessive. I'm not so naive that I don't know how rare it is for one special night to turn into the real thing. It's like when you're eating alphabet soup and you try to spoon up a five-letter word. These things just don't happen. If I were smart, I'd chalk up last night to experience. I'd pledge that next time, I'll give a guy nothing more than my phone number. Yup, if I were smart, I'd just lose hope right now. But of course, when it comes to men, I'm anything but smart. And when it comes to hope . . . I guess I follow my heart over my head in that department too.

'Here,' Cameron says, tossing a pair of white drawstring shorts and a white T-shirt on the bed, and then kissing my forehead. 'I don't want you to have to wear last night's dress again.'

I smile shyly. 'That's thoughtful of you.' It's times like these (okay, time like this) that I want to hug myself for always carrying flip-flops in my bag when I go out at night – just in case I can't catch a cab and have to walk home. Too bad I never worried about having to catch a toothbrush.

'Come on down,' Cameron says once I'm dressed, and last night's outfit is snugly folded in a paper bag. 'I'll make us fresh-squeezed orange juice.'

Okay, that's it. How am I supposed to fight orange juice? This guy is just too good to be true.

I follow Cameron down the wrought-iron staircase and into his sexy kitchen, where he deftly passes orange halves under a black and chrome machine, squeezing out the sweetest juice I've ever tasted. Then, once again, we sit side by side on his white sofa, and it's just like last night, except that everything has changed.

'I'm sorry to say, Isabel,' Cameron says, kissing my hand, 'but I've got a squash game this morning. I've actually got to be going in just a few minutes.'

'Oh,' I say, a bit startled. But, really, what did I expect, for us to spend the whole day together? Okay, yes, that's exactly what I'd expected. In fact, I hadn't imagined the day would ever end.

'But this was nice, you and me. Very, very nice.' He eyes me calmly and smiles. A sweet smile – the kind you give a baby niece, or a puppy. Hey, wait a second. Last night there was smoldering. Where'd my smoldering go?

'Don't worry,' he says brusquely. 'I'll walk you out.'

He'll walk me *what*? But I'm still . . . I'm not done with my juice yet. I sit there, my face wrinkled with confusion. I'm not done with *him* yet.

Just then the doorbell rings, a jingly ding-dong that has no right to sound so cheery, and Cameron raises and lowers his eyebrows, giving me a quick, 'All right, then.'

I watch from behind as he makes his way through the hallway, unbolts the door, and swings it wide open. I watch as two sets of bright red fingernails entwine around his neck. As his head tilts downward and becomes enveloped by a cascade of blond spiral curls. As he steps aside and reveals a woman so beautiful, with such flawless skin, that she might have stepped out of a Botticelli painting.

I watch as Cameron says, without even a glimmer of aren't-I-such-an-asshole-ness, 'Isabel, this is Jasmine, my girl.' And I watch, stunned into silence, as he passes a hand in my direction. 'And Jas, this is Isabel. My squash partner.'

You must be a light switch, baby,

'cause you turn me on.

His *squash partner!?* When Mr Slimy closed the door behind him, leaving Jasmine inside, I turned to look him straight in his remorseless eye. Then I said in my angriest voice, 'Oh, I'll show you a squash partner!' Which, of course, makes no sense. What was I going to do, hit a ball against him to death?

After meeting Jasmine, I was so stunned, I couldn't speak. And the worst thing was, she's really nice! Seeing me struck dumb – no doubt thinking I'm socially inept – she started making small talk. Turned out, Jasmine's an interior designer. So I replied with the first sentence that came to mind: 'My cousin's an interior designer. Mimi Duncan.' To which she, of course, said, 'I know Mimi! I hear she's working on an apartment for *David and Iman.*' Honestly, Mimi. Have you hired a plane to put it in sky-writing yet?

I had to get out of there as quickly as possible. Every moment was more unbearable than the last. I kept thinking – do I tell her? Would she even believe my word over his? Or, deep inside, does she already know? In the end, I wound up feeling a lot more sorry for Jasmine than for myself. Finally, I just said, a bit coolly, 'It was nice to meet you, Jasmine, but I've got some *squashing* to do,' staring all the while at Cameron's guilty, despicable head. What I wanted to say to him, though, was 'How could you?' Because, really, I don't see how he could. I just don't understand how he could be so . . . cruel.

I arrive home late Saturday morning to a blinking answering machine. *Beep! Saturday, three thirty a.m.* 'Well, look who's not home. I know where you a-a-are.' Dix's voice singsongs throughout my apartment. 'Iz is getting so-o-o-o-me! Call me, dearest.'

Oh, God, I feel like such an idiot. How could I have let myself become the other woman? Just the thought of those words makes me sick. Why didn't I even *think* to ask if he had a girlfriend? I tear off his stupid clothes, throwing them on the floor. Robbie slinks over tentatively, sniffing at them. That's right, Robbie. They smell like man. Assert your kitty domination and pee on them. But no, he just plops himself down on top of Cameron's T-shirt and shorts and rests his head on his paws, satisfied with his new napping space. Well, fine. But when they get smothered in cat hair, see if I go brushing it off.

This isn't the first time, I think numbly as I wrap my favorite blue robe around me. Not the first time I've let myself be duped. And after I found out that Seth, the artist I dated in college, had been cheating throughout our whole relationship, I asked myself the same question. How could I let it happen? How could I just have assumed he was being faithful? Dix told me then that it's a gift, in many ways, to be able to trust people so easily. One she sometimes wished she shared. But have too much faith in people, Dix said, and they'll walk all over you like the Brady Bunch on shag carpeting. So now, a few years too late, as I sit on my bed with my head in my hands, I take a vow. A vow of skepticism. From here on, it's going to take a lot more than sweet words to earn my trust. A whole heck of a lot more.

Except . . . that doesn't sound like a very fruitful way to live your life, does it? Going around wary of everyone you meet, staying aloof and distant from people who could actually become friends, if you let them. I mean, what if Lewis had never trusted Clark? What if FDR had never trusted Churchill? What if Batman had never trusted Robin? The United States would be half as large, World War II would still be going on, and the Joker would be president.

I shuffle in my fuzzy slippers toward the bookcase, fingering the tiny silver platters and porcelain vases in my dollhouse, running my hand over the spines of my books. I need some kind of guidance from these texts. Some words of wisdom from Tolstoy or Shakespeare or – let's be real here – Danielle Steel to divulge the secret to understanding relationships. I'm about to give up and go buy a *Cosmo* magazine, when I hear a faint metallic click, and my apartment lurches into darkness. Oh, crap.

Now, where did I put those extra lightbulbs?

If I ever want to see again, I'm going to have to tape a flashlight to my ceiling. Assuming, that is, I will ever be able to reach that high. Who keeps a ladder in a New York studio apartment? Even on a stool, standing on top of the Yellow Pages in my highest wedge sandals, I'm still not tall enough to reach the fixture. I *am*, however, about to plunge indelicately to my death.

'Ah!' I jump off the stool, and the cat runs for dear life toward the bathroom. 'Sorry, Robbie.' With a reluctant sigh, I pick up the phone. I have officially surrendered myself to at least a full week of jokes beginning with the words 'How many single girls does it take to change a . . .'

An hour later, Jamie and I are sitting on the bed, underneath a blazing glow, eating cheddar cheese popcorn and watching *Footloose* on DVD. 'You know,' I say, 'we'd see the picture better if we turned out the light.'

Jamie scowls, hits the light switch, and snuggles down next to me. 'So.' I poke his arm. 'When do you become too famous to watch classic eighties movies with me?'

He grimaces. 'Iz, you have no idea. It's only been three days since the column hit newsstands, and already I've gotten at least four hundred fifty emails from men with success stories, and another three hundred fifty from women thanking me for making the city's most desirable men become bolder.' Jamie shakes his head incredulously. 'Does that mean there are one hundred women out there who aren't satisfied? Or are *babies* being conceived because of me? How am I supposed to cope with that?' He twitches nervously. 'Dix is coming over later to help choose an outfit for the *Today* show. Get this – they want me to use a pickup line on Katie Couric.'

I rub his shoulder. 'Jamie, you're a star.'

He groans and throws himself back against the pillows. 'James D. Hunter is a star. Jamie Hunter hasn't got a clue.'

'Oh, come on, Jamie.' I give him a sly look. 'You seemed to be doing just fine at Shimmy last night.'

For a second his face lights up, but then his nose wrinkles, and his shoulders sag. 'She was only interested in the column. Nothing else. She kept saying over and over, "I have this really great idea!" until I finally asked what it was.'

'What was it?'

Jamie looks appalled. 'Date registries! She thinks every woman should have a registry at some major department store. That way, instead of bringing flowers, a guy can show up at the door with something she'll really appreciate, like tinted moisturizer or a French press for coffee. I mean, I don't even know what these things *are*.'

'Well,' I say academically, 'you can use a tinted moisturizer instead of foundation, and a French press has this pressy screen that goes over the coffee grounds –'

'Izzy,' Jamie interrupts, looking frustrated. 'That's not the point. The point is . . . she wasn't interested in *me*. Not at all.'

Jamie always does this – the better things are going for him, the lower his confidence sinks. I wish I knew why. When he started hanging out with us, I remember feeling entirely relieved to have found a new ally. Even as a PR assistant just out of college, Dix was already making a name for herself. She would get invited to every big party, even those her firm didn't organize, and she'd always want to bring me along for support. I don't know why, because inevitably, she'd know everyone there, and I'd wind up feeling like an unnecessary extremity, like a sixth finger or something.

At the time, I was working as an assistant at this gallery in Williamsburg, Brooklyn, where everyone walked, dressed, and spoke nothing but the height of hipness. Do you know how stressful that is? I was the only one actually *from* Brooklyn, and yet I might as well have been the clueless foreign exchange student you're forced to share your room with for a semester. I didn't know a single person who fit into the whole scene – either in Williamsburg or in Manhattan – as little as I did. Until Jamie came along.

We became very close, Jamie and I, very fast. At parties, when Dix ran off to talk to some agent or socialite, Jamie and I found ways to amuse ourselves. We'd stand near the gossip columnists and pretend to have scandalous discussions. Or we'd stock up on hors d'oeuvres, marveling that lamb chops and quiche could be so tiny. Or we'd wade through the crowds in a race to find the drunkest B-list starlet.

I've never said it out loud, but I love the guy. Not in a romantic way, but in the way you love your one friend who sees the world as you do. The one friend you don't have to explain things to because he feels the same way. The one friend who needs your shoulder as much as you need his.

'Jamie' – I cup his chin in my hand – 'you can do this. You can drive women wild. I know you can.'

Jamie leans forward, raising his eyebrows roguishly. 'Speaking of wild,' he says, 'why don't you tell me where you disappeared to last night . . . and with *whom?*'

Shit. I've been trying so hard not to think about Cameron. Is it so wrong to believe that if I keep the whole episode out of my mind, then it never happened? I know they say denial isn't healthy. But as far as I'm concerned, it should be the fifth food group. 'Let's just say,' I start reluctantly, 'that not every guy who successfully picks a girl up is going to be a winner.'

Jamie draws back, looking concerned. 'Iz, what happened?' His voice is soft, and he's lifted a hand to rub my back. Really, he's got this uncanny empathy.

I cuddle into Jamie's arm, letting his patient rubbing soothe me. I feel the beginnings of tears at the corners of my eyes, and I hold really still until they go away. Then, trying not to blush with shame, I tell Jamie what happened with Cameron.

'Gosh,' he says after I've finished. 'Men suck.'

'Yu-huh.' I nod, biting my lip. 'They suck buckets.'

'Listen, Iz, you didn't do anything wrong,' Jamie says into my hair, somehow knowing exactly what I need to hear. 'It's not your fault.'

'But I didn't ask, Jamie. I never –'

'No.' He sounds as forceful as I've ever heard him. 'What was your sin? Looking for someone special? Allowing yourself to hope?' He gives me a lopsided smile. 'Hey, I feel that way every day. I feel that way right now.'

I look earnestly into his dark brown eyes, so grateful for this man, my dear friend. 'Jamie, promise me you won't become one of them. Please say you'll never change, no matter how many girls come up to you saying, "*The* James Hunter?" I don't think I could take it.'

'Are you kidding?' He tightens his grip around me. 'You're stuck with me, babe. Glasses, skinny legs, and all. You're stuck with my whining, my corny jokes, *and* . . .' He wriggles his eyebrows. 'My newfound relationship wisdom.'

'So!' I say, slapping his arm teasingly. 'What's your next column about?'

Jamie returns my mischievous glance. 'I'm considering a riddle this time: How many postcoital girls does it take to change a lightbulb?'

'Ah!' I toss a piece of popcorn at him, laughing and blushing at the same time. 'You wish.'

For just a moment, Jamie loses his kidding expression, as if lost in a sudden, poignant thought. But then, just as quickly, he points at the television screen where Kevin Bacon is cutting a rug with Lori Singer. 'Hey,' he says defensively. 'At least I can dance.'

I'm so not touching that one.

Did it hurt when you fell from heaven?

There were a lot more couples than usual walking around the Upper East Side this morning. New couples, all glowy and goofy-looking. Hand-holding, coffee-before-work-grabbing, how-about-your-place-tonight-wink-wink-giving couples. It's like there's something in the air – an almost electric crackle, as waves of men and women are being drawn to each other like ions. Not me, though. Nope. I've erected an antimagnetic-field dome around myself, and I'll be darned if I let anyone through. See, I realized this weekend, I've been going about things all wrong lately. First, I let Mimi rile me all up, just like she used to – and in front of Grady Cole too. That's the worst part. My best defense against his sneering was to keep our interactions purely professional. Somehow, I doubt I'll be able to convince him that talk of ivy-strewn weddings, swing bands, and diamond rings are all business as usual here at the Emerson Bond Gallery.

Second, what was I thinking, to drown my sorrows in the bed of a man I'd only just met? No, not even a man! A sleazy, awful, slimebag son of a. . . . *ugh*, that look on his face when he introduced me to his girlfriend. Not a shred of guilt. But more, not even worry – as if the very concept of his cheating would be unimaginable to her. *Don't be a fool like I was, Jasmine*, I feel like saying. *Start imagining*. Not that I'm letting it get to me. Or even thinking about it. Nope. Antimagnetic-field dome.

I gather the pages of Grady Cole's press release, which I finished on Sunday, and place them on Freddie's desk for his approval. Contrary to the Tuesday-to-Saturday schedule most galleries keep, the Bond stays open on Sundays to take advantage of the foot traffic from the Whitney Museum of American Art, which is only a couple blocks away on Seventy-fifth and Madison. So while Freddie was here Saturday to call all his press contacts and herald Grady's show as his brilliant grand finale at the Bond, I was here Sunday to write words glowing enough to fit that description:

> The Emerson Bond Gallery is delighted to introduce Grady Cole, a graduate of the Ecole des Beaux-Arts in Paris, with a stunning debut solo show that's sure to be the must-see of the season. Mr Cole has long been fascinated with the semiotics of commercial culture, a theme he sets out to deconstruct in his paintings. Cole's work explores and upsets the visual power of a brand logo to impart meaning – not only about a product, but also about its history, the type of person who buys it, the company that makes it, and the society in which it's sold. By distorting even such a familiar logo as the Quaker Oats Man and transforming it into fine art, Cole has made his viewers rethink the everyday visual cues we all take for granted.

I won't lie. I'm pleased with the results. A good press release always has lots of academic lingo and important-sounding artistic and cultural language. That way, reviewers can quote or paraphrase it and sound really smart and important, like they're all art history professors. The more difficult to understand your descriptions are, the more likely you are to get a long, complimentary review.

Little do these reviewers know that in this case, the artiste walks around in tattered pants and Puma sneakers smirking so much, you'd think half his mouth was permanently higher than the other. Luckily, I was able to refrain from writing, 'Mr Cole, himself, suffers from acute delusions of grandeur that promote excessive narrowings of the eye, obnoxious turns of phrase, and a prodigious dose of just plain jackassiness.'

With the press release done, I pledge to devote the rest of my week to preparing for Avery Devon's arrival on Friday. It's Tuesday now, so that gives me three days. Three days to memorize all the information I can about our artists, their works, our past sales, and anything else I can cram in my head and make stick. Three days to prove I'm indispensable. What was it Dix said? Worry about the first impression. Somehow, when I meet Avery, he's got to love me on the spot. I've got to appear suave, intelligent, and art savvy. Like Jackie Kennedy meets Georgia O'Keeffe, or Nicole Kidman meets Grandma Moses. A *young* Grandma Moses, that is. Mama Moses. Just thinking about it makes me feel shaky with nerves. Because considering Grady and Cameron, when it comes to meeting new men, I think it's safe to say I am not on a roll.

I scan the to-do list taped to my computer: (1) Choose an image for Grady Cole's postcard. Today, Freddie and I've got to select the painting we feel best represents Grady's work so we can print it on a thousand invitations to his opening. Poor Kimmy will be pasting on mailing labels until her fingers stick to everything she touches. (2) Finalize plans for Freddie's going-away party. Kimmy's done most of the work, but I just want to check that everything's going smoothly. Thursday night has to be as special for him as possible. (3) Order new letterhead. That one's going to be heart-wrenching – seeing Freddie's name replaced on all the Bond stationery. But the new guy's got to write letters. And if all those boxes of new stationery also list my name as gallery director, well . . . it'd be an awful inconvenience to have to throw them all away.

I grab one of our elegant pens, which have THE EMERSON BOND GALLERY embossed in gold along one side, and begin doodling on the Emerson Bond stationery, trying out the new masthead. *Dealer: Avery Devon.* Jeez, the name sends a shiver up my spine. What if he's as stern as Kimmy and I imagine? What if he really *doesn't* have a sense of humor? A picture surges into my mind of an albino giant with cold, colorless eyes and massive fists. Oh, God, what if the new boss is a yeti? No, no. I laugh out loud at myself. Honestly, I don't know where I come up with these things. It's like I'm six years old again, convinced there's a monster in my closet. Which – by the way – is *not* the reason I still keep that Snoopy night-light by my bed.

I grip the pen tighter and scratch out, in neat capital letters, *GALLERY DIRECTOR: ISABEL DUNCAN.* That's right. Have been for two years now. Plus, with Freddie gone, I'll be the only one here who knows our collectors. The only one who's worked side by side with our artists. So what am I worried about? When all's said and done, I *am* indispensable. In fact, maybe Avery Devon will be so impressed by me that I'll still get my promotion! How cool would that be? I write out *ASSOCIATE DEALER: ISABEL DUNCAN* on the page, and I must say it looks stunning. Dazzling, even.

Isabel Duncan, Associate Dealer. I even love the sound of it. I lift my head confidently and push back my hair from either side of my face. *Eww.* What on earth was that? Something warm and wet has settled on my forehead and my cheek. I reach up, but realize it's on my hand too. Blue and sticky and . . . oh, *shit.* It's the pen. Our own Emerson Bond friggin' pen, the one I've been doodling with. It's cracked, and the ink is all over my hand and . . . *uh-oh.*

I stare at my reflection in the bathroom mirror. After half an hour of scrubbing, this is as good as it gets, I think. And it's not good at all. I've got a huge blob of light blue on the left side of my forehead, an oblong blue oval on my right cheek, a patch of blue in my hair, and a few swatches of it on my hand. I look like something out of a low-budget sci-fi movie. I should be wearing a skimpy silver outfit and go-go boots, crying 'Take me with you, Earth man.'

What am I supposed to do? I can't walk around like this. I've got alien vitiligo! I grab another wet, soapy paper towel and go at my head for one final, valiant effort before heading dejectedly back to the office. Now I'm blue *and* wet.

When I open the glass doors, Kimmy's busy arranging slides of Grady Cole's work neatly on Freddie's desk. She stares at me strangely before breaking into a good-natured laugh.

'I like it!' She giggles. 'Very *W* magazine. Smurfette chic.'

'I didn't mean to,' I say bleakly, sitting at my desk and hiding behind my – oh, God – blue computer. 'My pen exploded.'

'On your head?' She straightens up to get a better look.

'Stop!' I wail, covering my face with my hands. 'I'm blue!'

Kimmy crosses the room and throws an arm around my shoulders. 'Don't worry, Iz,' she says lightly. 'I'll make sure Papa Smurf doesn't get too randy.'

'Shut up!' I say firmly. But it's too late. We're both crying with laughter. Great. Now my mascara's probably smudged too.

Kimmy and I are just regaining our composure when Freddie swoops in. But we lose it again when he exclaims dramatically, 'And I thought *I* was feeling blue!'

Soon, though, Kimmy returns to her position out front, the silk laces of her corset top flowing behind her. I gesture to the slides on Freddie's desk, he nods, and we get to work on Grady's postcard. After about half an hour, we come to a consensus that the bold red, white, and black of the enlarged lower halves of the *A* and *Y* in *Ben-Gay* will best fit a shiny, four-by-six postcard. Having seen the label from which Grady took the detail, I can't help but chuckle – the graphic we chose to represent his show promises 'Ultrastrength, nongreasy pain relief.' Considering what it's like to work with Grady, I might have to get me some of that.

'Grady's the best, isn't he?' Freddie gushes.

I suppress a wince and cross my fingers under my desk. 'He sure is!'

'Just make sure to give him a call today,' Freddie says, shuffling some papers in front of him.

'O . . . kay . . .' I work on keeping the disappointment off my face. 'Any special reason?'

Freddie eyes me frankly. 'I'm all but gone, Izzy. You've got to take over now. We need his approval ASAP for the Ben-Gay image. These postcards should have been printed already.'

I lower my head, chastened, regretting my selfish hesitation. 'You're right, Freddie. I'll call him right away.'

He winks at me and then repeats, sadly, 'I'm all but gone.'

But despite his tone, there's a hint of a smile around Freddie's cheeks, and the worry lines on his forehead have smoothed. He seems to have regained some of his old positivity.

'Freddie!' I cry. 'What are you hiding from me!'

His hesitation lasts half a second. '*You*, my friend, are looking at . . .' He pauses for effect. 'The new dealer for the *Albemarle*!'

'Oh, Freddie!' I clap my hands. The Albemarle is one of the country's most prestigious contemporary galleries, right up there with the Gagosian or Mary Boone. It's the perfect place for Freddie – he'll be creating new stars right and left, like an artistic fairy godfather. The only thing is . . . jeez. The only thing is that the Albemarle's in Los Angeles. Three thousand miles away. 'Oh, *Freddie*.' My tone says what I can't bring myself to.

'None of that!' He waves the thought away. 'Or I'll start to cry right here. I don't even leave until after the summer season. And I'll e-mail you every day, and you better come visit me, you bitch.'

'I will,' I promise faithfully. 'I'll bring bagels. And lox.'

'Nova?' he says in a small voice. 'With cream cheese?'

I nod.

Freddie dabs at his eyes with his sleeve. 'Look at me. I'm such a sap.'

'No, Freddie,' I say, cupping his cheek in my hand. 'You're a gift.'

Freddie heaves a sigh, and I see tears rolling down his cheeks for real now.

'Smurfette, be a dear and let a man collect himself, okay?' He goes for a smile, but manages only a grimace.

'Sure, Freddie,' I say softly. 'Congratulations.'

And for the first time, as I walk toward reception, I'm actually imagining this place without him. Really, finally without him. It scares the crap out of me.

All I can think, as I lean against the ledge at reception, is thank *God* I don't have any appointments today. Kimmy's teasing doesn't quite end until she gets in a final 'What's your favorite movie, *The Blue Lagoon*?'

As usual, she's been drawing in her notebook with colored pencils, and when I look down at the page, I break out in laughter. There's the Bond town house as a grand tower, with ivy twirling downward and New York City's office buildings standing like weird and wonderful mountains in the background. A misty fog rolls between them, interrupted only by an occasional ominous-looking pigeon. Inside the tower, on its highest floor, stands the damsel – me – wearing a long chiffon gown with a little Gaultier label at the bottom (how cute is that?). Behind me, Freddie clasps his hands to his heart in dismay. He's wearing a black monk's robe adorned with a little Prada label. All around us are paintings and sculptures from the Old Man's collection. A fine detail, I think, considering that the upper levels of the town house actually are devoted to art storage. What makes me laugh, though, is the villain at the bottom of the tower, pulling desperately at the door. He's hunchbacked, with evil eyebrows knit into a frowning vee. The name *Avery Devon* is written in block letters near his feet. A long, thin stick protrudes from his rear.

Between her drawing and my blueness, Kimmy and I are now laughing so hard, we're gasping for air. And I have to admit, I do not have the most delicate laugh. In fact, at this moment, I might possibly be creating the world's most unattractive image since Michael Jackson's fifteenth nose job. Besides the patchy face and hand, and the soggy blue hair that's drying in knotty clumps, I'm also hiccuping and snorting like a mad-woman. But you know what? I actually like sharing these silly, unpolished moments with friends. There's a kind of purity to letting your guard down and not worrying about someone else's judgment. I'm blessed, I realize, to have friends who laugh at me only when they're also laughing with me.

Meanwhile, since Kimmy and I are having so much fun with her drawing, I don't notice when the town house door opens. And since my laughter is loud enough to drown out the sound of footsteps, I fail to realize that someone is approaching Kimmy's desk. So when I turn around, I am entirely unprepared to be standing face-to-face with the most handsome man I've ever seen *in my entire life*. My eyes still crinkled and tearing, I go mute midsnort.

'Hello,' he says, with a sharp nod.

'Hello,' I say back, because every other word has escaped my memory.

Here stands a man straight out of a childhood coloring book – the prince at the end of the 'Cinderella' story, for whom you save your best crayons, the ones you try not to wear down. He has flaxen-colored hair that seems to have been spun from gold, and eyes that could be made of aquamarine. His black suit seems to have been sewn onto him – it fits so well – and he's got the kind of muscular frame that comes from country-club athletics, not meaty gym workouts. And his face. My goodness. I didn't know they made them that beautiful. His skin is just slightly bronzed, as if he's spent a spare day in the Caribbean, and his cheekbones alone could make you stare, mouth open, for hours. *Izzy?* Shut your mouth.

The Adonis looks at me with those aqua-emerald eyes, as if waiting for me to snap out of my sudden idiocy. When that doesn't happen, his brow wrinkles slightly in amusement, and he turns away.

I swivel my body toward Kimmy, eyebrows at my hairline and eyes as big as pancakes. She just shrugs casually. 'Damned if I know.'

Adonis inspects our exhibit closely, wearing a slight frown. Ah! What if he turns out to be a collector? I'll have to be in the same room with him, and talk coherently, and be witty and completely unflustered. Oh, please don't let me have to. I watch the mystery man from behind as he walks deftly into the main gallery space, disappearing from view. Finally, I blink. Could I have dreamed it all?

But all too soon, I hear his footsteps coming back toward us. I run my hands frantically through my hair. 'Do I look okay?'

Kimmy offers a strangled smile. Then Adonis materializes in the doorway, first as a sharply tailored pant leg, then a single-breasted jacket and gray silk tie, and then hair, cheekbones, tan, and all. I can almost hear the angels singing.

He heads right for me, step by perfect step. He looks me in the eye. A rushing sound fills my ears, like the ocean in a shell. His lips are parted, and I think he's saying something, but I can't make it out.

'I'm here to see Frederick Barnes,' I finally hear. He says it slowly, like he's talking to someone foreign, or stupid. 'And . . . pardon me, but . . . are you *supposed* to be blue?'

Ooops. I had forgotten. For a moment, I had actually forgotten. I feel my whole body heat up and realize I must be blushing profusely red. Which, of course, would make me purple.

I glance at Kimmy, gripping her desk so hard, I'll probably get a splinter. Kimmy picks up the phone, as cool and collected as a Mondrian. 'I'll just see if he's free.'

The phone. What is it about the phone that I'm supposed to remember? *'Damn!'* I exclaim before I can stop myself. 'Grady!'

Adonis stares straight at me. 'Excuse me?'

'Oh, no!' I say quickly, waving my hands at him. 'I didn't mean *"damn* Grady." ' I try to laugh it off. 'We don't wish anyone to hell here at the Bond!' He tilts his head, and I can see him wondering if the brain damage is congenital or the result of an accident. 'I just meant "damn" *comma* "Grady," who I've forgotten to call.'

Adonis frowns slightly. 'Grady who?'

I squirm in my ballet flats, wishing I could will myself to disappear. 'Grady Cole.'

'Grady Cole,' Adonis repeats slowly with a subtle, but oddly knowing, smile.

Kimmy rises from her chair. 'Uh, why don't I show you to the private salesroom?' She shakes her head at me and surreptitiously points to her notebook.

Once they start walking away, Adonis leans toward Kimmy and says quietly, 'Performance art?'

She nods her head firmly. 'We like to push the envelope.'

'Hmm,' he says, lifting a finger to his chin. 'Quite interesting, actually. So, would the blue be a reference to Yves Klein?'

My eyes travel down to Kimmy's notebook, where she's written *Izzy. Stop. Talking.* But she doesn't have to worry. The next time I meet a gorgeous stranger, I'll be cementing my mouth shut.

My telephone conversation with Grady is mostly painless. He says whatever image we like works fine for him, and I have the okay to order the invitations to his opening. The only time I think he's mocking me is when he asks, 'Do you have your outfit picked out for Freddie's going-away shindig?' As if all I think about is clothes and parties. Then, instead of good-bye, he says, 'I'll be seeing you Thursday night, Izzy,' all sinister, like he's already planning ways to vex me. Of course, I could be reading into things. But I don't think so.

Meanwhile, Freddie's still meeting with Adonis in the private salesroom, which lies between the office, where I am now, and the escape zone by Kimmy's desk, where I want to be. If I can just reach the doorway without being seen, then I can run away until he leaves.

I sneak out of the office and tiptoe, hunched over, past the private salesroom. I bump into a waxen forearm on the way, and like a ninny I apologize to it. But I don't think anyone sees me.

I crouch toward Kimmy's desk quietly, popping up like a spring when I get there.

'Ah!' she screams. 'Izzy, what are you doing?'

'Shhh,' I say. 'I'm being covert.' Kimmy gives me a baffled look, and my shoulders sag. 'Oh, Kimmy. Don't you ever have those days when you just wish you could be invisible?'

Her expression softens, and she nods. 'Look, why don't you run home, take a nice hot shower, and, like, deal,' she says, tugging on one of her black lace gloves. 'I can totally cover for you.'

'Kimmy,' I cry. 'You're wonderful.' I can see the door to the outside world, and the brightness peeking out from under it like a beacon. I'm just about to walk toward the white light when I hear two sets of footsteps making their way methodically toward the reception desk. I freeze. Do I run? Duck behind the desk? Drop to the floor and curl myself into an inconspicuous ball? Before I can decide, Freddie and Adonis appear in the doorway. Freddie looks kind of tense, actually. His mouth is set in a tight line, and his hands are repeatedly clenching and unclenching. *Oh, no*, I think. Adonis has asked about the performance art in the lobby. And now Freddie's got to explain that I'm not officially on display. There will be no photo documentation of the event for sale. Why? Because I'm not art. This is actually just how I *am*.

But Adonis doesn't seem to be making any inquiries. In fact, with one eyebrow raised in our direction, he still has that amused expression on his princely face. He rests his eye first on Kimmy, then on myself, examining each of us for a good ten seconds or so before he turns to Freddie and nods curtly. 'Would you do me the honor?' he says.

'Kimmy, Isabel,' Freddie says formally, 'allow me to present Avery Devon, your new boss.'

*Let's have a party and invite your
pants to come on down.*

He was supposed to come on Friday! *Friday*! I was
going to wear my best suit and my Christian
Louboutin heels, and I was going to look very capable and
professional, and Avery Devon was going to know in an
instant that he wanted to work with me. What I was *not*
going to be was a blithering idiot talking about sending
Grady Cole to hell. And what I *really* was not going to be
was blue.

I'll never forget the look on Avery Devon's face when
Freddie introduced me as the gallery director. I now know
what the corresponding facial expression is for the words
Oh, dear Lord, no. Not that he would be so uncouth as to
actually say it out loud. Somehow, I managed to extend my
hand, smile confidently, and say, 'Well, Mr Devon, I look
forward to working under you.' Which, of course, provoked
another disbelieving smirk from him, and another moment
of absolute mortification for me.

The worst part is – I haven't had a single chance to
redeem myself! What little time Avery's spent in the
gallery since Tuesday has been with Freddie, 'gleaning
from his expertise,' as he put it, which was the whole
reason he arrived early in the first place. And short of
tugging at Avery's elbow and crying, 'I've got expertise

too!' how could I mend my stunningly bad first impression? I feel like a contestant on *American Idol*, the one Simon scowls at and says, 'You make me wish I had no ears.'

I gaze at myself in my bathroom mirror, knowing tonight is my only chance. My one shot to show Avery Devon that I'm not a big screwup. I silently rate my appearance – the smoky eye shadow, the sleekly straightened hair, the clingy black cocktail dress. Not bad, actually. For a final, offbeat touch, I place an antique pearl broach below one of the spaghetti straps. Perfect. Kimmy and I are picking up Freddie at his place in twenty minutes, and we've been warned repeatedly that there'd better be no surprises. In fact, just today, when Kimmy and I were discussing the RSVP list, there was our Freddie, inching toward us with a sidelong glance.

'You're not *planning* anything, are you?' he said suspiciously.

'*Duh*, Freddie, *no*,' Kimmy covered, rolling her eyes. 'You told us not to.'

'That's right,' Freddie said, pointing one finger at Kimmy and the other at me. 'No party. No.'

Which, of course, in Freddiespeak means *Can I have a party? Please? With streamers and balloons and a hot piece of ass who does magic tricks?*

So tonight, while Freddie thinks the three of us are off for intimate drinks at the Flatiron Den – surprise! – we're actually being joined by forty of his closest friends.

And Avery Devon.

I couldn't help it. There Kimmy and I were at the reception desk this afternoon, and there Avery was passing us by on his way out. Come tomorrow, he's officially our new boss. If I was going to redeem myself, it had to be today. So I invited him. I told him that our best artists and collectors would be there, and that I'd introduce him personally. And when I do, he'll see how well we get along. He'll see that not every word out of my mouth makes me sound like an incoherent dimwit. He'll see that when it comes to work, I can be poised and collected. At least, that's the plan.

I grab my wrap and beaded purse, shout a good-bye to Robbie, who gives a gaping yawn before returning to his nap, and rush out to find a cab. Let the celebration begin.

'You *guyyys*.' Freddie's hugging me with one arm and Kimmy with the other, marveling at all the guests standing up to applaud him. 'I can't *believe it!* I had *no* idea.' He holds his hankie to his eyes, dabbing at the corners.

I beam at him, absolutely thrilled. 'Come on, Freddie,' I say, resting my head on his shoulder. 'You think we don't know you? The more you insist against something, the more you want it!'

'That's not true!' He draws back in mock offense. 'I *also* said I didn't want a cake. Under no circumstances. And I still mean *that*.'

Kimmy and I just look at him.

Freddie claps his hands. 'There's cake too!?'

I kiss his cheek. 'Oh, Freddie. I'm going to miss you.'

The room we've rented looks gorgeous, all red velvet drapes and deco accents, like something out of an Erté drawing. The floor is dotted with cocktail tables covered with red tablecloths, where our guests are sitting down again after their rousing (for an art crowd, that is) surprise. I gaze across the dimly lit space, seeing the faces of dealers, artists, patrons, curators, and friends socializing and sipping colored drinks. Already, the party's a bustling success. Kimmy deserves the credit, though. She saw to every detail in that magic notebook of hers. Even her outfit – a shimmery flapper-style dress and black pageboy wig – enhances the retro-glamorous atmosphere.

My eye catches a few people I should say hello to right away, including Deidre Gayle, my absolute favorite client. Noticeably absent from the party, however, are Grady Cole and Avery Devon. I know I should be relieved about Grady, but I'm not. In fact, I'm angry. I thought his concern for Freddie was his redeeming quality. I should have known better. As for Avery, I can understand he'd want to put in a later appearance, after Freddie gets his time in the spotlight. He would be considerate that way.

Oh, good! A seat has opened up at Deidre Gayle's table, and I hurry over, my arms thrown open. Deidre is the most likable person in the whole world. Not only is she one of our biggest buyers, but she's also sharp, funny, and drop-dead gorgeous. *And* one of the most talented people I know. Deidre was a ballet prodigy as a child, which brought her to New York from Jamaica at the age of eight. Now, twenty years later, she's a principal dancer with the American Ballet Theatre. I saw her dance in *Coppélia*, and it was so beautiful, I had to repeatedly stop myself from nudging random strangers and asking, 'Did you *see* that?'

'Izzy!' Deidre exclaims as we hug. She lost her Jamaican accent long ago, but her consonants remain gently cushioned, as if even sound becomes more refined when it comes from her.

'You look more elegant every time I see you,' I say, and it's true. Tonight, she's wearing wide-leg gray trousers and a coral silk camisole that drapes down her back. Her soft, dark skin smells faintly of freesia.

'Consider it a testament to your art,' she says, smiling warmly, 'which inspires me.'

'You can expect the postcard for our next show soon,' I tell her, knowing she'll enjoy Grady's work. 'Keep the date open.'

'I'm already excited!' she says animatedly. 'Who's the artist?'

'Well . . . actually –' I point resignedly toward the entrance. The red velvet drapes cordoning off our room from the rest of the Flatiron Den are now parted, and Grady Cole's head is peeking in, soon followed by the rest of his body. 'He's right over there.' I check my watch. The invitation said eight fifteen, and it's now nine o'clock. Any decent person knows that when it comes to surprise parties, there's no such thing as fashionably late.

I watch Shady Grady make his way over to Freddie,

grasp his arm, and shake his hand. Freddie hugs him eagerly, patting his back like the two have been friends for years. I find myself wondering what inspires Freddie's devotion. Beyond Grady's art, what likable quality can I be missing?

'The last party I went to, darling' – Deidre's melodic voice turns my attention back to the table – 'it was so bizarre, I didn't know what to do.'

'What happened?' I lean toward her.

'I'm at a benefit,' she says, like we're two teenagers gossiping in the girls' room, 'when all of a sudden that channel four news anchor, what's his name?'

'Thin Lips or Helmet Head?'

'Helmet Head,' she says. 'He actually comes up to me, holding probably his tenth Scotch and soda, and says, "I'll be your ship, honey, if you'll be my harbor." '

'He did not.' I cover my mouth with my hand.

'Sweetie, he went there with *no* plans of turning back,' she laughs. 'But the strange thing is, that was the third pickup line I had gotten at that party – and the fifth in a week. Can you imagine?'

Oh, I can imagine. Keeping an innocent look on my face, I respond, 'I'm surprised it's only been five. You're the most gorgeous woman *I* know, that's for sure.'

Deidre laughs, motioning to the waiter for another glass of champagne. 'Darling, I already spend a fortune at the Bond. Save your flattery for a new recruit!'

A tuxedoed waiter arrives at our table with a tray of champagne flutes. Over his shoulder, I see Grady running a hand through his interminably messy hair, and Freddie scanning the room, probably for me.

'Deidre, forgive me,' I say, placing one hand on her forearm and grabbing a glass with the other. 'But I should go say hello to our new artist. Please don't go anywhere – I'll be back!'

'Of course, sweetie!' She kisses both my cheeks before I leave. 'If you believe in his work, then I'd love to meet him.'

'Indeed, my dear, you will.' I give Deidre's shoulder a squeeze. This'll be the ultimate test: Zoologists can teach apes to speak in sign language, but can I teach Grady Cole to speak in civilized conversation?

I take a deep sip of champagne. Okay, two sips. And one for the road. Oh, screw it. I drain the glass. Then I head to a long table where more glasses are laid out in sparkling, bubbly rows, pick up two, and head toward Freddie.

'Izzy!' he cries when he sees me coming. 'Look who's here!'

'I *saw*.' I try to sound enthusiastic. 'I thought you'd like this.' I give Grady one of the champagne flutes, and he accepts it with a bow of the head.

'Thank you, Isabel,' he says. 'That was thoughtful of you.'

I can tell we're already putting up a front for Freddie, trying to sound as polite as possible. 'It looked like we might not see you tonight,' I say, with a tiny edge to my voice.

Grady smiles sweetly – though he's probably sneering inside. 'As I was telling Freddie, I got caught up at the studio before I realized what time it was.'

I nod, as if convinced. But he's wearing a crisp white T-shirt that I promise you has never seen the inside of a painter's studio, a navy blazer, and jeans that actually aren't torn. Uh-huh, sure you came from the studio.

'And then, of course,' he says pointedly, seeing my expression, 'I had to change.'

'No matter,' Freddie gushes delightedly, throwing up his hands. 'You're here now.' He swings one arm around my waist, the other around Grady's. 'I'm so glad you two have gotten close. Now I *know* your show will be perfect, even if . . .' He breaks off and sighs. 'Even if I won't be there to curate it.'

I rub Freddie's shoulder. 'It *will* be perfect.'

'Yeah,' Grady says sheepishly, passing a hand in my direction. 'I mean, look who I've got to work with.'

'You two are so cute,' Freddie effuses. 'You don't need

me getting in the way! I'm sure you've got *loads* to talk about. Ta! I'll be mingling. Ooh, those look good!' He rushes off toward a waitress with a tray of canapés.

I can't believe it. The way he tried to pull us closer, the way he rushed off so we'd be alone . . . Freddie's trying to set us up. He actually thinks we're *interested* in each other. Okay, it's official. Freddie's just become the only guy I know with worse taste in men than my own.

'So, Izzy. Where's your friend?' Grady's chiding voice interrupts my thoughts.

'What?' I spot Kimmy a few feet away, talking to a curator from the Whitney. 'She's right there. In the black wig.'

'Not Kimmy,' he says, like I'm an idiot. 'I know where Kimmy is.'

Oh, of course. He means Mimi. 'You must mean my cousin. She's . . .' I clear my throat. 'She wasn't, um, invited.'

'So.' He lowers his head, gazing up at me. 'You two are close?'

Really, *why* does he want to talk about Mimi? Is it just because he can see it bothers me? Because he wants me to get all flustered and trip over my words? I think back to the Izzy in the mirror earlier tonight – calm, sophisticated Izzy – and I know in a flash, she's receding. She's allowing herself to get worked up at the slightest goading from stupid Grady Cole.

'No, not really,' I say, exasperated. 'Maybe we once were. Maybe not. But, look. Why do you even care?'

He gives me a slow, sly smile. 'Just curious.'

What is *with* this guy! Honestly, most people I can read. In fact, it's one of my strengths. I can tell when someone's thinking of buying a painting or just admiring it. I can tell when they're willing to pay top price, even as they try to bargain downward. I know these things. I can *feel* them. But with Grady, all I feel is confusion. I never know what he's trying to get at. I just know he's trying to get it at my expense.

I shake my head and grab Grady by the arm. 'Oh, come here.'

'Hey.' He draws back. 'What are you going to do, make me stand in the corner?'

I make a face. 'Will you just come *on*?'

He takes a gulp of champagne and lifts his hands in defeat. 'Okay, bossy pants. Lead the way.'

I pull Grady around the various tables toward Deidre, my friend, my salvation. When we get to her, I present him with an arm flourish worthy of Vanna White. 'Deidre,' I say, 'this is Grady Cole, our newest artist. And Grady' – I give him a stern glare that I hope wills him to behave – 'this is Deidre Gayle, a principal dancer for the American Ballet Theatre, and one of our top collectors.'

Grady gives a charismatic smile and stretches out his hand. 'Hi, good to meet you.' And I don't know how, but the guy's a pro. He turns a chair to face Deidre, sitting forward with his elbows on his knees. 'I confess I don't know much about ballet, but maybe you could enlighten me?'

'Oh, no.' Deidre dismisses the thought with her hand and crosses her muscular legs. 'You mustn't bore yourself with me. Please, I'd so love to hear about your work.'

I remain seated by Deidre's other side, nibbling on a cheese puff. Normally this is when I'd jump in and steer the conversation toward a collector's particular tastes. For instance, I know Deidre prefers abstract work, so I'd mention something about Grady's form and color, and let him go from there. But Grady doesn't seem to need the help. He's already rambling away, and Deidre's staring speechlessly, transfixed.

'Beauty is important to me,' I hear him say. 'I like to infuse my paintings with a sense of humor: I like to uncover the absurdity of commercial culture. But in the end, I want to create a piece with strong color and line. I want to look at something beautiful.'

'I'm intrigued!' Deidre says excitedly, gripping the tabletop. 'I can't wait for the show!'

Grady smiles humbly. 'Thanks, I hope it lives up to your expectations.' Jeez, he can even fake humility. It's like he's had PR training. He's wrapping Deidre right around his little finger.

For the first time, I find *I'm* looking at Grady with my eyes narrowed, in that signature hawkish look of his. There's something about this guy. It's as if he has a pocketful of faces that he rotates through, depending on the situation. Charmer. Adversary. Friend. So far, I don't trust any of them.

Grady catches me staring at him, and he returns the stare. We're just sitting there across from each other, locked in an eye battle that may last through eternity. But finally, he lifts a drink in my direction. 'Cheers,' he says, before swigging the rest of his champagne. 'Ladies?' He pushes back his chair. 'I'll return with more presently.'

Presently? Who does he think he is, Mr Belvedere? I watch him walk to the drink table. His stride is casual and unhurried, but purposeful too. And when he picks up three champagne flutes, he has no trouble balancing them in his hands. The liquids barely even move. He seems to be suaveness personified.

Grady returns to our table with a man-about-town smile, placing one drink in front of Deidre and another in front of me. He's still standing, about to place the last drink down, when his body freezes midmotion. My eyes turn to his face, which quickly runs through a full palette of emotions – white, sickly green, and finally fiery red.

'Grady?' I say cautiously. 'You okay?'

He redirects his gaze toward us, bringing the last glass down so hard that the narrow stem breaks, spilling champagne over the side.

'Shit!' Grady yells as I reach for a bunch of cocktail napkins. And then again, more softly, '*Shit.*'

Deidre dabs quietly at the spilled drink while I stand up to see what – or who – has pushed about every one of Grady Cole's buttons. There by the velvet curtain, handing Freddie a bottle of wine wrapped in red ribbon, in a light gray suit stylishly without a tie, is none other than Avery Devon.

When I turn back, Grady's helping Deidre mop up the spill, laughing at himself. 'That'll teach me to down a glass of champagne in one go,' he's saying. 'Guess I got dizzy for a moment.'

'Do you know him?' I ask calmly, pointing toward Avery.

'Who?' Grady's eyes betray nothing, and his tone is flip. 'Avery Devon, Freddie's replacement.'

He flinches. It's the slightest, split-second movement – just the twitch of an eye and a stiffening of the neck. But I see it.

'Nope.' He grins, stuffing the soggy napkins into the mouth of the broken glass. 'Never met the guy. But I look forward to it.'

'Well, then,' I say, feeling my heart race. Grady, if you ruin this, I'll throw food at you. 'I'll bring him over. You can both meet him.'

Okay. Here's my chance to impress Avery Devon. I go over what to say in my mind. *Avery! I'm glad you decided to come. There are so many people I'd like you to meet.* Except that sounds so cold, with Freddie right there. I don't want him to think I'm *happy* he's leaving. I just want to sound ... competent. Expert, even. When did that become so hard?

I smooth down my straightened hair, tug my dress into place, and stride on my black strappy heels toward Freddie's side. Kimmy's just a few feet away, talking with Adrienne Brewster, one of our artists. She catches my eye and nods her support. I grab Freddie's hand and lace my fingers through his.

'Are you having fun, Freddie?' I ask, not yet able to look Avery in the eye.

Freddie throws his head back and lets out a whoop. Hmm. Someone's been drinking. 'You girls sure can throw a party!'

I gaze shyly toward Avery. 'I'm glad you could make it.'

Hey! Six whole words and no fumbles!

Avery lifts his chin gallantly. The top buttons of his shirt are open, and I try not to stare at his tan Adam's apple. 'And I thank you for inviting me.'

I did it! I spoke to the unthinkably attractive man who also happens to be my boss. And he responded! Whew. Oh, wait. My turn again. Crap.

But like my guardian angel, Kimmy swoops in and saves me from a next sentence. 'Freddie!' she exclaims, her hand on his shoulder. 'Adrienne's been dying to talk to you all night.'

'Adrienne!' Freddie's eyes go wide. 'Where! Let's bring her some champagne! Ta, darlings.' He waves down a waitress with a tray full of glasses. Then he exclaims to Avery, 'Mingle! Mingle!' before following Kimmy into the crowd.

'You're fond of him,' Avery's even voice rings in my ears, separate and above the room's vibrant chatter.

'Of course. He's the best,' I say without thinking. And then, quickly, 'Except . . . I'm sure you're very good too.'

Avery laughs, his teeth flashing white in the dimly lit room. 'I will hope to live up to my predecessor.'

I smile up at him, eternally grateful for this small show of apprehension. 'Come on.' I gesture toward where I left Grady and Deidre. 'I'll introduce you to one of our best collectors and to the next artist we're showing.'

'Splendid,' Avery says, but his lips are twisting together, as if he has more to say. 'That would be Grady Cole, correct?'

Oh, God. He's remembering my humiliating outburst the other day. He's seeing me in his mind's eye, all blue and knotty-haired, shouting out, '*Damn Grady!*'

'Um . . . right.' I look solidly at the floor.

'Yes.' Avery grins at me. 'The name sounds familiar.'

I would kill for a cloak of invisibility right now. That, or a Valium.

'You'll love him when you meet him.' My words tumble out. 'Everyone does. He's so talented, and very charming with the collectors.' I start walking toward the table, hoping Avery follows me. 'You couldn't ask for a better first show.'

He falls in beside me. 'Then I look forward to meeting him.'

'That's exactly what he said about you.'

'Did he, now?' Avery keeps his eye on me as we pass through the maze of tables, amusement still apparent on his face.

He thinks of me as a punch line, I say to myself. But I'll change that. He'll watch me interact with Grady and Deidre. He'll see how I can sell paintings even before they hit the gallery walls. He'll see. He has to.

'Here we are!' I say brightly as we reach the cocktail table. But instantly, my heart rises in my throat. The table's empty.

I look up sharply to see the back of a navy blazer, no doubt Grady's, disappearing through the red curtain toward the exit. When I swivel my head to look for Deidre, I find her at the other side of the room, talking intimately with Adrienne Brewster, Freddie, and Kimmy. I've come all this way. And no one's here.

'So,' I say, defeated.

'So,' says Avery Devon, unsurprised. 'Champagne?'

'Yes.' I sink into a seat before realizing it's still wet from Grady's spill. 'Ohhhh, God, yes.'

14

I'm not drunk. I'm just intoxicated by you.

There's an evil sound near my ear, demanding, shrill, and insistent. I throw my arm off the bed and search around for the phone. I check the clock – seven a.m. My head is pulsing with pain. Must. Stop. The ringing.

Finally the answering machine picks up, and I can hear my own obscenely cheery voice belting out, 'Hi! It's Izzy! Leave a message!' Little did I know when I recorded that innocent ditty that someday it would be blaring through my crippling champagne hangover. I don't even know how much I drank. He just kept putting the glasses in my hand – Avery, that is. *Ohhhh, no.* Avery. He had to put me in a cab, didn't he? *Wait.* Was that him helping me up the stairs to my apartment? I look down to see I'm wearing a skimpy silk slip, and my cocktail dress is slung over a chair. *Oh, my God, no.* Did he *undress* me?

'Iz!' Dix's voice yells over the answering machine. 'Wake your ass up, turn on the TV, and press record. Don't make me call again.'

Why is she torturing me? Why is my best friend yelling at my poor, pounding head? There must be a good reason. What is it about today? *Oh!* I know! *Today!* My hand finally makes contact with the cordless, and I mindlessly stab at the buttons until I hit TALK.

'I got it!' I croak. 'I'm up!'

'Ooh,' Dix exhales. 'You sound like you've been dead awhile.'

'Honey, it's not good. I'll tell you later.'

'You better. Go watch, and we'll talk soon. Kisses.'

I throw the phone onto the bed and drag myself up with my arms. My mouth is all dry, and my eyelids are heavy. I move as fast as I can to the television, popping a tape into the VCR with one hand and turning on the cable box with the other. According to the VCR clock, it's 7:14 a.m. I couldn't have missed him yet. I jab at the channel switcher until a no-longer-portly Al Roker comes on, saying, 'And here's what's happening in your neck of the woods.' How can the man seem so chipper this early in the morning?

I turn the volume up and trudge to the bathroom. One look at myself in the mirror is enough to make me grimace. I may actually never approach reflective surfaces again. My hair has matted around my head, its usually ginger hue now closer to a tarnished rust. The dark bags under my eyes could carry sacks of flour, and my lips are so dry they're starting to crack. Last night's champagne has left me as dehydrated as a piece of beef jerky. Lovely. I mentally vow that I will never again drink to the point of hideousness.

For the next hour, sipping massive amounts of water and coffee, I watch the *Today* show. I see a segment on summer makeup (who knew peach blush was so flattering?), an exposé on women's hormone therapy (gosh, I'm going to have to worry about that in twenty years), and the miraculous tale of a rescued puppy (he limped ten miles before someone found him, poor sweetie). Wow. All you have to do is wake up a little early, and there's all this really interesting stuff to learn. Like, did you know the ancient Olmecs in Mexico were the first to cultivate the cocoa tree? Without them, there'd be no chocolate!

Finally, Katie Couric's bright smile pops onto the screen. 'And now,' she says, twinkling her eyes at the camera, 'we have with us an acclaimed journalist whose column, "Getting It", has been lighting the New York dating scene on fire. The column's latest installment, by far its most popular, called for men to revive that age-old dating institution: the pickup line.' Here, she turns to someone off camera and calls, 'Is that how you won over your wife, Matt?' and he calls back, 'If only I had tried, maybe it wouldn't have taken so long!' Cameraman guffawing ensues.

'According to the *Wall Street Journal*,' Katie continues, 'in only the eight days since this column was printed, the city's restaurant reservations for two have gone up twenty percent, movie ticket sales have increased by ten percent, and flower and chocolate sales have soared a whopping thirty percent.'

My God, I think. Jamie has single-handedly united hundreds and hundreds of people into coupledom. Just by telling men to suck it up and approach us. Can it be that easy? Of course not, I think cynically. Most of these new couples are probably doomed from the start. After all, once the initial flattery and physical attraction fade, what's left between them? And what about all the Camerons out there, using this new dating craze to cheat on their girl-friends? That's what men do, isn't it? I feel a shudder go through me. Jeez, I don't sound like myself. It's like I've been so hurt that I've finally stopped believing. *You'll find someone better than Jared Anders. Someone intelligent, dashing, and classy in a way Mimi will never be.* After thirteen years of hope, have I finally lost faith in Dix's promise?

'And now' – Katie Couric's ever-present smile lures my thoughts back to the television set – 'Mr "Getting It" himself, James D. Hunter.'

The camera pans to the cushy chair opposite Katie's. There's Jamie!! And he looks *so* great! He's got on the outfit Dix picked out for him, dark jeans and a white untucked button-down shirt. Boy, what they say about television is true – Jamie looks about fifteen pounds heavier, but in all the right places. His usually unruly hair falls in smooth, dark waves down to his collar, and he's got on his contacts instead of his glasses. Jamie's face looks a little tan too, which must mean he's wearing makeup. Must remember to tease him about that.

'So, James,' Katie Couric is saying, 'how did you get so wise to the ways of women?'

Jamie smiles and sits up straighter in his chair. 'Well, Katie,' he says, laughing a bit, 'I don't think any man can call himself wise when it comes to women. Insightful, maybe. Curious, certainly.' He shakes his head. 'But you women *always* defy explanation.'

Huh, that was a good answer. This is beyond weird. Jamie Hunter, who hasn't had a date in over six months – and even then, it was a blind setup – being interviewed as an expert on women. I know he must be nervous, but somehow, it doesn't show. He so looks the part and seems so confident that even I'm starting to believe he knows what he's talking about.

For an instant, I get the feeling that I'm watching a stranger, and a coldness passes through me. Can this be the same Jamie who gets flustered when even looking at a woman? The Jamie who likes to curl into a ball on my lap, ready for comforting? The Jamie most people think is secretly *gay*?

Finally, Katie starts to wrap up the segment, thanking Jamie for his advice *and* for being so charming. 'I have to confess,' she says to him, 'I used to think pickup lines were a little sleazy – before I read your column, of course. I don't get that feeling now. You have an honorable aura around you.'

Jamie leans forward in his chair. 'Do you know what I'd like around *you*, Katie Couric?' he says, like he's spent a lifetime sweeping women off their feet. 'My arms.'

As I push open the gallery's weighty wooden door, I'm paralyzed by an all-consuming feeling of dread. So much of last night remains fuzzy. I remember Avery telling me about growing up in Massachusetts, and then going to

Oxford, where he got his master's degree in history of art. I remember talking about my college job at Brown University's David Winton Bell Gallery. I remember eating tiny crab cakes. But that was all before the sixth glass of champagne. Before I got home. Before I got – somehow – defrocked. And I thought I couldn't face Avery Devon *before*.

'Morning, sunshine!' Kimmy beams at me. She's got on a gauzy turquoise minidress over gray pin-striped pants and a white tank top – really, as officelike as I've ever seen her.

My own outfit took twenty minutes to choose. I had to look businesslike, but mostly I had to look *covered up*. If I find out that Avery Devon took off my dress and put me to bed last night, I'll . . . oh, God, it's too awful. I can't even think about it. Of all my outfits, the finalists were a Chanel-style suit (a knockoff, but only $59.99!) and what I'm wearing now – a fitted long-sleeve white button-down and a black pencil skirt. This outfit went better with my shoes, which are really Dix's shoes, and which are so high and pointy, I wonder if my feet will ever unclench again. Dix says nothing screams capable like a 'power shoe.' Because, apparently, the key to convincing a man you can do anything is to look comfortable in a Jimmy Choo that can accommodate only three toes.

'*Ouch*.' I wince at Kimmy. 'Head hurts.'

'You must have had some time,' she says from the filing cabinet behind her desk. 'When I left, you and Avery were still having a cozy *tête-à-tête*.'

'We were?' Oh, right, we were. I mean, I remember the look on his face, and that bit of neck he exposed without his tie. I just don't remember . . . exactly . . . what I *said*. 'Is he here?' I whisper, squinting toward the office.

'Yup. I'm collecting materials on our artists to help ease him into our inventory. I'm sure he'll be counting on you for most of his information, though.'

'Did he say anything?' I ask, tucking my shirt more neatly into my skirt. 'Anything . . . out of the ordinary? About me, I mean.'

'No. Why?' Kimmy's eyeing me suspiciously. 'Ooh!! You two didn't wind up . . .'

'No!' I cry. 'God, Kimmy, of course not! I mean . . . at least I can't *imagine* . . .'

'Wow, you sure did have a good time last night,' Kimmy laughs.

'I didn't!' I reach plaintively for the reception ledge. 'I did not!'

'Izzy.' Kimmy returns to her desk with an armful of file folders. 'I'm teasing.'

'Oh, right. Heh heh.' I feel queasy, and I don't think it's because of the hangover. 'Here, I'll take those.' I reach for the files, balancing the heavy stack in both arms. Except I forgot which shoes I'm wearing. I can barely manage my own weight without spraining an ankle.

I take a deep breath. Better to just . . . get it over with. Now's as good a time as any. I wobble toward the office, each step an exercise in torture for my poor toes. I nearly drop the whole pile of folders trying to open the French doors, but luckily I manage to keep it together.

'Hi,' I say boldly, seeing Avery Devon seated at Freddie's desk. Except, of course, it's no longer Freddie's desk. 'Hi,' I repeat, with less bravado. 'We've, um, got some files for you to look at.'

'Thank you, Isabel,' he says smoothly, reaching to take the pile from my hands. 'And hello to you as well.'

How can he look so good? His coloring shows no sign of hangover pallor; his eyes still have their gallant twinkle. His suit jacket is open to reveal his sculpted torso in its wrinkle-free shirt. And here I can barely walk. Who am I kidding? I'll never be slick, like those girls you see striding down Fifth Avenue with their designer sunglasses and flawless tans. Like Mimi. What makes me think, even on my best day, that I could ever impress this man?

'How are you feeling?' Avery smiles up at me from his desk. 'Not so good, I would imagine.'

Since impressing him is out of the question, I go with my one other option. 'I'm sorry,' I plead, dragging my desk chair closer to his desk and sitting down. 'I'm *so* sorry. I don't ever drink that much. I don't know what got into me!'

'No, stop,' he says quickly. 'I take the full blame. Living in Europe for so long, I'd forgotten that Europeans drink more than Americans. I should have realized I was offering you too many glasses. I should have realized that *you*' – he inclines his head respectfully in my direction – 'were just being too polite to refuse. Please, Isabel, forgive me.'

'Oh,' I say in surprise. *He's* taking the blame? For my worst professional indiscretion ever? Can I really – for once – be this lucky? Gosh, I almost feel like singing. He doesn't even care! Except, there's just that one more teeny thing. . . . 'Avery, do I, uh, remember correctly that we shared a cab home?'

His lips twist in that amused way of his. 'To *your* home, yes. I've been staying at the W Hotel on Lexington until I find a proper flat.'

'Right. Okay. So, um . . .' I cross my legs, letting Dix's Jimmy Choo dangle off my foot. I must be blushing wildly. 'When I woke up . . . I was . . . I mean, did you . . . so, Avery, remind me.' I lean in a bit. 'Did I give you a grand tour of my apartment?'

He laughs, clasping his hands together on the desk. 'As much as I'm sure I would have enjoyed your sense of decor, Isabel, no. I saw you to the top of the stairs, and then I said my farewell. Whatever happened next' – his eye glints – 'I'm afraid I cannot take the blame for.'

'Great!' I say as relief washes over me. Well, that's not so bad! Here I thought all I did was embarrass myself. But from the look of him, you'd think he actually enjoyed our little escapade. 'Thank you for being so considerate and for making sure I got home okay.' I look down at my lap and then up again, at him. 'I'm touched by your concern.'

Avery pushes his chair back from the desk and crosses his legs. 'So you forgive me.'

'Yes!' I smile wide with joy. 'I mean, there's nothing to forgive!'

'Excellent,' he says succinctly. 'So then you *won't* be

poking my back with your finger only to yell at me for something I haven't done, correct?'

Wait. What did he just say?

'I . . . won't . . . what?' I feel a plunging in my chest.

'As you told me you did with Grady Cole.' He touches a finger thoughtfully to his chin. 'I wouldn't want to incur the – shall we say – misplaced hostility you described upon your first meeting.'

I am *never* drinking again. Not even a glass of wine. Not even a Diet Coke, lest the caffeine make me loopy. *How* could I have told him what happened with Grady? What on earth would prompt me to say, 'Guess how I met Grady Cole! It all started on the platform of the six train . . .?' He'll think I have anger management issues. He'll think I don't know how to treat our artists. He'll think . . . what he's probably thought all along. That I just don't know what I'm doing.

'Avery,' I plead, sitting primly at the tip of my chair. 'Do you think we could start over? That you could just forget the day we met outside at reception and the way I acted last night?' I try to sound confident. 'I promise you. I'm not usually so . . . incompetent.'

'Of course you're not,' Avery says softly, his eyes warm. 'If you were incompetent, I wouldn't hear every collector tell me how much they trust you, how they think of you as not only a businesswoman, but also a friend. If you were incompetent' – he gets up and walks around the desk toward me – 'Kimmy wouldn't be answering "Izzy would know" to every question I ask her. Freddie wouldn't have spoken of you with such immense fondness. If you were incompetent' – he's standing right over me now, looking down into my eyes – 'I wouldn't be so looking forward to working with you.'

I gaze up at those green-flecked eyes, and I'm struck completely speechless. I'm sure my cheeks must be fiery red, but I resist the urge to turn away from his gaze. It's then that I realize – I haven't lost hope. In fact, I'm looking at it right now. I hear the rushing in my ears, and I feel it in my chest. Even my fingertips tingle. *You'll find someone better than Jared Anders. Someone intelligent, dashing classy.* The antimagnetic dome I vowed to maintain crumbles around me. I think I've found him.

'Thank you,' I say, feeling flushed. 'So much.' And then, shyly, 'I look forward to working with you too.'

'All right, then,' Avery says, sitting back at his desk and picking up a file folder. 'Shall we?'

'We sure shall!' I hurry up from my chair, sending it rolling behind me. 'I'll just get some of our slide books, and we can get down to business.'

'Excellent.' He smiles.

'I'll be right back!' I teeter out as fast as I can in Dix's shoes, wondering which of our artists I'll start with. We keep slides of an artist's entire body of work on file, whether we've got pieces available to sell or not, in order to present a complete sense of his or her work.

I scan the shelves in the storage niche behind Kimmy's desk, running my fingers over the black binders. Avery's taste tends toward the avant-garde, so I should start with someone more outré, someone a bit shocking. Oh! I know. Dennis Barana, an installation artist who reproduces the public spaces our government would most like to remain hidden – prisons, state mental asylums, homeless shelters, and so on. Critics either love him or hate him, never in between – the sure sign of a truly controversial artist.

As I pull Barana's slide binder from the shelf, I feel almost giddy with happiness. Here I've been so worried about winning Avery Devon's approval, and so sure with every passing moment that I never would. Even just a couple hours ago, I would rather have spent the day wedding dress shopping with Mimi than be in the same room with him for one minute. And now look! Here I am positively in raptures over the idea of spending the afternoon just the two of us alone in the office, our heads inches apart as we peruse the work of our artists. I haven't felt this much joy since Robbie Williams announced his next U.S. tour! (In September! I already have tickets!)

'Iz,' Kimmy calls in a loud whisper, sounding nervous. 'You might want to –' Then I hear her cry, 'Grady, please, I'll just let Avery know you're here first!'

Grady? What's he doing here? And why does Kimmy sound so – I rush out from the storage space to see Grady Cole in his characteristic T-shirt and paint-stained pants striding quickly toward me. 'Grady!' I say, blocking his path. 'What can we do for you today?' He's got a frazzled look to him, his eyes blazing and intent. I've never seen him like this before.

'Stand back,' he says heatedly.

'Everything's okay.' I try to keep my voice soothing, as if I'm talking to a bear I've met in the woods. 'Whatever you need, we can help you.'

'No, you can't,' he says harshly, circling around me and resuming his purposeful stride toward, I now realize, the office.

'Grady!' I call after him, running to catch up. 'Ouch!' My foot buckles in my ridiculous heels, sending me nearly to the ground.

Grady stops suddenly and turns to see me bending down to grip my throbbing ankle. A look of regret passes over his face, but soon he's off again, gripping the French doors with both hands and pulling them forcefully open.

Damn it! I bite my lip and limp painfully toward the doors, arriving to see Grady standing over Avery's desk.

'I'm sorry, Avery,' I cry, despairing that yet again, I've got to apologize to him. 'He got past us, but probably because he was so eager to meet you! This is Grady Cole.' I'm panting now, and tears of pain are smarting in the corners of my eyes.

'Thank you, Isabel, for your diligence,' I hear Avery say calmly, though I can't see his face behind Grady's back. 'I can manage from here.'

Utterly confused, I've no choice but to close the doors behind me and limp back toward reception. Once Kimmy sees me coming, she leaps up and rushes to my side.

'Jeez, Izzy, what happened! Are you okay?' She pulls

her chair from behind the ledge and eases me down into it.

Gingerly, I take off my shoe and roll my ankle around first one way, then the other. The pain is easing up. 'It's okay, just twisted, I think. Don't worry.'

Kimmy grabs a first aid kit from her desk, punches an automatic ice pack until the cooling fluids rush together, and hands it to me with a look of concern.

'Really! It's okay,' I assure her. 'I'm more worried about Avery than anything else.'

'What is *with* that!' Kimmy leans back against the high reception ledge, looking like she could be in a fashion magazine. 'What freak demon turned Grady into Possession Central?'

I shake my head, remembering Grady's expression when he first saw Avery at the party last night. Something's going on between them. Grady Cole can be obnoxious, yes, but he's no raving madman.

'You've got no right!' we hear him yell from the office. He continues, hot with emotion, but too muffled for us to hear.

Kimmy and I stare wordlessly at each other, our ears straining to make out what the two men could be saying. My mind is racing with possibilities. Did something happen last night that I was too tipsy (all right, fall-down drunk) to notice? Or do Grady and Avery have some secret, tumultuous history between them? I rack my brain for any tidbit of gossip I might have heard. The art world is so small and insular that it takes only one person to start a flaming rumor – like that time Freddie kissed our artist Sarah Van Ange platonically on the mouth, and soon galleristas across the city were switching him to the 'straight' column on their lists. Really, as if!

But my contemplation is cut short when I see Grady Cole racing toward us, his face red and brow knit. He stops short when he sees the ice pack in my hand.

'I'm sorry about your leg,' he blurts out. And seconds later, the door is squeaking shut behind him.

'Friggin' Tasmanian devil,' Kimmy exclaims.

This has got to be one of the weirdest days I've ever had. Jamie an expert on women. Avery complimenting me as soon as I walk in the door. Grady turned into a whirling dervish. I'm tempted to call my dad and see if he's hanging out at the local disco. What is it, male opposite day?

'Are you going to ask Avery what happened?' Kimmy says, nodding in the direction of the office.

'Would *you*?' I ask.

'Hell, no,' she says.

So we just stay where we are, she standing against the ledge, me sitting with my ice pack, under such a cloud of confusion that we're sure there's no alternative but for it soon to pour.

15

Would you like a raisin?
How 'bout a date?

'So he just continued on like nothing happened?' Dix is sprawled out on Jamie's sofa, propping herself up on an elbow to sip her Martini.

'Totally!' I exhale in disbelief. I'm sitting in an easy chair with my ankle resting on Jamie's coffee table. The swelling's gone now, and it only hurts when I walk. Truthfully, the most painful part of the day was holding in the enormous outbursts that threatened to pop from my mouth at every moment. *I'm glad you like that print, Avery. We sold out the entire edition last year. WHAT IS UP WITH YOU AND GRADY? You might find this sculptor's work quite stimulating. Uma Thurman's a big fan. HELLO, DID YOU SEE HIM? We gave that painter his first show five years ago, and now he sells at fifty thousand dollars a piece. CAN'T YOU TELL I'M DYING HERE!!* But then, I'd feel Avery's breath on my shoulder, or catch him eyeing me with that twisty-lipped smile of his, and I'd feel a nervous flip in my stomach. Don't even get me started about the time he took my hand and moved it closer to the light so he could see the slide I was holding. That skin has known more moisturizer than most men see in a lifetime. Designer clothing, muscular definition, gentle tan, possible manicure . . . I'd be lying if I said I wasn't worried.

Could my Prince Charming turn out to be a Cinderfella?

'Here you go.' Jamie places a vodka gimlet on the table in front of me and scowls at Dix until she makes room for him on the sofa. Jamie's apartment is one of those rare great finds – a rent-stabilized one-bedroom near Central Park, with a study, fireplace, and original moldings – but it's also five steep flights up, with no elevator. You'd think with all the step classes I've taken at the gym, the trip up would be a breeze. It is so not a breeze. In fact, with a twisted ankle, it's more like a hurricane. And that's not even counting the fact that the Upper West Side is like the Arctic Circle for someone from my neighborhood. I have to take three trains to get here!

But the effort was well worth it when Dix and I saw the joyous expression on Jamie's face as he opened the door. We had decided to surprise him with a congratulatory bouquet of flowers for his stunning spot on the *Today* show. I half expected Katie Couric to grab him right there the way she was flirting! The only problem was that we couldn't actually find any flowers. The florists were already closed, and this being Friday night, the delis had sold out of all their pretty bouquets, leaving only the brown tattered ones. How ironic is that? Jamie's got so many more people dating, we can't even get him a decent bunch of flowers! Finally, we settled for a large handful of baby's breath, most of which now litters the five flights up to Jamie's apartment like the urban equivalent of Hansel and Gretel's bread crumbs. But even with our dry, shedding bouquet, Jamie was thrilled. I can't remember a time when he seemed so upbeat. Even his voice sounds different, like it's been recharged after a lifetime of losing juice.

'I've got an interview with salon.com lined up for next week,' Jamie's telling Dix, waving his arms around as if he can't keep in the energy. 'And the *News* has set up a photo shoot for me. They want a picture to accompany my column.'

'Find out who they're using,' Dix says, her brow creased. 'They've got some crap photographers, but I'll make sure you get someone good.'

Jamie laughs incredulously. 'They started calling me "pretty boy" at the office today,' he says. 'It used to be when someone gave me a nickname it was because they couldn't remember my *actual* one.'

'We've got to capitalize on this.' Dix pokes Jamie's thigh with her finger. 'If we don't milk your current fifteen minutes for all they're worth, you may not get the next fifteen.'

As Dix and Jamie lapse into PR strategies, I let my mind wander to thoughts of Avery. I get a tingle of anticipation just thinking about the next time I'm going to see him. Which, actually, is tomorrow! Avery wants to put the Bond on a normal Tuesday-to-Saturday gallery schedule, eliminating our Sunday hours. At first, I protested, pointing out that some of our regulars come only on Sundays – like Mrs Jacobs, who stops by after walking her teacup terrier Bunny (who doesn't fit in an actual teacup – we tried). But Avery countered that we've never once made a sale on a Sunday, which is true, and that we'll probably just get more traffic on Saturdays now. Besides, I'm sure he'll change the hours back to normal if it looks like our regulars can't make it any other day. He's reasonable, after all.

'So am I your client now?' I hear Jamie saying to Dix, and I lean my head back in the cushy chair, stretching my legs out on the coffee table. I'm sure they'll appreciate the opportunity to talk business while I think of my own strategies to impress Avery. And I've got lots! Lots of savvy, impressive business strategies.

God, I can so picture it. Avery's initial amusement at my klutziness will soon turn into admiration. How genuine that Isabel is, he's been thinking. How unaffected and fresh. At work, he may seem standoffish. He may barely even say a word to me all day tomorrow. But inside, he'll be enjoying my company so much, he'll make excuses for more.

'Isabel,' he'll say to me, all serious. 'Would you mind terribly staying late tonight? I know it's Saturday, but I'd like very much to familiarize myself with the gallery's inventory.'

'Of course not, Avery,' I'll say, businesslike. 'Obviously I had many plans for an exciting Saturday night and was not at all planning to read a book in bed with my cat. But I'll cancel them at once. You know the gallery always comes first.'

So dreamy Avery Devon and I will spend hours looking at the paintings stored in the salesroom. He'll be impressed at my arcane knowledge of each piece and its creator, at my memory of what collector bought which artist. We'll have so much fun evaluating the art – and tingling every time our hands inadvertently touch – that I'll offer to take him upstairs to show him the rare and valuable pieces from the Old Man's personal collection. In the higher reaches of the town house, it will be dark, and misty (well, dusty at least), and I'll feel his presence behind me.

'Isabel,' he'll whisper in my ear. 'Isabel.'

'What is it, Avery?' I'll ask innocently. 'What could it be?'

'You, my darling.' He'll push the hair back from my neck and press his lips against it. 'It's always been you. It *will* always be you.'

'*Izzy!*' I hear. '*Hello?*'

Poof. Exit rolling mist and dashing suitor.

'Are you even listening?' Dix is headed toward Jamie's kitchen, which is separated from the living room by a low half-wall.

'I'm sorry, Dix!' I say, brushing away the phantom memory of Avery Devon's lips.

'Dix, that's *amazing*,' Jamie's saying excitedly. 'What's he like?'

Oh, dear, I missed something big.

'He's ravishingly handsome, of course, and . . . well . . . a bit demanding, but I'm hoping to change him.' I can see Dix over the half-wall, rifling through Jamie's liquor cabinet as she speaks. 'And it *is* possible to change a man, no matter what they say.'

'New boyfriend?' I venture feebly.

'New *client*, Iz.' Dix comes back from the kitchen with a fresh drink. 'I'm not supposed to say anything until the contract's final, but I can't hold it in any longer!' Dix seems exuberant. Her usually porcelain cheeks are flushed, and her eyes are almost teary with excitement. She perches on the edge of the sofa, as if she's about to impart the secret location of Atlantis. In a whisper, she exhales, '*Arden Moore*.'

'Oh my *God*, Dix!' I'm stunned. 'That's astounding!' To say Arden Moore's a big star would be like saying Harrison Ford's been in a few movies. In fact, Arden Moore is fast becoming one of Hollywood's biggest box office draws. Right now, his career's at its peak – sort of like Tom Cruise's post-*Top Gun* and pre-*Eyes Wide Shut*. *Entertainment Weekly* just named Arden the hunkiest star of the millennium, and he's been linked with no fewer than five top actresses – including Halle Berry! – this year alone.

I drag my legs down from the coffee table, straining forward to achieve maximum gossip-hearing posture. 'Dix, how did you get him!'

She mock shrugs and says gaily, 'I'd like to say it was my hot body and expertise in seduction, but I'm afraid I have to give all the credit to brain-power and business sense.' She smiles as widely as I've ever seen.

Jamie's cell phone chooses *now* of all times to ring – and honestly, with a hundred ring tones to choose from, he picks 'Row Row Row Your Boat'? I'm vaguely aware that he rises to answer it, but I'm too riveted to notice more.

'Arden's starting to get a bad rep in the tabloids,' Dix continues animatedly, 'mostly because he isn't exactly the *politest* man you've ever met. And since his former publicist also reps about ten other huge celebs, how could Arden be getting the undivided attention he so justly deserves? All I did was point out the obvious fact of how much he needed me.'

Gosh, I feel selfish. Here I am all wrapped up in Avery

Devon (hmm, actually, that would be nice), and ignoring the two people who are dearest to me. I mean, forget about Arden Moore – Dix should be getting all the attention *she* deserves too. I've got to think of a way to show her how happy I am – and how proud.

'Dix.' I take her hand. 'I'm in awe.'

She sighs. 'Look at these heels.' She lifts her leg to show me a pair of stilettos astoundingly higher than the ones she lent me. 'You raise that pedestal any higher, and I'm bound to lose my footing.'

'I don't believe it,' I say warmly. 'You amaze me every day.'

'*God.*' She winces in disgust. 'Take it to fucking Hallmark.'

But I see the slight welling at the corners of her eyes. And she sees me noticing. 'Shove it,' she says, by which I know her to mean, *I appreciate your confidence in me.* '*Anyway,*' Dix says pointedly. 'Arden Moore's next movie premieres in a couple weeks, and I've already been planning the event. To which you and Jamie will be invited, naturally. It's *huge!* Total blockbuster. Iz, I'm so excited I might *piss* myself!'

'Not on the couch, please,' we hear Jamie call out from his bedroom. In all the excitement, I hadn't even realized where he'd gone. I glance questioningly at Dix, but she's already getting up, her long black hair bouncing behind her. I follow her to the bedroom, where Jamie's standing in front of his closet, examining his suits.

'Dearest,' Dix says tentatively, 'you did the *Today* show this morning. You already wore your specially chosen outfit. And you were fabulous.'

'Does this look okay?' Jamie holds a black suit against himself. 'If I gel up my hair, wear a slender tie.'

'Gel?' I feel my brow rise to my hairline. 'Like, the styling product?'

'Jamie,' Dix says frankly, her hand on her hip, 'why are you standing here, playing outfit?'

'For the same reason you would,' he says cagily,

admiring the suit in his closet's full-length mirror. 'Because I have a date.'

My eyes bug open, and my mouth goes slightly ajar. Even Dix seems struck dumb. Jamie starts to choose a tie, obviously enjoying our reactions.

'Jamie, that's wonderful,' I manage. 'A blind date? Like last time?' Well, hopefully *not* like last time – Jamie described her as a bony, large-headed locust lady.

'Actually, it *is* kind of a blind date,' he says, unconcerned. I wish I could feel the same way. I see worry flash across Dix's face as well – sometimes we wonder if Jamie's guy friends hold auditions to find the least attractive women to set him up with. 'But I know what she looks like. . . .'

Dix and I aren't sure how to proceed. We can sense from his flippant tone that Jamie's playing with us – which is, to say the least, unusual. 'I got a call from her manager after the *Today* show,' he says. 'And just now she called me herself, to confirm. Seems her escort for tomorrow night bowed out, and now she's left without a date for a benefit. She thought I'd be perfect.'

Jamie. Date. Perfect. It feels like a game on *Sesame Street* – which of these words is not like the other?

'You may have heard of her,' Jamie adds nonchalantly. 'Svetlana Pavlovov, the model? You know, the one in this year's *Sports Illustrated* swimsuit issue, whose bikini is *painted* on?' He winks at us, more lasciviously than teasingly.

I'm not sure why, but Dix and I both take a step back. Maybe we're just in shock. Or maybe it's more metaphoric.

'She needed someone tall,' he continues, straightening his shoulders and lifting his head to his full six-foot-three height. 'And charming.' He flashes us a Mentos-commercial-type smile.

'But what about the whole . . .' I pause, not wanting to hurt his feelings. But even with new posture and trendier hair, Jamie's still Jamie, isn't he? 'I mean, do you think you'll be able to *talk* to her? Without, you know . . .'

'Puking up a lung?' Dix finishes, shaking her head at the tie Jamie's got in his hand, and pointing to a darker one on the bed.

'That's the best part!' He puts on the black jacket and tie, shooting his cuffs and spinning around. 'She barely speaks any English! I don't even *have* to talk to her!'

I almost don't know who I'm looking at. Hipster suit, hair styled to look unstyled, cocky grin . . . how many times have I seen this look in the pages of *People* magazine? God, if I squint a little, Jamie almost looks like Orlando Bloom! How could I never have seen the resemblance before?

'So what do you think?' Jamie spreads his hands out at his sides, like the Fonz.

'I'll tell you what I think,' Dix says, nodding her head. 'Jamie, you've finally arrived.'

Baby, if appearances are deceiving,
you can lie to me all night.

I'm feeling very proud of myself when I arrive at the gallery at eight thirty A.M. on Saturday morning. We don't even open for another hour and a half. How conscientious am I? See, the plan is that by the time Avery arrives I'll be typing swiftly at my computer, consulting my deal notes, and drafting the last sale contracts for the John Teller show, which closes early next week. And Avery'll say, 'Isabel! You're looking quite efficient this morning.' And I'll say, 'I'm just finishing up now, Avery. Soon I'll be *all yours.*' And then he'll say—

I freeze midmotion with my key in the gallery door. It's already open. A cold feeling passes through me. Avery was the last to leave last night. But do we know if he has keys? Did we even bother to give him the alarm code! Oh, God. The realization hits full force. No one locked up last night!

I throw open the door, half expecting to find everything gone. But before I even step over the threshold, a terrifying thought pops into my head. *What if the robbers are still here?* They could be right beyond the door! Looting away! I peek my head in, listening for the footfalls of enormous, steeltoed boots.

AH! I hear them!! Distinct, echoing footsteps, coming

right for the door. Except they don't really sound like boots. But maybe *art* robbers wear Prada! Or. Wait. Maybe . . .

I am such an idiot.

'Isabel?' Avery's clear voice rings out just as I'm closing the door behind me, and he soon appears in person, looking casual yet sophisticated in a blue dress shirt and deep brown flat-front trousers.

'Yup!' I answer, trying to hide my embarrassment. 'I had no idea anyone would be here so early. I got a little . . . er . . . scared for a moment there.'

Avery takes in my flushed face, his eye passing over my little skirt and capped-sleeve shirt and down to my favorite pink ballet flats. I can't quite tell whether he's glad I'm here early or annoyed by the interruption. But then he laughs softly. 'You're sweet.'

Right. That's me. Watch out for toothaches.

'I'll just, uh –' I hurry past Avery and into the office, where I park myself at my desk and bury my head in this month's *Artforum*. There's got to be some juicy article in here I can bring up in casual conversation so Avery realizes I'm up on all the latest gossip and trends. Ooh! Here we go. Art smugglers in Europe. I'm sure that's something Avery had to deal with, working in Germany and all.

'Anything good this issue?' Suddenly, Avery's leaning over my shoulder, and his hand's on the back of my chair, an inch away from my neck. I can feel the little hairs there jumping to attention.

'Smuggling in Europe,' I say gravely, shaking my head. 'Hundreds of priceless works illegally leaving the country.' Oh, crap. 'Er, *continent*.'

Avery gives a derisive grimace. 'And what's new about that? Art's been changing hands illegally for hundreds of years. These articles are getting so sensational, building on the fears of a bearish market. It's reprehensible, really.'

'I know!' I shut the magazine briskly, rolling my eyes. 'I don't know why I even bother reading the trades anymore.'

Avery tilts his head thoughtfully. 'Well, clearly, the reviews are crucial. Did you read the one of Elspeth Worth at the Eaton Bosc? *Artforum* compares her to Rauschenberg.'

'They *do*?' I think back to the Elspeth Worth show – her honey imprint on the bed, Cassie Arnell's cheesy poem, my little plastic Winnie the Pooh.

'Apparently every addition to the bed was a well-thought-out statement,' Avery goes on. 'Like a Winnie the Pooh figurine as a symbol of childhood nostalgia, and a satirical poem as an example of the limitations of the written word.'

'Right,' I draw out the word, barely holding in my laughter. If Freddie were here, we'd be rolling on the floor, in hysterics over the cluelessness of art critics. But something tells me Avery's not the type to laugh at the pretensions of our profession. 'I've seen the show,' I manage, selecting my words carefully. 'It's very moving.'

'I'm sure,' he replies earnestly, crossing the room and pulling out his big padded desk chair. 'I've been wondering, Isabel.' He sits down, straightening an old-fashioned inkwell with two fountain pens and crystal pots of ink. Definitely not something Freddie left behind. 'What do you think of *this* show? Of the John Teller exhibit?'

Oh. That's a bit startling, actually. I hadn't expected to be quizzed on our very own show. Okay, so what does Avery want me to say? Does he love it or hate it? I turn my head back toward the various body parts in our exhibition rooms, the same ones I've been uncomfortably creeping around all month. Avery's testing my taste, I realize. He wants to see if I like what he likes. Do I try to puzzle out what he wants to hear? Or do I just tell the truth?

'Well, Avery,' I begin hesitantly, scanning his face for clues. 'To be honest, I don't think I *get* it. If Teller's message is literal – that his body is his art – I think he could have portrayed that more cleverly. But if he's doing a Duane Hanson thing and trying to startle the viewer with the sheer familiarity of the object, then I think perhaps he's achieved his purpose. But . . . I still wouldn't want his ear in my house.'

'Nor I.' Avery's smiling wide, keeping his eyes fixed on me. Did I pass the test? He leans back in his chair and crosses his legs. I'm barely keeping myself together here. I'm not sure whether it's his movie idol looks, his stylish sophistication, or just the respectful way he acts. But something about Avery Devon is affecting me in ways I've never felt before. It's like some sandman took an image from my subconscious and sculpted it into life out of clay. Or something finer than clay – like crystal, only manlier.

'Isabel, forgive me for asking you this, especially on a Saturday night,' Avery says, with his subtle British inflection. 'But might you be able to cancel your plans for this evening?'

Might I be able to . . .? Oh, my God. I swallow a big lump in my throat. It's happening! Just like I imagined! I nervously run my hand through my hair, smoothing down the waves. 'I could probably, um. I might be able to be . . . *free for you*, Avery.' Nice, Iz. Why don't you just whip out the bright red lipstick and tight black miniskirt?

'Oh, good.' Avery seems relieved. 'I didn't want to be without you tonight.'

I feel my heart pumping faster, and I lose my breath for a moment. He's asking me to spend the night with him! Well, I mean, not *spend the night with him*.' Or . . . *is he?*! Not that I would! Because, you know what? I've been there, done that, and bought the squash-appropriate T-shirt.

What should I do? The last thing I want is to insult Avery, but this is all too soon! We haven't even shared a meal together yet, or caught a movie. There haven't been flowers, or sweet little e-mails, or kisses. What *is* it with men and skipping all the important parts!

'Avery,' I say firmly, standing up at my desk. 'I appreciate your interest – I really do. But frankly, this is all happening too fast for me.'

He eyes me quizzically before frowning in realization. 'You're right. Of course you're right. I've been very insensitive. Here you are used to working with Freddie, and you know nothing about me or my methods. You haven't a clue what I expect from you or how closely I plan to involve you in our future shows.'

'*Come again?*' The words are out of my mouth before I even think them. It's what my deaf grandfather used to say when he couldn't understand you. *Come again?* he'd say, followed closely by, *What fool thing are you saying, young whippersnapper?*

'I want to make it clear, Isabel.' Avery stands now too, planting his hands firmly on his leather desk blotter. A piece of blond hair falls sexily on his forehead. 'You're a crucial piece of this operation. You've been Freddie's right-hand woman for a long time now. Our collectors trust your taste and judgment.' His voice softens. 'So do I. That's why I need you tonight . . .'

He needs me!

'. . . at Grady's studio.'

What fool thing are you saying, young whippersnapper?

'Grady's studio!' I'm sure my face is frozen in surprise. A million thoughts rush into my head at once. To be in a room alone with the two of them! Are they going to fight? Because I'm not sure I want to be in the middle of the screaming again. Am I going to have to referee or something? Ooh! Are they going to wrestle?

'I've scheduled a studio visit this evening to choose the paintings for Grady's show,' Avery says calmly, betraying no hidden emotion. 'Of course your input will be pivotal.'

'Oh, right.' I sit down, disappointed. There goes our special private night together.

'I won't be coy, Isabel,' Avery says, crossing the room toward the French doors. 'I know you were expecting a promotion before Freddie left. And though I can't make any promises, if you prove yourself the equal of my expectations, I don't see why that promotion has to fall by the wayside.' He turns to open one of the doors, offering me his Calvin Klein model profile. 'Now, if you'll excuse me, I think I hear Kimmy arriving, and I've got some assignments I'd like to go over with her.'

As Avery leaves, I stare blankly at my computer screen, trying to work out my jumble of feelings. I've wanted this promotion for months, and now that it's back within my grasp, I feel a sense of elated hope. I'm *almost* there! But then I feel a stab of sadness. Freddie was supposed to be picking out the paintings for Grady's show with me. Two weeks ago, I couldn't imagine that he and I would never collaborate again. And now look at me. I'm such a traitor, sucking up to Avery every chance I get. *I'm free for you, Avery*! God, I sound like a band groupie. But I can't help it. After wading for years in a pool of hurt and betrayal, this is the man who's inspired me to start swimming again. This is the man for whom I'm willing to crack open my defenses, maybe only to be clobbered – or, worse, ignored. And okay, so tonight won't be just the two of us, as I had imagined. But that doesn't mean we can't have our moment together another time. And when we do, I've already made a promise to myself, one I absolutely refuse to break: I'm sure as hell not going to fuck it up.

I can't remember a busier day at the gallery. Everyone who's anyone – and a whole lot of people who aren't – came by to gawp at the new dealer. Seems our humble corner of the world has become the nexus of New York art gossip. Dealers, gallerists, artists, and collectors from uptown and down all clogged our doorstep, rubbernecking to see Avery in action. I only hope the increased foot traffic lasts through Grady's show – and leads to some actual sales. Thankfully the phones were pretty quiet, so Kimmy could answer questions while I finished up my work in the office. I barely got a chance to look at Avery all day, let alone talk to him.

But now it's six P.M, the gallery's closed, Kimmy's gone for the day, and Avery's helping me into my little crochet jacket and grabbing his own brown blazer. Soon, we're walking down Seventy-third Street toward Madison, and the city's still bathed in sunlight and dusky summer air. If only Avery and I could spend the evening with Grady's art

. . . and *without* Grady. But at the very least, I'm hoping our artist has turned off his crazy button.

Our taxi takes us downtown, below the city's familiar grid, where the streets strike out at diagonals and the tires bump along neglected cobblestones. Grady's studio is located in Tribeca (the famously abbreviated 'Triangle Below Canal'), where you can still find massive artists' studios protected by New York's loft laws. I once heard of an artist who had a thousand square feet for 350 dollars a month! I know people who'd donate a kidney for half that space! But few of the studios I've seen are as nice as Grady's. A huge picture window lets in the golden evening light, bestowing a sense of shimmery magic on the paint-spattered walls. What's even more impressive, though, is the view of the Hudson River almost smack-dab in Grady's backyard, with the beginning pinks and oranges of sunset coloring the gentle, cresting waves. It's a studio any artist would die for. Yet, somehow, Grady's still managed to muck it up. He's got a lumpy black couch in one corner, with the imprint of his body pretty much seared onto the cushions, a tarnished hot plate with God knows what burned onto the dead heat coils, and a sink full of dirty dishes and plastic deli containers filled with paint-stained water.

The studio's saving grace, however, is Grady's art. Along every wall, interspersed with studies on paper and various images tacked up with pushpins, Grady's paintings shine with bold fields of color and meticulously clean lines. I'm seeing them life-sized for the first time, and I can barely hold in my excitement. This may be the Bond's finest show yet.

'These are amazing,' I hear myself saying to no one in particular, though I'm flanked on the left side by Grady and the right by Avery.

'Thanks.' Grady gives me an uncharacteristically friendly smile. 'I'm really glad you like them.'

Honestly, it's like the man's a different person. Just yesterday, he was an enraged bull charging at Avery's red cape. But in the ten minutes we've been here, Grady hasn't yelled once. He hasn't even snorted or stomped his foot. And look what he's wearing – khaki pants and a button-down shirt, not a paint stain to be found. Has Grady actually dressed up for us?

'What were you thinking,' Avery's asking, a pensive finger on his chin, 'when you chose to put the action of this painting down in the corner here?'

'I was thinking, this is where the image goes.' The statement's dripping with sarcasm, but Grady's voice sounds light and cordial.

'So it's representational.' Avery too has an affable lilt to his voice, like he's talking to a tennis mate.

'*And* abstracted,' Grady shoots back with a pleasant grin.

I'm thinking the real Grady's stuffed in a closet somewhere, and cyborg Grady's wearing his only pair of Dockers.

'Avery, look at this one.' I step back from the buffer zone between the two men and saunter toward the opposite wall. That's where my favorite painting is – the *Quaker Oats, 2000* I referred to in the press release. 'It's like a skewed Warhol.'

I catch Grady blushing out of the corner of my eye. When did he become humble?

'Not bad,' Avery says. Truthfully, I think he could show a bit more enthusiasm, but then again, I don't know his style yet. 'How many paintings do you think we can use, Isabel?'

But I barely register the question, because suddenly I'm feeling a warm hand on my shoulder. Avery's got his arm around me. He's got his arm around me!! Oh! He's waiting for an answer. Paintings. How many? Right. I tally it up in my head, trying to ignore the all-consuming sensation of Avery's warm hand. One or two paintings in the reception area, maybe seven in the first room, and – depending on size – four or five in the smaller second room. 'We can safely estimate twelve to fourteen on exhibit,' I say.

'But let's take fifteen and we'll keep the extras in the private salesroom.'

Avery licks his lips before answering. He's focused entirely on me, his head tilted down intimately. 'Excellent,' he says softly.

'I need a cup of coffee,' Grady barks out, his eye fixed almost wildly on Avery. 'Anyone else want some?'

I jump a little, suppressing a sigh of disappointment when Avery's arm returns to his side. Looks like the old Grady's back. 'You're not going to poison it, are you?' I let out under my breath.

'Funny girl!' He snaps his fingers. 'That's my Izzy.'

'*Your* Izzy?' I retort with a stern look.

'What about you, Devon?' Grady's tone has an air of familiarity. 'I've only got coffee, but I imagine you'd like tea. With cake, right? That kind of cake you can have . . . and eat too?'

'Coffee will be fine.' Avery's voice is low and dry. He shows no evidence of aggravation. 'I'd welcome the opportunity to discuss your work over any beverage.'

'I'm sure you would.' Grady's words are tinged with irony.

Oh, for God's sake. Let's just choose the paintings and get out of here before they start nonfighting about dinner.

Once we're settled, though, no one discusses anything. No one's even saying a word. Grady and I are sitting on the lumpy black couch with two chipped mugs of coffee, and Avery's facing us, the only one who asked for a saucer, still managing to look elegant in an old thrift-shop-looking wooden chair.

'Shall we begin the selection?' I offer brightly.

I get no answer. Grady and Avery are locked in some kind of Stepford staring contest. They're just smiling at each other sweetly. And silently. I can hear them breathing, for God's sake. Grady crosses his legs in imitation of Avery's own. Avery counters by putting his coffee mug down and lacing his fingers over his knee. It's awful. I can't take it. How can I get them screaming again?

I'm saved by the chillingly loud tweet of a cell phone, which provokes a little yelp of surprise out of me. Avery deftly produces a tiny silver phone from his jacket pocket, glancing briefly at its screen.

'Forgive me.' He nods his head formally. 'I've got to take this. Some unfinished business in Berlin. Please excuse me; I'll be right back.'

I watch with a mix of dismay and relief as Avery disappears into the large warehouse elevator. Nothing's going as I planned today. Even Grady Cole won't act like his usual snarky self. What's with this placid, sugary attitude he's suddenly acquired? I mean, I've known temperamental artists before, but this guy changes his mood as often (at least, I hope) as his underwear.

'Listen, Izzy.' Grady springs to action, placing both our mugs on a rickety coffee table, as soon as the elevator doors close.

'Oh, *now* you're Mr Talky?' I throw up my hands.

He lets a brief grin play over his face but then jets up from the couch. He's turning away from me, toward the window. We're full into sunset now, and the sky's a miasma of swirling color.

'My mother used to tell these wonderful bedtime stories,' Grady finally says, his face still hidden from me. Great. We're already into the gallerist-as-therapist phase? Usually I don't have to lug out the psychoanalysis until an artist's show is up, at least.

'She did?' I use a sympathetic tone.

'There was this one about a hungry wolf, stalking a farmer's herd of sheep fruitlessly for days, dreaming about devouring them.'

'Mm-hmmmm?' Devouring? Is Grady going psycho killer on me? I rise inconspicuously from the couch, sidling step by step toward the elevator, keeping my movements small. You know, just in case I have to make a run for it.

Grady faces me now, and I see some sort of emotion in his eyes that I can't quite make out. There's anger there. Maybe regret. Fear. But above all, a fierce intensity. He's willing me to halt right on the spot, my feet fixed to the worn floorboards.

'The wolf knew that to get what he wanted,' Grady goes on in that same fervent voice, 'he'd have to use some sort of disguise. And one day the perfect opportunity arose in the form of a discarded sheep pelt.'

'Jeez, Grady,' I let out, rolling my eyes. 'All this drama for the wolf-in-sheep's-clothing story? No offense to your mother or anything, but Aesop got there way first.'

He continues, unfazed. 'There's a moral, see?' He takes a step forward. '*Appearances are deceptive.*'

I think back to the many faces of Grady I've seen in the past few days, remembering all the times he's confounded me. I see again his cordial smiles at Avery just minutes ago, his buddy-buddy *That's my Izzy*, his reluctance to talk even about his own artwork.

'Fine, Grady,' I say, keeping my voice even. 'I get it. You're warning me.'

He seems to relax, his shoulders visibly slumping. But I'm crossing my arms, and I feel my jaw clenching. 'Just tell me one thing,' I say, maintaining a steely gaze. 'Between you and Avery . . .'

Grady raises a quizzical brow. 'Yes?'

'Which one of you is the wolf?'

*Your legs must be tired, because you've
been running through my mind all night.*

More than anything, I want to ask Avery what's
happened to make Grady — for lack of a better
phrase — cry wolf. Whatever it is, I refuse to believe
Avery's at fault. Look at the evidence here. We've got a
sometimes sarcastic, sometimes charming, sometimes
madly raving artist on one hand, and an ever debonair, ever
understanding, ever considerate dealer on the other. But
more, I feel safe around Avery. Well, I feel blissful, but
that's beside the point. I've always trusted my feelings
about people, and everything in my being tells me that
Avery's as genuine as they come. And freaking hot too.

It's nine o'clock by the time Avery and I get back to the
gallery. Our cab ride took a good twenty-five minutes in
the downtown Saturday night traffic, during which we
worked out some final details for Grady's opening. I'm
getting kind of nervous about the show, actually — after all,
my promotion depends on it. I'm determined not only to
live up to Avery's expectations, but to surpass them.

My cause is not being helped, however, by the gaping
yawns that contort my face every five minutes. Avery asks
me what art movers we use, and I yawn. He asks how many
cases of wine we should order for the opening, and I yawn
twice. But my exhaustion makes sense when you think

about it. I've been at work for over twelve hours now. Not that I'm . . . *yawn*.

'Tired?' Avery's features lapse into an easy smile. We're in the main exhibition room now, imagining what painting will go where, and he's tapping notes into his Palm Pilot.

'Not at all!' I blink back residual yawn tears. 'Just haven't caught my second wind yet.'

Avery pockets his Palm Pilot and gazes at me in that way of his – like I'm the only other person in the room. Never mind that I actually *am*. 'Isabel, you're an angel,' he says. 'You never take me to task when I'm being an insensitive brute.'

'But you're not!' I lean against the wall, shaking my head. 'Of course you're not!'

Avery moves closer to me, his tall frame towering over my slouching one. In my fantasy, this is where Avery would cup his hand to my face, lean down, and kiss me. But I know he won't. He'll just say something like, 'What price point do you figure for the smaller paintings?' Because if there's one thing I've learned today, it's that fantasies don't make the enchanted leap into reality.

'I've got an idea.' Avery smiles down at me, looking every bit the dapper gentleman with his shirtsleeves rolled up and one hand in his pocket. 'I think we've both done enough work for the day – and well-done, I must say.' He's twisting his lips together playfully. 'So why don't we reward ourselves with a trip upstairs to look at Emerson Bond's famed private collection. If you're not too tired, that is.'

Enchanted leap! Enchanted friggin' *leap!* God, this is *just* how I pictured it back at Jamie's apartment! Soon, Avery will be saying my name over and over, calling me darling . . . and there must be a wind machine upstairs, because I totally see my hair flowing outward. And where'd Avery's shirt buttons go?

'I think that's a *great* idea, Avery,' I respond, barely above a whisper. 'No one's been upstairs for months. It'll be like a secret rendezvous! Er . . . with the art!'

Avery rests his free palm against the wall, moving his

body only an arm's width from mine. 'Sounds just how I'd imagined.'

When the bottom floor of the Bond town house was converted into a gallery in the 1980s, the architects built a wood-paneled wall to hide the building's grand staircase. For the next two decades, few people ever noticed the hidden entry, carved right into the pattern of the paneling, which leads to the rest of the building. It's through this doorway that Avery and I now pass. We're ascending the white marble staircase in near darkness, and I feel just like I'm Mrs Peacock with the lead pipe. Except instead of murder, all I've got on my mind is a romantic tryst with Colonel Mustard.

At the top of the stairs, I turn on the light and disconnect the alarm. Here, in the hallway, the floor is covered by a light coating of dust, and the air is stale and humid. But behind the next door, I know, the air will be cool and regulated, the light won't ever rise beyond a hazy glow, and not a speck of dust or dirt will be found. The conditions of Emerson Bond's private collection rival some of the world's best museums. As well they should, considering the many millions of dollars' worth of art stored here.

'Ready?' I whisper to Avery. The whole excursion has this guilty, clandestine feel to it. Like we're sneaking away from the high school prom to make out in an empty classroom.

'I am,' Avery whispers back with mock solemnity. I can tell he's feeling sneaky too.

I ease open the door and shut it quickly behind us, preserving the controlled atmosphere. Usually when I'm up here, it's by special appointment with an art historian or a museum curator hoping to borrow a piece. The Old Man would come up too during his annual visit. He'd spend hours with his treasures, in what I'm sure was an experience of true love. I remember my first time seeing the collection, a few weeks after I started working at the

Bond. Freddie took me on the grand tour – the one I'm about to give Avery – and I don't think my mouth ever closed once. Some of the world's best art from the last half of the twentieth century hangs right here, every day, separated from my humble little desk by just a ceiling.

'Here are the Rothkos,' I gesture toward a wall of large color field paintings, stopping at one in particular. 'This is the only one from the Four Seasons commission that's in private ownership. The others are all at the Tate in London. But then' – I smile shyly – 'you'd know that.'

Avery nods admiringly, moving slowly toward the back wall, where there are some haunting de Koonings and a couple of early Pollocks. He looks shadowy and mysterious in the dim light. I narrate the origins of a Rauschenberg mixed media and a rare version of Jasper Johns's famous flag. Somehow, though, I'm getting the feeling that Avery's already familiar with these paintings. Maybe it's the lack of raw wonder on his face, or the way he keeps nodding at the works, as if revisiting old friends. Usually when I show someone the collection for the first time, they examine every detail on the surface so closely that the tour can take hours. Don't get me wrong – Avery's enjoying it for sure, just not in the way I'd expect.

'Ah, right,' Avery says to himself, stopping below a geometric Alexander Calder mobile. 'The Warhols are further upstairs, aren't they?'

'Yes,' I exclaim, perplexed. But then I remember – Avery's known Raymond Bond, the Old Man's son, for years. The Bond family must have arranged a private showing for him.

Up another flight of stairs, we're in the Warhol rooms, stepping around a big Brillo Box sculpture. Avery's head careens right and left, taking in the vivid paintings, a myriad of images each in five or six different colors.

'But where's the –' Avery pauses, scanning either side of a bright red Warhol self-portrait. The painting he's probably looking for – the one that's been moved just round the corner – is one of Warhol's famous Elizabeth

Taylor silk screens. Rumor goes that the movie star herself gave the portrait to Emerson Bond during their secret, torrid affair in the sixties.

'Do you mean this one?' I direct Avery farther on to the Elizabeth Taylor, watching for his reaction.

'Look at that! I didn't know Emerson Bond had one of these,' Avery says lightly, his eyebrows raised. 'Between you and me, I like the Elizabeths even better than the Marilyns.'

Hmm. He seems genuinely surprised to see the painting. Which *would* be convincing if he had shown any surprise at even one of the others before it. But why on earth would Avery lie? Why wouldn't he just come out and say he's seen Emerson Bond's private collection before? I'm racking my brain, trying to think of an excuse. There's *got* to be a reason.

'Elizabeth Taylor had such a regal beauty,' Avery's continuing, gazing now at me instead of the wall. 'Would I make you blush if I said I noticed a resemblance?'

My heart absolutely flips, and all of a sudden my head feels light. Who cares that Elizabeth Taylor's hair is black and mine's auburn? Or that her eyes are lavender and mine hazel? If he wants to turn me into a regal beauty, who am I to argue?

'There, I've done it. You're blushing.' Avery's manicured finger brushes my cheek, where I'm sure I'm as red as Andy Warhol's self-portrait.

Hours of anticipation are rushing to the forefront, almost too much to bear. Could it be possible – and here I'm just weighing the idea in my head, flipping it over and over like a lucky quarter – but could it be possible that Avery hasn't told me he's seen the collection before just so that he'd have an excuse for me to come up and give him the tour? Did he orchestrate this moment for the sole purpose that he and I would be alone together, among some of the best art in the world, with his hand caressing my cheek?

And brushing the hair off my forehead. And tracing the line of my jaw.

Oh, my God, this is it! This is the moment I've been dreaming of, finally happening *right now*. I close my eyes to savor every feeling – the jumpy flips in my stomach, the happy haze clouding my head, the almost ticklish softness of Avery's touch. *He's going to kiss me*.

But then an image pops into my head that has *no right* to be there. It's just floating around, all interrupting and unwelcome. I see his face, with its serious expression. His hair spiking out in all directions. His mouth, narrating the age-old story of the wolf in sheep's clothing like it's a missing piece of *The DaVinci Code*. *Appearances can be deceptive*. Yeah, well, *duh*! But the phrase won't stop rattling round my head, its tone getting more ominous each time. Why can't he just shut up! Suddenly, he's joined by a second voice, higher and more timid. *You should ask Avery about Grady*, it's saying. *C'mon, just bite the bullet!* And, okay. Fine. I'll ask him. But does it have to be *now*? When Avery's waiting for only the slightest encouragement? When I'm so close to *finally* getting what I want so very, very deeply? *Ask him*, says the annoying, unrelenting, maddening voice. Oh, crap. I know that voice. That's *my* voice.

'What's up with you and Grady?' I blurt out, my eyes still closed. Avery's hand pauses mid-cheek-stroke.

I open my eyes to see Avery no longer standing over me. He's pacing, artwork to artwork, clearly trying to formulate the right words before speaking. (Would it kill me to try that sometime?) More than once, he seems ready to open his mouth, but then he closes it again with a slightly frustrated expression, and he continues to pace – in silence.

Oh, God. *What have I done?* 'It's just that –' I offer feebly, struggling to fix my obvious gaffe. 'It's always hanging in the air, this unspoken past you two seem to have. And I feel like' – and here I'm struck by a small bolt of genius – 'I should know, for my *work*, in order to be as helpful as possible to both Grady and *you*. Because . . . that's my job!'

Avery finally stands still, his chest rising and falling in a big sigh. 'Grady and I have known each other for years,' he says in a resigned tone. 'In fact, we were once close friends. Very close, I'd say.'

'Really?' My head snaps back involuntarily.

'I think Grady would say so too,' Avery continues, with an edge of nostalgia. He shrugs a shoulder and cocks an eyebrow. 'But time passes, and things change. People change. Someone whom you once trusted, well, one day you realize you can't trust him anymore. And it's . . . unfortunate.'

'That's it?' I exhale, almost on tiptoe waiting to hear the rest. 'That's all you'll tell me?'

Avery gives a weary smile that speaks of a long and complicated past, of corners turned and doors shut, of hopes elevated and dashed. It's a smile full of knowledge not to be revealed.

'I'm sorry, Isabel,' he says earnestly. 'But it's not my story to tell.'

In a blink, I'm looking at Avery Devon's back. Just like that, without another word, he's navigating his way past the oranges and pinks of the Warhols, toward the door to a much more mundane reality.

I can still feel his papery-smooth touch on my cheek.

You look like a masterpiece — so how 'bout
I be the master, and you give me a piece?

Game on. Don't be nervous, Iz. Big smile, back
straight, lipstick off teeth. I take a minute by the
reception ledge to make sure everything's in order. We've
got Grady's bio, heralding his education at Paris's École
des Beaux-Arts and whatever honors he's garnered before
now. There's a fresh sign-in book, open to a pristine blank
page with a crimson ribbon snuggled in the center crease,
waiting for visitors to write their names and addresses for
future mailings. And next to that book, inconspicuously off
to the side — but totally available to all interested parties —
is Grady's title and price list.

Usually before a show opens, we've already sold two or
three works, and their cheery little red dots decorate the
page. Today, fifteen minutes before Grady's opening
officially starts, only one little dot interrupts the paper's
white background. I must have shown at least ten people
the exhibition before its official opening, but only Deidre
Gayle took the risk of purchasing a piece by an unknown
artist before his first show. How I wish she could have
attended the opening! But Deidre's dancing in *Giselle*
tonight, and so her unending support for the Bond will be
here in spirit alone. Her red dot looks so lonely hanging
out with all that black print. *Don't worry*, I feel like

whispering to the little fellow. *We'll get you some friends.*
And boy, we better. The careers of more than one person
depend on it.

'We need some music!' I hear coming from the
exhibition rooms. 'Like, some Blondie or – ooh – Duran
Duran.' Grady comes at me backward, moonwalking his
way into reception. 'How's about that?' he says, obviously
thrilled with himself. 'I can do the snake too.' He lifts his
arms out to each side and starts undulating as if in the
midst of a seizure.

'Grady!' I plead, 'Please behave. *Please.*' I glance over
his outfit – jeans, T-shirt, black blazer, and those old Puma
sneakers. I just hope collectors find the look boyishly
irreverent rather than plain obnoxious. 'There's no music.'
I lay a pacifying hand on his arm. 'Just stimulating conversation.'

He rolls his eyes. 'Spoilsport.'

'But we have refreshments!' I offer brightly, leading
Grady toward the back room. We always put the wine and
cheese at the end of the exhibition, sort of like a carrot
dangling in front of a moving horse. See all the art, and you
get a treat!

'Izzy, want a cracker?' Grady's following beside me, his
gait more bouncy than usual. I can tell he's in a good mood,
and he should be – his first solo show looks entirely
gorgeous. Now, if only the rest of the world can agree.

When we get to Kimmy, she's putting the finishing
touches on a beautifully arranged cheese and fruit platter,
with crackers laid out in ornate spirals. Grady starts to
reach for a cracker, but seeing Kimmy's look of utter
despair, he retreats. She hands him one from an opened
package instead.

Kimmy looks dazzling in a snug T-shirt dress with a
Flashdance-style neck exposing one shoulder. What's really
eye-catching, though, are her bright purple lizard-skin
high heels, which complement her purple hair winningly.

'But look at you!' Kimmy exclaims when I compliment
her on her outfit.

I'm wearing a pale peach chiffon dress, with a darker peach velvet ribbon lacing round the bodice, at a short enough length to avoid being too formal. Dix picked it out. She said if I'm going to wear pastels, they might as well be saucy.

'It's true,' Grady says as he helps himself to a clear plastic cup of red wine. 'You're looking hot, Izzy.' He grins, stretching cracker crumbs across his lips, and raises his cup to me. 'Well, almost, anyway.'

'Oh, shut up.' I turn my head so he can't see me blushing. The opening hasn't even started and already he's trying to get to me.

'Is it time?' Avery opens the office's French doors, stepping through them with the grace of a modern-day Cary Grant. He's wearing the same light gray suit he wore to Freddie's going-away party, this time with a royal blue tie. My stomach does a little flip. It's Wednesday now, and Avery hasn't made one mention of the advance he made upstairs on Saturday. Or *would* have made, had my big fat mouth been sewn shut. I try to gauge from Avery's expression whether he still might hold any affection for me, or whether I've truly ruined everything.

'Ten more minutes,' I say, trying to appear confident and self-assured. Our openings run from six to eight, but if the group is lively, we don't flash the gallery lights – a sign to move the party elsewhere – until eight forty-five.

'Right.' Avery turns to Grady. 'I've got some very important collectors in from London,' he says sternly. 'You'll treat them well, I presume?'

Grady doesn't respond, but I see his breathing quicken. 'Any friend of yours . . .,' he finally says.

'Come, now,' Avery chides. 'Let's be gentlemen.'

Grady's laugh is tinged with bitterness. 'Why start now?'

I see a spark in Kimmy's eye, and I know she's as determined to get to the bottom of this secret feud as I am. Kimmy's mind works like her drawings – wildly imaginative, but well-defined and precise. She'll immediately opt for the most unlikely explanation, and then she'll make it seem entirely plausible. Like, she'll figure that Grady and Avery were born as fraternal twins in the hills of Switzerland and separated after their parents divorced. Then, she'll find the Auntie Helga who took Grady to New York and Avery to Massachusetts under the veil of night, knowing that each brother would be raised to hate the other. Hey! Actually, when you think about it . . . . oh, wait. Grady's only twenty-nine, and Avery's thirty. Can you be that premature?

The front door chimes, and we all swivel our heads toward reception. Our first guest! *Oh, please let it be a good crowd*, I think, balling up my fists in anticipation. We need good word of mouth to sell out this show. We need as many people to see it as possible. We need . . .

'I am *soooooo* unfashionably early!' I hear coming from reception.

'Freddie!' I cry before I can stop myself.

'The show is stunning,' he exclaims, appearing in the doorway and striking a dramatic pose in his (naturally) black outfit. 'Whoever discovered this guy is a genius!'

Kimmy and I rush over to hug him, followed closely by Grady, who shakes Freddie's hand vigorously, and Avery, who does so with more muted enthusiasm.

Freddie shoos us away, eyeing the wine and cheese table. Then he throws up his hands and gives Avery a suggestive wink. 'So who do I have to screw to get a cup of wine around here?'

Over the next hour, I'm being pulled right and left by dozens of people kissing me hello and fawning over the show. Juggling a roomful of important people has always been a strong point of mine. I throw out a lot of exclamations like 'Don't you dare leave because I'm *dying* to see you,' and 'Go have a look at that painting, because I've been saving it just for *you*.' Out of the corner of my eye I see Avery expertly introducing himself to as many people as possible, clearly winning them over with his dashing smile and gallant manner. Kimmy's busy too, I notice, making sure the other dealers and gallerists are happy. A very important task, when you consider that tomorrow, their gossip will filter through the art world before any review does, proclaiming our show either a smash success or a limp washout.

I give Martin Feinberg – the successful New York restaurateur – a kiss on each cheek, leaving him to admire a painting called *Dunkin' Donuts, 2002*. And then, finally. A free moment. The gallery is so packed that the air conditioner's on its highest setting and still I'm wiping beads of sweat off my forehead. I scan the room, paying close attention for anyone who seems particularly enthralled by a specific work. And I *do* see someone pausing for a good while by the *Quaker Oats, 2000* painting. Someone I'm truly ecstatic to see. It's Dix! And she's got the prettiest male-model type on her arm too. Leave it to Dix to find a younger man at the ripe old age of twenty-seven.

'Hi!!' I cry out when I reach her. She's got on a clingy black jersey dress and, as usual, gravity-defying high heels.

'Dearest, the show is amazing.' Dix kisses my cheek and gives my hand a supportive squeeze.

'Thank you!' I can feel my smile spread across my entire face. 'I'm so glad you think so!'

'Jamie's just outside, but he'll be here in a moment,' Dix continues. 'He's sucking face on the street corner.'

'He's *what?!!*' My jaw opens so fast it almost disconnects.

Dix makes an exasperated expression. 'He's with that model. You'll see.'

I'll see? I don't think I want to see! *Jamie?* For whom *PDA* usually stands for 'pretty depressed, actually'? Dix isn't one to exaggerate, but I can't imagine Jamie has turned into one of those people who just *make out* in front of you. I mean, what do they expect you to do? You can't look at them, you can't walk away, and you can't scream out fervently, *'Hello, I'm right here!'*

'Darling, this is my closest friend in the world, Izzy.' Dix is talking to her arm candy, who's got flowing corn-blond hair and high cheekbones. 'And darling –' Now she's talking to me. 'This is Wednesday.'

I've scolded Dix before about her tendency to call her cache of boy toys by the days of the week she takes them out. But Dix explains that the arrangements are as much business as pleasure. She's got tons of events to go to, and they're at the beginning of their careers and need exposure. She assures me that as long as she uses each Day of the Week's real name when talking to press or bookers, they wouldn't care if she introduced them as 'Donkey Butt' to her friends. Which, she points out, she's too polite to do.

I reach out my hand to the pretty boy, wincing a little. 'Nice to meet you, uh, Wednesday.'

Dix gestures with her head then, nudging me to turn around toward reception. There, almost strutting through the doorway, comes Jamie. He's wearing dark jeans and an expensive-looking striped dress shirt, and attached to his hand is a woman who seems way too tall and skinny to have such a pop-your-eye-out chest. Compared with her frame, her breasts look heavy enough to upset her balance, if not topple her over. Jamie's preening and parading like a proud rooster, as if he expects everyone in the room to be watching him. And in fact, people *are* turning their heads and staring – even while pretending not to. How can we resist? His hen's eggs look like they were laid by a dinosaur.

'What's goin' down?' Jamie greets me with a caddish wink.

'Just, you know, the opening of the most important show of my career,' I toss out teasingly.

'This is *Svetlana*,' Jamie presents his platinum-haired companion. His voice has a licentious tone to it that makes me want to cringe. But I force myself to cut him some slack. Jamie's never had success with women before. Not ever. I mean, take a guy who's been stranded in the desert and put him next to a trough of water. What's he going to do, *sip*? And besides. It's *Jamie*. Sensitive, sweet, caring

Jamie. I know what he's like below the surface.

'Nice to meet you, Svetlana.' I work very hard at keeping my eyes steered toward her face. I do find myself wondering, though, what her shirts look like at the end of the day. Do they deflate?

'*Privyet*,' Svetlana says, giving me a cheery smile. I'm hoping that doesn't translate into, 'I'm going to make out with your friend now. Want to watch?'

'Thanks for coming, Jamie,' I offer sincerely.

His expression softens, taking on the warmth I know so well. 'Aw, Iz,' he drawls. 'How could I not? It's important to you.'

There's my boy. I give him a grateful hug.

'I want it!' Dix exclaims over my shoulder, pointing to the *Quaker Oats, 2000*. 'Can't you see it in my office? Right across from my desk, above the white carpet and black Eames chairs? *Arden Moore's* PR firm needs original art on its walls, after all.'

God, Dix is the most supportive friend ever. She knows I need to sell out this show to ensure my promotion, and she's willing to shell out upward of fifteen thousand dollars just to help. 'Dix,' I say, my voice filled with gratitude, 'I wouldn't expect you to actually buy! Just your being here is enough.'

'Fuck your expectations.' Dix waves her hand at me. 'I want this painting. What's your best price for the thing?'

She's really serious! She wants to buy the painting! And not just any painting, but my favorite one in the show. I can't think of anyone I'd rather sell it to.

'I'll talk to Avery and see what discount he's willing to part with,' I assure Dix, already lifting my head to look for him. I'm sure I can get her at least ten percent off, if not the twenty percent we reserve for our most frequent collectors.

'Ooh!' Dix wiggles her arm out of her date's grasp. He doesn't say much, that Wednesday. Maybe Dix should rename him Bracelet. 'Point this supposedly luscious Avery out! I want to see!'

I pass my eye over the front exhibition room, searching for Avery. There's Freddie deep in a tête-à-tête with an editor at *Artnet*. There's Kimmy, bravely listening to Cassie Arnell, the director for the Eaton Bosc, as she no doubt prattles away about the sociological depth of the art while secretly plotting to steal Grady for her gallery. And then I finally catch him. There's my Avery, gesturing to one of Grady's paintings while talking to a curator from P.S. 1. That would be a good match, I think to myself. P.S. 1. exhibits such edgy contemporary art. Good job, Avery.

'Right there.' I surreptitiously point him out to Dix.

'Oh, *honey*,' she says in her sultry voice. 'You should *totally* make him your Saturday.'

I give a girlish giggle and am about to respond when I'm halted midthought by the horrifying sight of Jamie and Svetlana. Their mouths are suctioned to each other as if at opposite ends of a vacuum tube. Oh, God. No. Anything but that! *Visible tongue!* I feel like if I close my eyes, I'll see colored spots, like my corneas have been permanently damaged. *Ewww*, There are *sounds*. I can't take it. This is so, *so* wrong!

'I'll just go talk to Avery!' I blurt out. 'So we can work out the details.'

'Oh, fine,' Dix throws out wryly. 'Leave me with the spit swappers.'

'Okay!' I cry, feeling my whole body shudder. 'Be right back.'

'Coward!' Dix calls after me, but I'm already easing myself through the crowd.

I don't have much luck finding Avery, who's no longer where he was just a minute ago. I figure he's taken the P.S. 1. guy to the private salesroom. I do see Kimmy, though, now freed from Cassie Arnell and slinking her way through the room in her purple lizard-skin heels. Every few steps, she hesitates, sticking her head forward. I watch her casually flit from group to group, pretending to admire a painting or look for someone. But I know she's really eavesdropping on any conversation she can find. Kimmy's up to something, all right.

Kimmy notices me watching her, and her eyes light up. She's beckoning me frantically with her hand, as if she's got something dishy she's dying to spill. I feel torn. On the one hand, I should be finding Avery and getting a best-price offer for Dix. (A) That's my job. (B) She's my best friend. Easy. That's my priority. But *come on*. Maybe Kimmy's found Auntie Helga! Maybe the whole secret's about to unfold! I rush over to her before I can reconsider.

'Okay,' Kimmy says eagerly, keeping her voice low. 'Think back to every show you've ever done. Hell, every one you've ever been to. *Especially* a debut show.' She's getting into it, drawing out the suspense.

'Yeah?' I'm totally hooked.

'How many friends and family of the artist would you say usually attend the opening?' She leans back, planting her hands on her hips.

I take a moment to think. 'Let's say twenty-five,' I offer, trying to gauge if I've given her the answer she wants.

'On a bad night!' she exclaims.

'Right,' I agree.

'So guess how many people Grady has here?' Kimmy's so bursting to get to the point, she's almost jumping.

All right. Let's estimate the very minimum. One best friend, two family members, maybe a girlfriend – poor gal. Figure in five struggling-artist friends who secretly hope they hate the show, one mentor figure trying not to be jealous, and one person Grady hasn't seen in years who read about the opening in *Time Out* magazine. 'Eleven,' I say.

Kimmy's face beams with satisfaction. 'Zero,' she says keenly. 'Nada. None.'

'What!' I cry a bit too loudly – a couple of people turn and stare. One of them's Freddie. His ears have perked up like a French bulldog's, and I can see him excusing himself from his conversation with the *Artnet* editor.

In a moment, Freddie's huddled beside us, as if he's

been a part of the conversation all along. Honestly, he smells gossip like one of those pigs they use to sniff out truffles.

'So I've been keeping an ear out all night for Grady's friends,' Kimmy begins her narrative. 'Just in case I might overhear – accidentally, of course – what this secret past is between Grady and Avery.'

Freddie gasps, holding up his hand. 'Grady and Avery have a secret past?! Hello! Why has no one informed La Freddie of this shocking development?'

'Long story, honey – details later.' I motion for Kimmy to continue. This is getting good.

'I've been keeping tabs on everyone here. *Everyone*.' Kimmy points a finger for emphasis. 'Grady hasn't got a single personal guest. Not one friend, not a brother, not a neighbor, not the local butcher. *No one*.' She's clearly enjoying the startled look on Freddie's face. 'It's like he *didn't even tell* anyone about the show.'

'I never in my *life*!' Freddie exclaims, a hand cupped over his mouth. 'Even when your artist's *dead*, he's still got friends at his opening. What did Grady do, tell his people not to come?'

'But why would he do that?' My mind is racing. What could Grady Cole be hiding that's so important he's willing to sacrifice the support of his friends and family on the biggest night of his career? Immediately, I imagine the worst. Forget Auntie Helga. Grady's a criminal. He's got some horrid past of murderous sprees – in Europe! And Avery . . . and Avery knew one of the victims! No, wait. He would have said something if our lives were in danger. What was it Avery told me about his past with Grady? 'It's not my story to tell.' Could Grady have done something so bad that he alienated himself from every friend he ever had? Is that the reason he's got no one here? But he seems to have such a way with people – other than me, that is. Surely Grady Cole has at least *one* friend in this world. Why isn't he or she here? It's enough to make your head spin entirely around.

'What does this mean?' I whisper eagerly to Kimmy.

She looks back at me with wide, fervent eyes. 'I have absolutely no idea.'

'Leave it to me.' Freddie nods solemnly, his voice full of foreboding. 'After all, you know that female curator at the Museum of Contemporary Art? The bed-hopping nymphomaniac? Who do you think found out she was born with the name Charles Hooper? *No* secret rests uncovered in my wake. I will master the mystery. It will be mine.'

I feel like we should join hands in the middle of a circle for a team huddle.

'Ooh, who's that!' Kimmy exclaims, grabbing my shoulder and whipping me round toward Grady, whom we can see through the archway to the second exhibition room. He's talking to two men I've never seen before. They're both slim, in tightly cut suits, with trendy-looking haircuts. 'Could those be his friends?'

Hmm. Mod-style suits and careful grooming? Not what I'd expect from Grady's friends. And their conversation doesn't seem to be of the most amiable variety. Grady's making pointed gestures toward one of his paintings, and the two men are shaking their heads. Now one of them's taking out a cigarette and tapping it on top of a cigarette case. Oh, my God. Someone who thinks you can smoke indoors in New York!? Those must be Avery's important London collectors!

'Uh-oh,' I exhale. 'Grady is *not* making nice.' I give Freddie and Kimmy a rueful look before rushing back headlong into the crowd. I'm used to juggling ten things at once, so why do I feel as if all the balls are about to come crashing down on my head? I take a moment to adjust my face into a no-we-weren't-talking-about-you-Grady expression, which would be a lot easier if I had some Botox.

'Well, it's about consumer culture,' Grady's saying to the two men when I finally get to him. He sounds frustrated. 'How these brand labels become so seared on our minds that when you see them just a bit distorted, you've got no idea what you're looking at.'

The men stare at the painting in front of them – the one titled *Skippy Peanut Butter, 2004* – with critical expressions on their faces.

'It's just so . . . *American*,' the one with the cigarette says, almost sneering.

'Yeah, well, I *am*,' Grady retorts with a sarcastic shrug.

'David Hockney has an American sensibility,' I throw out, inserting myself into the conversation. Although – and I really hate to say it – I think I'm siding with Grady here. I love English people more than anyone. (And it's not just the sexy accent! I'd totally get dual citizenship if, for instance, I were to marry Robbie Williams.) But these particular guys seem to have some sort of giant chip on their shoulders. 'And the British love Hockney, don't they? I saw an amazing piece he did on the Grand Canyon at the Royal Academy. Really, I think the Academy's underrated, wouldn't you say?'

The other Brit shakes his head, ignoring me entirely. 'Avery was showing such daring work in Berlin. Shame, really.'

Cigarette Guy nods to his friend, giving Grady one last dismissive frown. 'Right, shall we head out for a fag?'

Hee-hee. (Oh, you try and help it.)

The other Brit clasps his slender fingers together. 'Let's.'

Grady and I watch as the two trendy collectors head out the door, frowning at the crowd as they go. Frankly, I'm not sure I care if they come back. Did Avery search out the crabbiest English people in New York? Because I've known lots of Brits, and they're usually very laid-back and sociable. More than you'd ever expect! You know, as long as there's a pub around.

Grady's got his head down, unwilling to look at me. Whether he's angry or repentant I can't tell, but I can see he's agitated.

And why shouldn't he be? The poor guy hasn't got any friends here cheering him on. He can't even take solace in his own dealer. God, I think. *I'm* all he's got. Acting on instinct, I lean in toward Grady's ear, closer than I'd usually let myself get to him. 'Fuck 'em,' I whisper.

Grady looks at me with more shock than I've ever seen on his face – more, even, than when he realized that Miss Jabby Finger from the subway was the director of his gallery. 'Thanks,' he says with genuine feeling.

'See?' My voice takes on a jocular tone. 'I'm not always the Wicked Witch of the Upper East Side.'

'Hey, of course you're not.' But Grady's not joking back. In fact, he's sounding kind of . . . well . . . heartfelt. And then he does something that just floors me. Something that comes out of *nowhere*. Like, from the outer reaches of a far, unknown galaxy. He leans over and kisses me on the cheek. Grady Cole. *Kissing me*.

'Er. I, a –' I take a few steps backward to a safer distance, stopping when I see Grady's hurt expression. Jeez. I am so overreacting. I've kissed every single one of our artists on the cheek – straight and gay, women and men. That's what gallerists *do*. I don't think the art world could exist without cheek kissing. It's like art *oxygen*.

I'm about to laugh off my freakish reaction and set things right again when I feel a hand wrap around my waist and pull me in. Ooh, is it Freddie? But then I press up against a firm torso and inhale a faint scent of expensive soap. Mmmm. Avery.

'Well-done, the both of you!' he's saying, and I look up to see his beaming smile. 'We've just sold another painting!'

'Two actually!' I cry, letting my free arm wrap around Avery's waist. Look! We're hugging! And it's a total couple hug too, like we're so used to having our arms around each other. 'My best friend is interested in the *Quaker Oats*.' I lift my face up toward his.

'Splendid, Isabel.' Avery's praise feels nearly as exciting as his touch. 'Martin Feinberg, the restaurateur, is buying the *Dunkin' Donuts*. He said your presentation of the work was spot-on and that you've "outdone" yourself this time.' Avery's features take on an affectionate tenderness. 'I couldn't agree more.'

'No, no,' I insist, seeing Grady's scowling expression from the corner of my eye. He should be ecstatic! He just made over twenty-five thousand dollars! Good Lord, what does it *take* with him? 'The work speaks for itself, as does Grady's talent. He deserves the praise.'

'Yeah, thanks,' Grady responds flatly, his eye flitting from me to Avery like we're all at a poker table and he expects one of us to palm a card.

'Now, Grady.' Avery releases his grip on me, and for the first time tonight, the air feels cool against my bare skin. He's facing Grady now, with his arms behind his back. 'Have you spoken to Casper and Oliver, as I'd asked?'

Casper and Oliver? Is he for real? Those are names for makeover show hosts, or, like, children's-cartoon bunnies. Casper and Oliver should be returning home from a day in the forest only to find that their tree-stump house has been refurbished with all new twig furniture! I think back to the two men, with their matching skinny brown suits and carefully sheared hair. And I thought Avery's buddies were farcical *before*.

'Devon, you've got to be kidding me.' Grady tugs at the sides of his blazer with frustrated, jerky movements. 'Those guys are such –'

'I don't think they're interested!' I pipe in, resting a hand on Avery's elbow. 'I don't think we've quite . . . honed in on their aesthetic.'

Grady shoots me a tight-lipped, angry look. 'Izzy, they're ass—'

'*Ass*pecially keen on what you've done in Berlin.' I nod reverentially at Avery. 'But unfortunately not in tune with this particular show.'

'It's a shame.' Avery's brow is furrowed, and the corners of his mouth draw down in discontent. 'They're such spenders – like money's going out of style.'

'Why don't you speak with them?' I try to convey hope. I know what Avery's going through. He's the dealer. The burden of success rests on *his* shoulders, not mine, and yet he's had nothing to do with our three sales. Not that it's his fault! He's just relocated to a new *continent* and hasn't had time to forge new contacts. But I can imagine he wants to prove his worth to the Bond family. Of course Avery wants to get his snotty friends to spend a ton of money. I should support him in that. 'Surely they're worth a second go.'

Avery tilts his head down toward mine, and I think I see a flash of the desire he seemed to show this past Saturday. 'If you'll excuse me, I'll see if I can find them.' He shakes a reluctant Grady's hand, offering him congratulations again, and then Avery's walking away, his tall, regal form standing out among the crowd of arty revelers.

'I don't believe you!' Grady spits out at me, looking pained and angry.

'We're just trying to sell your paintings!' I shoot back, wondering why I'm feeling guilty. Why shouldn't I encourage Avery? His success with these collectors would be for the good of all three of us! 'What do you want me to do, Grady, tell Avery that his high-rolling friends are rude and unwelcome?'

'For a start.' Grady's shaking his head, telegraphing his disappointment in me. It's spread all over his face, like an oil spill on the highway. 'You're such a hypocrite.'

Ouch. That wasn't called for. 'He's my *boss*,' I insist. I'm fidgeting now, brushing a stray hair off my forehead, shifting my weight from heel to heel. Why should stupid Grady's disappointment affect me so much? Why should I even care what this sarcastic – and possibly two-faced – scrappy artist thinks of me? Look at everything I've done for him tonight! Except . . . I haven't really done it for him, have I? I've been working my butt off so I'll get my promotion. But *still*. He's benefiting too, by thousands of dollars!

'You're not kissing Avery Devon's ass like it's the pope's ring so he'll give you a raise, *Isabel*.' Grady's voice is dripping with resentment. He gives a sour laugh. 'Look, when you get hurt, don't come to me.'

His smug expression, his relentless berating, his sarcastic accusations, all finally hit me right then. Hard, in the gut. When I get hurt? *When I get hurt?* 'Grady Cole, I have been *nothing* but hurt,' I hiss at him. I'd be yelling if I weren't surrounded by every colleague I've ever had. 'By almost *every* man I've ever been with. *Liars*, all of them. Hell' – I snort indelicately – 'not even two weeks ago, I let some guy seduce me only to wake up and meet his gorgeous blond girlfriend!' Okay. Too much information. Way too much information. 'Not that it's any of your business!'

Grady's eyes are wide like an owl's, and he's giving me the 'Okay, crazy person' look familiar to all schizophrenic bag ladies. 'You're right,' he says placatingly, 'I uh . . . didn't mean to . . .'

'So *of course* I'm going to be wary!' I resist every impulse to wave my hands wildly, realizing that this would *not* be the best time to draw an audience. 'I'm wary personified. I'm Wary Wary Quite Contrary.'

Grady lifts a hand to his mouth, but he can't quite hide his smile.

'And why *do you care* anyway, Grady?' Now I'm the one with vitriol in my voice. 'What are you hiding that will make or break my opinion of Avery, huh? For all your proselytizing, when do you plan to *come clean*?'

'Forget I said anything!' Grady backs off, raising his hands in supplication. 'Forget I said one damn thing. Never mind.'

Never mind?!?

I don't know what to say. I'm just standing there, stupefied, in my girly peach chiffon dress, like I've just arrived at a party only to find I've gotten the date wrong. 'Grady, you're too much,' is all I can finally manage.

Grady gives me that characteristic icy, narrow stare of his, the one I haven't seen for days now. 'So are you, Izzy,' he says quietly. 'So are you.'

Baby, if you were words on a page, you'd be what they call fine print!

I can't believe it. I grab the magnifying loupe we use to look at slides and hold it over the newsprint. There's Jamie in his smart black suit, with his hair all gelled, holding Svetlana's hand as he pulls her purposely past the cameras. Right there on the *New York Post*'s 'Page Six', the most read newspaper page in all of New York City, if not the world! He's in 'Sightings' – and with a photo, no less! *New York's savviest bachelor, James D. Hunter, looking cozy with Russian swimsuit model Svetlana Pavlovov as they breezed past paparazzi on their way into the Bathing Suits for Children benefit.* Jamie! Breezing! On *'Page Six'*!

Yesterday was the second Thursday after his now infamous pickup line column, which meant another installment of 'Getting It' – only this time, Jamie's column got a mention on the *New York News*'s front page! Right next to a headline about Lindsay Lohan eating pizza! Jamie's photo appeared with the caption 'New tips from the city's hottest dating guru. Details inside.' This time around, Jamie's focus was the 'Wingwoman.' *Your boy used to help you out,* Jamie wrote. *He'd spend hours chatting up 'the ugly one' so you could go home with her hot friend. You lived for the time he'd casually say, 'Have you met my buddy?' In the good old days, out on the town on a Saturday*

*night, all you needed was a Wingman and a prayer. But, my
friends, the age of the Wingman has flown. That girl in the
designer jeans and sparkly tank top knows what you're up
to, and she's not trying to hear it. Nothing will get through
her icy exterior – not your friend, not your most charming
smile, not even your best pickup line. Nothing, that is,
except a good Wingwoman. The door has been closed to
you. Her own kind knows the password.*

Sitting at my desk Friday morning, I read Jamie's
column over again, wondering if I should be offended.
That's *me*, the Wingwoman. Well, me and Dix, really. How
many times have we made friends with random girls in
bars just so Jamie could get their phone numbers? Not that
he ever got up the courage to actually *call* any of them, but
still – he totally could have. Oh, *God*, I feel so smarmy
right now. Like I should be in a beer commercial
presenting a guy with two blondes on a platter. Jamie's
voice sounds so cold and calculating. But like it or not, I
have to hope that people keep lapping up Jamie's advice
like honey – his continued success depends upon it. And as
one of his closest friends, I've *got* to wish him every
success in the world . . . haven't I?

I turn to my computer, scanning my e-mails for the
morning. (No, I don't want to enlarge my penis, thank you
very much. Really, someone should do something about
that! The spam messages, that is, not the penis enlarging.)
Wow, there are a lot of messages this morning! It's not even
ten A.M. and yet it seems the whole world has written me.
I scroll down, reading the subject lines. Nearly all of them
say 'Congratulations' or 'Great job!' or 'Well-done!' Oh, my
God, are people crediting me with Jamie's column? Are
they just assuming that I'm, like, the best Wingwoman on
the planet?!

I'm looking at my computer screen in horror, about to
click on one of the bold black names in my inbox, thinking
of a way to tell everyone I know that I'm not free for
weddings and parties, when I hear the French doors
swoosh open behind me. Avery bursts through, moving

more quickly than I've ever seen him, and he's taking my hands and lifting me up from my chair, and he's spinning me around in a big bear hug.

'You're brilliant!' Avery rests my feet back on the ground and stands back, reassuming his usual dignified posture.

'I am?' I've nearly got the wind knocked out of me. Okay, this can't be about Jamie's column. What's going on?

'Didn't you see?' Avery's looking at me like it's raining jelly beans and I'm the last to notice. 'You mean you haven't read the *Times* yet today?'

Ohhhh, no. I've committed the ultimate cultural sin. I read '*Page Six*' before the Friday *New York Times*. But I can't be blamed! One of my best friends was right there – with a photo! (No one needs to know that I *always* read the gossip column before the art section. Like no one needs to know that at the gym, sometimes I just watch the TVs.) The Friday *Times* Arts section is the art world's bible – and I read it as religiously as anyone, I swear! Because, see, that's where the reviews are. Hang on a sec. *That's where the reviews are*.

'Grady?' My voice cracks like a teenage boy's. I'm digging under the *Post* and the *News* for my copy of the *Times*, frantically flipping through the sections. 'So soon? But how!' There's just no way I would have missed a *New York Times* critic at Grady's opening – Holland Carter, with his white hair and diminutive stature, or Roberta Smith, with her distinctive round glasses, or Ken Johnson, with his flowing blond mane. I don't care how many people were there. When it comes to the most important opinionmongers out there, I've got bionic vision – sound effects and all.

I'm scanning the 'Art in Review' page, my eyes moving fitfully over the eight or so listings of artists with their galleries. But there's no Grady. He's absolutely not here. What is Avery talking about?

'Avery,' I say soothingly, running the words round in my head until they form just right. 'I'm not sure I . . . see the review you mean.'

Avery's green-flecked eyes shine like signal flares. His elegant cheek-bones bunch into an enormous, euphoric smile. 'Not the "Art in Review,"' he says patiently. 'The front page. The *featured* review.'

I'm frozen still, blinking maniacally. '*Nuh-uh*', is what finally comes out when I'm able to make sound again. But sure enough, there it is. Grady's two-page *New York Times* review, with a huge picture of the *Quaker Oats, 2000* right on the section's front page. The piece starts by heralding the fact that June – usually a slow month, with the whole art world at Basel – is no longer dead. 'The summer scene has been resurrected in stunning fashion . . .' someone named Leland Caldwell writes. How were we supposed to know the *Times* had a new critic! Shouldn't they be forced to announce these things? Not that I'm complaining. Gift horse, mouth, I got it. '. . . by the current rapturous exhibition at the Emerson Bond Gallery.' And that's just the beginning. Leland Whoever is so filled with praise for Grady Cole, it's like we paid him.

I'm so shocked I don't know what to say. I'm holding – right in my quivering little hands – every gallerist's Holy Grail. No artist even dares hope that his debut show will get the featured review in the Friday Arts section. It's like winning the lottery with your first ever ticket. It's like getting an Oscar for your first ever role. In truth, I'm looking at what should be the impossible.

'It's ten o'clock,' Avery says, straightening his tie and smoothing his hair. 'We've officially just opened. Get ready for the mayhem.'

Avery's not kidding. When I go to unlock the door to the public, there's a line. Right down to the bottom of the town house steps. An *actual* line. Full of smart-looking women in silk blouses and men in linen jackets, mopping their faces in the oppressive humidity. And these people aren't just curious to see the show, I can tell. They're straining forward, eyes filled with hunger. I've seen that look before – on the line for a designer sample sale. Scores of women with straightened hair and logo handbags will have that same air of extreme longing, knowing they're steps away from the finest merchandise at the lowest prices. Every person in this line knows Grady's work will only appreciate in value from now on. They're just itching to snatch out their checkbooks. And I'm using every ounce of restraint to keep myself from jumping up and down and shouting, 'Wheeeeeee!'

'Make way,' I hear from the bottom of the town house steps, and my exhilaration instantly plummets. 'Excuse me. I said *excuse me*. No, I'm not cutting! I'm *family!*'

That pushy, high-pitched squeal could belong to only one person. I feel my forehead wrinkling up, and I automatically start chewing on my thumbnail – a nasty childhood habit I thought I beat long ago. My cousin Mimi is bounding up the limestone stairs, her shiny brown hair glinting in the sun. She's followed by an older, more reserved woman in oversized Chanel sunglasses and what looks like a Chanel suit, with the skirt cut just below the knee. A fortunate length, considering the woman is so painfully thin, her knees must look like doorknobs.

'Izzy, *darling*,' Mimi's exclaiming as she kisses me on each cheek. Her luggage-sized Louis Vuitton bag thuds into my hip. 'How lucky are you today? *How lucky are you!*'

I take a deep breath and work on keeping my smile fixed in place. 'Thanks, Mimi. Yes, we were more than overjoyed to see Grady's review.'

Mimi *tsks* at me like I just misspelled *and* at a spelling bee. 'No, you silly! I mean, look who *I've* brought you! *Look!* Catherine Wollcott herself! Right here, at your little gallery!'

Thin Lady manages a slight elongating of her tightly pursed lips, which I assume must be a smile, and then thrusts out her veiny hand, palm down, like she expects me to kiss it.

'Nice . . . to meet you,' I say, grasping her down-turned fingers and jostling them up and down in what could loosely be called a handshake. I hear the people on line beginning to rumble, and one of them throws out an 'All right already.' 'Er, why don't we continue inside.'

Walking through the gallery door, I feel like a glorified Pied Piper, except instead of rats, I'm leading a pack of art connoisseurs. I'm hoping their teeth will be less sharp.

'Catherine is my *boss*, Izzy,' Mimi's saying as we get to the reception ledge. 'She is *the* premier interior designer in New York.'

Mimi grabs the laminated copies of Grady's bio and title list and places them gingerly in Catherine Wollcott's bony hands. Thankfully, I see Kimmy already putting out new copies for others who might be interested. She gives me a scared look, pulling back the skin on either side of her face in an eerily accurate imitation of Catherine's face-lift. I have to swallow a few times before I'm sure I won't snort with laughter.

'I *knew* Grady Cole's show would be a smash hit. Didn't I say so, Izzy?' Mimi looks at me expectantly but doesn't wait for me to respond. ' "Offers a profoundly dark vision of consumer culture with the deceptively decorative hand of a Pop Art master," ' Mimi's quoting the *Times* review. 'Didn't I say that *exact same thing* myself, Izzy?'

Actually, no, Mimi. You've never even seen the show.

'I can't say I remember . . .,' I drift off.

Mimi gives me a sharp look and rolls her eyes. 'Well, of course I didn't use those *exact* words,' she backtracks. 'But the minute I met Grady I knew he would be a star, and my aesthetic sense is *never* wrong.'

Catherine offers her strangled version of a smile, and I'm wondering if Mimi's sole job is to talk for her. I'd give anything to be able to skip out on the pretense of other business, but I've got a gnawing feeling that this Catherine Wollcott could become a significant client. *Associate dealer*, I keep saying to myself, like a Zen chant to combat Mimi's poisoned chakras. Not that I know what a chakra is, but in Mimi's case I imagine it fits into an LV-logoed wallet.

'Guess who we're here for?' Mimi's grabbing my hand with both of hers, again slamming her bag into me. 'I bet you can't guess. Try!'

I glance toward Kimmy, desperate for an ally here, but she's on the phone, and I can see there's at least one other line on hold. I twist my head round to look for Avery, but he's positioned himself in the exhibition rooms, at the ready for anyone who might be showing serious interest in the available pieces.

'You're here for Grady, aren't you?' I take a stab, figuring it's easier to just play along. 'Though I would be more than happy to show you any of our other artists, should you be interested,' I make sure to tell Catherine.

'No, Izzy!' Mimi drops my hand, giving an apologetic look to her magnanimous boss. 'I meant our *clients*. Susan and Tim! We're buying for Susan and Tim!'

'O . . . kay . . .,' I say, wondering how I can steer this conversation toward the actual paintings. And the part where they get bought. And Mimi leaves me alone.

'*Sarandon and Robbins!*' Mimi nearly shouts. 'They love this critique-of-commercial-culture stuff. They can't buy enough of it!'

I hear a throaty chuckle coming from behind me and figure someone's been listening in on our conversation. I feel like crumbling with embarrassment. The entire art-savvy world is buzzing about this show right now, and here I am talking about celebrities. I can feel my heel fretfully lifting in and out of my slingback, and I will myself to stop fidgeting.

'Grady Cole!' Mimi squeals. 'I was *just* saying how amazing it would be to see you here!'

I spin quickly around to see the source of the chuckle – Grady, leaning against the wall behind me, biting his cheeks to keep from breaking into full-on laughter. For once, I feel elated to see him.

Suddenly, I'm almost jogging the few feet from the reception ledge to the wall by the doorway. 'Grady,' I say his name softly, so the others can't hear. 'Congratulations.

You deserve every bit of it.' Taken by an impulse spurred on by the joy of our success, I reach my arms around Grady's neck and give him a hug. I feel the soft cotton of his vintage T-shirt and his unexpectedly defined musculature. I smell a mixture of Ivory and turpentine that's surprisingly not unpleasant. I do *not*, however, feel him hugging me back. There are no grateful arms wrapping around my back; there's no Grady stubble brushing against my neck. In fact, he seems to be remaining as still as possible – like my war buddy has turned into a tin soldier.

I take a step back, and Grady passes by me without even a glance. But I thought – how could he not be – oh, *come on*. He's not still angry, is he?

'You're the friend, aren't you?' Grady nods his head at Mimi, then seeing both our mouths quickly opening, 'The cousin, right, I got it.'

'We *love* your work,' Mimi coos, clasping her hands together. Of course, she still hasn't seen the show.

I watch as Mimi introduces Grady to her boss with the kind of ceremony reserved for royalty, and as Grady chivalrously bows over Catherine Wollcott's outstretched skeletal hand. He's in his charming-artist mode, wooing this patron with his uncanny (and woefully intermittent) social skills. In fact, as Grady leads Catherine through the exhibition, I can see him closing the deal. We'll make this sale for sure. I should be glowing. My feet should be barely touching the floor. And I am! I'm ... ecstatic. Except Grady can't bear to look at me. He hasn't even said hello yet. For some reason, his silence upsets me more than his teasing ever did. Because after all, the Eaton Bosc isn't going to be the only gallery angling for Grady's next show after today. If we're going to keep our latest phenomenon at the Bond, we'll have to keep him happy.

Grady halts our little troupe in front of one of the more colorful paintings in the exhibition – *Mr Clean, 2003*, with its deep blue background and the detail of Mr Clean's bent elbow.

'How festive!' Mimi chirps. She's got her palms upraised, and she's breathing deeply. 'I can feel this in the guest room, Catherine, can't you? Or would you say over the fireplace?'

For the first time, I hear Catherine's voice. It's uncharacteristically deep and mannish, like Marlene Dietrich's without the accent. 'I'm communing, Mimi,' she says, shooing my cousin away with an outstretched chopstick of an arm. 'With the art and the artist. And no one else!'

Mimi mutters a quick 'Of course!' and scoots herself backward, obeying the order as swiftly as possible. 'Decor for Catherine is a *spiritual* matter,' Mimi whispers in my ear, as if speaking of the Dalai Lama. 'She mustn't ever be disturbed.'

This is where I'd expect Grady to swivel his head back toward me and mouth mockingly, 'We're *communing*, can't you tell?' But he doesn't budge. I might regret saying this later, but I'm missing that roguish smirk of his.

'Can you believe they printed the wrong date on the invitations?' Mimi's at my side now, flinging her long silk scarf over her shoulder indignantly. These last fifteen minutes must've been the longest she's gone without wedding talk since the engagement. She's so swelling from the effort that if she doesn't speak soon, I'm sure her cheeks will pop like a balloon. 'Everything's in such a rush! Did you know the waiting list at the Puck is *two years* long? Of course, when they had a cancellation for August *I* got the first call. The building's owner is a devoted client of ours, and he said my wedding would be his special project. Flowers, food, music – all in two months! And now a *mistake!* I don't have time for mistakes! Thank *God* we sent out those save-the-date cards.' She pauses, finally, for breath. 'You got yours, didn't you?'

Did I ever. The announcement of Mimi's wedding was more elaborate than any invitation should be – with ribbons, gold writing, and paper laser-cut to look like lace. 'Yup,' I say, trying to sound nonchalant.

'The invitations will be appallingly delayed!' Mimi's got a petulant frown on her rosy face. 'Which is *shocking*, if you ask me, considering what my mother's paying for them. You wouldn't *believe* what this wedding is costing! Honestly, my parents are spending the equivalent GNP of a Third World country!'

'There's a clever theme,' I interject. Really, I'm not sure I can endure another monologue on how rich Mimi's parents are. I raise my hands and wriggle my fingers to imitate sunbeams. 'The Third World! Palm trees everywhere!'

Mimi cocks her head and widens her slate-gray eyes. 'Ooh! I *love* it! . . . Maybe for the bridal shower! Because we've already got the perfect wedding planned.' Her focus sharpens here, as if honing in to drop a missile. 'The wonderful evening of romance I've been dreaming about for years.'

'I remember,' I say with as little despair as possible. I made a vow to myself back in high school when Mimi started dating Jared Anders – I'll never again let her see me vulnerable. 'Looking forward to it!'

Mimi scrunches up her shoulders in anticipation. 'Soooo? Who are you bringing as your date!'

I'll tell you. A week ago, that question might have floored me – a sucker punch from far left. But now I've got the beginnings of a plan rattling round in my head. Do I dare hope . . . it's not *entirely* unlikely . . . Couldn't I ask Avery? I get a longing feeling in my chest just thinking about it. There'll be dancing, and flowers, and formal wear. It'll be just like the prom! Except without the puking in the limo.

'I've got someone in mind.' I let my adoring expression tell Mimi all she needs to know.

'It's not that journalist you said you were dating, is it?' Mimi says archly, tossing her hair. 'Because have you seen "Page Six" today? Your James Hunter seems to have left you for a *model!*'

Oh, crap. Back when Mimi called to tell me about her

engagement . . . I told her I was dating Jamie, didn't I? I had forgotten about that. But no matter. With Avery on my arm, I'll feel like Cinderella at the ball – and when the clock strikes midnight, the magic will be just beginning. I hear someone call his name, and my attention's nabbed. There's my Avery now, shaking the hand of a man in boxy glasses. I give him my best, most dazzling smile, and he winks back at me, gesturing with a surreptitious thumbs-up. Look at the team we make. We're even beyond words.

'Is that the dealer?' Catherine Wollcott's masculine monotone draws my attention back to our little foursome. She's pointing a crooked finger across the room at Avery.

'That it is,' Grady says tightly. He's almost glowering at me. I'm actually flinching from the coldness coming off him.

I didn't do anything malicious, Grady. I didn't! Okay, so I told you to forget about Avery's collectors and then I encouraged him to go after them. Where's the awful transgression there? *You're such a hypocrite*, Grady seems to be telling me again with his eyes. And all right, fine. I confess: Losing his approval has hit me like a slap in the face. Which doesn't even make sense – because when did I have it to begin with?

'I've got business to attend to with that man,' Catherine declares, speaking of Avery as she might a courtier.

'What a coincidence.' Grady's heated gaze transfers to Avery's profile. 'So do I.'

He does? What kind of business could Grady have with Avery that doesn't include me? I'm just about to ask that very question when I feel Catherine Wollcott's frigid grasp on my arm. I almost gasp out loud. Gosh, that old lady's strong. I don't think I could wrest away even if I tried.

'Fetch your boss for me,' she commands. 'I will speak with him at once.'

Who *is* this woman? I mean, she looks like Helen Gurley Brown and speaks like a Klingon! Mimi's gesturing frantically at me, muttering, 'Go, go!'

I work on keeping the look of revulsion off my face as I

ease myself into Avery's conversation. He's making small talk with a haughty woman wearing a rhinestone broach the size of a watermelon. I compliment her on its originality before assuring her I'll return in just a moment.

'That's Catherine Wollcott,' I say into Avery's ear when I've dragged him away. 'She's interested in the *Mr Clean*.'

'I've heard of her,' Avery says in his crisp business voice. God, he's sexy when he acts all formal.

'And apparently' – I'm using my professional tone too, hoping it'll quell the mix of frustration and distress boiling up inside – 'Grady has business with you today as well.'

Avery pauses here, giving me a reticent nod. 'I'm aware.'

He is? Oh. Well, okay, then. I start to respond, but I'm not sure how. It's silly really, but I kind of feel left out. We're a team, all of us. Granted, our most valuable player can't stand the manager and now holds a grudge against the coach too, but we're a team nonetheless. Aren't we?

Avery seems to intuit what I'm thinking. I watch his eyes relinquish their keen, stoic gaze. His forehead smooths, and his lips relax into a pouty smile. Without meaning to, I shiver. I recognize this manifestation of Avery. This was how he looked upstairs in the private galleries.

'Save a late dinner for me tonight.' Avery's keeping his velvety voice low. He takes the first two fingers of his right hand and brushes my hair behind my ear. 'You and I have something special to discuss.'

Across the room, I see an agitated Grady leaving Catherine Wollcott's side, running his hands repeatedly through his hair. He's headed toward the office, I'm sure. For that crucial business meeting I'm not invited to. But really. How can I still care?

Would you like gin and platonic or do you prefer Scotch and sofa?

Two hours to go! T-minus two hours and counting! And okay, so I've never known what the *T* stands for, but tonight, we can make it *A*, for Avery and dinner at Chelsea's trendy restaurant Cafeteria at nine o'clock!

Kimmy and I have just arrived at Freddie's luxurious Chelsea apartment, where we've been summoned on very important business. Freddie's call came earlier this afternoon, while the gallery was still swamped with people. We've never had such a busy Friday. Or any day, for that matter. Grady's show sold out! (Except for one small drawing, and heck, I'm thinking of buying it.) That's right! We've sold *every single painting*. Eleven of those in one day alone! Avery was brilliant. Masterful, even. He's doing for Grady exactly what Dix is for Jamie: taking every advantage of his current fifteen minutes of fame. Avery's arranging for Grady to appear on symposium panels, he's got *Artnews* writing a feature article on Grady's work, and he's in talks with the New Museum of Contemporary Art for a possible commission piece! How unbelievably cool is that?

Kimmy and I are sitting side by side on Freddie's charcoal couch with enormous smiles just plastered on our faces. For hours, our eyes have been widened with shock. Our cheeks are flushed with exhilaration. A couple of curly wigs and red noses, and we could be driving the clown car at the Big Apple Circus. What's more, just a few blocks away, Avery and I will soon be celebrating on our own – finally the private, wondrous night I've been waiting for. I don't even dare hope this day could get any better. Or at least, I don't dare admit it.

'Crudités!' Freddie calls out as he emerges from his stainless-steel-outfitted kitchen carrying a lacquered tray of vegetables and herby dip. 'I checked with South Beach, and these carbs are absolutely doable.' Freddie rests the tray on his titanium coffee table and tweaks my knee. 'Just like Avery Devon.'

'Freddie!' I scold, arranging my features in an expression of beatific innocence. 'I haven't a clue what you mean.'

'Ha!' Kimmy erupts, her back slamming against the couch. She's wearing a T-shirt with the word *HOT* written out in hundreds of safety pins, and they're all jiggling merrily. 'Iz, you know we love you,' and here Freddie enthusiastically nods his agreement, 'but you're about as good at hiding your feelings as Pamela Anderson is at keeping her clothes on.'

Am I really that transparent? I grab a carrot stick and nibble, resting my elbows on my thighs. 'You try looking unaffected with Avery's arm around you!'

'Honey, I'll take that request,' Freddie chimes in. 'I had all kinds of plans for that lover boy.' He scoops up a huge glob of South Beach-approved dip with a celery stalk. 'The birds were not chirping in Freddieland when I found out Avery cuts a straight edge. Look at his suits alone! It's not right for a straight man to have that exquisite taste. Or that exquisite ass.'

Kimmy wrinkles her nose. 'I guess, if you go for someone that stiff. . . . Wait!' She throws up a hand in front of her. 'Freddie, don't answer that.'

'How do you know?' I'm scooting off the couch and sitting cross-legged on the floor across from Freddie. 'I mean, about Avery being straight for sure?'

He gives a huff. 'Darling, there's *no such thing*. But look –' Freddie lifts up a folder from under the coffee table and rests it on the sleek metal surface. 'This is why I called you here today.'

'Ooh! Goody!' Kimmy joins us on the floor, tucking her black-legging-clad legs under her. 'Espionage!'

Freddie lets out a wicked grin as he opens the folder. Inside are a handful of neatly stapled printouts, articles, it looks like. Freddie sifts through the pile and lifts one up for me and Kimmy to see. 'Exhibit A,' he says with gravitas, pointing to a low-res color photo on the page.

It's Avery! Kind of blurry, perhaps, and with a bit longer hair that curls cutely at the ends, but definitely Avery. In the photo, he's got his arm around a beautiful woman with long, straight, ash-blond hair and a friendly smile. On her other side stands an unsavory-looking man with a black monobrow, weaselly little eyes, and bulbous lips. No joke, he looks like a *Dick Tracy* villain. I strain forward to read the article, but I quickly see that's not going to happen.

'It's in German!' I almost wail.

'Unfortunate, isn't it?' Freddie agrees. 'But look at the names in the caption. Herman Munster on the end here is Raymond Bond, the Old Man's son. And this' – Freddie points at the blonde – 'is the Old Man's *granddaughter*, Constance Bond. Which brings me to ... Exhibit B!' Freddie draws out another article with a flourish, this one without photos. 'A profile of Avery Devon in *Art Monthly*, dated almost a year ago. *In English*, thank you very much.'

Kimmy claps her hands like she's watching a magician at a child's birthday party. I'm scooching myself forward as much as possible. The hard, cold coffee table presses into my rib cage.

Freddie scans the article for a moment, then continues. 'See? It's right here,' he says, pointing at the page. ' "*The young dealer was formerly engaged to New York heiress Constance Bond.*" So there! Proof of Avery Devon's heterosexuality *and* unattachment. Izzy, dearest' – he puckers his lips at me – 'go wild.'

Avery was engaged to the Old Man's granddaughter? Huh, that's a new one. But we knew Avery had some kind of connection with the Bond family. That's how he got Freddie's job, after all. I do have to wonder why Raymond Bond would make his daughter's *ex*-fiancé the dealer of his gallery, but then, who knows what Avery's current relationship with the family might be? I'm surprised, yes, but not quite stupefied. Nope, Freddie's going to have to dig up a lot more dirt before I crown this detective the Ellery Queen.

'Listen to this,' Freddie continues, wriggling his shoulders excitedly. 'I'm getting to the good part! Let's see ... "Making a name for himself at the Shtutman-Devon Gallery in Berlin with his provocative exhibitions," yada yada. "Grew up in Massachusetts," blah-blah. "Master's in history of art from Oxford," how la-di-da for him. Oh! Here it is. "Completed his undergraduate degree at Paris's *École des Beaux-Arts*." '

Now, *that's* interesting. Better than anyone, I should recognize where Grady went to college. I wrote it on the press release: 'Grady Cole, a graduate of the École des Beaux-Arts in Paris.' So that's how Grady knows Avery. Because what's the likelihood that two Americans only a year apart wouldn't find each other at a Parisian university? I try to imagine Grady and Avery in matching berets, drinking Bordeaux and dangling their feet in the Seine. There's Grady's hair, sticking out around the black beanie, and there's Avery cupping the mouth of his red-wine glass like he might a woman's cheek. Hey, I bet that's where he got that move from – the whole caressing-the-cheek bit. And if so, then I say, *Vive la France!*

'Avery and Grady are old college buddies?' Kimmy scrunches her nose, sounding skeptical. 'Don't you think their connection seems more epic? Like they're jousting knights or something?'

Leave it to Kimmy, master of medieval-fantasy art, to go straight for the epic. But I get what she's saying. Somehow, I doubt Grady's animosity toward Avery has to do with cheating on an exam or violating the age-old maxim that friends shouldn't room together. If we're putting together a jigsaw puzzle here, Freddie's gathered up the straight-edge pieces and made the border. The picture remains to be filled in.

'Is there more?' I ask eagerly, resting my forearms on the cold surface of the coffee table. 'Anything about Grady in there?'

Freddie pouts, his eyelids drooping. 'Nothing. The rest of the profile focuses on the damn art. I must say, Devon's taste tends toward the macabre. Get this – his most popular artist in Berlin used a medium of paint mixed with his own blood.'

'Ich!' Kimmy puts down the cauliflower blossom she was about to eat. 'Grody.'

I sneak a peek at my watch – eight o'clock. A-minus one hour and counting! Although I'm hoping Avery's taste in food proves less gruesome than his taste in art. Hmm. How rare can you order meat?

'Where did you find all this out?' I ask Freddie, who's searching through the last few articles for anything remotely juicy. 'You must have spent the whole day at the library!'

Freddie *tsks* at me in disbelief. 'Darling, I have two hundred ex-boyfriends to stalk. You don't think I'm *all over* google.com? Hell, tell me Avery's middle name and I'll find you his underwear size.'

'Don't bother.' Kimmy punches my upper arm playfully. 'Once Izzy gets into his briefs, she can just check the label!'

'It's not like that!' I cry, no doubt wildly red in the face.

Freddie and Kimmy break into uncontrollable giggles, bent over from the force of their teasing. Two backs heaving on either end of the coffee table, one in white, one in black.

'It isn't!' I call out again. But it's no use. They're just sitting there, unable to respond, convulsing. I might as well be speaking in tongues.

Besides, I bet he wears boxers.

*

Avery Devon is speaking. I'm transfixed by his Adam's apple rising and falling above the open buttons of his polo shirt, and I'm seeing his bare arms for the first time. Look at that short cotton sleeve hugging that shapely bicep. Actually, pretty much all of the diners here at Cafeteria have already noticed. We make an odd couple, Avery and I, in this part of Chelsea. Me being a woman and all. Right now, Avery's telling me about the restaurant in Berlin where he used to go after all his openings, which is called something like 'Schtichergartenschtacher,' and which I'm hoping I never have to repeat.

'Wow,' I say animatedly, taking a ladylike sip of my chilled cucumber-basil soup. 'I'll definitely have to try schnitzel soon. The Viennese way, as you suggest, with veal.'

Why do I do this? Every time I have a crush, I hang on every sentence the crushee says, then wind up hardly hearing anything. My mind just wanders off on its own accord. Like one of those children you see at the supermarket attached to the mother by a leash. I start out by promising myself I'll listen intently the whole time – because how else can you shoot back a clever, informed response? Except then the guy I'm listening to gets this hazy sheen around him. Like, Avery's not an attractive, sophisticated man sitting opposite me anymore. Nope. He's someone looking at me for a prolonged period of time, judging me moment by moment. Which means I've got to eat as daintily as possible, making sure nothing falls off my fork or – God forbid! – drips down my lip (why'd I order *soup*?). He's someone raising an eyebrow or smiling in a different way – and what does that *mean*! In the end, I'm left grasping at the very last thing I heard before or after I spaced out. Which, in this case, is Eastern European meat preparation.

'Excellent!' Avery's pleased by my sudden interest in schnitzel, though he seems happy enough with his calamari appetizer. I notice he eats the European way, without switching his knife and fork. He's leaning back in the restaurant's white leather banquette, against which his tan looks even bronzer. 'You do strike me, Isabel, as a woman who's graciously open to new experiences.'

I do? 'Er . . . sure!' I swirl my spoon around the soup, creating a basil eddy in the center. 'Try something new every day, is what I say!' I hold up my hand to display my fingernails, which are painted lavender. 'Like new nail polish!'

Just once, can I consult between the ears before I open my mouth?

Avery gives a good-natured chuckle and a twisty-lipped smile (what does that *mean*?). He finishes chewing a piece of calamari, and says at last, 'It's lovely. Very daring.'

I may just plunge through the ground with embarrassment. Any minute now . . .

'Which brings me to the reason I've asked you here, Isabel.' Avery rests his fork neatly by his plate.

Here it is! The part where he confesses his feelings for me! He's got this expectant expression, like he's imagining our future together, the It Couple of the art world, side by side at every auction and benefit. See? I knew guys daydreamed about relationships too!

'I've got great plans for the Bond,' Avery says assuredly, tenting his fingers together over his plate. 'I'm going to put us firmly on the map. Soon, we'll be a must-see for any gallery tour. Or any tour of New York, for that matter.'

Hang on, what's he saying? He's talking about the gallery. Not about us at all. But what about the way he brushed my hair back when he asked me to save dinner for him? The way he said we had something special to discuss. What's special about putting the Bond 'on the map'? Weren't you there today, Avery? We're already *on* the map. We're smack-dab in the middle of the map!

A waiter in a black 'Cafeteria' T-shirt comes to take our plates away, leaving me with my spoon paralyzed midmotion in the air. 'Avery.' I hear the concern in my voice. 'I'm not sure I see what you mean.'

Suddenly, he's all eagerness, like a puppy let loose in a field of squirrels. 'I hope to continue the work I started in Berlin,' Avery begins. 'From now on, the Bond will skew our exhibitions a bit more avant-garde, along the lines of, say, Marc Quinn.'

'Marc Quinn?' I repeat, my voice rising in both pitch and timidity.

'You know his work, of course?' Avery's forehead creases.

'Yes, I do,' I respond carefully. In Marc Quinn's most famous work, *Self*, he created a bust of himself using eight frozen pints of his own blood. What *is* it with Avery and blood? Since when is there anything wrong with plain old reliable paint and plaster?

'My model, of course, is the Saatchi Gallery,' Avery continues excitedly, oblivious to my dismay. 'We can foster our own breed of YBAs, only here in the States. We'll be revolutionaries, Isabel. You and I, together. True innovators.'

My head starts to spin, and I don't think it's from the wine. Charles Saatchi, who made his fortune in advertising, went on to found one of the world's most famous private galleries – the Saatchi Gallery in London. In fact, he's the one who owned Marc Quinn's *Self*. Until it became a puddle on his floor, that is. When Saatchi renovated his kitchen, the builders unplugged the freezer keeping Marc's head together, and, well, the poor guy kind of melted.

The Saatchi Gallery's troupe of YBAs – 'Young British Artists' – became instant sensations, and many critics still consider them the most provocative and daring artists of our day. Which is fine. Great, really. But the thing is, I'm not sure I'm entirely keen on the Bond showing that type of work. See, the most well-known of the YBAs, Damien Hirst, became famous for making sculptures out of embalmed dead animals. And Chris Ofili's *Holy Virgin Mary*, which Mayor Giuliani publicly declaimed when it came to New York, was made with real elephant dung. I mean, I *absolutely* stand up for freedom of expression. These works have every right to be exhibited. But still. *Ewwww*.

I'm not sure how to proceed here. Avery's fervor seems to ooze from every pore. One minute he's the picture of country-club gentility, and the next he's off-the-wall agog at the idea of . . . well, at the idea of I'm not sure what exactly. 'So, let me understand here.' I'm barely keeping the wince off my face. 'Do you mean you'd like the Bond to show . . . embalmed animal parts?'

'You said it yourself, Isabel' – Avery grabs my hand, clutching it tightly – 'when I asked how you felt about the John Teller exhibition. I remember word for word: 'If Teller's message is literal – that his body is his art – I think he could have portrayed that more cleverly.' I couldn't have agreed more! What if Teller had used his own hair on the sculptures? Or his own –'

Don't say blood! That is *so* not what I meant by clever! 'Avery,' I interrupt anxiously. 'I'm open to all your ideas. Of course I am. But I just can't see our collectors responding to . . . to elephant poo!'

'No,' Avery laughs now, the corners of his eyes crinkling adorably. 'Of course not. That's why I need you, Isabel.' His voice softens a notch. 'I want to push the envelope, but never to offend our collectors. You'll be by my side in this endeavor, reining me in when I venture out too far. You'll be my ballast, securing my feet to the ground.' Avery's fervent grip on my hand relaxes into something gentler. 'You'll be my partner, Isabel. As an associate dealer should be.'

My breath catches in my throat. Did I just hear correctly? 'Really?' Now I'm the one squeezing Avery's hand. I feel the elation bubbling up inside. 'I'm an associate dealer?'

'How could you not be?' There's nothing but affection and respect in Avery's eyes. He's proud of me, I realize. 'You've outshone yourself every step of the way. The Bond family would have been idiotic not to approve your raise –

and the budget for a new director. Isabel, you deserve every accolade I can throw at you.'

Oh, God. I'm almost crying. There's this well of emotion, like, right up there at my tear ducts. I didn't even dare dream . . . I mean, this moment is so much better than I'd ever thought! I tuck my head down, staring at the napkin in my lap. There's a waiter next to me, I realize, setting down my main course – sea bass on saffron rice, garnished with the teeniest baby carrots ever. But I'm afraid to look up. I pretend to readjust the napkin over my skirt until I'm more composed.

'There's more,' Avery says in that playful way of his. He draws his tongue across his lips, and I worry I may hyperventilate. 'I'll be going in mid-July to the Venice Biennale. I've got my eye on several European artists who will be showing there this summer, especially Lars Handelnik, who casts sculptures out of ice, right in the gallery, as the audience watches. He's got a special cooling chamber big enough for him and the sculpture.'

Hey, that sounds pretty cool, actually. Not even the least bit gory. 'I'd love to see his work,' I say eagerly, skewering a baby carrot with my fork.

'I'd love you to as well, Isabel,' Avery says suggestively, cutting into his tender-looking leg of lamb. 'I'm hoping you'll agree to accompany me to Venice next month. I'd be endlessly grateful for your input.'

'Venice?!' I nearly fall off my seat. My fish is forgotten, saffron rice and all. My napkin's somehow tumbled down to my ankles. Robbie Williams could be singing 'Angels' in my ear and I might not even notice. 'With the canals, and the bridges, and the vaporetto boats?'

'Yes,' Avery says calmly, pausing to chew. 'That's the one I mean.'

'I've never been.' I'm getting myself under control here, picking up my napkin, taking a swig of wine. 'But my cousin Mimi went last year and trust me, I've seen about a bazillion photos. Each one looked like a postcard.'

'I can imagine,' Avery says, and – I may be mistaken

here – but did his leg just move so it's touching mine? I'm sure I'm feeling the pressed cotton of his chinos. But then again, it *is* a small table, and a man's got to stretch his legs, right? He goes on, leaning toward me. 'I'll confess, Isabel, that I'm hoping . . . I'm hoping you and I . . .'

Yes? You're hoping what? Oh, don't trail off and twitch your lips! Finish the sentence! *Finish the damn sentence!*

'I'm hoping you and I will be able to foster a' – Avery bites his lower lip for just a millisecond, and it's the most provocative action I've seen in my life – 'a more than functional relationship.'

I'm swallowing every instinct to shout out in the middle of the restaurant. Literally, I'm using every bit of energy to quell the enormous exhortations threatening to burst out right here and now. Avery and I are going to Venice together! To one of the most prestigious exhibitions in all of Europe! I'll be his associate dealer! This sea bass is remarkably fresh! And finally, overwhelming every other thought: *What's a more than functional relationship?!*

21

You're so hot, you must be the reason for global warming!

'**Y**ou have to!' Dix scolds in the middle of Barneys. She's holding up the tiniest string bikini I've ever seen. The bra looks like it would have trouble holding in a pair of grapes. 'I don't know why you're scared of your figure.'

'I'm not *scared*,' I insist, testing the fabric of a navy-and-white bikini that's made to actually cover one's assets. 'I just want a simple, classy new bathing suit for Venice. Is that so hard?'

'Hel-lo!' Jamie calls out a few racks away. He pulls out a hot pink and denim bikini with ruffled boy shorts. 'Maybe I should get this for Patrice.'

'Patrice?' Gosh, I hadn't noticed before how sunken Jamie's eyes look, like he hasn't slept in days. Poor sweetie. Could the Russian model have dumped him? 'What happened to Svetlana?'

Jamie gives me an impish grin. 'Nothing at all. She was Saturday. Patrice was last night.'

Dix jerks her thumb in Jamie's direction, rolling her eyes. '*Page Six*'s most eligible bachelor, can't you tell?'

The three of us have gathered for the most sacred of missions: a lunchtime shopping trip to prepare for my (whoopee! dance around!) trip to Venice with Avery. So far, I've already gotten the most Riviera-looking sun hat with a big white brim, new baby-soft leather driving moccasins, and a huge jar of Clarins self-tanner. Venice, you're going to have to search elsewhere for your token pasty American. I've spent a fortune I don't have, but I figure I've got a raise coming, right? And this is my *future* I'm investing in, here. My future as Mrs Avery D—

Okay. So I'm a wee bit ahead of myself. But lucky for me, Dix has almost finished planning her big premiere party for Arden Moore (at Rush! where P. Diddy had his birthday party this year!), and Jamie's between columns and – apparently – girlfriends, which means this Tuesday afternoon is completely free for the most important shopping journey of my whole life. Never has the notion of packing entailed such gravitas! Everything has to be perfect! Or, rather, *more than functional.*

'Are you bringing tampons?' Dix throws out, holding the skimpy swimsuit against herself in the mirror. 'Remember – they do random security checks. Your unmentionables could be spread wide open in front of Avery's eyes.'

That cannot happen. 'I'm sure I can buy some in Venice if I need to.'

Jamie's face scrunches up. 'Why am I here again?'

'For the male opinion!' Dix's arms are full of suits, hanging from her like tassels on a Cher jacket. 'And now, to the fitting rooms!'

I'm grabbing the black handles of my sleek Barneys bags, walking sideways through the racks of bikinis so the giant hatbox doesn't topple them all over. 'Dix!' I cry out. 'I'm not sure I feel comfortable modeling . . . I mean, do we need the male opinion on *everything*?'

Dix flashes her best 'trust me' smile, even as I nearly choke at the sight of the bikinis she's holding. What's the use of putting on a bathing suit if it's going to be see-through? And I'm sorry. No thongs!

The fitting-room attendant, dressed in Barneys black, tucks her glossy maple-colored hair neatly behind her ears and hands me the suits. Behind the closed dressing-room door, mirrors display my every angle. One thing's for sure.

Barneys is not for the weak of heart. Or, for that matter, the fat of thigh.

'Are we near the airport?' I hear Jamie ask on the other side of the door, his voice mellifluous and smooth. Is he mad? The airport's in Queens. When are we *ever* in Queens?

'No, sir,' the confused fitting-room attendant responds. 'We're at . . . Barneys.'

'Well, then.' Jamie doesn't miss a beat. 'That must have been my heart taking off.' There's a girlish giggle and a shy 'That's a good one.' In an instant, before my very ears, Page Six's most eligible bachelor has another date.

'Whatcha got on?' Dix calls out impatiently.

'Um . . . just a second!' I call out, trying to sound cheerful. I'm sifting through the unlikely pile of bathing suits in front of me, wondering how I can retain my decency.

There's only one bikini here that I'd actually wear. It's absolutely glamorous, so Saint-Tropez. The material is a textured white, but with enough lining to avoid the dreaded wet-T-shirt syndrome. The halter top at the neck and the straps at the back close with a chic gold hoop, as do the sides of the bottom piece, at the hip. And my goodness. I can't believe what I look like when it's on. My legs look inches longer. My waist curves more inward. Now, that's a girl Avery would squire about town. That's a girl . . . no, a woman . . . finally giving up her Peter Pan collars and pink shoes. That's the woman I've aspired to be for as long as I can remember.

My hand's on the lock. I'm gearing up my courage. Come on, if you can't show your friends . . . *ouch*. Something's jabbing at my back with the tenacity of a hungry mosquito. Undoing the suit, I realize it's the price tag. *Oh, my God. That's the price tag?* Two hundred and fifty dollars for a couple of scraps of fabric? Nuh-uh. Not when I already love it so much! Why couldn't I have looked at the price *before* I put the thing on? That's just . . . cruel chronology!

'Iz!' Dix yells again. 'I can feel myself aging. My boobs just sagged an inch.'

What the hell. Free trip. Free hotel room. Through-the-nose expensive bathing suit. I'm still getting a bargain. Besides, the look on Avery's face when he sees me in this getup will be worth twice as much.

I stand in front of my two best friends and Jamie's latest date, one leg in front of the other and slightly bent, like a Rockette. I don't even feel embarrassed. I feel empowered, with a self-confidence I never knew I had. This trip is going to be so cool! Avery and I in *Venice*, the enchanted city of islands, where it's always sunset – at least, according to Mimi's photos.

'Whoa!' Jamie exhales, to the obvious chagrin of his new paramour. 'Holy – Iz, you're burning a friggin' hole in the carpet.'

Dix has clasped her hands together and she's holding them to her mouth. 'Look at you,' she finally says, her voice sounding somehow far away. 'You're all grown-up.'

I'm beaming. Little rays of light must be shooting off me (I haven't used the self-tanner yet, after all). I feel just like a fashion pinup girl.

Dix sets her mouth into a tight, determined line. 'Avery better take damn good care of you,' she says.

As usual, she's right. He sure damn better.

I get back to the gallery overwhelmed by shiny black Barneys bags. I can't help but remember that day, exactly three weeks ago, when Freddie and I returned from the very same place to learn the Old Man was gone. For the first time since then, I've finally let go of my guilt and anguish. Freddie leaves for L.A. at the end of August, and he's completely thrilled. He's not sure which excites him more – the enormous pool of untapped artists, or the even larger pool of untapped men to date. I've never seen someone so pleased about losing his job. And look at me! I'm an *associate dealer*!

I cannot wait to show Kimmy my purchases. She'll be

so impressed! I'm not even letting myself think about how much I spent. Every time my mind wanders toward my credit card bill, I quickly shift to thoughts of moonlit gondola rides, or trattoria dinners, or Avery's hand passing over my cheek. Talk about worth it. And that's not even considering the vast array of contemporary art at the Biennale that will be spread out before me – like an all-you-can-eat buffet made up entirely of chocolate!

I've got my hand on the gallery's great wooden door, and I just feel like singing! Venice Venice Bo Benice Banana Fanna Fo Fen – Oh . . . hey. What's Grady Cole doing here? There he is, on the floor by reception, folding up the clear sheets of plastic he uses to cover his paintings during transit. I hesitate by the entryway, feeling oddly shy. I can't explain why, except that I've been getting these sort of – wobblies in my stomach when I think about Grady these past six days. Since his opening, that is. Since he stopped ribbing on me, or trying to embarrass me, or . . . paying any attention to me at all, really. I get the sense I've screwed things up between Grady and me. We used to support each other. Professionally, I mean. And in truth, I miss that. What's more, I'm actually sorry. Sorry that I ruined Grady's trust in me. Sorrier that I never realized I had his trust to begin with.

'This is a nice surprise!' I call from the doorway.

Grady's head swivels briefly toward me, a stony expression on his face. Kimmy's on the phone, but she waves an enthusiastic hello.

'Did you bring us more paintings?' I ask Grady excitedly. 'I'll go make space in the private salesroom!'

Grady gestures toward Kimmy with his chin. 'We already did. You weren't here.'

'Oh,' I say, a bit deflated. I'm shoving my bags behind Kimmy's desk as she peeks in at all the tissue-paper-wrapped delights. 'I would have been here – of course I would have been – if I had known you were coming.'

'Okay,' Grady tosses out nonchalantly, his focus riveted on the plastic sheeting. 'Whatever.'

I return from behind the reception ledge, and lean against it. 'I'm sorry,' I tell Grady. My voice sounds small and distant.

'Don't worry about it, Princess.' Grady's tone is acidic. Aside from the initial glance, he's barely even acknowledged my presence.

God, it's like the past month never happened. We're back at square one – or even worse. Now I'm the subway assailant *and* the hopeless hypocrite. The only difference is that instead of anger, I'm feeling this odd sense of loss.

'No, Grady.' I squat down next to him on the floor, drawing my skirt over my knees. I will him to look at me. '*I'm sorry.*'

Grady purses his lips. Somehow, I get the sense he's conflicted. Is he deciding whether I'm worth forgiving? I hesitate a moment, but then I put my hand on his shoulder. I'm reaching out, literally. I shouldn't have. Grady shoots up as if I've burned him. He's grabbing his neatly folded plastic and rushing toward the front door.

Before I can even try to stop him, Grady turns suddenly around. There's a beat of awkward silence as his forehead creases. When he finally opens his mouth, he takes a deep breath. He says quietly, 'I know.'

I watch through the gallery's one window as Grady bounds down the limestone stairs, leaving me in the wake of yet another tumultuous mood swing. Will I ever be able to do anything right in his eyes? Because the thing is, for all the times I've wished he'd leave me alone, now that he actually *is*, I'm wondering if that's what I really wanted. Perhaps the gratitude just hasn't sunk in yet. Come on, gratitude. Sink faster.

Grady reaches the bottom of the stoop just as an elegant light-haired woman rests her satin shoe on the first step. Ooh! I know that shoe. It's been in W magazine at least four times this season. Louis Vuitton! And not Mimi's version of Vuitton, splashing the name around like a Times Square billboard. No, this is the tasteful, haute couture variety. Jeez, I think I'm salivating. Grady's exchanging words with the woman. She's resting her hand on his arm, and even making him smile! Does he know her? Could this be one of the friends who skipped out on his opening? But no, after just a moment, Grady's off again, his powerful stride taking him and his ratty cargo pants down Seventy-third Street and out of sight.

'Love, love, love!' Kimmy cries behind me.

When I turn around, she's got on my new oversized white sun hat. With her pixieish features and waify frame, Kimmy looks just like Audrey Hepburn in *Breakfast at Tiffany's*. You know, if Audrey had been wearing an orange bubble skirt minidress. Kimmy rises from her chair, throwing her arms above her head in a triumphant 'Ta da!' pose just as the blond woman from outside steps over the threshold.

'Oh! Er . . . welcome!' Kimmy covers, sheepishly drawing her arms back to her sides and removing the huge hat as surreptitiously as possible. 'To the Bond Gallery!'

'Thanks!' the woman says, tentatively stepping forward in her luxurious pink satin shoes. 'I didn't realize. . . . How do you know . . .? *Do* you know who I am?'

And as I look closer, she does seem familiar. Pretty features, friendly smile, ash-blond hair. Where do I know that face from?

'Hi.' I hold out my arm. 'I'm Isabel Duncan, the dir – the associate dealer.'

'Oh, yes!' the elegant woman says, shaking my hand. She's got on the sweetest lacy silk camisole with a simple heather gray pencil skirt. 'I just wanted to ask first . . . I hope you don't mind . . .' She seems uncomfortable. Reluctant, even, to fully enter the gallery space. 'Could you tell me if Avery . . . if the dealer's here?'

'He's not, actually,' I say, using an authoritative tone. 'He's conducting a round of studio visits today. But I'm sure I can help you with whatever you may need.'

'That's great!' The woman relaxes at once. Her shoulders loosen, and her smile widens with delight. 'Oh, I should introduce myself, shouldn't I?' She laughs good-naturedly, offering me her hand as if she's forgotten we've just shaken hello. 'My grandfather was . . . this was my grandfather's gallery. I'm Constance Bond.'

'Wow!' Kimmy rises from her seat again, this time with less 'Ta da!' 'What an honor to meet you.'

'It certainly is!' I second. Now I know why she was asking about Avery. I'd want to avoid my ex-fiancé as well, if I were in her gorgeous shoes. So this is the former love of Avery's life. And she's beautiful, elegant, and flawlessly dressed. No need to be insecure, Iz. Maybe he just . . . got tired of all that perfection. 'We've never met any members of Emerson Bond's family, Ms. Bond.'

'Constance, please!' she insists eagerly. 'I know, my family hasn't been too visible in the past. My father had been estranged from my grandfather for years. He's a *difficult* man, my father, and everything was all . . . kind of a mess, really. But now I felt I just had to come visit.'

Of course she did, I think to myself, feeling sympathetic. She's just lost her grandfather, and she's paying respect to his memory. What a gracious woman! Not at all stuck-up. You'd never know she was an heiress to a fortune estimated at over a billion dollars!

'I'm happy to give you a tour of our current exhibition, if you're interested.' I gesture toward the gallery's other rooms.

'Only if you're not too busy!' Her face lights up. 'I saw the *New York Times* review. He seems pretty fantastic, this artist.'

'He is,' I say, with a hint of melancholy I hope I've hidden. We pass through the doorway into the first exhibition room, pausing at the *Dunkin Donuts* that now belongs to Martin Feinberg. 'Grady Cole's lines are playful, but there's sociological depth to his message,' I begin, using my rehearsed collector presentation. 'His paintings are so eye-catching because they're based on commercial design – whose sole purpose is to catch the eye. However, once Grady holds your attention, he won't let you feel secure.'

'I can't believe it,' Constance exhales. 'They look phenomenal. So he's a success, right, this Grady Cole?'

'Entirely.' I nod. 'You actually just saw Grady, on your way in.' I'm directing Constance toward the private salesroom. 'As he was leaving. You two seemed to . . . do you know each other?'

'Is that who that was?' Constance's voice rises. 'How . . . nice he seems! Have people bought all of his paintings?'

'The show has sold out, but he's just brought us more pieces,' I say encouragingly. 'We have a long waiting list, but who should get preference if not the owner of the gallery?'

Constance gives a bemused smile. 'That's my father really. He's the one who . . . he's always liked Avery Devon. That's why he instated him as the gallery's dealer, despite my own . . . well . . .' She gives a laugh tinged with distress.

Despite your own *what*, Constance? Sadness? Anger? Regret? Lordy, and I thought I was curious about Avery's past with *Grady*.

But to my chagrin, Constance never finishes her thought. She sits on the beige couch in the private salesroom, her legs effortlessly crossed. I'm pulling out two of Grady's newest pieces. One of them I've never seen before – it's a detail, it seems, from some kind of hair care product, rendered more realistically than Grady's other work. A woman's red, wavy hair tumbles down the plane of the painting. Even though we can't see her, there's a feeling this woman has somehow seduced the viewer, like Eve in Milton's *Paradise Lost*.

'Look at that,' I say under my breath, in wonder.

'So you like his work. Personally, I mean.' Constance is examining me, her eyes sharp and astute.

'I do.' I join her on the couch after resting the paintings against the wall before us. 'He's remarkable.'

'And as a person?' she continues. 'Do you think he's . . . a good man?'

Is Grady a good man? Huh. That's a question I've never

been asked about an artist before. Let's see. He's sarcastic, highly irreverent – and talk about an unpredictable temper. But Grady's got his good points too. He's managed to overcome his personal feud with Avery in order to make his artwork the priority. He's agreed to everything we've asked him to do, without a single argument. And most importantly, he treats Kimmy as a vital member of the team and not 'just' a receptionist, as I've seen other artists do.

'I think he is,' I tell Constance, facing her keen gaze. 'I think he is, at heart, a good man. What makes you interested?'

'Nothing!' Constance breaks eye contact, uncrossing her legs and drawing her palms over her skirt. 'Just curious! You know, this being my father's gallery now.'

Your ex-fiancé's gallery as well, is what I'm thinking. What about Avery has this elegant woman as jumpy as a grasshopper? I finish showing Grady's pieces to Constance, but she seems more guarded now. Her questions avoid mention of both Grady and Avery, and I swear, if one more iota of mystery surrounds either of those men, I may just faint from the stress of not knowing. If I were Nancy Drew, things would be so much easier! There'd be clues everywhere – like, I'd be walking down the street, and look! There would be the stationery store where the kidnapper bought the paper for his ransom note! And lucky me, the shopkeeper would remember his name, and address! But I guess, like good old Nancy, these neat, tidy endings vanish after childhood. The grown-up world becomes something scarier, and more uncertain. You're no longer guaranteed that at the end of the novel, no one will get hurt.

As I show Constance Bond out of her grandfather's town house, and as she hugs Kimmy and me with all the informality of friendship, I realize that's what's got me so keyed up. Not the mystery, really, that lingers between Grady and Avery, but the whole new uncertainty I'm now plagued with. Constance Bond is attractive, warm, intelligent, gracious, and in possession of hundreds of millions of dollars. What *possible* reason could there be for Avery Devon to break up with her? Or, even more troubling, what could he have done to make her break up with him?

I nibble at my thumbnail, planning to stop off at Barnes & Noble after work to buy a whole slew of comforting Nancy Drew novels. For the first time, I'm really wondering, When it comes to the Mystery of Avery Devon . . . should I be worried?

22

Stop, drop, and roll baby,
'cause you are on fire!

Jamie's turning right and left, waving with one hand, and
guiding the teeny-waisted Celeste with the other.
Flashes are popping on either side with the rhythm of
microwave popcorn. Flash! Flash flash flash! Flash! Then,
suddenly, they stop. Or, rather, they turn away, toward the
man behind us, who's – ooh! – Joaquin Phoenix. Jamie
seems befuddled. His hand's still in the air, which makes
him look like a bit of a fool since no one's watching. Of
course, fewer people have noticed me. We're on the red
carpet – which is navy, go figure – and I've arrived just a
few steps ahead of Jamie. Actually, I did get two or three
flashes before anyone realized I wasn't Julia Roberts (who
I could totally resemble! You know, if she had a different
face).

Dix couldn't have hoped for a nicer night for her first
big A-list premiere party. The day's heat has given way to a
lively breeze, and there's not a cloud in the sky. The cosmic
stars above are twinkling over the Hollywood ones below
like a giant connect-the dots puzzle. I'm wearing a white
goddesslike gown, with long, billowy fabric that falls in
ruched folds, and it makes me feel like a Roman empress.
The real attraction, though, is the dress's back, which
plunges dangerously low in a pointed vee. Jamie's got on

his signature black suit, with the skinny hipster-style lapels. His date, Celeste — whom I just met tonight (since when do we bring dates to Dix's events, Jamie?) — has on a spandex, light blue tube dress that I'm pretty sure was meant to be a shirt. You know how your mother always said Barbie's proportions would be impossible on a real woman? Well, I'm thinking Celeste must not be real.

We're at one of the three check-in tables now, where Dix's assistant, Larissa, is presiding over a black binder full of names. Her supershiny hair falls forward against her cheeks, and she keeps a pen clutched tightly in her fist at all times. I'm fishing around in my beaded purse for the silver coin I'm supposed to give her. Each invitation came with one, like an entry token. The silver relates to the alchemy theme of the movie, which is called *Ashes to Dust*. Dix's client, Arden Moore, plays an L.A. cop who gets caught up in an evil alchemist's scheme to turn the world to ashes. It was described as *Beverly Hills Cop* meets *Lord of the Rings*. Although we're just coming from the screening now, and I've got to say the film struck me as more *Miami Vice* meets *Dungeons and Dragons*. But Arden Moore looked entirely dreamy in every shot. Like when the evil alchemist burned off his shirt. And then his pants. Come to think of it, all those fireballs ever destroyed was Arden's wardrobe. So why did the world need to be saved again?

'Hi, Larissa!' I call brightly, holding out my silver coin, which has tonight's date, Thursday, July 6, embossed on the front. I love Larissa. She's totally my partner in crime. Like, she's promised that if Robbie Williams ever steps into Dix's office for any reason (and it's not improbable!), she'll immediately text message my cell phone with the code 'RW here 4 U' and I will drop everything and run. Faster than light, even on its fastest day. I've got a pair of Air Jordans under my desk just in case.

'Izzy!' Larissa stands to kiss me on the cheek. She always manages to look happy and calm even when a hundred people are trying to get her attention. 'Dix should be right inside. Have a great time!' She crosses out our names with her omnipresent pen, and that's the end of our navy-carpet journey.

Jamie's sulking as we approach the sleek steel doors. He seems frustrated – angry even – that the press and paparazzi haven't made more of a fuss over him. Jamie, what's happened to you? Has this celebrity fantasy become what he expects of everyday life? That photographers will fawn over him every second, snapping away at his merry-go-round of barely clothed dates? I can't keep ignoring all the fears that have been flitting around inside me. For his sake, if I'm to be a true friend, shouldn't I be saying something?

But in an instant, we're through the heavy doors, and my breath is catching in my throat. Dix has created an absolute wonderland! Rush has been transformed into an opulent array of luxury and color, rousing every sense to full attention. The trendy meatpacking-district restaurant's tables have been cleared away, and the marble floor eagerly awaits the eminent guests on their way from *Ashes to Dust*. A long, sparkling bar is stocked with every imaginable type of liquor and dozens of crystal glasses. Toward the back, the DJ is hunched over his lush leather booth, listening to a headset as his hands fly over the turntables. Red, orange, and yellow flowers entwine around the banisters of a double staircase leading upstairs to the lounge, which Dix has reserved for VIP access. The whole place is decorated with vibrant reds and oranges, making the space seem alive with magic flame. Ooh! Maybe Arden's clothes will get burned off again! Truthfully, that was my favorite part of the movie. Well, that and the part where the alchemist turned Kathie Lee Gifford into coal.

Jamie and I (and Celeste) are among the earlier guests, having walked the two blocks from the movie theater instead of fetching a limo (parking's such a pain!). Jamie taps me lightly on the arm and nods toward one side of the room, where Dix is talking to an older man in a dark blue suit. Oh, wow. That's my best friend! Over there, with the brilliant glow all around her. The one who looks like a goddess! Dix is absolutely ravishing in a red-and-orange Roberto Cavalli gown that – no surprise – hugs her figure tightly. Her sleek black hair cascades down in all its glory, and ruby earrings dangle to her shoulders. She's smiling wide as she talks, and – again, no surprise – the gentleman in the blue suit is hanging on her every word. But unfortunately for him, Dix has spotted us now. So after kissing the man on each cheek, she's gliding our way. Her feet seem to barely touch the surface, like she's skimming across water. The man gazes longingly after Dix, pining for a lost treasure he never had to begin with.

'Dix,' I say in awe when she reaches us. 'You are the hottest thing since sunburn.' I give her the biggest hug ever, hoping she can feel by osmosis how proud I am.

'Can you believe I'm nervous?' Dix whispers urgently into my ear. 'I must be, because my stomach has been queasy all week!'

Dix? Nervous? Good Lord, it's like I've just been told the emperor's wearing no clothes. I give her hand a squeeze and whisper back, 'I would never know, promise.'

'Damn straight, you'd never know.' Dix tosses her silky hair over her shoulder, taking a moment to survey the scene with her expert eye.

Jamie's attention, meanwhile, seems to be focused elsewhere, at a point beyond Dix's shoulder. 'Isn't that Richard Johnson?' He's craning his neck forward. 'From "Page Six"?' Then, after a beat of awkward silence, 'Oh, right! Dix, this is Celeste. She's an actress.'

Dix gives Jamie a smile I've seen many times before. The fake one, where her teeth don't show. It's the smile she uses with her clients. 'Don't be too obvious, darling,' she tells Jamie. 'If you court the press too hard, they'll forsake you like last season's shoe style. You'll be less popular than Uggs.'

Jamie recoils, instantly transforming his features into a look of studied nonchalance. He may as well be whistling with his hands clasped behind his back. Soon, though, Dix has to be off, greeting a new guest with a kiss and a smile. At her firm's functions, we get her for only a few minutes. There are too many other people who need her, too many details to oversee. No matter how many times I see her in action, Dix always floors me. I truly believe the woman is invincible. And if Jamie weren't being so selfish, he'd agree with me.

'Jamie.' I rest my hand on his shoulder as he's pretending to ignore the 'Page Six' guy. 'What the hell has gotten into you?'

'What are you talking about?' Jamie's hair flops forward, his warm brown eyes flashing confusion. For a second, he looks like the Jamie I remember.

'You've changed,' I say softly, feeling concern spread across my face. 'Jamie, you were my pillar of everything decent and kind. Now you're becoming so self-involved, I don't even know how to talk to you anymore.' Saying the words out loud is so much harder – and *realer* – than thinking them in my head.

Someone famous must be coming through the doors at just this moment, because Celeste is making these yappy noises and jumping around so much, I wonder if she doesn't have some Chihuahua in her.

'I haven't changed!' Jamie insists, actually seeming offended. How can he be so blind to himself? 'I'm just catching up, Iz. Come on. Add up all my dates in the past five years and compare the number to any normal guy's. I'm still behind.' His pained expression exposes ages of want. 'I'm still so behind.'

'Jamie, I'm not begrudging you your success,' I say sympathetically. 'How could I? I've hoped for it almost as long as you have.' I can see his eyes glazing over, like he's mentally shutting me out. 'Look around you!' I finally cry. 'Have you even congratulated Dix? Have you noticed how nervous she is? No! Your first instinct was to talk about yourself. If you were the old Jamie, you would have been *supporting* her. Like she's supported you since the day you two met. She's never been anything but there for you. And now when she needs us, you've got nothing to give.'

I'm almost panting. My face feels hot, and I realize my nails are digging into my palm.

'My God.' Jamie's head is tilted down now, the bravado seeping out of his shoulders. 'You're right. I'm an ass. I'm a total ass.'

'Arden Moore!' Celeste shrieks beside us. She's still jumping around, holding up her tube dress with both hands. She's had her eyes glued to the front door this whole time, waiting for a bona fide Grade A star. 'Can we meet him? I want to meet him!'

'Let's find Dix.' Jamie's nodding his head humbly. 'I've got to congratulate her.'

'What a good idea,' I say reassuringly. I'm feeling more relieved than the time my parents promised me that my first cat, Mr Pooky, hadn't run away at all, but was at kitty sleepaway camp. He sent me a lanyard bracelet that summer, which I found pretty impressive given his lack of opposable thumbs.

'I promised you I'd never change, didn't I?' Jamie's voice sounds husky. He rubs at his face with the back of his hand. 'I've snapped myself out of it. I promise.'

The crowd has thickened now, mostly with people I don't recognize. Could that be Elton John? No, wait. Just a man in a hot pink suit. There are sparkly dresses everywhere, and silky ones, and men wearing everything from crisply tailored jackets to leather pants (in the middle of summer?). I'm catching snippets of conversation as I pass by various champagne-swilling clusters. 'Her dress is so sheer you can see her stretch marks.' 'Wait, are you talking about his wife or his boyfriend?' 'I'm working now on *Desperate Housewives, the Musical – Wisteria Lane Sings!*' But most often what I hear on our way through the party is, 'Of *course* they're fake.'

At last, we catch up with Dix, who's fawning over a man with his back turned to me. One shriek from Celeste, though, and his identity is immediately revealed.

'Arden Moore!' she cries, skipping forward. 'I'm your biggest, biggest fan! I've seen *Road Hog* five times! I own the special-edition DVD of *Moon Rocket*!'

Arden Moore's been in some pretty crappy films, I'm realizing. But he sure is pretty in person. He looks taller than he does on-screen, if a bit less muscular, with caramel-colored hair and about three days' worth of stubble. He's wearing a rumpled suit without a tie, and his shirt is opened enough to display his hemp-rope necklace. On anyone else, this outfit would scream 'aging surfer.' On Arden Moore, it looks like a fashion ad. Arden's giving Celeste a smirk now, drawing a black felt pen out of his jacket pocket.

'Where do you want it?' he says lazily. 'Breast or leg?'

'Ooh!' Celeste pulls down her tube top to an almost indecent level. 'Right here! Eeeeeee!'

Arden Moore is signing a woman's breast. Jamie's looking on, unsure whether to be offended or just plain horrified. But then, I guess this is what life's like for a movie star. I try to picture an art groupie squealing at Grady Cole to sign her leg. But I'm pretty sure art lovers prefer their signatures on canvas.

'There you go, kid.' Arden winks at Celeste.

'Arden, these are my dearest friends, Jamie and Izzy.' Dix sounds so calm! Like she introduces movie stars to her friends *every day*. How cool is this!

'Hello.' Arden's attention is suddenly pinpointed – directly, without wavering – on me. '*Izzy*, was it? Izzy. I like that.'

Get out. Is Arden Moore . . .? No way. Arden Moore *cannot* be flirting with me!

'I like *Arden*, too.' I mimic his tone, willing my heart to slow its pounding.

'Then that makes two of us.' He arches an eyebrow suggestively. Okay. Pretty, yes. But not too bright.

Out of the corner of my eye, I see Jamie expressing heartfelt apologies to Dix, who's giving him her dazzling, real smile. Celeste is still fixated on Arden, a droplet of drool escaping one corner of her bright red mouth.

'The movie was a lot of fun!' I tell Arden, hoping I sound more like an equal than a fan. 'Your portrayal was really . . . powerful.'

Arden lifts his head toward the VIP lounge, up the flower-strewn double staircase. 'Join me at my table.' He's reaching his hand out for mine. 'You can tell me all about it.'

Really? I'm going to the superstar table? Well, sure. Why not? I've got on my swank empress-style dress, my hair's all smooth and neat, and after all, I am the associate dealer of one of New York's major galleries. Hey! Maybe I can get Arden interested in buying art! See how good at networking I am? Avery will be so impressed!

As Arden Moore takes my hand, I see Jamie trying to budge Celeste. But she's still riveted, stock-still, her hand holding the place where Arden's pen graced her skin. Dix has moved by now. She's kissing Joaquin Phoenix's cheek, like he's just another friend stopping by the party.

Arden Moore raises my hand as we approach the staircase. I can hear the flashes of the paparazzi snapping away behind us, sounding just like raindrops in a thunderstorm. Oh, my God, I could be in a magazine! Like, in *People* or *InStyle*, where they show pictures of celebrity parties! Or – I bet my back will be in a tabloid! Can't you see the headline now? ARDEN MOORE ESCORTS MYSTERY WOMAN AT EXCLUSIVE FILM PREMIERE. I go to lift up my long skirt with my free hand, because in movies, isn't that always the elegant way to ascend a staircase? But somehow my heel gets caught in the fabric. Oh, crap. Oh, *crap*. . I'm going to trip. Right here, on this marble staircase, in front of celebrity photographers and elite party-goers and the superfamous movie star holding my hand! New headline: ARDEN MOORE'S MYSTERY WOMAN FALLS FLAT ON HER MYSTERY FACE. Except I don't fall. Not even a little bit! Arden grabs my shoulders just in time and pulls me back, into his chest. He's *hugging* me. Flash, flash, flash, flash.

'I got you,' he says close to my ear.

'Thank you!' I cry gratefully.

'Oh, I've got you all right. Nice and tight.'

Um, yes, you do. And you may release me anytime now, Mr Famous Movie Star Who's Beginning to Sound a Bit Shady. There's something in Arden's tone that's putting me on guard. Like he's thinking about what parts of *me* he'll get to sign later on in the evening.

'See her?' Arden's leaning over the banister, pointing to a woman in a rust-colored cocktail dress. 'I hit that.' He turns to me with a crooked grin. 'Her too. And that chick over there? I hit that *twice*.'

He can't be serious. How am I supposed to respond here? *Gee, Arden, it's so refreshing to hear you speak of your sexual conquests as if you're physically hurting them. Can I get hit too? Pretty please?* We're almost at the top of the staircase, and all I want is to run back down.

'You know her, right?' Arden's pointing to a relatively famous independent-film actress at the top of the stairs. 'I hit that all over!'

We've barely stepped foot into the lounge area before Brittany Parker, Arden Moore's bubbly *Ashes to Dust* costar (she plays the alchemist's assistant, who gets hypnotized and tricked into . . . oh, it's so not worth it), bounds up to him, throwing her arms around his neck.

'Hey, baby,' Arden says flatly before wiggling out of her arms.

Brittany puffs out her lower lip, crossing her arms over her ample chest, as Arden grabs my hand again and pulls me toward the back of the room.

'Needy little wench,' he whispers.

That's it. There's my tolerance level, dozens of steps behind where I now stand. 'You know, I – uh –' I'm gazing longingly toward the staircase. How am I going to get away from this raging dickwad without offending him? He's Dix's biggest client, I keep telling myself. Your priority is to support her. Even if it means putting up with the mayor of Smarmyville. 'Never mind,' I say, almost cordially.

'What, you want me to sign you too?' He's actually pulling out his pen again.

'No, thanks.' I can barely hide the disgust in my voice. 'I'm not a huge fan of indelible marker.'

'No,' he says, licking his lips. 'You wouldn't be. You're classier than that, I can tell.'

Classier than indelible marker. Stand back while I swoon.

We're at a table now marked 'reserved,' with an enormous centerpiece of fiery flowers surrounded by a ring of votive candles. If I weren't so furious, I'd be memorizing every detail of the decor so I could praise Dix about it later. But I'm too busy keeping myself together. Arden Moore pulls out a chair from the table – is it for me? Ah, no. That would be too gentlemanly. He sits himself down, tapping his thumbs on his thighs.

I've got to join him. I've got to pull out the chair next to Arden – the one touching his leg, *ick*. I've got to smile politely and hide my waves of revulsion. I bet this is how those contestants feel on *Fear Factor*, when they're about to eat cricket brains or something. You can do it, Izzy. Just put your hand on the chair. See? That's not hard! Now pull it out. Come on. Pull!

But I don't even get the chance. Arden Moore is turning his baby blues up at me – at my breasts, actually – and letting loose a vulgar grin. 'Why don't you sit down,' he says, patting his lap with his palms, 'and we can talk *at length* about the first thing that pops up.'

I don't mean to do what I do; the impulse hits me before I can even regret it. An uncontrollable peal of laughter begins deep in my diaphragm and erupts so loudly that the conversation around us quiets. 'Are you for *real*?' I say, holding my stomach. Somewhere in my subconscious, I'm realizing that a few people are watching us. Okay, more than a few. Oh, shit. Everyone. 'Arden,' I hear myself saying, as if I'm watching the scene from the comfort of a darkened movie theater, 'you could be the biggest hammer in the world, and I the biggest nail, and you would still *never* "hit" this.'

And . . . oh, God . . . this mask of sheer rage passes over every one of Arden Moore's features. The veins in his neck are pulsing so hard that his rope necklace does a little dance. Arden's shooting up from his chair, and I swear, it looks like he's about to *actually* hit me. I stumble a few steps back. Then he turns on his heel, strides toward the staircase, and stomps purposely downward.

Oh, no.

Oh, no, no, no, no.

I start to run, pushing past people who have already moved aside. I grab the railing, absolutely paralyzed with terror, my knuckles turning white. Arden's cutting a straight line past the clicking photographers, past the sycophants trying to compliment him, past the many women with their many signable breasts. He surges past a dismayed Dix, who abandons Joaquin Phoenix to trail after him. But she's too late.

She's too late because Arden Moore's already on the other side of the heavy steel doors. He's already left his own party – which is Dix's party – which is now ruined. And it's all my fault.

All my horrifying, mortifying, unable-to-be-fixed, just-dashed-my-best-friend's-dreams, stinking fault.

*If this bar is a meat market,
you must be the prime rib.*

Pick up. *Pick up.* It's Friday morning, I'm at the gallery, and this is now officially the tenth time I've called Dix's home line. I haven't even been able to apologize yet, let alone explain that *I* was the one responsible for Arden Moore's fit of rage. With each unanswered ring, I feel another dart of dread. I can't close my eyes anymore without seeing Dix's look of horror last night. She must have spoken to a hundred reporters, but the damage couldn't be contained. This morning, both the *Post* and the *News* splashed the photos on their front pages: Arden Moore in his rumpled suit, storming out of the premiere for *Ashes to Dust.* The *News* couldn't resist the pun: HUMILIATED MOORE LEAVES PARTY IN ASHES.

It's possible she's just turned off her ringer, I tell myself. Because I'm sure publicists always turn their phones off in the middle of a crisis. Right. Or maybe she's at the office. I just can't believe she's ignoring me. If Dix knew I was responsible for Arden's early exit, wouldn't she have called? If for nothing else than to ask, *How could you?* That's what I've been asking myself, every single minute since last night. My desk is heaped with work for the day – I've got two collector presentations this afternoon, and I haven't even pulled any paintings from inventory yet. But how can I focus on *my* career, when I've quite possibly ruined that of my best friend in the world?

Biting my thumbnail, I pick up the phone receiver and dial Dix's work number. It's ringing. *And ringing*.

'Dorothea Dixon Public Relations,' Larissa's voice finally comes over the line. For the first time ever, she sounds harried.

'Larissa, it's Izzy.' I very nearly start spewing out a thousand *I'm sorry*s right away.

'Izzy, Dix isn't in the office right now.' I'm trying to gauge if she's been asked to hold my calls.

'Should I call her cell?' My voice is shaky. I feel tears pricking at the corners of my eyes.

There's a pause, and then Larissa says dryly, 'Now might not be the best time. But you could try.'

My hands are trembling as I dial Dix's cell number. More ringing. I leave a voice mail asking her to call me. Then I ring Jamie's cell. God, even *he's* not answering. 'It's Jamie,' says his voice mail. 'I'm out someplace that's too loud to hear you. So leave a message.'

'Jamie?' I nearly whisper into the phone after the beep. 'I can't find Dix.'

But what's worse, I don't know if she wants to be found.

'I've got the tickets.' I absolutely jump at the sound of Avery's voice as he appears through the French doors, holding his titanium briefcase. 'We're booked at the Villa d'Araggio, right on the water.' He's resting the briefcase on his desk, popping it open, and taking out a brochure. Avery's a vision in crisp white trousers and a light blue dress shirt that accentuates his tan.

'Great!' I manage, wiping my thumbs across my cheeks. I can't help but get excited at the thought of Avery and me sipping cappuccinos at a Venetian villa . . . but then I just feel even more guilty. How dare I fantasize about locking eyes with Avery over a bowl of gelato when I should be focusing on Dix. Oh, God, there's the panic again. The waves of dread. I've got to fix what I've done. I've just got to.

'Are you all right?' Avery's peering at me with concern. 'You don't look so . . . well.'

I give a halfhearted smile. 'Thanks, Avery. I'm okay.' The scourge of my best friend's career, but okay. 'A friend of mine's in trouble, and I haven't any idea how to help her.'

Avery grabs a tissue from his desk and crosses the office, handing it to me with an empathetic smile. 'Sounds dismal,' he says. 'But I bet I can take your mind off it, if that's what you're looking for.'

Do you see why I'm over the moon for this man? I blink my eyes a couple of times before answering. 'Maybe. I mean, if you've got something really good . . .' Like, say, unbuttoning your shirt?

Avery twitches his eyebrows. 'I do.'

He swings around, with a jaunt in his step that provokes me to follow. Avery situates his briefcase neatly at one corner of the antique desk, lifting out a brown file folder and opening the front flap. We're both leaning over the front of the desk as he pulls out a set of drawings – schematics, it seems, with measurements and notes along the edges – and lays them out one by one across the desk.

'What am I looking at?' I ask, trying to make sense of what looks like an architectural model. For a . . . for a bar? Actually, it looks like *two* bars. With stools, and slick surfaces, and mood lighting. Is Avery planning to moonlight as a nightclub promoter?

Leaning his frame against the desk, Avery crosses his arms. He's beaming with satisfaction. 'That,' he says, pointing to the series of drawings, 'is our next show.'

Hang on. 'We're having our next show . . . in a *bar?*' Although, when you think about it, that would save me the trouble of ordering wine for the opening. And, ooh! I could have vodka gimlets at work. And cocktail olives. Why haven't we thought of this before?

'No, no.' Avery gives a laugh. 'The bar *is* the show. An installation, right here in the gallery. One bar per exhibition room. The first one will be a replica of La Boom on West Twelfth Street, and the second will recreate the Huxley on Avenue A. One East Side, one West Side. You've got to love the symmetry.'

I roll the idea around in my head. An installation of two New York bars. Not something sellable, really, unless to a museum. But that's okay. With our previous installations, we've been able to sell photographic documentation. The thing I'm missing here is the *point*. Replication for its own sake? Strikes me as kind of boring. But look at Avery's face! He's so excited by the idea, so alive with the possibilities. Clearly, I'm missing something. Maybe the bar's made out of something organic, like . . . chocolate? Chocolate *and* alcohol. Now, that's something to get excited about!

'The artist is named Elmore Cowper.' Avery's peering closely at the schematics. 'The project will be combined installation and performance art, evolving every day it's in the gallery.'

Hey, that's interesting. A continual work in progress. And yes, Avery, you may keep brushing your arm against mine. And your leg needn't move at all. It's fine just where it is, touching my thigh. Because you know what? We leave for Venice next week. We're going to be more than functional.

'For one month, Cowper will be spending every night alternately at La Boom and the Huxley, in a perpetual search for female companionship. He'll document his successes the next day at the gallery, by pasting a souvenir of each encounter on the appropriate simulated bar top.'

Er . . . did I just hear that correctly? 'Avery.' I'm keeping my voice light. 'Do you mean that the artist will be picking up women every night? And using the evidence as his art?' I'm squinting now, waiting for him to laugh again.

'In a nutshell, yes.' Avery's gathering up the drawings carefully, his face still glowing. 'They'll be mostly phone numbers, we imagine. Maybe a lipstick-marked napkin here or there, or occasionally – Cowper hopes, at least – a forsaken item of clothing. There will be a small card included as well, with a narrative of the meeting – what pickup line he used, how far the encounter went. That sort of thing. Can you imagine anything more visceral?'

Visceral? I stand back, appalled. 'Will the women know they're only part of an art project? Will they be giving permission for their phone numbers to be exhibited? What if we get sued?' I can feel my head shaking back and forth with concern.

'Yes, I had thought of that.' Avery's giving me a reassuring smile. 'But the Bond family lawyers are the best in the world. I can't imagine the opposition would have a chance.'

I feel the revulsion rising inside me. How can we associate Emerson Bond's good name with this exploitation of women? 'Is Cowper looking for love? Will he be contacting these women ever again?'

'Don't know.' Avery's tone is breezy. 'Hadn't thought about it that far. But you see, *this* is the type of art I want to bring to the Bond. Art that raises questions, provokes discussion. Something daring.' He opens his briefcase again, returning the drawings to their folder and taking out another piece of paper. What now? An exhibition featuring *Playboy* photographers?

Avery hands me the sheet of paper and snaps his briefcase shut. I give the paper a quick scan. I know what it is. I'm just not quite believing it. A video artist who plants cameras in other people's bathrooms. A sculptor whose works include parts of endangered animals. A dealer known for bidding up his own artists at auctions in order to keep their gallery prices unjustifiably high. I'm holding in my hands a list of everything I hate about the art world. The heading reads, *Venice Biennale*.

Has Avery gone mad? Why does his list of meetings read like a Who's Who of scandal and deprivation? I'm scrambling to think of something positive to say ('What high-quality paper this is, Avery!') when I come to a sudden revelation. I don't have to! That's the whole reason Avery made me his associate dealer in the first place. So I could rein him in when his avant-garde ideas crossed a line our collectors couldn't tolerate. What was it he said to me at dinner? *You'll be my ballast. Securing my feet to the ground.* Well, get ready, Avery, because when I'm done, your walking days will be over.

'I admire your instinct to show an artist whose work is so profoundly personal,' I begin, stepping away from the desk. The authority in my voice surprises even myself. 'But I can't agree with you, Avery, that Cowper's work makes a good fit for the Bond.'

'Is that right?' Avery sounds taken aback. His eyebrows are sinking in the middle of his forehead, giving him an irritated expression. Which I'm sure just means he's having an intense thought. 'What makes you say that?'

'I'm not convinced Cowper's project is ethical,' I go on. How cool is this? I sound *just* like an associate dealer. 'Without full disclosure to the women involved – the women Cowper will be picking up – I don't see how exhibiting their phone numbers or lipstick smears or . . . whatever else can be anything other than exploitation.'

'But don't you understand?' Avery's pacing the office with swift, jerky movements. 'Cowper will be recreating his life experience as art, exhibiting a physical manifestation of his interaction as a substitute for the real thing.'

'I do follow your point,' I say, straightening my torso. 'But the Bond collectors will not respond positively to the project, I'm certain of it. There's something . . .' and here I have to wonder if I'm not superimposing my own feelings onto this exhibition. Have I put myself too much in the heads of these unsuspecting women? But no. My job is to follow my instincts. I can't start to doubt myself just because Avery has stopped casually brushing up against me. 'Avery, quite frankly, there's something seedy in the vision for this project. I know our collectors, and I'm sure that they too will be left with feelings of distaste.'

'I see.' Avery's eyes have taken on a stony glaze. 'And what of the list I've given you? The one you're holding now?'

Gosh, he sounds scary. So cold and hard! But what can I do? If I don't voice my opinion now, Avery will be spending the entire time in Venice meeting with artists entirely wrong for our gallery. When Avery promoted me, I made a promise – I vowed to curb him when he went too far. So if I'm going to do my job well, then that's what I've got to do.

'Avery, in my mind, you've crossed the line from daring to indecent,' I say, struggling not to sound like I'm chastising. 'You've asked my opinion, which I feel obligated to give as truthfully as possible. And I have to wonder if your strategy is simply to court sensationalism at every corner.'

Avery's breath quickens, puffing from his nostrils in staccato bursts. He's standing absolutely still. I've secured his feet to the ground, all right. But the last thing I want to do is anger him! I'm not trying to be harsh or argumentative, but I must be saying this all wrong. The words must not be coming out the way I'm thinking them in my head. I'll try a different track. It'll be okay.

'I like the ice sculptor still!' I blurt out, referring to the artist Avery first mentioned during our dinner, the one who sculpts ice while immersed in a freezing-cold glass chamber. Now, that's visceral. 'But Avery, think about it.' I'm keeping my voice soothing, conversational. 'We've got to honor the vision of a man now lost. We will always be showing under Emerson Bond's name. And I can't imagine he created this gallery for the purpose of displaying bathroom-themed video art.'

'I'm the dealer,' Avery says curtly, his mouth set in a firm line. 'Not Emerson Bond. I have a vision too, Isabel, and it doesn't involve remaining stragnant. Change will reinvigorate our work here.'

'You're right!' I nod rapidly. 'I totally agree! I just ask that you reconsider the *direction* of your changes. Considering our clientele and all.'

'Noted,' Avery says coolly. 'Duly noted.'

'Great!' I give him a big, enthusiastic smile. I'm

returning to my own desk, pulling out my chair. 'See? I'm reining you in! I'm acting as your ballast, just like you asked me to!'

Avery's focus remains riveted to his desk blotter, as if it's spelling out the final 'Who done it?' of a page-turning crime novel. He says simply, 'Indeed.'

Later, when we're actually in Venice, I know Avery will thank me for doing my job. He just needs some time to let go of his ideas, to open his mind to new ones. So for the rest of the day, I work on not regretting what I've said to him. I work on not letting myself worry when Avery won't meet my eye for the entire time we're in the office together. I work on not tensing up when he gives me nothing but a curt 'Well-done' after I sell paintings at *each* of my collector presentations. I know Avery will come around soon, maybe even tomorrow. He'll be drowning me in gratitude. Big, heaping barrelfuls of gratitude.

That's what I keep telling myself, anyway.

Total phone calls: twenty-six. Total voice mail messages: thirteen. Total e-mails: seven. Total handwritten, five-page letters pouring out my heart: one. Total times I've reached Dix to apologize hugely and repeatedly: zero.

By the end of the day, I'm convinced that modern communication has failed me. Clearly I've got only one alternative. I'll go to Dix's office myself. And if she's not there, her apartment. And if she's not there, her favorite bar at the corner that has all the hot bartenders. And if she's not there, well, I'm going to need a drink anyway.

I leave for Venice next week. I can't go without talking to Dix first. I just can't! What if, God forbid, something happens with the plane? And we wind up crashing on a deserted island like in that show *Lost*, stranded with a hobbit and the big brother from *Party of Five*? Then I'll *never* have another chance to apologize. And Dix will never know why Arden stormed out of her party! How can I let that happen?

I'm supposed to go to a handful of gallery openings

tonight in Chelsea, but I'll have to miss them all. Whatever Dix needs me to do, I'll do. Together, we'll find a way to fix the Arden situation. Because united, the two of us have always been invincible. Alone, however, I am much stronger after I've stuffed my face with junk food – for courage. So before I descend the steps to the 6 train station, I head to the news kiosk where I go occasionally – okay, fine, every day – for a Dove Bar or a Kit Kat. Or a Twix, or a Hershey's with Almonds. Oh, God, I can't wait. My mouth is watering so much I could irrigate the Sahara.

'Hi, Abdul!' I call to the ever-busy kiosk proprietor. Somehow, even though he's stuck in a box all day, Abdul never runs out of things to do. Right now he's reaching over his display, straightening the magazines so the stacks are precisely one inch apart.

'Hello, Chocolate Lady!' he greets me with a smile. 'No newspapers for you, I know. No magazines!'

Good Lord. Even Abdul the news kiosk man knows my greatest weakness. I'm Chocolate Lady! What's next? Will my dry cleaner start calling me Pastel Lady? At my local take-out place, will I be Vegetable Dumpling Lady? I cannot be this predictable. Not even the groundhog on Groundhog Day is this predictable. So, yes, I will have my DoveBar. I would be cruel not to, with Abdul so smiley about it. But I will *also* find a new and exciting publication to read, thank you very much. I've got a long plane trip coming up, after all, and what if the in-flight movie is something like *Gigli*?

'Actually, I think I *will* have a little look-see,' I say pleasantly to Abdul. 'Even though I get most of my newspapers from work.' There, see? I *am* highly literate and up on all current events. So I won't be missing anything if, say, instead of perusing the *New York Times*, I thumb through a tabloid or two. How can you resist the headlines? JUSTIN TIMBERLAKE AND CAMERON DIAZ SWITCH HAIRCUTS; JESSICA SIMPSON AND NICK LACHEY SAY: WE WERE NEVER MARRIED AND WE DON'T REALLY SING!; ASHES TO

DUST STAR ARDEN MOORE BURNED BY UNIDENTIFIED
MYSTERY WOMAN AT BIG PREMIERE.

Wait. What was that? Are those pictures of – ? No, it
can't be. . . .

Oh, holy mother of crap.

It's me. A whole photomontage of me, or rather my
back, in its dramatically plunging white goddess dress.
There's my back headed up Rush's staircase, my hand in
Arden Moore's. There's my back falling forward with
Arden Moore reaching to catch it. There's my back being
held in Arden Moore's arms. Then, at the bottom of the
page, there's Arden Moore by himself, his hands balled
into fists, taking the stairs down two at a time.

Two words pop violently into my head. When I close
my eyes, I see them pulsing there behind my eyelids, like
they've been written by the sun. *Dix knows*. I snatch up the
tabloid with all its condemning photos and bold lettering
and cheap color printing. I hold out my money with a
quivering hand, letting Abdul pick out the exact change
from my palm. What do I do? How can I show my face at
Dix's office, where everyone must hate me? Really really
hate me?

I grab at my purse, tugging open the zipper and
reaching around for my cell phone. My fingers are almost
too jittery to work, but all I need to press is redial.

'Dix,' I say into the receiver when her cell voice mail
picks up. 'I'll be at your apartment in twenty minutes. And
if you're not there, I'll be outside your door when you come
home. I am so, so sorry.'

As I turn my now infamous back to the news kiosk, I
hear Abdul calling out 'Good-bye, Tabloid Lady!'

If he only knew.

I wait almost all night in front of Dix's door. For hours, I sit
on the hard, high-concept-design floor of her SoHo loft
hallway. The air is cooler here than outside but still without
air-conditioning, and I find myself reaching an almost
trancelike state in all the heat and despair. At one point, I

must fall asleep, because suddenly it's five A.M. There's no way Dix could have gotten through the door without waking me, and I'm sure I don't hear her moving about inside. She's not coming home, I realize with a pang of hopelessness, and I've got to be at work in five hours. So I give up. I take the saddest taxi ride ever home and, when I'm in front of my bathroom mirror, realize I must have slept on the tabloid's front page, because it is now smeared all over my face. And sure enough, there's my sweaty cheek imprint on the newspaper photograph, right where my dress plunges at its lowest. I've slept on my own butt. I am literally a butt face.

I seize onto the one conciliatory thought that pops into my head. The one teeny ray of brightness in an otherwise dank and dismal wasteland:

How could I possibly sink any lower?

24

*You must be a stewardess, 'cause my
tray just returned to its upright position.*

Over the next few days, I feel more alone than I ever
thought possible, both at home and at work.
Whenever Grady's at the gallery, he can barely look me in
the eye. How ironic, I think to myself, that I would give
anything for him to start calling me Princess again. Avery,
meanwhile, is continuing work on the Cowper installation,
which he plans to open in early August. He's courting
every press contact he's ever made in New York and
throughout the world. The buzz has already started, and
the general consensus is that this show will herald a bold
new direction for the Bond.

We've also got a new employee. Beth. Beth with her
color-coordinated file system and freakish desire to do
more work than is on her daily to-do list. Beth with her
crease-free white shirts and tidy black leather pumps. Beth
is our new gallery director. Avery hired her without even
consulting Kimmy or me. I don't like her so much. Mostly
because she doesn't say things like 'Hi' or 'How are you?'
Beth's more of a first-thing-in-the-morning-before-coffee
'Do-we need all these slides or can't we store some as
JPEGS?' kind of gal. But I'm sure I just haven't warmed up
to her yet.

'*Time Out*' has asked for a press packet, and they're

considering an interview with Cowper,' Beth says in her staccato, computerlike voice. She's sitting in front of Avery's desk with her legs crossed, writing furiously on a legal pad. Her dark hair is pulled so tightly back into its bun that her eyes have a permanent look of surprise.

'Excellent, Beth!' Avery nods approvingly from behind his desk. 'Keep me informed of any new developments.'

'Of course, sir,' she says, with no hint of emotion.

I'm tapping loudly at my keyboard, trying to look as though I'm corresponding with a new and important artist I'd like to recruit for the Bond, when actually, I'm answering an e-mail from my mom. I've got my head lifted high, and I'm pausing occasionally to stroke my chin, all the while writing to my mother that I'm sure she has a summer cold and not, in fact, the Asian bird flu.

'Isabel,' Avery intones without looking up, 'you'll show Beth how to catalog new inventory? We're expecting about a half-dozen Cowper drawings next week.'

'Sure!' I chime out with feeling. See, Beth? *Feeling*.

Beth will be in charge of the gallery while Avery and I are in Venice, and I must remember to tell her she's not allowed to clean my desk, or for that matter touch my desk. Because she'll get efficiency cooties on it. I *have* a system, Miss Frownsalot. My own very effective 'if the boring work's at the bottom of the pile, then I don't have to do it' flawless-type system. And fine. I know I'm being too harsh. I'm sure Beth's very nice and smart and I just haven't gotten to know her yet, blah-blah. But still. Don't touch my desk, you unfeeling robot ice queen.

Avery and I haven't seen each other much this week. He's been relying on Beth to help him prepare for the Cowper installation, probably because he knows how I feel about it. Or maybe he just wants to give me time to create my own list of pavilions to visit in Venice – every country gets its own. I'm hoping to convince Avery that the Bond should lobby to get one of our artists in the American pavilion at the next Biennale. We can make Venice our special trip, just the two of us.

Because surely, once we're in Europe together, Avery's recent coolness toward me will fade. He'll give me those longing smiles again. He'll touch my cheek, my arm, my hair, just like he used to. Surely, when we've got no one else but each other, and we're looking out over the water at sunset, and we're working as a team to represent our dear gallery, surely then he'll stop treating me as something . . . *less* than functional.

And while I'm gone, Dix will have time to cool off and let things settle down with Arden Moore. She just needs her space for a few more days. When I get back, she'll be ready to hear my apology, and I won't be ripping my hair out with worry that I haven't spoken to my best friend for a whole week. In fact, I'm sure she'll be leaving a message on my answering machine the minute I hit Italian soil. Which will be . . . tomorrow! God, how can I wait? Come tomorrow, I will have in my grasp everything I've ever hoped for, both professionally and personally. Every dream I've held on to since I was a young girl bringing my Barbie and Ken dolls to the Museum of Modern Art so they could fall in love in front of Picasso's *Desmoiselles d'Avignon*. Truly, the anticipation is overwhelming. You know when you're so excited that you feel you're raising the very notion of excitement to a whole new level? That's where I'm at. That whole new level.

Oh, holy God, I am going to die.

My clothes have turned into stone. Because there is *no friggin' way* that fabric can be this heavy. I'm half pulling, half dragging my overstuffed suitcase up the Bond's limestone steps, convinced I will be in Venice with nothing to wear except granite. They will call me Signora of the Rocks.

I glare harshly at my bag. *Suitcase?* I feel like saying. *You don't want to mess with me right now.* It must get the message, because a final, desperate heave gets us up the last step. It's 7 : 50 A.M. and I'm due to meet Avery inside in ten minutes. We'll be sharing a town car from the gallery to JFK Airport, and all I can say is, that car better have a huge trunk. Venice is in the midst of a heat wave, so you'd think – easy! No luggage! Tiny tank tops and flip-flops galore! Which I've got. But there are also work outfits, and beach outfits, and party outfits, and dinner-with-Avery outfits, and 'What if the pavilions don't have air-conditioning?' outfits, and 'What if the pavilions have too much air-conditioning?' outfits, and pajama outfits, and sexier nightgown outfits, and 'What if those night-gowns are too sexy?' outfits. I've got day makeup and night makeup. Five pairs of shoes. My 250-dollar bikini. Every hair product I own. Three kinds of perfume. This month's *Lucky* magazine, which I will read if Avery falls asleep on the plane. *Art in America* and the *Wall Street Journal*, which I will read while Avery's awake. Toothbrush. Floss. Contact lens solution. And more. Much, much, much more.

Good Lord, how am I going to get it back down again?

Avery will help, I think to myself. He's a gentleman, after all. Perched on top of my suitcase near the Bond's reception ledge, I get this picture in my head. Avery's sliding into the leather town car seat, right beside me. He kisses my cheek, exclaiming, 'You look well, Isabel, for this early in the morning.' He puts his arm around me, we share a muffin from the local fancy patisserie, and our grand adventure has finally begun! Flying is so fun. And it's so much *more* fun when you're with someone you like. Sharing an armrest, maybe even a blanket. Quite intimate, really, when you think about it. So why is it eight o'clock? *And why is there no Avery?*

I give a self-deprecating laugh and roll my eyes. If I'm this eager now, how will I ever keep my cool once we get to Italy? I take a deep breath and vow to wait patiently. Which I do. For all of three minutes.

It can't hurt to give Avery a wee call. I've got his cell number in the office. After all, what if he's overslept? I scurry through the exhibition rooms and through the French doors, clicking on the light. Where's my Rolodex?

And *why is my desk so messy?* I can just see Beth's chilly lips mouthing 'I told you so.' Oh! Here it—

Hang on.

Why is there a note, written on Bond stationery, taped to my computer screen? And *oh, God,* why is it saying —?

I've got to sit down. Right now. I pull out my desk chair and sink into it, tearing the note down from my computer and reading it over, more slowly this time. I don't understand. How could he—

> *Isabel:*
>
> *Forgive me for misplacing your home phone number. I must make sure to get it from you again, please remind me. Reports from Venice indicate the heat wave has worsened to the highest temperatures in the city's modern memory. Lars Handelnik, the ice sculptor you and I were so excited about, will not be attending the Biennale due to a breakdown in his cooling equipment. Indeed, I have gotten word that several other of my meetings have been canceled, and my workload will be significantly decreased.*
>
> *In addition, even though I anticipate that next week will be a slow one for the gallery, I would feel more confident with you left in charge. And so, in light of these new developments, it only makes sense for you to remain in New York. I am certain you will agree.*
>
> *We will see you next week upon our return.*
> *Sincerely,*
> *Avery Devon*

No. But . . . *no.* I can't move. I literally can't even lift my arm. It's like every ounce of energy has fizzled from my body. How am I ever going to get out of this chair? *Oh, God,* how could this have happened?

But I know *exactly* how it happened. I screwed up. I thought — I *honestly* thought — that I was doing my job when I contradicted Avery's plans for the gallery. Was I even listening to myself? *Oh, no, Avery. Your ideas are such crap! We should do everything the way it was done before you became the dealer. I am not open to change. Not at all. So certainly don't take me with you to the Biennale. Because I'll probably just spit on your ideas there too.*

I'm not quite certain how to cope right now. Should I try to reach Avery at the airport? Maybe I can convince him that I'll be entirely responsive to his new ideas – no matter how disgusting they are. He said he would be – No, wait. Avery didn't say *he* at all, did he? I snatch the paper up, scanning the bottom lines. I'm right. He said *we*.

Who's we?

Who's WE?!!

I'm scrambling for my Rolodex again, flipping the cards to Avery's information. There it is, next to his home number. *Doorman: 212–555–9784.* My hand feels leaden as I pick up the receiver and start dialing. I don't even know what I'm hoping to find out. In fact, hope itself is a concept I'm altogether unfamiliar with right now.

'Twenty-seven East Sixty-fifth Street,' I hear a jolly voice say on the other end of the line.

'Avery Devon,' I blurt out, my vocal cords constricted. 'I mean, did you see him just now? Leaving in a town car, to go to the airport?'

'Indeed, ma'am,' the jovial doorman responds. 'Mr Devon's expected back by the end of next week.'

'I–I know, thanks. But did he –' I ball my free hand into a fist, squeezing as hard as I can. 'Was Avery alone? Because . . . my sister was supposed to go with him, and I . . . um . . . want to make sure she made it okay.'

'He did have a companion, ma'am,' the doorman answers casually. 'Fair skin, official-looking lass,' and here I realize what I recognized as enthusiasm in the doorman's voice was really an Irish accent. 'Your sister could stand to let her hair down some, don't you think?' He gives a friendly chuckle.

'Her . . . hair . . . down?' The words come out as a rasp, barely above a whisper. My stomach hurts. It hurts so bad.

'Was she wearing . . .?' Deep breaths. 'Tell me, was she dark-haired, wearing a white shirt and black round-toe pumps?'

'Can't say I looked so close, ma'am,' the doorman says. 'But now that you mention it, yes, I think so. White shirt, plain black shoes. You know your sister well!'

'Thank you,' I manage, letting the phone fall back in its cradle.

It's even worse than I thought. So help me, it's a million times worse. Avery's not going to Venice alone at all.

He's taking Beth.

The taxi deposits me, numb and shaking, on the curb in front of my apartment – a mere hour and a half after I finally finished packing. Never mind that it's Friday and I'm supposed to be in charge of the gallery. Never mind that Kimmy thinks I'm in Venice, so she won't be calling if anything goes wrong. I need to be in my bed right now. And quite possibly forevermore.

I'm working on instinct here. I'm opening the front door to my apartment building and getting myself through the door because that's what I always do. If I had to think about it, I would probably crumple to the floor with the effort. So when I get through my building's entryway, I find myself doing what I always do. I'm checking my mail. Here I am, pretty much emotionally destroyed – more than I ever was by Cameron, or my artist ex-boyfriend, Seth, or even Jared Anders. And what do I do? I check my mail. The sheer ordinariness of the action almost makes me laugh out loud.

But what's in my mailbox is anything but ordinary. It's a shiny sateen box, with grosgrain ribbons crisscrossing everywhere. And inside, it's tissue paper, and sequins, and fabric butterflies. When I open the folded paper, unleashing glitter all over my luggage, the tinkly sound of 'It Had to Be You' rings out through the hallway.

How wrong I was to think things couldn't get any worse.

I'm holding in my weary, feeble hands the singing invitation for Mimi's wedding. To which I had planned to take Avery. Mimi wasn't exaggerating when she said the invitations would be late. The wedding is two weeks from tomorrow.

I feel my back sliding down against the wall until I'm sitting on the cold, tiled floor. I cover my face with my hands, letting my head drop to my knees. There's no way to hold in the heaving, hiccuping sobs anymore.

There's just no possible way.

You'll do.

I eat a lot of chocolate over the next two weeks. That, and I thank God for Kimmy a whole lot. She's so angry at Avery, she draws a new series in her notebook entitled *The Bastard of the Bond*. Avery starts out as a golden-haired knight and ends up a heinous, knobby troll, transformed by the evil wizard, Venice.

Meanwhile, Wizard Venice also seems to have fused Avery and Beth into one being, albeit with two distinct heads. Either that, or their *I*'s never made it to baggage claim. Because since their return, the two of them speak only in *We*. As in 'We need you, Isabel,' or 'We're off to Cowper's studio,' or 'Look, we've formed this exclusive club that's only for the two of us, so buzz the hell off.' Avery's barely even looked at me since they got back. I swear, sharing an office with those two is like a constant slap in the face. I've been feeling as small and unwanted as the dust bunnies under my desk chair. Which, by the way, I keep picking up and throwing away. Because do I really need Beth scowling at me over a fleck of dirt that it's *her job* to prevent in the first place?

I force myself to focus on the figures on my desk – a list of measurements for the building materials we'll need. Today, Grady's show comes down, and next week, building begins on Cowper's installation. I've made sure the plywood boards will fit through the door and around the necessary corners – meaning, I've done Beth's job for her *again*. For all her clipboards and lists, all Beth really seems able to do is exclaim, 'Yes, Avery! Of course, Avery! You're so right, Avery!' And the sad thing is, that's all he seems to want. I've discovered the real reason Avery promoted me to associate dealer. Not so that I could participate in his aesthetic choices, or argue against their worth to the gallery, as he said. But so that I could make his ideas more palatable to our collectors. He wants me to agree with everything he does – and then sell it to our clients. I'm a glorified sales clerk. I may as well be working at The Gap.

As I'm getting up to give these figures to Kimmy, I catch sight of the plastic-wrapped dress hanging from the coatrack behind me. Right now, with Grady's show officially over and the gallery closed, I've got on jeans, a white tank top, and flip-flops. But tonight, I'll be wearing the beautiful creation hanging here. It's almost diaphanous, the way it falls in layers to the floor. A true gown, the color of barely brewed tea ('ecru,' the saleslady called it), with a deep V-neck vanishing into a satin-wrapped waist. And then the floaty layers of sheer fabric, not too poufy, cascading to the ground like an enchanted waterfall. I'm going to look amazing in that dress. Or at least, I better. Because that dress, and Jamie's support as my date, are all that are going to get me through Mimi's wedding tonight.

Thankfully, the 'We Brigade' are off to a long lunch with Elmore Cowper, so I can safely make my way through the exhibition rooms. Truly, if I have to overhear one more private joke about Venetian Chianti, I might just drown myself in it. But Kimmy's the only one here now, and she won't care if I let my brave front falter. So as soon as I reach reception, I lay my head down on the ledge, allowing her to pat my hair.

'He's such a jerk, Iz,' she whispers, standing behind her desk. 'Don't you see that now?'

'Kimmy, I was so stupid,' I hear myself saying. 'Because I *knew* I was going to get hurt. I had this dome around myself. This antimagnetic dome, with lasers and everything.' I'm lifting my head up now, brushing my hair off my face.

'Lasers?' Kimmy's looking at me funny. 'You had lasers?'

'No, I mean –' I take a deep breath. 'I knew I should have kept Avery at arm's length. That I trust people too easily.' I'm pushing against the ledge with both hands, letting my head sag down. 'Yet I still allowed myself to hope. And not just a little bit! I had these big bushels of hope, just bulging out of me. Like a moron. So now I'm paying the price.'

'Don't say that,' I hear softly behind me.

I spin around, taken completely off guard. It's Grady Cole, his arms full of glassine paper, plastic wrap, and cardboard. Of course. Grady's here to wrap his paintings so we can crate them for shipping. He's giving me that familiar smile – the one I used to think was smug. But now I see it's more easygoing than self-satisfied. Like he's waiting to see which of life's foibles will amuse him next.

'Eavesdrop much?' The barb is out of my mouth before I even realize. It's like my brain can't remember that Grady's already angry with me. Somehow, I've reverted to the antagonistic banter of two long months ago.

'I guess I do,' Grady shoots back harmlessly, making his way over the threshold and dropping his wrapping materials to the floor.

Hang on. Is Grady talking to me again?

'You know, we usually hire art handlers to prepare our paintings for shipping,' I try tentatively. 'You don't have to do it yourself.'

Grady tugs at his T-shirt, which has pressed against him in the humidity outside. 'I want to do it,' he says decisively. 'No one else would be as careful.'

I watch Grady through the archway as he gets to work, spreading a large sheet of acid-free glassine on the floor of the larger exhibition room. I admire him, okay? I admit it. His dedication to his work, the care he's showing the collectors who now own these paintings – it's not usual, I can tell you that much.

Kimmy's making these head motions at me, widening her eyes and pointing in Grady's direction. What's she going on about? Grady doesn't need my help. He probably doesn't even want it. Why is Kimmy trying to get rid of me?

'You've got work to do?' I glance at her desk, which looks pretty clean since she's already mailed out the invitations to Cowper's opening.

'Yeah,' Kimmy deadpans. 'Tons.' She juts her head toward Grady again. I must really be interrupting her!

'Sorry!' I whisper guiltily. Avery or Beth must have her on some sort of assignment. So . . . fine. I'll just hang out with Grady. Whether he wants me to or not.

'I've always loved that one,' I say, crossing my legs on the floor next to him. He's wrapping up the *Quaker Oats, 2000*. Which now belongs to Dix.

Man. At even the thought of Dix, I get this awful, plunging feeling. I can't imagine what she's going through right now. Neither Jamie nor I have seen her since the *Ashes to Dust* premiere. Jamie says I shouldn't worry, that she probably just needs time to work everything out, and did I see him and his hot date on 'Page Six' again? I won't lie. It's been hard to believe that Jamie's snapped himself out of his egocentric stupor. But I'll have another heart-to-heart talk with him tonight at the wedding. I mean, he's promised to be my date – for that alone, he deserves at least a dozen antiselfish points.

'You all right?' Grady's eyes are fixed on my face, which is no doubt telegraphing the concern I'm feeling.

I search his face for a moment. 'Why are you suddenly talking to me again?' I ask instead of responding to his question. I'm fiddling with the hem of my tank top. 'Is it to say "I told you so"? About Avery, I mean.'

Grady's deft fingers are taping up the corners of the packed-up painting, pressing delicately against the

protective cardboard. 'Nah,' he throws out. 'Not worth it.
The guy is . . .' Grady lets out a heavy sigh. 'Devon's hard
to resist. I know that better than most people. I've . . . been
there.'

He has? Oh, my God, *see*? I *knew* Avery was gay! And
Grady fell for him! So that's the big damn secret. How
could I not have admitted it to myself, about Avery? He
gets manicures! What was I waiting for, a plane to fly by
with a banner saying 'Izzy, snap out of it. Your hot boss is
gay!'? Total surprise about Grady, though, I'll give on that
one. But still . . . art world, man . . . not a huge stretch.

'*Not* what I mean, Iz!' Grady cries out, seeing my
expression. 'I'm not – I am *so* not – not that there's
anything wrong with—'

'Of course there's nothing wrong with –' I'm nodding
my head vigorously.

Grady stops his work, looking me directly in the eye.
I'd almost forgotten how pale blue his own were. 'Look,
Princess,' he finally says, and I get a stab of feeling at the
sound of my old nickname. 'Maybe you're right. Maybe all
men are liars.'

'I never said that!' I'm taken aback by the accusation. I
wouldn't say something that pessimistic! Would I?

'Grady Cole, I have been *nothing* but hurt,' Grady's
saying, his voice high like a girl's. Like mine, I'm gathering.
'By almost *every* man I've ever been with. *Liars*, all of them.'

Er, and now that he says it, I do remember having that
wee outburst in the middle of the gallery during Grady's
opening. I probably *did* say something about men being
liars . . . Oh, yeah. Right before I told him about going
home with Cameron and waking up to his girlfriend. Good
job, Izzy. Nice one there.

'You're making fun of me?' I hazard, biting the inside of
my cheek.

'Little bit,' Grady says, endlessly pleased with himself.

And I've got to say, in a month where every single thing
has changed for the worse, this one piece of life returning
to normal feels . . . well, to be honest, it feels more

comforting than any words of understanding ever could. It's like eating *two* bowls of chocolate mousse. With chocolate cake for dessert.

'Dickwad,' I toss out.

But I know Grady gets what I really mean. I see it in his smile. Not the usual half-lipped one, but a full, appreciative grin.

I know, because I get it too. He's saying, *You're welcome*.

This can't be happening. Not tonight. Not after Venice two weeks ago. Just . . . *not*. I'm shaking. It's ninety degrees outside, and I can feel my shoulders actually shivering. I'm alone here in the gallery, but I'm not supposed to be. Jamie's supposed to be here. Mimi's wedding starts in forty-five minutes.

No, calm down. God, look at me. I've gotten to the point where I automatically expect the worst. Jamie's just stuck on the crosstown bus, I tell myself. He'll be here any minute, and we'll have plenty of time to get downtown to the Puck Building. Still, I take out my nervous energy by pacing the floor at reception. I've got my gown on, and for all Grady's teasing, it really does make me feel like a princess. I've pinned the front pieces of my hair up, and the rest of it tumbles down my back in perfect, hot-curled waves. My makeup is dewy and elegant, not at all overdone. I'm ready to face my cousin. I think I'm ready, even, to be happy for her.

There's a rapping at the front door, and I let out a gigantic sigh of relief. See? All that stress for nothing. Jamie's not like Avery. He wouldn't let me down.

I grab my shawl and my beaded purse, scurrying to the entryway in my satin high heels. But *damn*, Jamie's not there. It's Grady. He must have forgotten something.

'Hi,' I say, swinging the heavy door open. 'I'm just about out the door. Did you forget something?'

'Wow.' Grady takes a step back, almost falling off the top stoop stair. 'You look—'

'Like a princess?' I finish, rolling my eyes. 'Like I didn't see that one coming.'

'Er, yeah . . . pretty much.' Grady's following me into the gallery, reaching behind the ledge to Kimmy's desk. He pulls up a silver cell phone. 'I took it out of my back pocket while I was sitting on the floor.'

'Okay.' I can feel the shaking start again. Where the hell is Jamie? 'So I'll . . . ah . . . see you!'

'What's going on?' Grady lifts an eyebrow. 'Why are you so jittery?'

'I'm not!' I'm pacing around the room again, clip-clopping my heels in the empty space. 'It's nothing. He's just late. He'll be here. He knows how important this is to me. He knows I will *never* ask him for a bigger favor. He knows! Okay?'

Grady comes forward, laying a steady hand on my arm. 'Avery?' he says quietly.

'God, no!' I'm momentarily snapped out of my panic. 'Jamie. My date for my cousin Mimi's wedding. Which is in –' I check my delicate dress watch. '*Shit*. Half an hour.'

Just then the phone rings. Oh, thank heaven. It's got to be Jamie. I grab up the receiver and shout, 'Hello?' not even bothering with the less insane 'Emerson Bond Gallery.'

'Iz.' It's Jamie, all right. Sounding like roadkill. 'I fucked up. I fucked up bad.'

'Jamie! What's going on? Where are you?' My heart starts to beat faster.

'I feel . . . like . . . an ass crack.' I hear him retching.

'Jamie, what *happened?*' In an instant, Mimi's wedding is forgotten. The dress, the late hour, all of it. 'Oh, my God, are you okay? Jamie! Talk to me. What's going on?'

'I haven't slept in four days,' he's rambling. 'I just kept drinking. And partying. And drinking. Iz, I was such a jerk. Svetlana won't have anything to do with me. Patrice too. Celeste. All of them.'

'Jamie, what are you saying?' I'm trying to keep up with his delirious train of thought.

'I missed my deadline. My editor says I'm writing crap. And now I've got so much alcohol in me, I smell it on my skin.'

'Jamie,' I'm struggling to understand. 'You did this to yourself?'

'I'm sorry,' is all he says, barely above a whisper. 'I'm so, so sorry.'

'Get some water,' I manage. 'I'm coming over to make sure you're all right.'

'No, please, no.' He's pleading. 'I don't want you to see me like this.' He pauses to retch again. 'I'll be fine. *You're* the one I've harmed here. More than myself.'

'No, Jaim. Hold tight – you might have to go to the hospital.'

'I don't,' he gags. 'I'm already better than I was an hour ago. Just need to . . . get out the rest of it.'

'I was counting on you, Jamie,' I can't help but let out.

'I know,' is the last thing he says before the line clicks and goes dead.

I lay the receiver gently back in its bed. I've never heard the gallery this silent before. Jamie'll be okay, right? Or should I call back and insist he let me check on him? I don't know what to do. Well, that's not entirely accurate. I do know. I just don't want to say it out loud. I've got to go to Mimi's wedding alone. My mother would never forgive me if I missed this kind of family affair. There'll be long-lost cousins there. Aunt Sheila, who hasn't seen me in twenty years. My hands rise involuntarily to my temples.

'I could take you,' I hear, somewhere in the middle of the room. Grady. Grady's still here. But oh, God, I can't. I *know* him. He'll use every chance he gets to embarrass me. 'Am I right? Your date canceled?' He's flashing a roguish grin. 'Who else do you know who owns a tux and can make it back here in half an hour?'

'You *own* a tux?' Torn-jeans-and-Pumas Grady Cole in formal wear? It's too outlandish to be true.

He winces, shrugging a shoulder. 'My mom. She doesn't believe you can call yourself a man until you've got your own tuxedo.' He lifts both hands, as if to say, *So?* 'Me, man. You, woman. Without date. Yes?'

I squint at him, biting my lip. I see the crinkly corners of his eyes, the bunching of his cheeks. Grady Cole is exceedingly amused right now.

'You're going to make this difficult for me, aren't you?' I say drily.

He punches my shoulder lightly. 'You've got no choice.'

Twenty-five minutes later, Grady Cole is standing in front of me in a gorgeous black tuxedo, with a shiny satin cummerbund and bow tie, luxurious mother-of-pearl shirt studs, and polished, see-your-face-in-them dress shoes. He's offering me his arm, gesturing at the cab waiting outside.

All I can think is, *who is this guy*? Grady looks like a different person. Gallant and dashing, but still down-to-earth, in a way Avery never managed. I feel a well of gratitude rushing up inside. Shouldn't I say thank you? Except this *is* Grady, after all. If I show one note of sentimentality, he'll be calling me Sappy McSappy Pants all night long. So looping my arm into Grady's and looking up at him shyly, I say the next best thing:

'You combed your hair.'

26

May I have this dance . . . horizontally?

According to the gilt sign in the Puck's lobby heralding the 'Duncan-Hewitt Wedding,' the ceremony will be held upstairs in the Skylight Room, with reception to follow in the Grand Ballroom. Which means my aunt and uncle have rented *both* rooms. They must have spent an unheard-of, absolute fortune . . . and I'm sure I'll be hearing *all about* that in only minutes now. Grady and I are in the elevator headed to the top floor, and I can't help but suppress an aching pang. When I used to dream of a wedding at the Skylight Room, *I* was going to be the one with the waves of shiny satin trailing behind me.

Grady's leaning against the elevator's deep wood paneling, his ankles crossed in front of him. He's got this mischievous aura coloring his features that I do not feel good about. What is Grady plotting behind those mirthful blue eyes?

'So,' he says, grinning, 'am I your date, or your sexy new boyfriend? Because I could do both, you know.' He shoots his cuffs, adjusting his shoulders in the finely fitted tuxedo jacket. Seeing Grady look so comfortable in a penguin suit is like . . . seeing a penguin look at ease in chaps and a cowboy hat.

'Grady, what are you talking about?' I throw back,

arranging the gauzy layers of my skirt so they hang most effortlessly.

'Obviously, we're here under false pretenses.' He raises his eyebrows, examining his nails. 'I just need to know how far I should carry the charade. Are we newly acquainted, or are we more . . . *intimate*?'

'There's no charade!' I cry out. 'Grady, just be . . . normal. For once in your life, *please*, just be –'

But I don't get to finish my sentence, because the elevator doors slide open, and we're deposited into the most sparkly, elegant, tastefully splendid room I've ever seen.

'Look.' I'm grabbing on to Grady's upper arm. 'Oh, God, look.'

This space is everything I ever imagined. Dusk is only just falling over New York City, and a hazy gold-purple glow pours through the dozens of windows that make up the Skylight Room's walls. The light streams up the aisle, on which white satin has been laid, leading up toward the flower-strewn altar. White lilies twine around the backs of the endless chairs on either side of the alabaster walkway, and green ivy curls down the white pillars beside them. Finally, hundreds of candles of various sizes border the entire room, giving the scene a sense of absolute enchantment.

'Come on.' Grady's guiding me to one of the few empty seats toward the back. 'It's about to start.'

He's right. There's no time to scoot up and say hi to my folks, or my other family, or the gaggle of Park Slope Ladies Who Lunch already gossiping across the aisle. No time to despair over the most gorgeous wedding setting in the entire world. The string quartet, all dressed in black velvet, have started to play a lilting melody. The first groomsman and bridesmaid pair is promenading down the aisle. And *how unfair is this*? I can't even sneer at the bridesmaid's dresses! They're deep burgundy satin, an elegant strapless sheath with extra fabric crisscrossing in back, at the tailbone. They're the kind of dresses . . . well, they're the kind of dresses *I* would have picked.

The quartet halts its playing, pausing dramatically with bows over strings. Then, after a nod from the cellist, they begin the opening notes of 'Here Comes the Bride.' My heart starts to beat faster. I don't know why, but I get this vision of Mimi interrupting her long-fantasized trip down the aisle to stick her tongue out at me and hop up and down screaming, 'I got here first!'

But instead, my cousin, flanked on either side by Uncle Pete and Aunt Barbara (who would be damned before she let my uncle escort the bride alone), performs the walk in the highest of style. Her Vera Wang dress could not be more gorgeous. Made of matte satin, with delicate lace straps, a mermaid silhouette, and a sweeping train, the dress hugs Mimi's lithe figure while at the same time moving fluidly around it. Behind her tasteful veil, I can see Mimi beaming with happiness. Her whole body seems to glow, backlit by the dusky sun. She looks perfect.

I feel Grady's eyes on me, and I move my head a fraction of an inch until he's farther in my peripheral vision. He's got this questioning expression, as if he's trying to puzzle out what I'm thinking. You know what I'm thinking, Grady? Stop staring at me, is what I'm thinking. Because it's making me uncomfortable. The show's out in front, at the altar, where Trevor's lifting Mimi's veil with the tenderness of someone deeply in love. The show is where rings are being exchanged, and Mimi's and Trevor's happy, tear-strewn faces are exchanging vows. You should be looking where ... where Trevor's holding both Mimi's hands, telling her how she's made his life complete. Where Mimi's responding, with a catch in her voice, that Trevor has given her everything she's ever wanted.

It's ... beautiful. And not just aesthetically. I'm actually feeling for these two people, wearing their new shiny platinum bands (in Mimi's case, bedazzled by diamonds). You can see the genuine, heartfelt love in their eyes, in their grasping hands, jeez – in their whole bodies. Of all the people in the world, they found each other – beating all the obstacles between them. God, it's enough to make you . . . come on, Iz, hold it together. Awww, *crap* it all to hell.

To my credit, I'm not the only one with fat tears rolling down my cheeks. In fact, it looks like I'm in the majority here. But I had planned to be so strong, steeling myself against any emotion that could lead to Grady's ridicule. Surreptitiously, I sneak a glance over at his face, which is still turned toward mine. He's giving me one of his intense gazes, the kind that pierces right through the skin. I soften a bit when I see what he's got in his hand. Grady's offering me his pocket square. Hang on. Grady's wearing a *pocket square*?

I take the soft silk and press it to my face. 'You're going to be able to wring this sucker out by the end of the night,' I whisper.

Grady shakes his head in mock exasperation. 'I expect it back cleaned and pressed by tomorrow.'

'Better get acquainted with your iron, then,' I retort in the same teasing tone.

The ceremony has ended now, and Mimi and Trevor are traipsing happily back down the aisle while the guests throw rose petals at them. I'm holding the plastic bag of powdery pink and white petals that was provided on my seat, but I just can't bring myself to grab a handful. It's not out of spite. I just don't feel . . . merry enough. It takes a certain degree of glee to fling out fistfuls of rose petals.

I feel a puff of hot breath on my shoulder, and I hear a low voice in my ear. 'Izzy, did Avery . . . did he hurt you very badly?'

Way to sneak up on a gal, Grady! I spin around, my head tipping involuntarily backward. 'Where'd that come from?'

Grady runs a hand over his smooth, tidy hair. His mother-of pearl cuff links catch the light, glinting with iridescence. 'You just seem down,' he's backtracking. 'And I . . . want to make sure you realize how much of a . . . a shit Avery is. That you didn't do anything wrong. In fact, you probably did something right. To save yourself, I mean.'

Up the aisle, I see my parents and family grabbing their

shawls and used tissues. I should rush over and say hello. But then I look at Grady's face, which is plastered with genuine concern.

I press my palm against my forehead, willing away the beginning of a colossal headache. 'Grady,' I say, letting my shoulders slump, 'can we just not talk about it?'

Grady nods firmly. 'Done,' he says, letting his face crease in an easy smile. 'Totally done. So you gonna introduce me to your mother now?'

I'm seized by a sudden wave of panic. 'Grady, I should warn you – I mean, you have to understand about my mother . . .' Oh, God, there's my mom now, waving at me from across the room, near the altar. She's wearing a low-cut dress, and let's just say I didn't get my modest bosom from her side of the family. Yup, that's my mom. And yup, that's her cleavage.

'Are you trying to say your mother's not normal?' Grady's smirking at me. 'Because, come on, whose is?'

'No, see, it's just that –' I'm wringing my hands together. 'My mother used to be a hippie, like of the' – and I wince in pain to say it – 'free-love variety. And, well, forty years later, she's never exactly lost that whole, um, *sensuality* of the sixties movement.'

Grady holds his stomach, doubling over laughing. 'You mean, your mom's into, like, *orgies*?'

'Ugh, Grady, no!' I've got to wash my brain out with lye. Right this minute. 'She's just a little . . . sexy.'

'Nothing wrong with that,' Grady hums in my ear.

Seriously, I'm going to toss my cookies. After twenty-seven years, you'd think I'd be used to introducing new people to my mom. Except I'm not. I'm just really, really not. And now she's kissing my uncle Pete on the cheek and coming over to us, her hips swaying as usual.

'Hello, *darling*,' my mother exclaims as she gives me a big hug. I flinch wildly as she cups one of my breasts and gives it a little squeeze. 'You're not wearing those silicone jobbies I got you!' she whispers in my ear. 'Tsk on you, Iz! They'd lift your little ones so nicely!'

'*Mom!*' I get out through gritted teeth. 'This is Grady Cole. He's an artist with the gallery.'

'Mmm, look at you!' My mother exclaims, eyeing Grady up and down under her red bob. 'Quite spiffy-looking for an artist, aren't you?'

'Just for tonight, Mrs Duncan,' Grady responds politely. Then he swings an arm around my shoulder, hugging me tight against him. 'Had to clean myself up for my little Izzy here.'

I jab my elbow into Grady's side, but he maintains his viselike grip, smiling wider as I struggle. Oh, for goodness' sake. What's worse – my mom jiggling her boobs at my fake date, or my fake date pretending he's the love of my life? Right, no question there.

'I'm sure we'll see you again soon,' I cry out to Jiggly Mom Boobs. 'You and Dad can save a seat for us at the table!' I whirl out of Grady's grip, grabbing his hand and pulling him. 'We'll just head down to the reception . . . get a head start!'

'And spend some *alone* time in the elevator!' Grady calls back to my mom as I tug him fervently to the back of the Skylight Room.

'Grady!' I hiss. 'That's my *mom.*'

He gives me a quick wink. 'I know. Me-ow.'

'*Shut up,*' I say, sulking, as we gather ourselves into the wood-paneled elevator for the second time in less than an hour. My entire life, I've been shielding my dates from my mom. Because – well, do I really need to explain? And even though Grady's not a *real* date, we're stuck here for a whole wedding reception – right at the same table! I *must* remember to sit Grady next to Dad. He's not too talkative, my dad, which can be the best blessing ever. If Grady was to sit next to my mom, I wouldn't be able to go to the bathroom *the entire evening.* Give Grady five minutes alone with my mother, and he'll be hearing all about the time two-year-old Izzy learned the difference between the sexes and then proceeded to ask every random person on the street, 'Do you have a penis or a vagina?'

The Grand Ballroom looks as extraordinary as I expect it to – all white chandeliers, and columns strewn with tiny white lights, and tables as far as the eye can see, with massive centerpieces of white and dark pink flowers. I've always loved this color scheme – white everywhere, with just the hint of a compelling accent hue. Needless to say, I had planned just these hues for my own . . . well, you know.

I tug Grady over to a seemingly endless massive table covered with obsessively neat rows of place cards. Rows, and rows, and rows. Mimi and Aunt Barbara must have invited every single person they've ever met. I can't help but roll my eyes. Of *course* they did.

'Here you are.' Grady's holding one of the delicate cards, where *Isabel Duncan* is spelled out in extra-swirly gold script, right above *Table 8*.

I stuff the folded card in my purse, stretching my neck in all directions looking for the bar. A drink. A drink will make everything better. I scan the enormous buffet of hors d'oeuvres lining the ballroom's back wall. There's an ice pyramid laden with fresh oysters, next to fruit sculptures shaped like birds, with cantaloupe beaks and black currant eyes. There are platters of shrimp cocktail, crackers, gourmet cheese, caviar, three kinds of foie gras. And that's not even half of it. At the very end of the table, there's a sparkling champagne waterfall, surrounded by mountains of chocolate strawberries. Then, finally, there's the fully stocked, oasis-in-the-desert, sweet-nectar-for-the-hungry, open bar. Champagne will do fine later. Right now I need vodka. As the uniformed bartender gives me my drink, I desperately thank him, telling him he's the Wizard to my Dorothy. He gives me a wink and says, 'You can pay attention to the man behind my curtain anytime.'

'Not too shabby,' Grady says a minute later as he appraises the room, swirling his brandy in its wide-bottomed glass. 'Good drink, good food, and – allow me to say – pretty fine-looking date. I've had worse evenings.'

I feel myself blushing violently, and I take a deep drink of my vodka cranberry to hide it. Yeah, I'm going to need a faster-acting alcohol. I don't know how to respond, so I just slap Grady lightly on his upper arm. 'Are you going to behave?'

Grady grabs my hand and pulls me in toward him. Close. Uncomfortably close, actually. Or . . . what I would *think* would be uncomfortably close. I can smell the aged liquor on his breath, and I can feel the heat of him. Grady's looking down at me, almost nose to nose, and I swear to God, for a minute I actually think he's going to – I know, crazy – kiss me. But instead, he shakes his head, giving me an impish, Han Solo grin. 'Am I going to behave?' He lets out a deep laugh. 'No way, Princess.'

Just then, I'm jolted into nearly dropping my drink when out of the blue (or in this case, white), a nine-piece swing band starts up a rousing rendition of 'In the Mood.' They're playing on a raised dais at one end of the ballroom – a splendid array of brass and drums. I realize with a start of embarrassment that Grady and I are standing on the dance floor. It's so big and wide, I'd just assumed it was the . . . regular floor. I sneak a glance at Grady and see he's as white with terror as I am.

'Should we find our table?' I'm trying to slink off as inconspicuously as possible.

Grady's backing away from the dance floor like it's a lion he's just met in the middle of the Serengeti. 'Um, yeah.'

I catch sight of my folks at a table on the far side of the dance floor. Dad looks pretty handsome in his tuxedo, I've got to say, with his shiny bow tie and cummerbund. My father, who works for the Brooklyn district attorney's office, usually dresses in suits whose style has come and gone at least twice. And he's got this enormous collection of the ugliest ties ever. Pea green, rusty orange, god-awful, nearly fluorescent paisleys. It's only because my mother used to work at Brooks Brothers in the early years of their marriage, and she got a huge discount on the merchandise. The ties *were* luxurious. In the *seventies*. But bless his heart, my dad still loves each and every hideous one of them – because they were all gifts from Mom. For all my dad's bad fashion and my mom's blatant bosom, I'm sure it's their constant, supportive love that's shown me what finding the right person can be like. Thirty-five years they've been married now. How could I ever find someone I'd be that compatible with?

'Hey, Iz?' I feel Grady tugging the tulle skirt of my dress. 'I don't think we're supposed to sit there.' He's peering at my parents' table number in the distance. 'We're at eight. They're sixteen.'

'What?' I fish out my place card from my purse and stare at the two disparate numbers. Hey, he's right. So if I'm not sitting with my family, where the hell did Mimi – suddenly, I'm struck by a horrific thought. Is there a *kiddie* table? Am I supposed to be the babysitter for the entire under-ten set?

But oh, God. It's worse. Five hundred times worse. Grady and I are weaving through the ballroom, and I think I've just spotted number eight. Please, *please* tell me that's not our table. There's Cat and Debbie and Becka and Heather, all in their burgundy dresses, next to their smug-looking dates. And . . . why . . . *why* . . . are there two empty seats – at the very table populated by my ultimate nightmare. Mimi's best friends from high school. The snobbiest, most vindictive, cruelest girls in the *entire world*.

'She put us with the *bridesmaids*?' I blurt out, feeling pinpricks of heat all over my body. But I set my jaw, swallowing all my desperate protests. There's nothing I can do.

Cat, Debbie, Becka, and Heather are all deliberately staring at me as Grady and I approach the table. I honestly expect one of them to put a preemptive hand on our seats and exclaim, 'Sorry, these are saved.' But then Cat whispers something in Debbie's ear, and she whispers it to Becka, who whispers it to Heather, and they all break out laughing. While still staring at me. Oh, I can feel the fun starting already. I take a few deep, steadying breaths and wonder if Grady can sense how nervous I am.

Step by torturous step, I'm getting flashbacks from years past. Heather spreading false rumors that my 'academic scholarship' was really extreme financial aid because my parents were destitute, and couldn't you tell all my clothes came from Goodwill? Debbie disinviting me from her junior-year holiday party because she expected everyone to play Spin the Bottle, and who'd want it to land on me? Cat cheating off my chemistry test senior year (thankfully *after* I'd already been accepted at Brown), getting us both suspended for a week. Becka hiding my shoes in the woods during our sophomore school retreat, demanding I do all her dish-washing duties or she wouldn't give them back. (Actually, that memory's not so bad. The look on Becka's face when Dix threatened to beat the living crap out of her made everything worth it.) Do you see what I mean? These are not women. They are succubi. Evil, soul-sucking succubi.

Except maybe I'm not being fair. Nine years have passed since we graduated high school. People mature, right? They grow out of their bullying days – and sometimes even regret them. I can be big about this, and gracious and courteous. We're adults, after all. So as Grady and I pull out our chairs and set our place cards down, I greet the table with a wide, open smile.

Until Becka starts singing that old *Sesame Street* song 'Which of These Things Is Not Like The Other?' and the whole table bursts out laughing.

'You're right,' I say, smoothing my skirt under me as I pull in my chair. I *will* be calm, no matter how far I'm goaded. 'You're all in burgundy satin, and I'm not. So . . . funny song.'

'Your dress is actually . . . pretty decent,' Cat offers reluctantly. If it can be said, she's the nicest of the bunch. By which I mean she'd kill just the mama bird, while the rest would also eat its young. 'Much better than your baggy high school wardrobe. Did you pick it out yourself?'

And though her tone is dripping with condescension, I

hesitate at the thought that yes, I did pick it out myself. I dressed myself for a major function *without* Dix's help. Granted, that's because she *hates* me right now, and if I dwell on that fact for even a second, I'll lose all the pieces of me that I'm just barely holding together to begin with. But, as mundane as it sounds, I'm kind of having a revelation. For the first time, all of my own doing, I feel gorgeous, sophisticated, adult, and accomplished. Or, at least, I *did*. Before I sat down at the devil table of the four succubi.

'So,' Grady says, that playful smile flickering on his face, even though none of the foursome have bothered to introduce us to their dates, or even asked Grady's name. 'What was my little Izzy like in high school?'

Oh, no. No no no no. I give Grady a kick under the table. We're not playing games here, Grady. *Not* this time. But instead of kicking back, Grady wraps his arm around my shoulders and squeezes tight. Because we're a couple. We're madly in love. That whole Fake Date Charade vs. Jiggly Mom Boobs decision? Boy, did I choose wrong.

Debbie's grinning wickedly, tucking her short corn-silk blond hair behind her ears. She's planning something; I can sense it. What's going on behind those cold, dark eyes? Deb reaches down beside her and cradles a shiny party favor bag in her lap. 'Mimi made copies for all of us. Just in case we hadn't saved ours,' she says, drawing what looks like a flat piece of paper out of the bag. 'Because, Iz, I'm sure you'd agree,' and here she gets this sugar-sweet lilt to her voice, as phony as her hair color and nose. 'Memories are such precious gems. And a picture's worth a thousand words. . . .'

What is she holding? And *why* is she handing it over to Grady? Oh, God. Oh, God. I swear, the band must be playing the theme from *Jaws*, because it's all I can hear, looming large and ominous in the foreground. *Duh* duh. *Duh* duh.

'Oh, man!' Grady's laughter erupts beside me, overwhelming the *Jaws* music. He's holding the stiff paper with one hand and his stomach with the other. 'Iz, this is priceless. I can't stand it, it's so good.'

'What is it!' I cry, snatching the offending evidence from his fingers.

It's a photograph, I see now, a five-by-seven matte. But not just any old photograph. No, *this* photograph is the most horrible, embarrassing, heartrendingly painful photograph I've ever taken. It's our freshman-year class picture. Taken the *very day* I found out that Mimi was dating Jared Anders. So, not only am I wearing my usual high school outfit of over-sized, monochromatic clothing, and not only is my hair flat and lifeless, with scraggly bangs (my fourteen-year-old self had not yet discovered deep conditioner and hot rollers), but also, my eyes and cheeks are red and raw from hours of crying and tissue rubbing. But you know what's worse? Worse than looking back at yourself thirteen years ago, on the most horrible day of what was already the awful experience of high school? How about if you *also* happened to have the biggest, reddest, most noticeable pimple ever on the very tip of your nose? No, really, if the *Titanic* had hit this zit instead of the iceberg, *no one* would have survived. Not even Kate Winslet. The class called me 'Rudolph' for *months* afterward. Truly, looking at this picture, you don't even see Mimi and her friends in the back row. You don't see Jared Anders in the middle row, or Dix sitting next to me on the floor. All you see is my puffy face and gigantic red nose. It's like an eye magnet. You're physically unable to look anywhere else.

'Let me see again!' Grady's nudging me, pulling the monstrosity from my shaking hands. 'Iz, what is that sweater you're wearing? Are you hiding someone under there?'

'You always were too far gone to be saved,' Heather says, tutting me with a shake of her head. Then she pats down a stray hair from her stiff chignon and promptly dismisses me from all consideration.

'Fine,' I say, lifting my head and squaring my shoulders,

demanding her attention back. 'Laugh away. Because, as you can see, I do *not* need saving anymore.' I rap my finger on the table for emphasis. 'Not that I ever did! From you, or . . . anyone!'

'Aw, Iz, don't be sore.' Grady's eyes are glowing warmly. He's laid a hand gently on my forearm. 'You look adorable in the photo! All young and, er, *rosy* . . . just waiting to blossom into my very own Lovey Dovey Bear.' He's cooing at me, batting his eyelashes. I can hear the succubi snicker, and I feel like cringing with mortification. 'You should see *my* high school class photo,' Grady continues. 'Damn, I was skinny. They thought I had an eating disorder!' He flinches at the memory. 'Not to mention how my ears grew *way* faster than my head . . . *and* I had braces! From the ages of ten to *nineteen*!'

'Hey, wait a second. . . .' The entire table starts with surprise as one of the guys halts his conversation with the other smug dates – something about the discount rate and equities – and fixes his gaze on Grady. 'I thought I knew you from somewhere. . . .'

'What?' Grady lets out, probably louder than he means to. He's staring back at the guy, brow furrowed, as if trying to place the face. Then, in a flash, his eyes widen, and I hear him take in a sharp breath.

'You know each other?' I watch Grady lower his head and grab at the napkin in his lap.

'Psssh,' Grady dismisses the thought. 'Not likely. You're a trader, right? Or in banking? Because I'm a painter. Kind of different social circles there, buddy.'

'Howard is *the leading* day trader for Goldman Sachs,' Heather pipes in haughtily. '*And* my fiancé.' She turns to Becka, examining her ring with a pout. 'And I don't care what Mimi says about the size of her center stone. I have a full *extra carat* in baguettes.'

Howard's still peering at Grady, his mouth slightly open to reveal his fat, swollen tongue. 'But you look so familiar. I could *swear* I've seen you before. Maybe at . . . wait! Did you go to Choate?'

'What's Choate?' Grady responds innocently, his eyebrows raised.

Howard makes a choking sound, as if Grady's just asked, 'What's toilet paper?' 'What's *Choate*? Only the *finest* boarding school in Connecticut, that's what.' He gives a disbelieving look to Heather. 'Who hasn't heard of *Choate*?'

'Whatever,' Grady mumbles gruffly, tossing his napkin on his plate and pushing back his chair. 'Iz, I'm going to find the men's room. You need another drink on the way back?'

'What do you think?' I answer resignedly.

'So, Izzy,' Cat purrs when Grady's left. She rests her left hand on the table alongside the other three girls', fanning out their huge diamonds like a jeweler's display case. 'When are *you* going to get engaged?'

I'm sorry. If Grady gets to leave, so do I. Equality of the sexes, and all that, right? 'Gosh, guys, I just realized!' I exclaim, resting my napkin next to his. 'I haven't even said congratulations to Mimi or her parents yet! Jeez, I'd better go do that.'

'What are we supposed to do if the waiter comes?' Debbie sneers. 'They might not bring us our food if you're not here to order yours.'

'You can order us the fish, please,' I say calmly. 'If you find you have no choice.'

'But the other option is *Kobe beef*,' Heather spits out, like I've just voluntarily downgraded myself from first class to coach.

'You know what, Heather?' I say breezily, giving her a dazzling smile. 'I think it's pretty obvious you and I don't share the same tastes.'

'Hello, understatement,' sniggers Becka.

I stand behind my chair, gripping the back for support. 'Because I value things like originality and creativity.'

'So do we,' Deb scoffs, giggling with the other girls. 'We are *all* designer originals.'

'Oh, yeah?' I offer a sympathetic look. 'Then why do all

your gaudy diamond rings look *exactly the damn same*?'

I turn my back on the table of doom, the click of my heels sounding especially loud given the stunned silence behind me.

I catch sight of Mimi and Trevor across the ballroom, making the rounds from table to table. Stunningly, I realize, I have yet to meet Mimi's new husband. With all my cousin's meticulous wedding preparations, you'd think introducing her fiancé to her family would have made the to-do list. Guess not. I figure it's best to meet my new cousin-in-law when I'm *not* fuming over my seating arrangement at his wedding, so I opt for congratulating my aunt and uncle first.

When I reach my parents' table, Aunt Barbara is giving a standing monologue about the cost of the dinner – 'Sixty dollars per person for the *beef alone*. And the flowers were imported all the way from *Hawaii*.' Instead of rolling my eyes, though, I put on an enthusiastic smile and lean down to hug my uncle. Like my father, my uncle Pete's a pretty neutral kind of guy. Their wives are the vocal ones.

'Great wedding, Uncle Pete!' I venture. 'You did a super job . . . er . . . making it so fancy!'

'*I* did all the planning,' Aunt Barbara intones, all deep and menacing. Her black eyes are flashing, and her wide hips braced as if for battle. 'You're enjoying yourself, Izzy?' She poses the question like it's some sort of test that if I fail gets me thrown in the dungeon.

'I was very touched by Mimi and Trevor's vows during the ceremony,' I manage truthfully, trying not to tremble. Aunt Barbara's kind of scary. She speaks in this booming baritone, and her features are hard and stony. No matter what Mimi's done, I've always felt kind of bad for her, having to deal with a fire-breathing mother and all.

'This wedding cost more than Mimi's high school and college tuition put together!' Aunt Barbara booms with fiendish glee.

'Wow, that's . . .' Obnoxious? Obscene? Disgusting? 'Congratulations!'

'Izzy, where's that hot little date of yours?' my mother chimes in, pulling my attention to the other side of the table. Of course my mother and Aunt Barbara would be separated by a floral centerpiece larger than some breakfast tables – the two have never gotten along and tend to antagonize each other whenever possible.

Aunt Barbara grimaces. 'Looks like your mother's calling. Tell her not to get cocktail sauce on her heaving bosom.'

And so summarily dismissed, I can say I've completed my duty congratulating the bride's mother. I'd rather have run barefoot in a rose garden full of thorns.

I find my dad behind the gigantic floral arrangement and kiss his cheek hello before settling down next to my mother.

'There, I've saved you from that gorgon.' Mom's flipping back her short red hair as I sink into an empty seat next to her. 'So consider me your hero. But darling, where's your man hunk?'

And now that she says it, I take a look around. Grady's spending an awful long time in the restroom, isn't he? Although he's probably just trying out all the personal-care freebies you get in swank bathrooms – mini deodorant, perfume, hair spray. Wait, do they have those in the men's room? Or is their goody basket all baseball cards and beer cozies? 'He'll be back,' is all I say, hoping I can end the conversation there.

No such luck. 'There's something about that man . . . Grady, was it?' my mother whispers excitedly. 'Looks like he'd be a minx in the sack. Is he quite creative?'

'Mom!' I'm using my firm, preemptive voice. 'We're not talking about my sex life!'

She pouts, rifling a fork around in the goat cheese and endive salad in front of her. 'Spoilsport.' But then she perks up again, her cheeks flushing. 'Look, darling! I've got the most fun thing to show you ever!'

Oh, God. The last time my mother announced she had

something fun to show me . . . how should I put this? . . . I wound up holding an object shaped like an enormous cucumber that made a loud buzzing noise and – according to my mother – would ensure *all* my needs could be fulfilled without a man in the picture. Although I appreciate her feminist ideals, nothing–*nothing!* – could be more profoundly, deeply wrong than receiving *that* from your mother.

Hang on, give me a chance to reconsider. Because what I'm looking at right now is giving the giant cucumber a hell of a run for its money. My mother has lifted her dress a few inches off the floor, and is modeling her lower leg in front of me, pointing her foot in its rhinestone-crusted strappy sandal.

'I wanted to show you first!' my mother coos happily, looking down under the tablecloth at her ankle. 'Well, after Dad of course, but before the other relatives.'

'You got a tattoo!?' I cry in dismay. It's jet-black, a hieroglyph or something, a loop on top of a cross thingie. *My mother got a tattoo.*

'It's an ankh!' she exclaims, her cheeks bunched with glee. 'On my ankh-le!'

And now she's making puns about it!

'My own fifty-fifth birthday present to myself.' Mom beams with satisfaction. 'And now that I've shown you, I can show everyone!' She's standing up, waving her hands, trying to get my uncle Pete's attention.

Okay. Let my mother have her tattoo. No harm done to anyone. But do I *really* need to stand here while she shows every relative we've got – including ninety-five-year-old Aunt Sheila, who's still getting over the fact that women can vote – her new piece of body art?

'You have fun, Mom,' I say supportively. 'I better find out what Grady's up to.'

'Oh, yes!' Her eyes gleam. 'Maybe he's waiting for you in the "elevator" – wink wink!'

I let out a strangled grin and pray to God she's not actually right.

*

What *is* taking Grady so long? Because I've still got to congratulate Mimi, and I'll be damned if I go it alone. I can just picture her self-satisfied expression. *Couldn't hold on to this guy either, could you Izzy?* Nope, Mimi, you're right – I lost Grady to his bladder. Taking a deep breath, I venture farther into the grand ballroom, looking for the bathrooms.

That's when I see her. Or what must be the *apparition* of her. Because certainly there's no way I'm seeing who I think I'm seeing. With the blond Botticelli spiral curls, and the perfect china doll skin. What was her name? I think back, to that horrible morning, remembering my fresh-squeezed orange juice and white terry cloth outfit. I strain my neck forward, squinting hard. See how awful this wedding has been for me? I'm hallucinating! Except . . . why isn't the taunting vision disappearing? Oh, God. She sees me. She's making eye contact, even smiling! She whispers into the ear of the guy beside her – a guy I know a little too well and yet not really at all. His face turns as white as I expect mine must be. But he has no choice. She's coming my way, and there's nothing he can do but follow. Cameron and his girlfriend – *Jasmine*'s her name. Headed right for me.

I can hear these panicky whimpering noises coming from deep inside me. Jasmine knows Mimi, doesn't she? That's right; they're both in interior design. How can I be expected to remember these things when I'm making small talk with the girlfriend of the man I've just unwittingly spent the night with? *How?* I'm just standing here, a phony smile splashed on my face, while inside, all I want to do is pull a Road Runner and sprint off in a puff of dust.

Jasmine and Cameron are only steps away when I feel a warm, steady arm wrapping round my waist. *What the* – But oddly, my first instinct isn't to wriggle away. Instead of irritation, I'm feeling . . . something pretty close to relief, if you want to know the truth. I lean against a firm chest, smelling the faint remnants of paint and turpentine.

'I gotcha, Princess,' I hear close in my ear.

'Thanks,' I whisper back, sneaking a peek at Grady's reliable, steadfast face. I never noticed that freckle he has by the corner of his eye, or the perfect Cupid's bow of his upper lip. He's kind of . . . well, he's actually kind of handsome, once his hair is combed and all.

Jasmine sticks out her hand then, giving me a warm grin. 'You're Cameron's friend, aren't you? It's good to see you again.'

I see Cameron – Mr Slimy – wincing guiltily, and I can tell he's silently praying I'll play along. But last time, at his apartment, I helped Cameron lie only because I was too shocked to do otherwise. I hadn't yet wrapped my mind around what was happening. Now I feel a whole lot less like making things easier for this cheating slimeball. If he's got to stew in his own shamefaced, dishonest juices, well, I'm okay with that.

'We've met before,' I say casually, nodding my head. 'But I wouldn't say we're *friends*, would you, Cameron?'

'I, uh . . . guess maybe not.' Even Cameron's Robbie Williams-y British accent can't save him now. I don't even know why I found him so sexy to begin with. Oh, fine. Of course I do. But whatever charm I saw in Cameron, is long, long gone. ' "Acquaintances" would be more appropriate, yes.'

'I'm Grady,' I hear behind me, as Grady steps forward, neglecting to shake Cameron's hand. There's something about his stance, the protective heft of his shoulders, that tells me somehow Grady's intuiting my discomfort. He actually seems ready to defend me. 'How do you two know my Izzy here?'

There's a beat of silence, until Cameron, still wincing, lets out a pathetic, 'We, er, met . . . um . . .'

'You're squash partners, aren't you?' Jasmine pipes up, wrapping a loving hand through the crook of Mr Slimy's arm. My heart goes out to her. I've been there. I know what it's like to love someone *so much*, completely in the dark about their extracurricular trysts with nubile young art models. Or, in this case, art dealers.

Grady's gaping at me, his mouth open in disbelief. 'You play *squash?*' He gives a guffaw and turns to stare Cameron in the eye. 'With those sissy-sized baby tennis rackets?'

'It's a very *manly* sport,' Cameron protests.

'I don't play squash,' I say softly, looking straight at Jasmine. 'To be honest, I'm not even sure what it is, exactly.'

'But then how –' She's scrunching her nose, turning her head up toward Cameron's. 'How are you two squash partners if you don't –' I watch as her face blanches with recognition. 'Oh,' she says, biting a trembling lip. Then, more quietly, 'I get it now.'

'*I'm sorry,*' I immediately say, as genuinely as I can. I don't know whether I should offer a hand of support or just vanish as quickly as possible. 'I'm so, so sorry. If I had only known about you, nothing would have *ever* happened. I swear it.'

I feel a supportive touch at the small of my back, and I realize how grateful I am to have someone here by my side. Someone who understands I never meant to hurt anyone. No, not just someone. Grady. For the first time, I'm actually thankful for Grady Cole. At least, I think it's the first time. Because . . . this is Grady. We're sparring partners, verbal adversaries, right? He annoys me. He teases me mercilessly. I dread spending time with him . . . *right?*

Jasmine's cheeks are reddening, and I know she's moved into the anger stage. A stage I know well. I remember throwing a tissue box at Seth's head – my college boyfriend, the artist who slept with all his models – and then not even feeling bad about the red mark it left on his cheek. My own anger stage was fleeting, though. The hurt part, and the sadness part . . . well, they kind of overwhelmed everything else. They still do if I let myself dwell on it.

Jasmine's setting her jaw, shooting imaginary laser

beams at Cameron with her eyes. 'You promised!' she hisses. 'You said there'd be *no more* women.'

'There haven't been!' He's pleading with her, grabbing at her hands. 'I lapsed once! Just one time!'

'What about the other squash partners, huh?' She pulls away from him, listing them on her fingers. 'All in those same terry cloth shorts, which you said were the athletic-club uniforms! All holding brown paper bags, no doubt with their clothes inside!'

I glare at Cameron with new disgust pouring down over the old. He is *devious!* I nearly crumple at the thought of how easily I fell into his snare – how I played into every part of his ruse. I can't help but visibly cringe, and I feel Grady's hands tighten where they're gripping my shoulders.

'I cannot look at you another second,' Jasmine says through gritted teeth. 'I need to go.' She's backing away from Cameron. 'Get your stuff out of my apartment – all of it. Or it'll wind up on the street.'

'Jasmine!' he cries after her, but it's lost in the music. The band's playing 'It Don't Mean a Thing If It Ain't Got That Swing.' Which, in Cameron's case, should be, 'It Do Mean a Thing If You Cheat on Your Girlfriend, You Asshole.'

'You're a real piece of work,' Grady says frankly to Cameron, shaking his head.

'Look what you've done!' Cameron shouts at me, surging forward.

Grady plants himself between me and Cameron, spreading his arms wide. 'You better watch it,' he says threateningly. God, he sounds scary. I wouldn't mess with him, that's for sure.

'We were going to get married,' Cameron moans, letting his head drop into his hands. 'You've ruined everything. Look how you hurt her.'

For just a second, I wonder if I should regret what I've done. I'm seeing Jasmine's face again, plastered with pain. I'm hearing the desperate croak in her voice. But what if I hadn't found out about Seth? What if *we* had gotten married, while all the time he was boffing other women right and left. Was that the life I wanted?

'*You* ruined everything,' I manage finally, spitting the words out with vitriol. '*You* hurt her. *You* did.'

'Come on,' Grady lets out under his breath. 'You don't need this.'

I let him tug me away from Cameron. Far from the hurt, the guilt, and that generally ewwy feeling you get when you've fallen prey to the charms of an expert gigolo. Not a pleasant sensation, I can tell you.

It's with a start of surprise that I realize where Grady's pulling me. We're not headed to the bar at all, which was my natural assumption, because – that's where the drinks are. Instead, we're almost smack-dab in the middle of the dance floor. And oh, my God. Grady's shimmying around, wagging his finger to that old standard, Duke Ellington's 'Take the A Train.' He's kicking his feet out, looking every moment like he's about to take a wild fall. Oh, it's too much to take. I squash down the giggles so violently that they erupt instead through my nose, in one of my resounding snorts.

Grady joins in my laughter, shrugging his shoulders at himself. 'Yeah, I'm not much for the jitterbug.'

'Oh, is that what that was?' I hide my enormous smile behind my hands.

'Shut up,' Grady says genially, latching on to one of my hands and drawing me up close to him as the music changes to a much slower 'Night and Day.'

'*Night and day . . .,*' Grady hums in my ear. '*You are the one.*'

Okay. Don't laugh. But there's something about the gentle way he's holding my hand, the way his arm is wrapped around my waist, guiding me deftly through the motions. Or maybe it's just being this close to him, letting my head rest on his sturdy, tuxedo-cushioned shoulder. But God help me, I'm feeling butterflies. What else could account for the nervous tingling in my stomach? For the self-consciousness that's making every sensation feel heightened? All of a sudden, the easy comfort I've been feeling around Grady vanishes. I'm too aware of every movement I'm making, of every movement *he's* making.

'Relax,' Grady's saying softly. 'Just follow my lead.'

I take a deep breath and try to ease the stiffness in my limbs. Grady's jerky flailing of just a moment ago has been utterly transformed. He guides me smoothly, fluidly, around the spacious dance floor, spinning with me as the gauzy layers of my dress flow between and around our legs. He dips me in a semicircle, and I let my hair swoop down and then snap back up. What's up with Grady dancing like a professional? I mean, how totally Fred and Ginger must we look right now?

'Hey!' I draw my head back to look Grady in the eyes. 'Where'd you learn to dance?'

He gives a sheepish wince, and I can see him silently debating whether to fess up. 'Dancing lessons,' he finally says. 'My mother again. Apparently, to be a man, one must both own a tuxedo *and* learn to dance in it. Too bad I quit before they hit swing dancing.'

'Pretty fancy mom you've got there,' is all I can think to respond. My entire book of knowledge on Grady Cole is being rewritten by the minute. The second, even. I've lost all frame of reference. 'You're pretty dashing when you play the hero,' I add shyly.

'It's just dancing,' he dismisses, spinning me around again.

'No, I mean' – and here I bite the inside of my cheek, wondering if I'm being too obvious – 'with Cameron. Sticking up for me and all. That was really . . . sweet.'

Grady rolls his eyes, tilting his head down modestly. 'Oh, that. I just . . . it's just that . . . I don't like to see people making you so upset.'

I nearly stop short as I give him the most disbelieving look I can drum up.

'Unless it's me, of course.' He grins widely, drawing me closer again until my head's back on his shoulder.

The music swells as it hits the bridge, all strings and soft brass. The hum of the bass reverberates through the colossal room, a low, mournful sound that somehow makes me feel more thoughtful than sad. The loss of Avery, my concern for Dix, my frustration with Jamie . . . it all seems to dissipate, carried away by the vibrating bass line. What's left is the firm shoulder under my cheek. The strong arm clutching my back. The touch of fingers faintly calloused by the grip of a paintbrush. And, go figure, this evening's first moment of contentment. I'm actually . . . kind of . . . enjoying myself.

Grady guides me out of his arms, pushing against my hand to perform some sort of agile foot maneuver. Show-off. I mean, it's not like anyone – hey. It *is* like anyone is watching us. In fact, *everyone* is. They're still dancing their stiff, safe moves, too aware of the formal setting, but now the couples on the dance floor are also staring our way. Ooh! Spin me around again, Grady! Spin!

And as he does so, and as I feel my dress and hair cascade out with abandon, I'm struck by an unexpected, overwhelming revelation. *This is not my wedding.* The stuffiness of it, the grandeur everywhere. Not one person besides me has even said a word about Mimi and Trevor's tender, loving vows. Everyone's too busy evaluating the cost of the food, or the rooms, or the band. How can you enjoy something when you have to worry so much about . . . breaking it? When I get married, I want people to dance so hard, they've got to take off their shoes. I want them to be joyful because of all the happiness of the occasion, not because I've got the band who played at Dustin Hoffman's son's bar mitzvah. I want everyone to be smiling, without a care in the world, at least for this one night. Mimi's wedding has been perfectly beautiful. Excruciatingly painful and mortifying, but nonetheless beautiful. It's just not, in the end, very . . . *me*.

The hushed rattle of a cymbal signals the end of the song, and as Grady and I part, people actually start clapping for us. All I can do is blush, but Grady waves good-naturedly at the small crowd, offering a modest head nod. He starts to sling his arm around my waist for the next number, but I press gently on his chest, indicating we should sit this one out.

'What's wrong, Princess?' he says, cocking an eyebrow at me. 'I tired you out so soon?'

'Dinner's served,' I point out. 'Why don't you head back to the table, and I'll join you in a minute? I've just got to take care of something.'

Grady's cheeks bunch up miserably as he gazes at the devil table of hell. 'Do I have to?'

'I'll be right back,' I laugh in sympathy. 'I promise.'

'Friggin' better be,' Grady mumbles, taking a small step toward our table. I might as well be sending him to purgatory.

It's not hard to find who I'm looking for. There she is with her new husband, grinning ecstatically at a table of immaculately groomed revelers. Mimi's veil has been removed to reveal the mass of chestnut curls pinned to her head in an ornate, sculptural creation. Up close, I can see how delicate the lace straps of her gown are, and how the fabric shimmers as it clings to her figure.

'Mimi, you look beautiful.' I give my cousin a hug once I get to her.

'Izzy!' Mimi clasps her hands together. 'Did you love the ceremony? I'm so glad you did! Everyone, this is my cousin Isabel,' Mimi announces. 'Iz, these are my coworkers from Wollcott Design. *You* remember Catherine Wollcott – I'm sure meeting her was the *highlight* of Grady Cole's show.' There's a beat of silence as I tactfully hold my tongue. 'Well, Catherine had to be in Hong Kong with a client this weekend,' Mimi goes on. '*Absolutely* broke my heart. But have you tried the Kobe beef yet?'

Good Lord, this beef better jump off the plate and perform 'Oklahoma' for all the applause it's getting.

Trevor clears his throat discreetly, and Mimi lets out a

whoop. 'God,' she says. 'I haven't even introduced you to my Trevsies yet!'

Trevor inclines his head respectfully, his handsome green eyes shining. 'I'm so glad to be a part of your family,' he says, giving me a kiss on the cheek. Gorgeous *and* nice. Mimi did, indeed, hit the jackpot.

But to my surprise, when I tell Trevor we're delighted to have him, I don't feel a whit of resentment or envy. I let out a deep breath, and it's like my shoulders are releasing a lifetime of tension. For once, when I look at my cousin, I'm not seeing everything I don't have. I'm not even seeing everything I want.

I rest my hand lightly on Mimi's arm and gesture toward a relatively private spot on one side of the ballroom, behind the pillars wrapped with twinkly lights. 'Can I snag you away for a minute?'

'Of course!' Mimi squeals, waving good-bye to the Wollcott Design brigade. 'Trevsies has to go say hello to his banking buddies anyway!'

Trevor gives me a genial look that seems to say, *I know, but I love her* before he excuses himself and ventures off where he's been sent.

'So here I am!' Mimi exclaims when we're off on our own. 'All yours.'

'Great,' I manage. 'Because I wanted to make sure I got to tell you –'

Mimi's looking at me with wide, glistening eyes. I've never seen her happier. She looks like . . . well, like every bride should look on her wedding day.

'Mimi,' I say earnestly, 'your ceremony moved me to tears, and the reception turned out perfect. Congratulations. I mean it.' And the thing is – I do mean it. My cousin looks so genuinely fulfilled and enthusiastic that I can't help but be happy for her.

'Oh, Iz, that means so much to me.' Mimi exhales, spreading a palm over her chest. 'More than you know, probably.'

And hold the phone; drop what you're doing; blow me

over with a feather. Because she sounds sincere. Mimi Duncan, or rather Mimi *Hewitt*, actually sounds sincere. I thought I'd see Bill Clinton become a priest before I heard the ring of truth spout from this girl's mouth.

'Your opinion matters more to me than anyone's,' Mimi continues while I'm frozen in flabbergasted silence.

'It does?' I hear the shock in my voice. The light's dimmer where we are, and I wonder if that's why Mimi looks suddenly vulnerable.

'Don't hate me for saying this,' she starts, leaning against a pillar and flicking a tiny white light with her finger. 'But I've always been jealous of you.'

'Hum-in-na-*wha*?' is what comes out of me. I am literally standing here, my mouth a gaping chasm – bats could fly around in there – and my features contorted into the most blatant expression of '*Huh*?' ever evinced in the history of humankind.

'It's just that you always did so much better in school than I did,' Mimi goes on, seeming distressed. 'And then you went to Brown, and I only went to Middlebury –'

'There's nothing wrong with Middlebury –' I interrupt, wondering what parallel universe my cavernous black-hole mouth has transported me into.

'It's not Ivy League.'

'Jeez, Mimi, who *cares*?' I nearly laugh at the absurdity.

'My mother.' Mimi gives me a regretful, lopsided smile. 'That's *all* she cared about, the whole time I was in high school. Her and those uppity Park Slope friends of hers.'

'Oh, Mimi,' I say, with genuine feeling. But then I get a sharp stabbing sensation in my side. I'm remembering the source of my own most intense high school anguish. 'What about Jared Anders?' I cry out. 'How could you care about grades and stupid colleges when you had *Jared Anders*?'

Mimi fixes me with a frank, how-could-you-not-have-realized gaze. 'Jared Anders is *gay*, Izzy. Extravagantly, outrageously, neon-bicycle-shortsy-gay. Always has been.'

'*What*??' I blurt out. Jared Anders? Of the sexy biceps

and the pillowy lips? I mean, sure he loved musical theater. And hair products. And he got his shoes shined professionally. *Holy crap*. 'But you guys dated for, like, *three years*!'

Mimi throws her hands in the air. 'I didn't say he admitted it right away!'

'Still,' I insist, sticking to the facts, 'he chose you over me. *I* wasn't the one he picked to see if he could ever make it with a woman.'

'That's not true.' Mimi's shaking her head, looking down at her pointy satin shoes. 'He always liked you better. Jared adored you. That's why he never *dated* you. He always knew we were a sham, even when I still clung to the notion that we were in love. Me, Jared could hurt. You, never.'

'Oh, my *God*.' I'm seeing the past thirteen years in a whole new light. My first heartbreak, what I've always considered the catalyst to all my following years of heartbreak, was actually . . . an act of tenderness? The only reason Jared Anders dated Mimi Duncan was that . . . he never really cared for her at all? 'No wonder you hate me, Mimi!'

'I don't hate you!' Mimi wails, grabbing my hand and squeezing it. 'I've just always wanted to . . . measure up. Make my parents as proud of me as yours are of you.'

'Look at them, Mimi.' I guide my cousin to where she can see my aunt Barbara and uncle Pete visibly beaming with joy. (Or rather, in my aunt's case, giving a Cinderella's Wicked Stepmother grin of satisfaction.) 'You've never had to measure up to anything.'

Mimi's forehead smooths, and I see her small frame relax. 'You and I used to be such good friends,' she says wistfully.

I smile back at her affectionately, nodding with understanding. Because, though both of us know we'll never be as close as we were as toddlers, I think we're feeling the same enormous relief. My cousin and I won't wind up like our mothers, snapping *at* each other in person and *about* each other behind our backs. Mimi and I can finally be – after so many years – family.

Not that I'll *ever* be able to love her friends. Out of the corner of my eye, I see Heather trotting over to us, taking manic steps in her tight, ankle-length bridesmaid dress. She's got this frenzied expression on her face, like she's just found out the fish tastes better than the beef after all.

Heather's breathless by the time she reaches us. She lunges right for Mimi's ear, cupping her mouth with one hand. She's sneaking furtive glances in my direction every half second, and I wonder with a stab of horror what Grady's done now. Did he fess up that he's here only because I got stood up? Or – worse – could he have told Mimi's friends what he actually thinks of them? Because he's got it in him; I know he does. I can just imagine Grady calling the four succubi 'as shallow as a puddle in the desert.'

I watch Mimi's eyes widen to Frisbee size as she gasps at Heather's sudden news. The two of them are just staring at me like I'm some spiritual guru, about to impart unto them the secrets of immortality.

'What's going on?' I keep my tone flip.

'Ohmigod, Izzy! If we hadn't just had that little discussion' – Mimi's voice is reaching its squealiest pitch – 'and if I hadn't found my own wonderful Trevsies' – and yet somehow, it's still going higher – 'I would be so *screamingly* jealous of you right now!'

There goes my eardrum. Completely torn. 'Mimi, what are you *talking* about?' I'm actually kind of scared here. I take a peek at the gigantic crystal chandelier to make sure Mimi's voice hasn't cracked anything important.

'Heather's fiancé, Howard, finally realized where he knew Grady from!' Mimi screeches, with Heather nodding feverishly by her shoulder. 'They went to high school together! Well, for one year at least.'

This is what sends Heather into an apoplectic frenzy? The fact that her exalted fiancé and my humble date could ever have studied under the same roof? Give me a friggin' break! If we were anywhere other than a formal, family-filled reception, I'd be telling Heather Taylor where she could stick her haughty, upturned nose. And I'll tell you, it would *not* be smelling anything sweet.

'How could you never have told us who Grady *is*!' Mimi continues excitedly.

'But . . . you know who he is!' I exclaim back. All this furor is over the fact that Grady's a newly successful, bona fide art star? Because I find it extremely hard to believe that anyone at my table gives a flying fig about the art world. 'Your boss even bought one of Grady's paintings, Mimi, remember? For '*Susan and Tim*.' You know all about Grady. You always have.'

'Oh, *I* get it,' Mimi says in a hushed but eager tone. 'We're keeping it on the . . . how do they say? The *down low*?'

Okay there, Snoop Mimi. Maybe I just don't have the right perspective here. Maybe it's like how Dix never gets keyed up by movie or music stars because she's around them so often. Maybe I've just been around famous artists so much that I'm jaded by the whole thing. Grady's the painter of the moment, it's true. But still – he just had his first show. Could you really call him *famous*?

All this talk of Grady has startled me into remembering my promise not to leave him alone for too long. I give my thumbnail a gulty nibble, thinking I may have already broken my word. 'I should get back to Grady, actually,' I tell Mimi and Heather, inching backward. 'He's expecting me.'

'Go, of course!' Mimi urges, nearly shoving me off as Heather keeps nodding madly.

What has gotten *into* these people? 'So, I'll just . . . catch you later, then!'

'Ta!' Mimi waves after me.

'Tell Grady hi!' Heather barks out, as if it's not Grady but actually Jude Law who's dining next to me.

'Sure thing!' I call back as I cross the room with what I'm sure is a look of utter confusion clouding my features.

From not ten feet away, I can already tell that the whole

tenor of my table has changed. Cat, Debbie, Becka, and their dates, including Heather's Howard (try that five times fast), have ceased their private, gossipy whispers and financial-gobbledygook talk. Instead, they're all staring at Grady. Who looks more uncomfortable and fidgety than I've ever seen him. He's pushing back in his chair, rubbing his palms on his thighs. He's focusing his eyes right and left, up and down, anywhere but at the faces of his newly captive audience. I don't get it. Since when are my high school nonfriends more enthralled by painting than by diamonds?

Inching nearer, I hear snippets of conversation, mostly obscured by the band music. They're talking about the Bond, I think, because I catch one of the girls mentioning it in between the drowsy bars of 'Stormy Weather.' For a second, I'm seized with dread. Is Grady telling some humiliating story about me? Is that why he seems so . . . well, so guilty-looking?

I quicken my steps, reaching the table just as Grady's saying something cryptic like 'I was living with constants.' What is that, a mathematical allegory? Was Grady shacking up with the number pi? I don't even get a chance to ask, because the split second I rest my hand on his shoulder, Grady jumps straight out of his chair. Literally – he bolts upright, springing forward and nearly knocking me to the floor. Easy there, tiger!

'Izzy! Sorry!' Grady's lunging to throw an arm around my waist before I can topple to the ground. 'You just . . . startled me.'

'Whoa! Remind me never to sneak up behind you in a dark alley.' I tug at my dress, which has twisted catastrophically close to a boob-revealing wardrobe malfunction.

'Let's go.' Grady grabs my wrist with surprising vigor and pulls me toward the dance floor.

'Not so fast, Fred Astaire!' I'm digging in my heels. '*What* was that all about?'

'What was what all about?' Grady blinks innocently, his

face blank. I give him a searing, don't-bullshit-me glare. 'They're impressed by art.' He shrugs. 'Who knew?'

Something here feels shifty to me, but I bite my tongue about it and try to scoot around Grady to get back to my seat. He parries to block, strengthening his grip on me. I can see a flash of panic in his eyes, even as he struggles to hide it.

'Grady, what is *wrong* with you?' I insist, eyeing him with heightened suspicion.

His head droops dejectedly. 'I don't much like it here,' he admits. 'To be honest, when I vanished to the bathroom for twenty minutes, I was actually taking a walk around the block, debating whether or not I should come back.'

'You didn't.' A knot of betrayal sticks in my throat. 'How could you?'

'That's the thing – I *couldn't*. I couldn't do that to you.' Grady's eyes shine with concern. 'Still, no offense or anything, but this whole place isn't very *me*. And I don't think it's *you* either. Am I right?'

'I wouldn't call this my first choice for a Saturday evening, no,' I confess diplomatically.

Grady tilts his head toward mine, giving me a scoundrel's smile. 'So let's get out of here,' he hums.

I take a step back. 'But I can't!' I'm shaking my head. What am I supposed to do, just leave? Before they cut the cake? Before they make the toasts?

'Sure you can,' Grady retorts, gesturing to a spot behind him. 'The elevator's right over there.'

And now that he says it, I take a pause to reconsider. *Do* I really need to be here? Haven't I already accomplished more than I anticipated? I fawned sufficiently to Aunt Barbara, got to see my folks and ancient Aunt Sheila, and even smoothed out my differences with the bride herself. That's a pretty complete evening, if you ask me. Except . . . there is still that one thing. . . .

'But I'm hungry,' I blurt out, even knowing my fish must be cold by now.

Grady gives me a slow, easy grin. 'I know just the

place,' he says, backing up toward the exit and pulling me along with both hands.

Gosh, this is kind of exciting, actually. Skipping out, without a word of good-bye to anyone. I'm escaping. With Grady Cole. A tingle of anticipation rushes through me. I follow his bold stride toward the elevators, managing to look back only once. But once is enough. There's my mother, catching my eye. She throws me a playful wink and an encouraging wriggle of her fingers. Oh, for goodness' sake. My mother thinks I'm stealing away to make out in the elevator.

Yup, I've made her proud.

27

If you were a new hamburger,
you'd be the McGorgeous

'Trust me!' I exclaim to Grady's disbelieving face. We're in the midst of a very serious argument here, but only because he refuses to admit I'm right. 'A real chocolate milk shake is made with *vanilla* ice cream and chocolate syrup. I know these things! I'm from Brooklyn! Home of the original Fox's U-bet milk-shake-making chocolate syrup!'

Grady takes a tentative slurp, his cheeks caving in as he draws the thick drink through its straw. 'I don't know . . .'

We're cozily ensconced opposite each other in a booth at the Renaissance Diner, just west of the Theater District, and – as Grady claims – home of the best milk shake in New York City. He's got his chocolate, and I've got cookies 'n' cream – vanilla with bits of Oreo blended in. And God, it's heavenly. I can taste the flecks of vanilla bean, alternating with the soft, chewy chunks of cookie. Mmmm.

'Stick to painting,' I insist. 'Leave the food expertise to me.'

'Whatever you say, Princess,' Grady laughs, rolling his eyes.

Just then the waiter arrives, a seasoned-looking veteran in a black vest with a stained apron tied round his waist. He plops probably his ten millionth and ten million and first cheeseburger deluxes in front of us, offering an accented, 'Enjoy your meal' before he shuffles off to chitchat with the cashier.

'Are you disappointed?' Grady asks, picking up a chunky French fry. 'You're expecting a swank night out, and I take you here?'

I can't quite answer right away, because my mouth is stuffed with a heaping bite of cheeseburger, which tastes so juicy and fresh and – ooh! – even has *bacon* on it! 'I love it here!' I beam, washing down the burger with a deep sip of creamy milk shake. 'I just worry we might be a bit' – I scrunch up my face – '*underdressed.*'

'It's true,' Grady deadpans. 'I should have worn my Cartier cuff links.'

We spend a few moments in comfortable silence, wolfing down the enormous amount of food in front of us. Grady's stuffed a napkin down his neck to protect his stiff white shirt, and I do the same, covering my shimmery ecru neckline. We must look like rejects from Carnegie Hall – the only two who didn't practice, practice, practice. I shove a salty French fry in my mouth. Usually on a date, I force myself to eat delicately, even if I do order a giant meal. But now I'm taking bites as big as I want, leaving the knife and fork untouched at the side of my plate. Somehow, I get the feeling Grady doesn't care about my being ladylike and genteel. Not that *we're* on a date, or anything. We're just . . . eating. You know. Together.

I let myself gaze upon Grady's face for a moment, taking in the bold jut of his chin, the defiant angles of his cheekbones. I notice his hair has started to get tousled again – as if it's got a will of its own – and I feel a stab of affection for its rebelliousness. I think back to the ballroom dance floor, to Grady swooping me around, my hair flying, everyone going gaga over us. They applauded! And I actually had . . . fun. Can you believe it? All the stars in the sky – and in multiple far-reaching galaxies – were conspiring to make this the worst night of my life, and yet I still wound up getting at least a modicum of enjoyment from it – all because of Shady Grady Cole. Who's seeming a lot less shady lately. Must be the tux.

Grady catches my eye, and feeling caught, I dart my gaze away. But not before I see the strained look on his face, as if he's struggling to break the silence. I give him a questioning glance. What's on Grady's mind that he can't just say outright?

Grady clears his throat, coughing into his hand. 'Are you still in love with Avery?' He squints with concern. 'Because I kind of . . . I feel responsible, Izzy.'

'*Huh?*' The sudden mention of Avery startles me. In truth, for the first time in two agonizing weeks, I'd sort of . . . *forgotten* about him. 'I don't think I ever loved Avery,' I say slowly, working out the thoughts as I'm speaking them. 'How could I, when I never really knew him? Don't get me wrong –' I add, seeing Grady's hopeful expression. 'I *wanted* to love him. I thought for sure we'd be the toast of the town, the two people invited first to every art gala, benefit, and exhibition. I guess you could say I had . . .' I feel a catch in my voice. 'I had a lot of hopes for me and Avery. But now that I think about it, none of them were actually *real*. Like Mimi's wedding, with all its polish and grandeur . . . on the surface, it's everything a girl could ever want. But what's the use of a fantasy that never touches the ground?'

Grady's pursing his lips across the table from me, and I can't tell if he's trying not to laugh or just baffled as all hell. 'Okay . . .,' he manages, scratching his head. 'So were these . . . very *juicy* fantasies you were having about Avery? Anything you'd like to share?' He's giving me a caddish smirk.

'Oh!' I cry before I realize he's just teasing. I throw a French fry at his chest, laughing as it bounces off the paper napkin and onto his plate.

'Thanks!' Grady munches on the torpedoed fry, wriggling his eye-brows at me.

'I didn't mean it *that* way! Avery Devon was the best part of a fairy-tale life I never really wanted in the first place. Don't get me wrong – I appreciate a fifteen-dollar cocktail, or a swank restaurant brimming with all the Kobe beef in the world. But in the end, I guess I'm just more of a burgers-and-milk-shakes kind of gal.'

Grady swallows, parting his lips. I find myself focusing on the bottom one, which is full and tender-looking. Kind of sexy, actually. I'm struck by an inner flush, the heat rushing to my face. There's that self-consciousness again. The ultra awareness of where my hands are, what I should say, how much I'm giving away by my expression.

'Sounds like you're my kind of gal, then,' Grady says, his voice gravelly.

I hesitate, shoving my hands in my lap so I don't have to worry what to do with them. 'I'd say you're a lot more champagne and caviar, now, Mr Rags-to-Riches Hotshot Artist,' I tease back. 'Just look how everyone at the wedding was fawning over you! And by the way? You're buying dinner.'

But Grady's not laughing. In fact, a spasm of pain passes over his features.

'Oh, fine,' I let out with mock exasperation. 'We'll charge the meal to the gallery!'

'No, it's not that,' Grady hastens to say. He swallows a few more times, and I can see the uneasiness spread over his face like a patchwork quilt. 'There's stuff I need to tell you, Izzy. Something you need to know about me . . .' He rakes his hand through his hair, ruffling the last carefully combed pieces. 'But I'm worried . . . I'm *scared* . . . that you'll never forgive me for it.'

'Come on,' I say softly, idly swirling a French fry through a river of ketchup. 'You don't care that much about what I think of you.'

Grady fixes me with a frank, and slightly sad, stare. 'You know that's not true.'

Oh, man, those are some butterflies. How do I respond? My breath is quickening, and I'm suddenly too shy to make eye contact. It's like if I let myself even look at Grady, I might step over some invisible line into territory too uncertain to tread upon. There might be minefields there.

When I don't say anything, Grady takes a giant, cleansing breath and lets it out forcefully. His half-eaten burger's forgotten, the fries getting cold. 'Avery and I went to college together,' Grady begins, like he's narrating an odyssey. 'We were best friends, back then. But you know that already, I think.' There's a pause, as if he's deciding whether to jump over the precipice.

'Yes,' I whisper my encouragement. 'I know.'

'Three years ago, Avery started going out with this girl,' Grady continues, the hurt coloring his face. 'Someone I cared about, very much. Someone more important to me' — he lowers his eyes. — 'than anyone.'

I bite my lip, willing Grady to go on. I'm waiting for the part where I'm supposed to never forgive him.

'After a long time,' Grady goes on, with obvious effort, 'I found out Avery had been cheating on her. During their entire relationship. With various different women. And without a shred of remorse. Of course, I had to tell her.'

'So that's why you hate him?' I wince.

'Because he's a spineless, cheating liar?' Grady says without flinching. 'Basically.'

Involuntarily, my eyes close, and I lay a hand on the diner tabletop to steady myself. That woman could have been me. 'So that's why you warned me against him,' I nod. 'Not that I listened.'

'You should have seen her, Izzy,' he says, nearly under his breath. 'She was so devastated. She still is. Even now, I can't look at her without seeing the pain she's feeling.' His face crumples with anguish. 'She and Avery were going to be married.'

She and Avery were going to be married.

Grady's words are echoing around in my head, trying to trigger something I know is in there. I've got a sinking, ominous feeling. Oh, God. There it is — a direct hit. I'm hearing Grady's voice again, from less than two hours ago. The evidence was right there in front of me — glaringly so.

Back at the reception, when I startled Grady at our table. When I caught those tiny snippets of conversation over the melody of 'Stormy Weather.' I had thought Grady was saying, 'I was living with constants,' a mathematical metaphor, all intellectual and mysterious. But what I really heard was *'Constance.' When I was living with Constance*.

I know why I'm never supposed to forgive Grady Cole. The woman Grady's talking about – Avery Devon's former fiancée – it's Constance Bond. I *knew* she and Grady had met before. Didn't I say so, back when she visited the gallery? Grady loves her. She's the most important person in his life. And here I've been laughing with him, dancing with him, *having dinner with him* . . .

I don't need to hear the rest of Grady's story, because I've already read the final pages. Avery stole Grady's girl and broke his heart, and then went and broke the girl's heart. But Grady made sure he was right there to pick up the pieces for her. Grady's in love with Constance Bond. I can *see* his feelings for her, all raw and at the surface. They might even be dating – hell, living together – as we speak. Or . . . if not . . . and here I just can't look at Grady, not even in my peripheral vision, so I stare instead at the red leather booth, focusing on a tiny tear in its corner. If Grady can't have Constance, then he's willing to settle for me.

But that's not good enough! I'm rising from the booth, grabbing the napkin from my chest and throwing it down on my plate. Is there really and truly not *one man* in this city – not Cameron, not Avery, not Grady, not even Jamie – who can stick to *one woman*? Is the very concept too foreign for them to grasp? Even *cave people* understood monogamy. I mean, when did Fred and Barney ever cheat on Wilma and Betty?

I storm out of the diner, taking long strides, feeling the gauzy layers of my dress trail behind me. I'm absolutely fuming.

'Izzy!' I hear Grady calling after me. 'Izzy, where you going? Hey, wait up!'

But I refuse to listen. I'm out the door with a brisk,

'Thank you' to the waiter (there's no need to be rude), and marching down Ninth Avenue, the indignation quickening my steps. It's kind of ironic, when you think about it. For the whole time I've known him, Grady's done nothing but irk me – and that, I handled just fine. But now that he's trying to befriend me – or be*whatever* me – I can't bear it. I'm about to give a sarcastic laugh at the thought when I feel a strong hand grasping my arm, spinning me sharply around.

'Izzy, what did I do?' Grady's face has adopted new levels of hurt. The kind that only comes from the inside out. 'Why'd you run out like that?'

The sight of him makes me waver. He's back to his old self now, even in the penguin suit, all frazzled and messy, and – okay, I admit it – damn cute. But he's made me feel like crap. And I don't need that. Not at all. So I waste no time with pleasantries. I spit it out. 'Is this about Constance Bond?'

Grady drops his grip on my arm. Every ounce of color vanishes from his face. He doesn't answer me. He doesn't need to.

'I thought so.' Spinning on my heel. I resume my purposeful escape, raising my hand to signal an oncoming cab.

'No! *Isabel*!' Grady calls out as the taxi slows in front of me. He motions for the cabbie to move on, and so to add insult to injury, now he's ruined my ride. We're standing in the gutter, between two parked cars, and Grady's behind me, blocking the narrow path back to the sidewalk. 'Why does it matter?' he whispers, close to my ear.

I tighten every muscle in my body for courage before I turn around to confront him. 'You're in love with Constance Bond. It's so obvious.' Just saying the words draws up this well of emotion right at the surface. 'Don't you get it, Grady? I can't be the other woman anymore. I'm so sick and tired of being in the shadow of someone else. You knew that. You *know* that.'

'Aw, Iz, no.' Grady shakes his head at me tenderly, a

measure of relief easing the creases in his brow. 'That's not it at all. There's no other woman.'

'You're hiding something,' I say flatly.

'You need to trust me first,' he responds.

'But I don't,' is what comes out of my mouth. Three words barely there, quivering in the atmosphere. It's like I've struck him.

Grady leans against the old Buick beside us. He's tenting his fingers over his nose, looking down at the asphalt. 'I tried to ignore you,' he finally says. 'When I saw you getting closer to Avery. I figured I'd just . . . get over you. Nothing had happened, you didn't know. No harm done.'

Wait. Grady had something to get over? 'Is that why you stopped talking to me?' I say tentatively, standing on the curb, a healthy distance away.

'Yeah, that really worked.' He kicks at a stray soda can with his shined dress shoe. 'God, Izzy,' and he's looking up at me with those big blue pools he has for eyes, 'I'm fucking *painting* you. You've *seen* it.'

Oh, my God. He's right. I just never thought . . . Grady's newest work, the red hair cascading down the canvas. What I took to be a detail from a hair-coloring product. 'My hair's browner,' I hear myself saying, and I can't help but smile.

'Artistic license,' he shoots back, rising from his perch on the Buick.

'Well, as your *associate dealer*, I'm supposed to be guiding your vision,' I insist, idly playing with a piece of the hair in question.

'Oh, but you are.' Grady takes a step forward, toward where I'm standing.

A few people pass by us on the sidewalk, but we don't seem to notice, and neither do they. This is New York. We could be having a knock-down, drag-out, hair-pulling fight and no one would lift an eyebrow. More so than at the diner, or at Mimi's wedding, or even at the gallery, out here on the street, we might as well be alone.

Grady's right in front of me now. I can see the sprinkling of stubble that's sprouting along his jaw, even though he just shaved hours ago. He takes another step closer, joining me up on the curb.

'You're not supposed to like me!' I blurt out, a last feeble effort at resistance. 'Remember, when we met? On the subway platform, I mean.' I can't help but cringe at the memory. 'You called me a brat! You think I'm spoiled!'

'I don't think you're spoiled,' Grady traces my collarbone with his finger, brushing away a stray hair. He's leaving bursts of sensation everywhere he touches.

'You don't?' My voice is small, the fight leached right out.

'I think you're very well preserved.' He's brushing his lips against my forehead. He's lingering gently on either cheek. 'I think you're wonderful.'

When Grady kisses me, all his weeks of want rush to the forefront. I'm sensing, through his lips alone – and the hands cradling my face, then descending to clutch me tighter – that there is no other person Grady would rather be holding, not anywhere. No place that would give him more pleasure to be than right here, with his adamant, devoted lips pressed urgently to mine.

God help me, I feel the same way.

Hey, Mother. Want Another?

Mmm. I'm taking a delicious morning stretch in a warm, hazy ray of sunlight, jostling Robbie from his perch on my chest, where he's been purring contentedly for who knows how long.

'*Mrawr!*' he cries as he hits the floor.

That's right. I'm in my own apartment. Alone, except for Sir Robbie. What, you don't think I've learned my lesson by now? Well, okay. Fine. Maybe I haven't. Because from the second my head hit the pillow to the second before my eyes even opened, I've been dreaming about nothing but Grady Cole.

In my pink fuzzy slippers, I shuffle over to the kitchen nook, a gigantic, goofy smile stretched across my face. And I haven't even had coffee yet! I switch on my Mr Coffee, and grab the Frosted Mini-Wheats from the upper cabinet, and without even realizing it, suddenly I'm singing a little song.

'*I'm gonna eat cer-e-al,*' I belt out, swaying my shoulders. '*And Grady likes me. He really liiiiiikes me.*'

What a night we had! After the diner – and the smooching – we just kept walking downtown. Grady told me all about Paris, studying art in the same city where Picasso strolled the dim, gaslit streets of Montmartre. And

I told him all about starting out as a gallery assistant in Williamsburg, Brooklyn, where I would be the only one going on studio visits while the dealers were off smoking at some warehouse loft. We talked about everything. Well, everything except Constance Bond. I want to believe Grady when he says I've got nothing to worry about. My every instinct is saying to give him a shot. Which is exactly why I should be fleeing in the other direction. Since when have my instincts *ever* been right?

Grady and I must have walked almost thirty blocks last night, because suddenly we were in Chelsea, and my feet were wrecked in their high heels, and we were stopping at a bar for a rest and a glass – or several – of wine. We stayed out until three in the morning, and then Grady accompanied me in a cab home, holding the car door open like a gentleman, and leaving me on my doorstep with one last, lingering, euphoric kiss.

So, yes. The evening turned out better than expected, to say the least. But that still doesn't let one self-destructive, floppy-haired lothario off the hook. Grabbing my Robbie Williams mug ($5.99 on eBay!) full of hot, black coffee, I plop myself down on the floor in my cotton nightgown, leaning back against the bed frame. Cordless in hand, I punch out Jamie's number.

'Hello?' Jamie croaks, sounding half dead and wholly miserable.

My heart instantly goes out to him. 'Aw, Jamie,' I sigh. 'What'd you go and do to yourself?'

'Iz!' He perks up a bit, then groans with regret. 'How badly did I screw things up for you? Did you make it to the wedding?'

'I . . . did,' I tell him, not yet ready to confess about my newfound . . . whatever it is . . . with Grady. But I give Jamie a few details about the evening, and I make sure he's no longer retching over a toilet bowl. 'You make me worry about you,' I finally say, hearing the distress in my voice. 'You're a different person these days, and not a better one.'

'You're right.' He sounds grim. 'I've behaved horribly

since that stupid pickup line column. You should be letting me have it right now, Iz. You're being too good to me.' He heaves a deep sigh. 'In the past week alone, I've lost all my girlfriends – they called *me* shallow. My writing has gone to crap, and I've hurt my best friend. How could I have let all of that happen?'

'I don't know,' I answer truthfully.

Jamie's pause on the other end of the line is suddenly cut through by the sound of the door buzzing downstairs. Someone's here to see me? This early in the morning . . . er afternoon?

'Jaim, I've got to call you back – someone's at the door, okay?' I trot over to the entryway.

'I'm sorry, Iz. I'm so sorry,' Jamie exhales through the phone line.

'I know you are, honey. Please, just take care of yourself,' I offer before clicking off, hoping beyond hope that I'll get my old Jamie back very, very soon.

The buzzer drones again, and as I press the intercom to say, 'Who is it?' I'm struck by an incredulous thought. Could it be Grady? So soon after our first date? Instinctively, I peer into the wood-framed mirror on the vestibule wall, gathering my hair into a ponytail. *Damn*. No time to brush my teeth.

'Izzy?' the familiar voice, much weaker than I remember it, crackles over the speaker. 'It's me.'

Oh, my God. Instantly I press the DOOR button, completely unprepared for whatever's about to ensue. What should I say? Should I just immediately drop to my knees? *Finally*, after all this time . . .

I throw open the door, contorting my features into the best expression of repentance I can possibly muster. But soon that expression vanishes, replaced by a full-body wash of concern. I can't believe what I'm seeing. Involuntarily, I take such a sharp breath I almost choke on it.

It's Dix. And she looks . . . *awful*. Well, awful for Dix, that is, which is still pretty gorgeous compared with most people. But still! She hasn't got a speck of makeup on, not even to cover the dark circles under her eyes, and her long hair's sort of half in, half out of its lopsided bun. She's wearing linty gray yoga pants, an oversized T-shirt, and sneakers. Dix owns *sneakers*? I would have sworn she even went to the gym in Jimmy Choos. I swear, if it weren't for the stylish, slouchy white leather bag slung over her shoulder, I'd be dialing 911 right now.

'Can I come in?' Dix sounds hesitant, almost shy even. Okay, now I'm scared.

'Of course!' I cry out, stepping away from the door. 'Oh, *Dix*. I've been trying to reach you for *weeks*.'

'I know.' She's biting the inside of her cheek, all guilty-looking. Wait. Why is *Dix* the one looking like she's got something to apologize for?

We head into my main room, Dix easing herself into my desk chair, and me flopping down on the bed. Robbie hops on the desk, eyeing Dix suspiciously. He and Dix have never had the most . . . adoring relationship. Not since baby-kitten Robbie threw himself, claws and all, at Dix's ponytail, grabbing on for dear life as she swung her hair around in circles. I'm convinced Robbie just thought he was reuniting with his long-lost mother. But Dix wasn't happy about becoming a one-woman kitten rodeo.

'Beat it, cat,' Dix warns Robbie, pointing her finger at him.

He mews defeatedly, jumping down to slink to my side.

'Dix, you've got to let me explain about Arden Moore,' I start immediately, finally letting the words pour out. 'I didn't mean to! He was just being so . . . sleazy, and I snapped! I could have been adult and mature about it, but instead I made him angry and ruined your party. And . . . I'm horrible!'

Dix is staring at me like I've just confessed to having twelve fingers. 'God, Iz, don't worry about it,' she says, giving a quick shrug. 'Arden's a total dickhead.' She reaches into her slouchy bag and pulls out a package of saltines, which she promptly opens with her teeth.

'So . . . you mean . . .' Hang on. Dix isn't angry with me?

'I didn't bankrupt your business?' I feel the urge to start singing again, but for Dix's sake, I resist. 'You want some water with that?'

'Please!' Dix says as I hop the three steps to my kitchen. 'Fucking crackers. Can't even keep *these* down.' She takes a reluctant nibble. 'Iz, my company is fine. In fact, the publicity actually *helped* Arden's reputation. Finally, we found a way to make him look sympathetic in the tabloids. He's been spurned by a woman! *Everyone* empathizes with that.'

I'm grabbing my water filter out of the fridge, fighting an inner battle between relief and utter terror. 'Dix,' I manage, spilling all over the breakfast bar as I pour. 'If you're not angry at me, and your business isn't in trouble –' I will myself to stay calm. '*Where the hell have you been?*'

Dix lets out a laugh, and I'm glad to see some of the old glow return to her face. 'I've been in Brooklyn,' she admits more somberly. 'At my mom's house. Hiding out.'

Hiding out? Oh, God. What has Dix done? I wonder if it's tax evasion. I *knew* she shouldn't have expensed all those hundreds of cocktails. I *begged* her to let me pay! At least once!

'I needed to consider things,' Dix goes on, drawing her long legs up under her. 'To decide what to do.' She looks down at her hands, which are fidgeting in her lap. Dix *never* fidgets. 'I needed time alone.'

I hand Dix her water, resting my palm on her shoulder. I don't even need to know what she's done. Whatever it is, I'll stick by her. I'll offer character witness testimony. I'll conduct a sit-in protest at City Hall.

'Whatever you need from me,' I whisper, bending down in front of my best friend so we're at eye level. 'Anything at all. You got it.'

Dix gives me a strangled smile, uncertainty clouding her face. 'You up for being a birthing coach?'

'*What?*' I stumble backward, winding up in a tangled heap on the floor. Robbie screams and sprints in the other direction. '*Dix*, you're –'

'I'm pregnant,' Dix says, shaking her head nervously. 'Eight weeks now, if you can believe it.' She seems, herself, not quite able to. 'And I've decided to keep the baby.'

'But who ... I mean ...' I might be treading on forbidden ground here, but my thoughts are just racing too quickly. 'Do you know who the father is?'

'I do, actually,' and Dix seems to brighten. 'It's Julian, the guy who owns East of Eden, that speakeasy-type bar down the block from me. He's a really nice guy.'

I know just who she means – Julian the hot bartender, who seems to live permanently in 1935, with his sleeve garters, suspenders, and everpresent fedora. Dix is having a baby with Clark Gable!

'He asked to marry me,' Dix says, rolling her eyes.

'Oh, my *God*,' I'm shouting, still splayed on the floor. 'Are you going to?'

'Of course not!' She gets up, briefly pacing the length of my bedroom-slash-living-room-slash-study before easing herself back down in the chair. 'But you know him, Mr Old-fashioned and all. He had to offer.'

I'm only just now wrapping my mind round this. Dix! Having a baby! In seven months! An actual, live, squishy, helpless little baby! But you know what? The idea kind of makes sense. She'd never admit it, but Dix is a natural nurturer. To those who don't know her, she can seem harsh and tough on the outside, but Dix has done nothing but take care of people since the day I met her.

'You're going to make such a good mom,' I tell her honestly.

'You think?' Dix's voice is small. For once, she's the one who needs the advice, the one without all the answers.

'Hell, yeah.' I rise to convey all the support I can with a big, comfy hug.

Dix swiftly pushes my arms away, squirming out of the chair and hauling herself into the bathroom. 'Fucking crackers,' I hear her moan.

I rush in to hold back her hair.

*

Kimmy's blinking at me, her face a total blank. 'Well, duh,' she says, and returns to stuffing envelopes with press releases. Elmore Cowper's show opens on Thursday, only two days away.

'Kimmy, did you hear what I said?' I'm leaning over the reception ledge, keeping my voice low so Avery and Tight-Ass Beth, who are busy in the exhibition rooms, can't hear me. 'Grady and I kissed! Like . . . a lot! It turns out he's *totally sexy*.'

'Freddie wins the pool after all,' Kimmy says with a sigh of disappointment. 'I didn't think you guys would get together for at least another month.'

'The pool? There's a *pool*?' I look at her in disbelief, gripping the ledge with white knuckles.

'Well, no, not really.' Kimmy cocks her spiky purple head. 'Just him and me. But I'm out twenty bucks, thanks a lot.'

'But . . . but . . .' My whole face is scrunched up. 'It was a total fluke!' Grady and I were *so not* supposed to be making out! There's just no way Kimmy and Freddie could have had *any* idea . . .

'You two are really cute together.' Kimmy smiles coyly.

My resolve melts away, and I lapse into a girlish giggle. 'Aren't we?' But hastily, I add, 'Not that we're together, or anything! We're just . . .'

And here, I find myself at a loss. It's been three days since my fake-turned-possibly-real date with Grady Cole, and since then, he called Sunday to say what a good time he had – something we both laughed over given the obstacles that sprang up every step of the way. That night, talking to Grady just felt so natural. Whenever I lapsed into those nerve-racking neuroses that always pop up with a new crush – what's he thinking of me? am I playing it cool enough? – Grady would immediately soothe my worry with some affectionate comment or gentle teasing. God, I can't stop thinking about him. But every moment I start feeling giddy about Grady, I have to check myself. I can't shake the nagging feeling that he's hiding something. It's like he's got some sort of street sign plastered on his chest, and I can't figure out whether it reads YIELD, STOP, or MERGE.

Kimmy looks up at me understandingly. 'I get that you'd be wary, Iz, but I don't think –'

'*Isabel*,' Beth's brusque, monotone voice cuts through from the neighboring room, causing Kimmy to break off midsentence, cringing. 'We need you.'

Oh, God, what now? What insignificant detail of Elmore Cowper's exhibition needs my immediate attention? So far today, I've been summoned by Beth to inspect the barstools (should they be farther apart?), the lighting scheme (how dim can we get away with?), and – most crucial by far – the honey-roasted peanuts (will viewers know they're invited to partake from the bowl?). What's worse, with every word out of my mouth, Avery's frown deepens. He just stands there, scanning Beth's ubiquitous clipboard and scowling at me. Meanwhile, all I want to do is scream out, 'This is a bar top! Strewn with crumpled napkins showing real women's names and phone numbers! Women who aren't going to be called! And everyone's in on the joke but them! *How can this be ethical*?' But Avery's not interested in discussing the concept of the exhibition. He's too busy bugging out over the peanuts.

'The Bride of Frankenstein calls,' Kimmy whispers, her eyes wide in mock fright. We haven't dared mention it – because that would make it real – but I can tell Kimmy's as dismayed by the Bond's current direction as I am.

When I reluctantly cross the threshold of the larger exhibition room, I see Avery, hand on chin, scrutinizing the simulated bar of La Boom, all cherry colored fiberglass and turquoise backlighting. Not a bar I can see myself rushing to any time soon.

'Yes, Beth?' I work on keeping the frustration out of my voice. 'Avery?'

But despite a slight lift of the eyebrows, Avery won't even acknowledge my presence. That's how it's been since these two got back from Venice. Avery speaks to me through Beth, when he bothers to at all.

'We're getting in another artifact today from Elmore,' Beth says efficiently, looking as out of place standing next to a bar as Big Bird might slogging down a Jack and Coke. 'And Avery would like to know your opinion, from a formal standpoint, of where it should be placed.'

'Artifact?' I run my eyes over the litter of phone numbers, drink receipts, and recorded pickup lines. What, is Cowper adding a historical viewpoint now? Sleaziness through the ages? 'I'm not sure I understand what you mean.'

'A relic.' Avery's crisp voice is tinged with impatience. 'Of his social experiment.'

Oh, is that what we're calling it? 'And, this . . . relic, Avery' – I lick my lips – 'you want me to tell you where to put it?'

Avery manages a tight-lipped smile. 'Never mind, Isabel. We'll ask the artist himself. I believe I hear him at the door.'

With that, Elmore Cowper comes surging through the archway, a look of avid excitement splayed over his pockmarked face. He's got long, greasy hair, and a lizard's shiftiness to his eyes. No offense to the lizard. In his hands, he's clutching something that looks like a balled-up piece of netting.

'Bingo, Avery,' Cowper yells indelicately. 'I've got pay dirt. Let me tell ya,' he's panting. 'It's bull's-fucking-eye.'

Cowper unfurls the netting in his hand, and when I get a glimpse of what it really is, I suppress a gasp of disgust. He's holding a pair of women's panty hose. The artist lays the 'artifact' on the bar, draping the fabric so it dangles down over one of the stools. Looking at those wrinkled hose, the imprint of someone's feet still visible, I feel a wave of such revulsion, I wonder how I don't actually double over. It's not the sexual subject matter I object to – because what about Tracey Emin's *Everyone I Have Ever Slept With (1963–1995)*, which is just a camping tent filled with men's names? No, what makes me so appalled right now – to the point of physical nausea – is that yesterday, there was a body in those panty hose. A woman. Seduced by a man. Never knowing that the whole time, she was really just an art project. Elmore Cowper isn't airing his own dirty laundry. He's seeking out other people's. And I think that's despicable.

'Those East Side Girls.' Cowper gives Avery a lascivious smile. 'They like to party.'

'I live on the East Side,' I say boldly, meeting his shifty eye. I don't care if Avery wants to shut me out of the gallery's most important decisions. I've got a voice. And a pretty damn good one at that.

'Well, hel-lo, missy,' Cowper drawls at me, a faint trace of spit on his lower lip. 'I think you're on my list of things to do tonight.'

My eyes narrow as I hear Beth and Avery chuckling like sycophants. But you know what? Thank God for Elmore Cowper. Because suddenly something clicks in my head, and I'm suffused with a sense of inner calm. I've been worrying so much about the future of the gallery and Avery's vision, but that's completely out of my hands. As I let myself gaze over the walls of the Bond, remembering all the beloved works that have graced these surfaces, I'm hit with the full force of realization. If I can't recognize substance in an artist's work, then this gallery becomes nothing but a glorified display case. Which makes me nothing but a salesgirl. And not even a good one, because I don't believe in my product.

'Avery, may I have a moment?' My voice sounds cool and unfamiliar in my ears.

Avery huffs dismissively. Honestly, it's as if my eyes have been squeegeed clean. I see clear as daylight – the only thing that was ever classy about Avery Devon was the cut of his suit. 'I'm a bit tied up here, as you can see,' he says patronizingly. 'Beth, could you help Isabel?'

'No, actually.' My voice rises with insistence. 'I need a moment of *your* time, Avery. In the office, please.'

I see him flinch with surprise. 'Very well,' he says tightly. 'Elmore, excuse me for just one second.'

I catch Beth sneering at me as I turn on my heel. It's a shame, really, that the girl doesn't smile more. I guess it's not in her programming.

As soon as the glass doors shut behind us, Avery's nostrils flare. 'Isabel, this is *un*acceptable,' he begins in a hushed, angry attack. 'As you could see with your own eyes, I was –'

'I quit,' I interrupt, my voice ringing out steadily.

There's a beat of stunned silence.

'Isabel, don't be ridiculous.' Avery shakes his head at me. He sounds frustrated, as if I'm a toddler who's finger-painted the family dog. 'You're not quitting. You've got more of yourself invested in this gallery than any of us.'

'How nice of you to acknowledge my contribution,' I offer dryly. 'But indeed, as of today, I no longer work for you, Avery.' I don't think he notices, but I give the teeniest tremble as the words leave my mouth. Avery's right. I've given everything I have to the Emerson Bond Gallery – my time, my eye, and, above all, my passion. But the gallery as I know and love it exists no more. The tremble I've given isn't one of fear, but of relief.

Avery reaches out a hand, resting it lightly on my bare arm. That touch used to provoke waves of pleasure. Now it feels as cold and limp as a damp washcloth. 'Isabel.' A familiar charm softens the sharp consonants. 'This isn't because . . . I mean, you know how important you are to me, don't you? I need you. Here, where you belong. By my side.'

I take a step back, forcing Avery's hand to drop. 'Your *arm* belongs at your side,' I tell him archly. '*I* belong somewhere that shows work I can believe in.' I start to move purposely past him.

'The customary courtesy is to give two weeks' notice,' Avery booms before I can get to the door.

'You're right.' I turn to face him directly. 'That would be common courtesy. As would calling your travel companion to say you're leaving without her. Instead of, say, writing it in a note. For her to read while surrounded by her luggage.' I watch Avery's eye twitch. 'But then, you always were an expert in courtesy.'

'Just stay for this show,' I hear Avery call in desperation as my hand rests on the double-door knobs. 'We need your contacts! We need your relationship with the Bond's collectors! Isabel! *You can't just leave!*'

But that's exactly what I do. To the sound of Kimmy's applause, I exit the heavy wood door of Emerson Bond's limestone town house without looking back.

*If I could rearrange the alphabet,
I'd put U and I together.*

If I had time, I would be freaking out right now. Or rather, freaking out *more* than I am right now. Because what did I just do? I quit my decent-paying, prestigious position at one of New York's best galleries. *Am I crazy?* Jobs like that do not pop up every day. Or every year, for that matter. Most people go from being a dealer at someone else's gallery to opening their own gallery – but that takes enormous capital, and the ability to go without solid pay for who knows how long. I've got about two months' worth of rent in the bank. That, and one unused 250-dollar bikini. I don't need a Magic 8 Ball to tell me the Outlook Does Not Look Good.

But all that panic and stress has to be squashed down right this minute, because I've got a gala to go to. I know – how Upper East Side Socialite do I sound? Two formal events in one week! I'd almost *forgotten* about the gala tonight, what with the wedding horror and the everything-else horror going on behind the scenes at Izzyland these past few weeks. Tonight's party is being held at the Metropolitan Opera, honoring a new gagillionaire donor for the American Ballet Theatre. Deidre Gayle generously invited me to sit at her table, and even better, Dix will be there too, because she's friends with the party planner. And

Jamie's coming along as my date. He's asked for a second chance, and how could I possibly deny him that?

Besides, I wouldn't feel comfortable asking Grady anyway. What would I say – hey, want to be my default date again for another black-tie affair? As long as you've got the tux and all? No. For our second date, which I'm pretty sure will happen soon, I think we've got to take it down a notch. Maybe see a movie. Grab a slice of pizza. Something that doesn't involve ballroom dancing or champagne fountains.

God, I haven't even told Grady yet about quitting the gallery. Or any of our artists, for that matter. I feel the inner terror starting to bubble up again. I've got to call them all. And the collectors, curators, dealers, gallerists. I take a few nervous swallows. Focus on tonight, Izzy. One step at a time. I quickly slither into the dress that's been lying on my comforter – a tight, long black strapless Armani gown that Dix has lent me for the next seven months. She's convinced the clingy fabric shows off her belly, even though at eight weeks, her stomach's still as flat as a board. But I can't complain. I look fabulous in the silk crepe gown. It's giving me curves I've never seen before, and elongating my frame so I look taller even without heels. Too bad Grady won't be able to see me in this getup after all.

I'm rolling myself with the adhesive lint remover familiar to all cat owners, marveling over how much of Robbie's hair is continually repelled by his body, when I hear the door buzz downstairs. Aw, Jamie's ten minutes early. He's really trying.

I buzz him up, wobbling as I pull on my strappy heels. Quick check in mirror – no mascara smudges, not too much eye shadow. Hair falling over my shoulders in Veronica Lake finger waves. All in all, I'd say I look pretty great.

Jamie apparently thinks so too, because the first thing out of his mouth when I open the door is, 'God, you're gorgeous.'

I swat his arm with my evening bag, feeling my face flush. I have never been able to take a compliment. But as for getting my mind off my sudden unemployment? Oh, we're getting closer.

How am I supposed to take this all in? It's overwhelming. Utterly, entirely, these-people-are-worth-more-than-the-entire-borough-of-Brooklyn overwhelming. I've been invited into the New York of legend – of coffee table books, artistic lore, and W Magazine. With every second, I expect some illustrious matron in an Oscar de la Renta gown, with a tight face and spun hair, to point her finger at me and cry, 'Imposter!' Because here I am, on the Grand Tier of the Metropolitan Opera house, rubbing elbows with the highest of the high of New York Society. Hmm, I wonder if any of them own galleries.

I can think of no more luxurious place in the world for a party than the Metropolitan Opera, with its towering Marc Chagall murals depicting the 'Sources' and 'Triumph' of music – two dreamy, folkloric paintings whose passionate swirls of yellow and red make even the most stoic heart beat a little faster. The Grand Tier has been outfitted with dozens of white-clothed tables, and we'll be dining within sight of the famous snowflakelike crystal chandeliers, overlooking Lincoln Center and its majestic fountain surging upward against the summer night sky. You couldn't imagine a more magical sight.

As Jamie and I look for our table, a glamorously sophisticated woman with a blonde updo catches my eye. She's got on a lush-looking black satin gown paired with a white satin capelet. She fixes me with her regal gaze. Uh-oh, here it comes. The part where she shouts accusatorily: 'What are you doing here! And in someone else's Armani no less!' Ooh! She's coming this way! I grab at Jamie's arm, trying to pull him in the other direction, but he stands firm, riveted by the sight.

When she steps toward me, I'm surprised to see the woman's painted red lips are drawn back in a smile. 'Darling,' she says in an accented tone, 'your dress is divine.' And as she speaks, some guy behind her with longish dark blond hair is rapidly snapping pictures – of the both of us.

'Thanks!' is all I can think to say. To be honest, ever since the whole Arden Moore debacle, cameras in public have given me the shivers. 'Your capelet is just grand!'

The woman gives a low laugh and moves on, followed closely by the photographer, who tosses me a charming, 'Thanks, doll' before continuing his snapping and schmoozing.

'That was Carolina Herrera!' Jamie cries when the woman's out of earshot. 'The überdoyenne of society designers!'

'It *was*?' My eyes bug open. 'God, she's *gorgeous*.'

'And the photographer was Patrick McMullan!'

I give a scrunchy-nosed shrug. 'Okay . . .'

Jamie's gaping incredulously at my ignorance. 'You know, the über-photographer of the überdoyennes?'

Now that he says it, I'm pretty sure I've seen that McMullan guy at the bigger art openings – the Gagosians, the Mary Boones. And I might be mistaken, but I think Freddie sold a sculpture to Carolina Herrera about a year ago. So, see? I fit right in here, don't I? Ooh, look! That's Sarah Jessica Parker!! In a pink ball gown! I have got to get a look at her shoes . . .

'Patrick McMullan didn't even ask for my picture.' Jamie's sagging morale draws my attention away from celebrity footwear. 'A couple of weeks ago, I was drinking Bellinis with Patrick and a bevy of supermodels. Now he won't even acknowledge my presence.'

A look of sheer dismay darkens Jamie's face. I've been so happy to have my dear friend back that I'd almost forgotten how he must be feeling. In my eyes, Jamie's been rescued from the clutches of fame and excess. From his perspective, it's all been wrenched from him. I hadn't considered that, to Jamie, returning to his old self might be a less-than-thrilling notion.

'I don't want this Patrick to notice you,' I say playfully, lacing my fingers through Jamie's. 'Because I want to be selfish and keep you all to myself. My handsome date in his handsome tux.'

'Yeah.' Jamie nods, perking up a bit. 'Flattery works.'

'A-*fucking*-mazing!' I hear, coming round the corner toward our spot near the double staircase. 'That dress fits you better than it ever did me, you whore!'

'Dix!' I give her a big hug, relieved beyond words that she too looks like her old self, all glamour and effortless perfection. Dix is wearing a white tuxedo, with nothing on under the low-cut, finely tailored dinner jacket. Her hair is drawn back into its sleek, straight ponytail.

'I tell you.' Dix exhales a puff of air, cocking her hip. 'It's the no-drinking thing that's going to get me. Can you imagine? Not one cocktail – not even wine – for seven more months. I might as well be at the Betty fucking Ford Center. At least there, I'd get some new industry contacts out of it.'

'What about coffee?' Jamie asks. Dix clued him in to the big news right after she told me. She said his eyes went so wide, she worried the lids might never make it down again.

'Thanks for mentioning it!' Dix rails, rolling her eyes. 'You two are going to be dealing with one crabby bitch for a while.'

Jamie gives her a wide smile. 'I can't wait,' he says sincerely.

Dix groans and motions with her finger for Jamie to follow. 'I'm borrowing him,' she says wryly. 'I've got someone I want you to meet, Jamie. A radio guy – he thinks you might be right for a regular spot about the New York dating scene.'

I clutch Jamie's hand so hard he actually yelps.

'Do we really think that's a good idea, Dix?' Jamie cowers away from her. 'Look what the column did to me. How do you think I'm going to react to being on the airwaves?'

'It's NPR!' Dix shakes her head impatiently, dragging him off. 'You can't get a swelled head from public radio!'

I laugh as Dix drags Jamie off toward the wall of windows. *God*, I think as it hits me again. I can't believe where I am! I lean with my elbows on the railing, gazing down at the dramatically curved, red-carpeted stairway leading to the orchestra level. Above my head the modern Swarovski crystal chandelier, with its ethereal, airy design, sparkles like the first warm ray of sunlight after a winter storm. I feel as though I'm an extra in a movie scene. Any second, Sarah Jessica will be running down these stairs below me at lightning speed, leaving behind one perfect, glass Monolo slipper.

As if the director's just yelled, 'Cut', my reverie is broken by the realization that someone's leaning against the rail next to me. I inhale the heady scent of freesia and instantly, a wide smile spreads across my face.

'How long have you been there!' I chide, reaching over to embrace Deidre Gayle.

'Sweetie, it's a joy to see someone actually appreciating the scenery.' Deidre squeezes my hand. She's dressed in the most romantic-looking lavender dress, dramatically slit on one side to show off her sculpted legs.

I go through the formalities of thanking Deidre for the invitation to her table, silently debating whether I should tell her I've left the Bond. I had planned to inform our artists first, as a professional courtesy. But Deidre's been there with me from the beginning. So much of where I've gotten to today (except for that whole no-job thing) I owe to her.

'Deidre,' I say in a hushed voice, glad to be away from the thick of the crowd, 'I have to tell you something.'

Deidre gives me a knowing smile, her coffee-colored eyes taking on a mischievous glint. 'You were very naughty to keep it from me! But don't you worry. I understand your motives fully.'

I take an involuntary step back. How could Deidre have heard so soon? I know art world gossip spreads like wildfire, but I only quit four hours ago. What did Avery do, hold a press conference? Or was it Tight-Ass Beth?

Parading around the city with a megaphone, shouting, 'We got rid of Isabel! *Ha-ha-ha.*'

'My God, Deidre.' I'm truly flummoxed. 'I only just left today! And I haven't told a single soul!'

'Left?' Deidre looks at me in sheer confusion. 'Sweetie, what are you talking about?'

'Er . . .' I squint my eyes up. 'What are *you* talking about?'

'I was referring to ABT's newest thirty-million-dollar donor,' Deidre answers, clearly puzzled. 'The honoree of this party. But now you've got me all concerned, Izzy! Have you *left* the Bond?'

'Actually,' I say steadily, 'yes, I have.'

And as I explain why, I'm endlessly relieved to see Deidre nodding her approval. Even though I've spared her the worst details, like Elmore Cowper's forlorn panty hose, Deidre's dismayed gasps tell me she's as appalled by the nature of his 'social experiment' as I am.

'Sweetie, wherever you go next, I will follow.' Deidre's voice is kind and melodic, as comforting to me as my cozy blue bathrobe. 'To the ends of the earth if need be.'

'You are the best,' I say warmly. For a moment, I feel a stab of guilt at the possibility of stealing one of the Bond's best collectors. But I get over it.

A distinguished-looking man waves at us then from the other side of the Grand Tier. With his gray-flecked hair and rakish smile, he looks vaguely like a combination between Pierce Brosnan and the Old Spice man.

'Someone's got an admirer,' I tease Deidre as she waves back with a forced smile.

'They're all the same,' she dismisses, turning her back on Pierce Spice. 'Financial wizards eager for a prima ballerina to hang from their arms like an ornament from the Nutcracker. Your fellow, though' – she whacks me playfully on the hip – 'he's a cutie all around. Tall, lean, with that thick curly hair!'

My fellow? Could she be talking about Jamie? 'Do you mean my date?' I point to where Dix, Jamie, and the radio guy are huddling by the windows. 'Because Jamie's just a friend! He's not my . . . fellow . . . at all!'

'Really?' Deidre gets this hopeful look in her eyes.

'Really and truly! Jamie's one of my best friends!' I hear my voice rising with girlish excitement. How cool would that be? Deidre and Jamie! 'You should totally introduce yourself,' I urge, almost psychotically enthusiastic. 'Lookie! He's done talking to that radio guy. Perfect opportunity.'

Deidre throws back her head with her tinkly laugh. She's stepping away from the railing, looking both confident and a little shy. 'Maybe I will, sweetie.'

'Hey, Deidre?' I ask just as she's about to take off. Something's not quite gelling in my mind, about Deidre's reaction when I mentioned I had news. 'What'd you mean about understanding my motives fully? When you said I kept things from you?'

Deidre searches my face, her brow furrowed with contemplation. She opens her mouth, but seems to think the better of whatever was about to escape it. 'Table twenty,' is all she says. Then she and her perfect posture vanish into the crowd.

I fish out my place card from my evening bag, and sure enough it says table four, just as I remembered. So who's at table twenty? Ooh! Maybe it's Katie Couric! I saw her before, in a rather scary-looking, Pucci-type dress, but boy does she look good for her age.

I'm atwitter with curiosity, sneaking peeks at the table numbers nestled in dripping floral arrangements on each table. God, this setup makes Mimi's wedding look positively bohemian. Glasses and silverware must give a keener sparkle when surrounded by rich people. Let's see. Table nineteen's right here, with its stunning view of Avery Fisher Hall. So there! There's table twenty! Now, if only Caroline Kennedy weren't smack in the way . . .

Now I get it. There she is, at table twenty, with her sweet smile and straight, ash-blond hair. Constance Bond is ABT's new thirty-million-dollar donor! Instantly, my pulse quickens. What should I do? On the one hand, I want to tell Constance how sorry I am that I won't be working for her family anymore. On the other hand, I want to bum-rush her like a madwoman asking every question I've ever had about Grady Cole. I hesitate, remembering how nice Constance was to me when she visited the gallery – and how hurt Grady said she'd been by Avery. I think Constance Bond and I must have a lot in common – aside from the gigantic fortune, that is. Maybe for now, I should just say hi.

But as I edge closer, I see this might not be the best time for chitchat. There's a man next to Constance with his arm around her shoulders, whispering intimately into her ear. I can't help but feel glad for her. See, Constance? There *is* life after Avery. I can't see the man – he's being hidden by Caroline Kennedy's elbow – but I'm hoping he's got a kind face. Because, after all Constance has been through–

No way. In a millisecond, my heart plummets to the floor, where all the fancy shoes mash it to a pulp. I don't believe it. I close my eyes to regain my equilibrium, and try to swallow, even though my throat is drier than lint. The man who was just whispering in Constance's ear, who's now kissing her forehead? It's Grady Cole.

I can't move. I can't lift my feet. Not even when Caroline Kennedy nudges me aside after her repeated attempts at a polite 'Excuse me.' My first instinct is to run as far away as possible. But what if forgoing a scene in the face of male treachery isn't mature, as I've always thought? What if it's just plain cowardly? How can I let Grady, with all his seducing and promising and fake sincerity . . . how can I let him get away with playing me for a fool?

I clear my throat a couple times until I can swallow again. I'm lifting one foot, then the other, willing myself to walk right up to Grady with my head lifted high. There will be no girlie tears escaping these eyes. Mustering all the dignity I can, I continue with solid, even steps until I'm right in front of him.

When he sees me, Grady's face turns deathly gray. I can see his mouth opening, his hand rubbing fiercely at his lower lip. I don't take notice, this time, of how good he looks in his tuxedo. Or fine, maybe I do, but with a heavy dose of regret. I don't pay attention to Constance, who's gripping Grady's arm with taut fingers. I've got to get out what I'm going to say right now, or I swear to God my nerve is going to poof away like the flame on a soggy candle.

My voice is low and gravelly with hurt. 'Ask me again, Grady, why I don't trust you.'

And that's the extent of my noble bravery. I only glimpse the flash of pain in Grady's eyes before I spin around and run. I dash past all the important people, with their sequins and bow ties. I'm headed toward the lobby, where if I can only get out the door and into the fresh air, maybe I'll be able to breathe again. But I don't make it past the staircase. I'm halfway down, just under the cluster of twinkling Swarovski crystal lights, when I hear Grady's anguished voice call my name.

'Izzy, stop. *Please*,' he calls again. 'I'm just going to keep on chasing you. And I'm not the one in heels!'

I'm not sure why I turn around. Maybe because the alternative would be always wondering what Grady had to say for himself. Let's just get this over with, I think, bristling. And then I can join a convent and begin my new life of utter chastity.

Grady jogs down the stairs to me, his hair bouncing over his forehead. He looks both defeated and determined at the same time. 'Thanks for stopping.'

'You're a liar,' I respond bluntly. I sound collected, but inside I just want to curl up with kitty Robbie and have a good sob.

'You're right.' Grady lowers his head, shoving his hands in his pockets. I hear the guilt in his voice. 'I've been lying to you. And it's been tearing me up. I'm a wreck. I'm a lying wreck.'

To my utter surprise, a bark of laughter escapes my lips,

soon escalating into a torrent of manic giggles. 'No,' I say between gasps. 'You're a lying piece of crap.'

'*Okay* . . .' I see Grady trying to puzzle out the reason for my hysterical giggle fit – am I overwhelmed by anger, or is there a shard of a possibility for forgiveness? Or, quite frankly, am I just mad?

I wish I knew the answer myself.

'Iz, it's not what you think.' Grady grabs my hands tightly, resisting my struggle to release them. His grasp is firm, but tender, like he's trying to tame a beloved wild colt. 'Connie's my sister. Constance, I mean. She's my sister.'

'*What?*' The giggles break abruptly, and my hands go limp in Grady's clutches.

Grady takes a deep breath, apprehension flooding his pale eyes. 'Emerson Bond was my grandfather,' he says slowly, earnestly. 'My full name is Grady Cole Bond.'

I give a hiccup. I've got so many thoughts rushing around my head that I don't know which one to pluck at first. I do find myself wondering, though: Back when I first met Grady, on the 6 train platform? What on earth was the heir to billions doing riding the subway?

'I dropped my last name so I could be judged by my work alone,' Grady goes on when he sees me physically unable to form words. 'I didn't want to have to fight off the prejudice of nepotism – "Oh, he's only being shown at a major gallery because it belongs to his grandfather."' He rubs at his eyes with the heels of his hands. 'Yes, my grandfather asked Freddie to visit my studio, but Freddie had no idea who I was. The decision to show my work was entirely his own. God, if people knew my name, every review would have focused on who I was, rather than what I painted. Do you get that, at least?' I see him searching my face for a reaction.

I nod my understanding. I don't quite know how I should be feeling. Enraged at being lied to? Relieved that Grady's not in love with Constance Bond? Embarrassed? Happy? My head feels like it's been stuffed with cotton, dulled by a haze of shock and confusion.

'Will you walk with me?' Grady holds out his hand, waiting to see how I'll respond.

I could listen to my head, telling me that if Grady lied about something as basic as his name, what's to stop him from hiding everything else from me too? Or I could listen to my heart, which is thumping in overtime just being near him. With Avery, all I could do was dream about the future, what a good couple we'd make. With Grady, I only ever want to be in the present – to be exactly where I am, whenever I'm with him. I want each second with Grady to be tangible, so I can paste the moments in my scrapbook to look back on years from now, running my fingers along the worn edges. Before I can realize I've made my decision, my hand is nestled warmly in Grady's.

We stroll along Lincoln Center Plaza, circling the fountain, gazing up at the boxy sixties architecture of Avery Fisher Hall. Grady tells me everything. Every little detail about himself, Avery, and Constance. Probably more than I need to know, actually. Like the part about his sister sticking a LEGO up his nose in third grade? I could have done without that. Got to save some of the mystery, you know.

I listen as Grady's whole story unravels under the August night sky, with his dinner jacket flung over my shoulders to protect against the faint chill. Of course Grady had no friends or family at his opening – they would have given away his secret. The only person at the gallery who ever knew Grady's true identity was Avery, his former college chum. Grady tells me about the guilt he still feels over introducing his sister to a man who caused her nothing but pain. Apparently, Avery seduced Constance while she took him on a tour of the Bond's private art collection. As the two stood before Warhol's portrait of Elizabeth Taylor, Avery compared her beauty to that of the legendary actress. Needless to say, Constance was immediately hooked. (That rat bastard!)

Grady explains how he worked out a deal with Avery, to ensure his silence – both to me and to the press. When

Emerson Bond died, the contents of his will were the ultimate thumbed nose at a son whose selfishness had alienated him from his whole family for years. Raymond Bond may have inherited control of the Bond Gallery, but Constance and Grady inherited all the money that kept it going. So in exchange for Avery's keeping quiet about Grady's identity, Grady agreed to continue forking over the endowment needed to keep the gallery afloat. He felt the Old Man would have wanted him to anyway.

'I'm really sorry about your grandfather,' I say softly, drawing Grady's jacket closer round my shoulders. We're standing on the east side of Lincoln Center, near Columbus Avenue, with the fountain and the Metropolitan Opera House forming a picture-perfect tableau behind us.

'Thanks,' Grady replies wistfully. 'I really loved him, despite his ability to hold a grudge past eternity.' He gives a genial laugh. 'The men in my family can be very difficult, Izzy. Just a warning.'

'You think?' I chide with mock sarcasm. But then my mood takes on a more sober cast. Sure, Grady's story makes sense, and he *seems*, at least, to be the same person I've known these past couple months. But something still sticks in my craw – the only question Grady hasn't yet answered. The most important question of all.

'Why didn't you tell me?' I ask, my face lifted toward his. 'After the opening, once your paintings were selling off the walls no matter who you were. Why not tell me then?'

Grady presses a hand to his forehead. For a moment, I'm sure he's going to blurt out, *I was having too much fun messing with your head. Like I'm doing now. I can't believe how gullible you are.* But, after raking his hands through his unruly hair, Grady seems to lose his resistance. He takes a step closer to me, rubbing the fabric of his jacket lapels through his fingers.

'I wanted to,' he says, raising his eyebrows. 'I almost did. But then you started going off on how much you hate lying, and how you value honesty above all else.'

I feel myself squinting. 'You listened to that?'

'I sure did,' Grady admits. 'The last place I wanted to be was on the giant heap of men you can't stand.'

'I wouldn't call it *giant*,' I protest, despite the fact that Grady's arms are now around my shoulders, drawing me into his chest.

'You endured all my gibes so well,' Grady goes on. 'The more you fought back, the more I admired you.'

'Really?' My voice is muffled by Grady's crisp white shirt. 'You must have admired me a ton.'

Grady laughs, easing his grip a little so I can lift my head and look him in the eye.

'I did.' His face lights up. 'I do.'

Grady rests his palm lightly on my cheek, leans down, and kisses me. And as I let myself sink into him, losing my breath in a whirl of exhilaration and hope, I realize that I could love this kind, classy, considerate man.

Epilogue

You look like you've heard every line in the book. So what's one more?

'We've got a *very* interested collector,' I'm telling our artist, nearly clapping my hands with excitement. 'He says your work redefines the boundaries of fine art, and he's never seen anything so original!'

'That's so cool!' The artist actually jumps up and down in her four-inch silver wedge boots, her purple hair not budging a millimeter from its cemented spikes. 'God, I cannot believe how many people are here!'

'I know, right!?' And now we're both jumping together, Kimmy and I, like we've just won concert tickets on the radio.

It was Grady's idea to open the Duncan Bond Gallery. He wanted a space that would preserve the legacy of what his grandfather really stood for: supporting fresh, vibrant talent, a notion that's been lost over at the other Bond on the Upper East Side. The Emerson Bond Gallery's still in business, but just barely. Grady pulled the funding, hoping to pressure his father into letting him and Constance find a new dealer. Eventually, he's sure they'll restore the Bond to its former glory. But the Duncan Bond will be my baby, and I'll be its sole dealer. Grady surprised me with the new space at what I thought was going to be our three-month anniversary dinner. Instead of a restaurant, I was ushered into a far different building. My favorite in all of New York City. The Puck Building, of course. We picnicked that night on the floor of our future gallery, with candles all around, drinking the chilled bottle of champagne that had been awaiting our arrival.

The Duncan Bond's situated in a loftlike space on the top floor of the Puck, with a full wall of windows that lets in sheets of natural light, and mobile walls that can adjust as needed for each exhibition. Every detail, from the restored original moldings to the futuristic multimedia alcove, combines a rich sense of artistic history and a forward-thinking contemporary outlook. Grady and I have poured our hearts into these few rooms, and from the look of things, the enormous crowd that showed up for our first exhibition is appreciating each nook and cranny almost as much as we do.

As I wade through the throngs of people – hey! there's that Patrick McMullan guy, the celebrity photographer! – I'm being tugged at right and left. Unfamiliar guests are interested in Kimmy's work, asking to see press packets, marveling over our exhibition space. And my friends and family are tossing their support at me like rice after a wedding. Mimi's over there, with her arm laced through Trevor's, seeming – well, a little lost, actually. I'm not sure medieval-fantasy graphic art is exactly her thing. Still, my cousin beams at me as I catch her eye.

'Where's that billionaire boyfriend of yours?' Mimi bursts out after the initial congratulations. Even after six months with Grady, Mimi still hasn't gotten over the fact that I'm dating a member of one of *Forbes*'s one hundred richest families in the country.

'Meem, Grady's not a billionaire,' I tell her for the, well, billionth time. 'His *grandfather* was. A lot has gone to charity, and the Bond Family Foundation for the Arts, and he shares the legacy with his sister. Really, he lives pretty normally. We both do!'

Mimi tilts her head in contemplation. 'So would you say he's a hundreds-of-millions-aire?'

I give up. 'I guess so. Kind of. Oh, look! I *must* say hello to one of our collectors. You'll excuse me, won't you?'

Even though Mimi and I have reached something like a real friendship, I have to say – I don't think we're *ever* going to speak the same language. Still, in her own way, I know Mimi's saying she's happy for me. I give her hand a squeeze of thanks before I head off into the crowd.

I wasn't lying when I said I'd spotted an important collector. In fact, I see two of our top buyers right now, examining Kimmy's fantastical, richly colored drawings. Dix has her arms wrapped around her enormous belly, gazing up at a scene where an ethereal wood nymph sits with a dashing knight by the side of a gently rippling pond. Right next to her, Deidre Gayle's admiring the drawing she's already bought – the dance of a twinkly fairy wearing glittering sapphire toe shoes.

'Hello!' I wrap my arms around Dix's shoulders, hugging her from behind.

'I'm giving you one more hour of standing,' Dix warns grumpily, her face flushed. 'And then I am sitting my ass down in your office with a cheese plate in front of me.'

'Whatever you need is yours,' I say, rubbing her back. Dix is due in only three weeks – she's having a boy! And though her tone is brusque, just one look at her face would tell anyone how blissful she feels. Well, aside from the bloating, achy back, and swollen-feet bits.

'What do you think –' Dix waves at the drawing she's been admiring – 'for the nursery? Looks like something that would foster a kid's imagination.'

'Sweetie, I think it's wonderful!' Deidre pipes in. She's let her hair down from its usual bun, and it falls down her back in tight waves. 'I almost bought that one myself, but how could I resist the dancing fairy?'

Jamie wraps his arm around Deidre's shoulders, pulling her toward him. They've been dating as long as Grady and me, and still, Jamie's face just radiates light whenever Deidre's around. Do you want to hear the cutest thing ever? They started seeing each other right after the

ABT gala, where Deidre approached Jamie and said, *I hope you've got a library card, sweetie, because I'm checking you out*. For that result alone, Jamie's pickup line column turned out to be the best thing that ever happened to him.

Soon, our little group is joined by Grady, looking mighty sexy in his dark jeans and Diesel jacket, and his sister, Constance, who I've come to know as Connie. She's the shy one in their family, which makes no sense because she's the sweetest, prettiest, most genuinely kind person I've met in a long time. In fact, I'm angrier at Avery for screwing over Connie than I ever was for the way he treated me. Grady's such a caring brother too. Connie's got a standing invitation to come to our place every Sunday night for an evening of comfort food, DVDs, and lots of wine.

God. 'Our place.' How crazy domestic does that sound? But it's true! I just moved into Grady's building this month. And when I say 'building,' I don't mean 'the apartment complex he lives in with many other owners lining the hallways.' I mean his nineteenth-century Tribeca brownstone row house, a few blocks from his studio, which has been gutted and transformed into a modern, minimalist enclave. The street is so lovely and quiet, lined with cobblestones and the faint remnants of old trolley tracks. And the house is nice too, with all its Eames, Le Corbusier, and Mies Van der Rohe furniture. I mean, it's gorgeous. It's just still kind of . . . *male*. But we're working on that.

Grady drops a kiss on my forehead, giving me his usual impish smile. 'You've sold more than half our inventory,' he says. 'And we only just officially opened two hours ago. You didn't sell half *my* paintings before the *Times* review came out!' He pouts teasingly. 'What, I wasn't good enough for you?'

'Oh, right.' I slap at his chest. 'Poor neglected artist. With a waiting list sixty people deep.'

Grady nods over at Kimmy, who's rushing toward us from across the room, her space-age boots thudding on the light wood floors. She's followed by an elated Freddie, who's come from L.A. especially for the exhibition.

'Izzy, Izzy!' Kimmy's crying as she hops over to us. The petticoats under her miniskirt are bouncing dangerously high. 'Guess what? It's so friggin' cool!'

'I'm so proud,' Freddie gushes. 'Look at me, I'm like the uncle at the school play giving a standing ovation for the third daisy from the right!' He's wearing the most luxurious black cashmere sweater, a gift from his boyfriend of the moment. After all these years, Freddie's finally shied away from artists. Now he dates only fashion retailers. He's currently seeing the head buyer for L.A.'s prestigious Fred Segal. You'd think that in L.A., Freddie would have discovered color. Not so much. 'Our baby's making it, Iz!' His cheeks shake with excitement. 'She's a *star*.'

'What's happened?' I say, unable to hold in my laughter. 'Besides the whole instant commercial-success thing?'

'Oh, my God, so this guy? With the black glasses, that one over there?' Kimmy points surreptitiously, and we all turn to gape. 'He works in Marvel's graphic-novel department, and they're going to start a new fantasy line.' Kimmy's breath is quickening, her spiked head bouncing back and forth. 'They want mine to be the debut novel. I'm going to be published! It's finally going to happen!'

'Kimmy! That's amazing!' I cry out. See? I always knew how talented she was. When Grady gave me full creative control of the gallery, it was a total no-brainer who should be shown in our debut exhibition.

'And it's all because of you, Iz,' Kimmy says, taking it down a notch. 'You and Grady.'

Grady waves the notion away with a modest pshaw.

'You've earned everything, Kimmy,' I say earnestly.

'Love, love, love,' Freddie bursts out. 'All this love in the room makes me want to gag! You two alone.' He wags his fingers toward where I've got my arms around Grady's waist. 'What's this about moving in together?'

'I get to redecorate half the house!' I exclaim, unable to hold it in. 'With as much Pottery Barn as I want! And

Grady has fresh flowers *delivered* every week for my glass wall vases.'

Grady winces with embarrassment. 'The florist's just around the corner. It's not like he's traveling from Mozambique.'

'Oh, shut up. I know you're a secret romantic.' Freddie rolls his eyes at Kimmy, who's nodding her agreement. 'You two are so happy it's sickening.'

'He's right,' Dix says sarcastically.

'Mm, kinda.' Even Connie's in on it!

'*Happy!?*' Grady seems wounded with offense. He holds out his arms, which are crisscrossed by thin red scratches. 'Have you met her *cat?*'

I sling my arm through Grady's, resting my hand on his bicep. 'Robbie's like me,' I say sweetly, giving Grady a look of innocence that dares him to reproach me for anything. 'He just needs to get to know you better, and then he'll fall instantly in love.'

The resounding groans and gagging noises lets me know that all our friends agree.

Acknowledgements

I'm indebted to many rocking people for their support. Sheri Pasquarella proved invaluable during my research, and the brilliant Susan Kamil whipped my earliest drafts into shape with admirable insight.

Many thanks to my enthusiastic early readers: Vera Zlatarski, Marianne Power, and my hero, Madeleine Wickham. I'm indebted as well to the publishing professionals who offered me their expertise gratis: Elizabeth Kellermeyer and the wise and precise Margo Lipschultz.

I'd be nowhere without my devoted friends and family, including but not limited to my best friend Zaira Zafra, my book party thrower Joan Ai, my Grandpa Hy and beloved Grandma Eve, my love and my rock, Robert Grunder (who's also a damn talented painter), and the two most supportive parents ever, Mom and Dad, whose pride in me overflows no matter what I do.

Finally, I continue to be awed by the smartest agent in the business, Kim Witherspoon, and her flawless right hand gal, Alexis Hurley. In the US, I'm lucky to have New American Library as my publisher, and I thank my editor Anne Bohner, and the whole team. And in the UK, I've fallen in love with Little Black Dress, and I'm thrilled to work with Catherine Cobain, her assistant, Poppy Shirlaw, and everyone else involved with what I'm sure is a very well-dressed imprint.

Now you can buy any of these other
Little Black Dress titles from your
bookshop or *direct from the publisher*.

FREE P&P AND UK DELIVERY
(Overseas and Ireland £3.50 per book)

TO ORDER SIMPLY CALL THIS NUMBER

01235 400 414

or visit our website: www.madaboutbooks.com

Prices and availability subject to change without notice.